Cooch

COOCH

AN ALEX CUCHULAIN NOVEL

ROBERT E. COOK

ROYAL WULFF PUBLISHING

www.robertcooknovels.com

Printed in the United States of America

ISBN: 978-0-9843155-0-5

Acknowledgments

AS a first time author, I needed a lot of help, and got it, from friends as first readers and commenters. My sincere thanks for the efforts and contributions of, among others, Art Allen, Jack Bray, David Campbell, Gay Wind Campbell, Bruce Coleman, Bob Corman, Bruns Grayson, Judy Hamilton, Pam Hunter, Stan Joosse, Lee Keet, Jim Loy, Peter Palmisano, Leslie Rudd and Rex Swain.

For Paula

The love of my life

The president of the United States, Reverdy Hendrix, turned slightly toward the window. Thick bulletproof panes bent the sunlight and washed color from his face; he nodded at his visitor and waved the Secret Service agent from the room.

"Have a seat, MacMillan," the president said, as he dropped into a deep, high-backed leather chair and picked up a pen, idly spinning it in his fingers. "The National Security Advisor tells me, rather urgently, in fact, that you may be able to help with a serious problem that's on my table right now. Before I discuss that problem and make a decision about how to handle it, I thought I should get to know you a bit, since I've ignored you until now."

Hendrix leaned forward and said, "I have a half-hour. I have an idea of what you do—sort of a tame thug, I guess. How can a man like you help me do my job better?"

Mac nodded, and said, "What you call the 'tame thug' bit, the special-ops thing is, in my mind, just a small part of what I bring to your table. I view myself as more of a problem illuminator than a solution provider. I think I bring a different perspective to national security matters."

The president nodded, held out his hand, and moved his fingers impatiently in a "let's go" gesture. "We don't have a lot of time. Take a few minutes and broadly frame a situation where you might be useful to me. Something that you have been thinking about lately. Give me some reason to keep you at my very crowded table."

Mac nodded and said, "Israel is the topic."

The president sat forward a little, paying more attention.

"Israel is having a kitten over Iran building a bomb. They think they simply can't tolerate Iran having even a nuke or two, for fear Iran will match bombast with action and send two their way; two would wipe out about 90 percent of Israel's population. To attack Iran, they need to safely bypass our air defense over Iraq, which is formidable and effective."

Mac turned a little in his chair and gathered his thoughts. "The Israelis are tough beyond American perspective. There is no ethic in Israel that says one should trust in fellow man. They tried that; it didn't work."

The president leaned back in his chair and was silent for a few seconds, then asked, "And for this little piece of speculation, why do I need you, and what is your advice to me today concerning Israel and Iran? "

Mac nodded and said, "My advice to you is that you should consider that you may receive a call at 0300 some morning that says Israel has called on the hotline to notify us that they are coming over our defenses in thirty minutes to get Iran, and they will use all of the fighter cover in their arsenal to protect their bombers. They say if we want to mix it up with them that would be unfortunate, but necessary, as they see it."

The president reached into his desk drawer, stood, shook out a cigarette from a half-empty pack, and lit it with a cheap gas lighter. "Well, that's a little harsh. Go on."

Mac went on, "My advice is that we will lose a bunch of airplanes and maybe a ship or two, guided missile cruisers in particular; the Israelis are very, very good and well-equipped. We'll get them all, even if it's not until they're on the way out; their pilots will expect to die and will get their job done first."

"So, in that scenario I still consider somewhat likely, 'what therefore shall we do?' as the critical thinkers like to ask," Mac said. "I don't know. But I doubt that you want that decision made, or want to make it, in the fog of a 0300 awakening, without the advantage of intelligence or background discussion."

"Dammit, MacMillan," the president snapped, "How is it that I hear this first from *you?*"

"Mr. President," Mac said, "I can only assume that you didn't ask or it didn't come up, and that's no surprise, given the huge numbers of things going on here. I don't have a full-time job involving bosses and conflicting priorities. I gather data, read reports, and just crunch things around in my head and draw tentative conclusions. That's my job."

The president stared at Mac for a second, and then asked, "And what opinion would I get from the chairman of the Joint Chiefs on your opinions, your advice?"

"That's above my pay-grade," Mac said. "He knows vastly more about the execution of a thing like that than I do, and how we would fare against an all-out effort by Israel to destroy Iran's nuke capability. I imagine the chairman has an informed opinion about what that sort of combat mix-up would do to our readiness if we took predicted losses, and how Israel would survive without an effective Air Force that the US destroyed. On that issue, someone else will likely have an opinion about the stability of the Middle East. The whole topic seems worth early, thoughtful consideration. That is my textured advice."

"Okay. Got it. Any comments or questions?" You have eleven minutes left," the president said, as he began to move folders on his desk and flicked some ashes into a hexagonal glass ashtray with *Put It Out*! engraved on its base. It had been a gift from his wife.

"No, Sir," Mac said.

"Okay, I understand who and what you think you are. So, let's move on. As I mentioned earlier, we have a particularly nasty and immediate national security issue," Hendrix said, as he picked up one of the thick folders. "As I said, I'm led to believe that this kind of thing is down your alley. I'd like you to read through this and come up with solid advice or a solution. If you come up with a solution, you'll be provided with whatever assets you need, given deniability."

MacMillan said, "Yes, Sir," as he took the package.

"No Questions, MacMillan?"

"No, Sir. Maybe later, but probably not," Mac said.

"You're growing on me, MacMillan," the president said. "That's scary. Advise me on this issue; then we'll talk about your future." He picked up the briefing sheet for his next appointment and stubbed the cigarette into the ashtray. "You are dismissed."

"Yes, Sir," MacMillan said as he stood and spun, then walked briskly to the door.

The president watched, somewhat bemused, as MacMillan walked out with his shoulders squared, but with little apparent sign of tension in his stride. He looked down at the briefing sheet for his next appointment. *Gear change*, he thought, and let a little grin slide out. *Damn! I like this job. Never a dull moment.* Then his head snapped up.

"MacMillan!" Hendrix said.

MacMillan stopped, and spun to him. "Yes, Sir?" he said.

"Just curious. Do you see yourself as the Gunny in Eastwood's *Heartbreak Ridge*, or what?"

"Aha, another Eastwood fan," MacMillan said, with a grin. "I liked that Gunny, Tom Sunday, as I recall, but he's a little out of control early on for me. We need those guys on the ground, but I'm well past that. If I had to pick, I actually see myself more as a William Munny, in *Unforgiven*. You do what you gotta do when things get ugly."

The president gave a little grin, and said, "Do you think Eastwood has popular influence, beyond the obvious? And what do you think his broad message is, if he has one?"

"Yes, Sir, I do think he has broad popular appeal," Mac said. "I think he is a very talented chronicler of our times, just as Louis L'Amour was for the nineteenth century and a little more. Hell, Louis L'Amour won a Presidential Award of some sort for his tales. Eastwood is telling stories of today. Maybe you'll give Eastwood a medal."

Hendrix let go with a snort and a grin. "Hell, I'd at least be selling to the middle of the voter market, bent to the right."

MacMillan stood quiet.

"You are dismissed," the president said with a smile and a nod.

MacMillan spun and walked through the White House and from the West Wing across the small, paved pathway to his tiny office in the Old Executive Office Building next door. He sat down and began to read, and quickly began to consider how to best use his lethal little band of warriors.

New York
West Side

THE late afternoon crowd was thinning around Columbus Circle, as rush hour faded into early evening and the pigeons settled on the head and shoulders of Christopher's statue, busily ridding themselves of the late-day's pickings. A sliver of new moon was peeking over Central Park, and the view across the Park from the mezzanine of the Time Warner building was stunning. Inside *Per Se*, a tall man in a suit leaned casually against the wall, talking to the restaurant's host. He was dark, with a slightly crooked, hooked nose, and an old thin scar running from above his right ear to the corner of his upper lip and a scattering of small irregular scars across his forehead. His hair was thick and black, worn long but expensively styled. He wore a grey suit, with pink pinstripes, and a pale pink shirt with a spread collar. His tie was a deep scarlet, tied four-in-hand and pulled snug to his throat.

A tall, thin blonde woman hurried through the door. She looked around and smiled when she saw Cuchulain standing to her left, talking to a man in a tuxedo. "Alex. I'm sorry I'm late," she said. "I couldn't find a cab."

"Hi, Caitlin," he said. "It's not a problem. I was just gabbing a bit with my friend, Jesus. He's the guy who did the magic of getting this reservation on a week's notice. Someone cancelled and he grabbed it for us."

"Good for you!" she said to Jesus, and reached to shake his hand. "I've been dying to eat here since you opened in New York. I ate once at your French Laundry in the Napa Valley, and it was probably the best meal I've ever had. The good news is that I skipped lunch today and I'm fucking famished!"

Jesus looked a little startled, then grinned and said, "Let me show you to your table, *Senorita*. We'll try to make you a little less hungry."

They walked from the foyer into the restaurant, where tables were arranged on three levels, gently elevated to permit each table an unobstructed view of Columbus Circle and Central Park South. It was quiet and elegantly furnished, with dark walls set off by Arctic white table linens. Like Jesus, the entire staff was dressed formally with white shirts and bowties, and moved about so smoothly that at first there seemed to be more staff than diners.

As they settled into their table and looked around, a waiter appeared and exchanged their white napkins for black ones to prevent white lint on dark clothes, then took a cocktail order. He put a thick wine list on the table, a menu in front of each, then faded from sight.

Alex Cuchulain was a professional investor who had made a big investment in Axial Systems, a public company with an exciting innovation in computer software. Unfortunately, he had made the investment a few months before the economy started turning sour. Alex was now actively trying to salvage his investment, but still had a deep conviction that Axial's product could be a huge winner. The fact that he was attracted to its CEO was a bonus.

Caitlin O'Connor was the Chief Executive Officer of Axial. Cuchulain's reasoning for making such a big commitment had as much to do with O'Connor and her reputation as it did with the enormous size of Axial's potential market. Caitlin O'Connor had a Ph.D. in computational physics from Caltech and had obtained a MacArthur "genius" grant at the age of twenty-three. She had used the time and money from the award to develop a new theory on using neural networks for the design of complex networked computer systems for corporations and government. Axial was founded on that theory, and the bet was that her technology would lower the cost of developing and maintaining internet-linked computer systems in corporate America and around the world, plummeting costs by at least a fifth. She had spent some time during and after Caltech working for the Feds as a consultant, and on their grant money to develop her ideas. Now thirty-six, O'Connor had brought her company to $80 million in sales in three years and was struggling to make a profit, burning corporate cash to support expansion and enhance product, even as a weak economy suddenly drove down sales. If she could keep it together until her worldwide sales offices were productive, the company would be a big winner, and its stock would follow.

O'Connor knew almost nothing about Cuchulain, other than the fact that he was very bright, moderately handsome, knew a lot about technology investing, and was reportedly quite successful. He had a thick upper body that made him appear to be in extraordinary physical condition, but she wasn't even sure about that. He also had a sort of brooding, dark aura about him that made him seem faintly dangerous. She found that curious, and a little exciting. Alex also had impeccable, almost old-worldly manners. That appealed to O'Connor, despite her aggressive feminism.

Caitlin had asked around about Alex after he had called her at home in California several times, trying to arrange a dinner with her when he was in California. Their schedules hadn't meshed, but they had spent a few group lunches together on business, and met over drinks several times at industry gatherings. No one knew much about Cuchulain, and what one person thought he knew conflicted with another person's information. After a few acquaintances said they thought that Brooks Elliot, an investment banker whose firm had taken Axial public, had been in the Navy with Alex, she had found an excuse to walk beside Elliot from a meeting at his investment bank, and had asked whether the rumors were true. She had been at Princeton with Brooks and had dated him seriously then, and again a couple of times after he had gotten out of the Navy. They had both given it up when it became clear that he was looking for a wife and a mother for his children-to-be; that was not her agenda. She had been surprised at the way Elliot's face had closed up when she had asked about what she had heard regarding Cuchulain in the Navy.

"I don't know where you heard that, Katy," Elliot had said. (He *knew* she hated to be called Katy). "It's not quite true, and if it were, it would be none of your business. That was a long time ago." Elliot had almost been rude, which was entirely out of character for him, particularly given their history together. This had only made her more curious about Cuchulain. Cuchulain was clearly much better friends with Brooks F.T. Elliot IV than were many of the people who had been kissing his privileged ass for years, yet the two of them appeared to have very little in common. O'Connor rarely faced problems she found difficult to solve, and this one was beginning to irritate her.

At *Per Se*, Cuchulain was once again stunned by O'Connor's physical beauty. He thought how was rare it was for an intellect to grow as powerful as Caitlin's when it was required to exist and grow in the shadow of great beauty. Ordinarily, a stunning woman can get what she wants without relying on a strong intellect, and intellectual activity is consequently given short shrift. Caitlin seemed clearly an exception.

Caitlin O'Connor looked more like a runway model than a Caltech Ph.D. She was at least 5'10, with wide shoulders, wide flat wrists and muscular, long-fingered hands. She wore a black Armani suit, fitted at the waist. A blue silk blouse, jewel-necked, was draped with a single strand of pearls, shimmering white and hinting pink against her dark clothing. With the exception of an incongruously large rubber dive watch with bright yellow numerals, she wore no other jewelry. The overhead lighting cast small shadows under high cheekbones and washed color from thick, shaggy blond hair, cut short for low maintenance. She had the fair, almost translucent skin that seems to bless only the Irish. A sprinkle of freckles splashed across her nose, accenting her blue eyes—so light that they looked washed with ice, tiny arrows of green and amber winging out from their centers.

Just then a waiter appeared bearing a silver rack with holes drilled through it, and what appeared to be two tiny ice-cream cones set into the holes. "Compliments of the chef," he said, and served two cake cones filled with a mixture of smoked salmon and crème fraiche. Caitlin took hers and consumed it in two large bites, then said to Cuchulain around it, "I love these things!" He took a third small bite of his cone, watching her, amused and a little disconcerted.

She abruptly wiped off her mouth with her napkin and pushed it back into her lap, then interrupted his thoughts. "Tell me about yourself, Alex. I'm curious, and no one seems to know jack shit about you."

He shrugged. "There's not much to tell. My father is dead and my mother now lives in the South of Spain, with her sisters. I have an older sister in New Jersey, who teaches eighth-grade math. I grew up in South Carolina, joined the Marine Corps young and stayed for a while. When I got out, I went to Carnegie Mellon and double-majored in electrical engineering and computer science. It took a degree in that stuff to convince me that I didn't want to make a life of it. I did some post-grad work in England— Arabic studies and modern history, mostly. Then I came to New York and worked up through the financial analyst training program at Merrill Lynch for awhile and took a bunch of finance courses at NYU, mostly at night."

O'Connor leaned back in her chair and took a sip of her cocktail, studying him. She had a sense that there was a lot more to his story than he was telling. *Fine*, she thought. *I suppose we're just trying to get each other's scent right now.*

The waiter appeared again, to take a dinner and wine orders. Caitlin ordered the special, a braised veal shoulder, Alex a veal chop. For wine, he chose a 2006 Dancing Hares, a Napa red table wine in a lovely bottle, etched with hares standing on their hind legs, holding paws and dancing around the bottle. The waiter brought it quickly, opened it, and poured a little into a large wine glass and smelled it. He offered the glass to Alex, who swirled it around in the glass a bit, inhaled the scent deeply and nodded to the waiter. The waiter decanted the Dancing Hares at the table, then swirled it before setting the decanter on the table.

"I don't know this wine, Alex," she said. "The bottle is certainly beautiful. What's the wine like?"

"It's Cabernet Sauvignon, Merlot, and Cabernet Franc, with a little Petit Verdot, blended like a traditional Bordeaux," he said. "It's is not as bold and in your face as some of the wines that are cabernet only, but I love the smoothness and complexity of it. It takes a few minutes to open up."

Cuchulain interrupted her thoughts. "And about you?"

Caitlin picked her chin up from folded hands. "You probably know most of it about me. It's more public—I'm more public. The loss of personal privacy is what I like least about running a public company. Your salary, your history, your education, and your stock holdings in the company are only the beginning of what people can easily find out about you, and government rules demand that I supply the information."

She grinned at him. "You're reputed to be a very thorough researcher and successful at beating the market as a result. Tell me what you know about me, other than that I have a trash mouth, which I've been told a thousand times. Fuck 'em."

That was nicely done, he thought. *Keep me talking, and give me a little verbal hip fake with the potty mouth. I don't think I'll bother telling her how many otherwise interested investors are turned completely off by that.*

Alex leaned back. "And if I do, will you tell me what it is about you that I missed, in your opinion?" he said.

She thought for a few seconds. "Not this time. I'm not sure of your agenda, or if you have one. Let's just see where it goes."

"Okay, fair," Alex said. "I don't have an agenda that you don't already know about, which makes it easier. I'll just paint the description a little more broadly."

"Go for it," she said. "This is a Thomas Keller restaurant, so we'll be here for at least three hours."

Cuchulain nodded, amused. "Okay, your parents are college professors. Two younger siblings—one of each. Summa in physics at Princeton, varsity swimmer, passionate scuba diver, Master's and Ph.D. from Caltech. You ended up at the top, without apparent effort, and Caltech's the toughest. You got a MacArthur grant—pretty amazing, given your age. Dissertation had to do with dynamic building and connection of virtual neuron receptors in hardware, based on statistical projections of growth patterns under various stimuli. I didn't understand all of it, but I see how you got the process from hardware to software; software is more flexible and adaptable. Better yet, software is cheap to duplicate and ship to customers."

"You read my dissertation?" Caitlin said. "Whatever for?"

Cuchulain shrugged. "It's not rocket science as to my motives. I have a lot of my clients' money invested in your company, and the market for tech stocks right now is not great, so I have to be super careful. It's my job to dig as hard as I can. If I'm to outperform the market, I need to know more than the other money managers, and there is a big bunch of very smart people managing money and looking at technology companies. If I get out of a suddenly troubled stock thirty seconds before anyone else, I win. Thirty seconds late—I lose. If I sell and then short the stock before the others get out, and I'm right, I win big-time. So, you can see that I play both long and short. I'm a hedgefund manager; that's what a hedge player does."

"You'd short Axial? My baby? That's sacrilegious!" Caitlin snapped in mock horror.

Cuchulain laughed. "Only to you. This is what I do for a living. My clients and I are just as much owners of Axial as you are; you sold us that right when you went public. We have the independent right to buy or sell the stock as we see fit. I exercise that right aggressively."

O'Connor shook her head ruefully. "I'm too close to Axial to think like that. Have you ever sold Axial short?"

"Not yet," he chuckled. "But your last calendar quarter was close. If you hadn't closed that Daimler deal in the last few days, you would have missed the financial expectations the market holds for Axial. That would have hammered your stock price by at least 20 percent, maybe 50 percent in this market, even from this depressed level. The good news is that the Daimler deal closed, even though you gave them a nice discount to get it in."

"Jesus," she sighed. "You know a lot more about my business that I dreamed any outsider knew. But we have a deal working with Airbus in Toulouse. That could have just as easily closed as Daimler. You missed that one didn't you, Cuchulain?"

He sat silently for a moment, thinking. It had been a long time since he had met someone who attracted him the way Caitlin did, but it wasn't his practice to arm CEOs with any more knowledge about him or his methods than was essential. Then he decided. "That deal with Airbus may not happen at all. It certainly won't happen any time soon. Your French country manager is in over his head; he's slippery, and the customers there don't trust him. Things there will progress very slowly. Don't depend on him."

Caitlin's temper flared. "You're a money manager who has never produced anything, and you have the unmitigated gall to tell me that you know more about my management team than I do? Who the hell do you think you are? You just sit there on the sidelines, smug, and tell others how to do things that you've never done yourself. Get a life, Cuchulain!"

Damn! Cuchulain thought, *Now you've done it!*

He shifted slightly, then said, "It's what I do, Caitlin, and you asked. I dig and dig and dig, and have employees who do the grunt work and like it. You don't have time to do that. No, I've never run a company, and I don't plan to. I like what I do. I'm good at it and it pays the bills."

"Oh, no!" she fumed. "I want to hear more than bullshit platitudes! Just how do you pretend that you reached those conclusions when you're 3000 miles from the source? Are you fluent in French?"

"I wish," Alex said. "I speak only schoolboy French. But I hire people in France to ask questions. I mostly use university professors in the summers to make calls, talk to customers and company people and provide some oversight perspective on a short list of topics we suggest. You would be amazed at how many people in Europe will open up to college professors, plus the professors are smart, articulate and can usually write their reports in English. Sometimes I hire what you might call financial detective agencies. One of those detective types gave me written evidence that your manager in France got caught with his hand in the cash register at another company where he worked a few years back, so I watch Axial France pretty carefully."

Caitlin's face went cold. "I don't believe you," she said. "I can't believe that you're sitting here bullshitting me about something like that, for no reason. You're an asshole, you know that?"

Cuchulain was fighting his irritation. "Check it out. If you can't find it, I'll e-mail you a sanitized version of the report. I have no reason to bullshit you. I'm telling you things tonight that I almost never discuss with anyone. It may have been a mistake."

"And how did I get favored with all this disclosure? Dumb luck?" she said.

Here we go, he thought, standing up.

"Worse yet," Alex said, "I think you should close your European offices and pull back. Europe is in worse economic shape than the US, and no one there is buying much of anything they don't have to have. Save your cash."

Cuchulain said softly, "You are drop-dead good looking, drop-dead smart, drop-dead successful, hard body, good jock, and an articulate and interesting conversationalist. I wanted to tell you as much about the way I think and work as you wanted to hear. I took a risk. I'd like to see more of you, and this was my shot to get you interested. I'm sorry it didn't work out, and that I ended up irritating you. That was not my intention. I just tend to plunge right down the middle on things that interest me."

'Sit down, Cuchulain," Caitlin said with a smile and a wink. "I'm not done with my wine. This Dancing Hares is great wine, by the way. Good choice. Besides, I think it worked out just fine, at least so far. I'm interested—at least a little. So, I guess we are now officially on a date. Where are you going to take me when we finish dinner?"

"All right!" Alex said enthusiastically. "I'll take you wherever you want to go!"

"I know!" she said excitedly. "I heard today that there's a biker bar downtown that's hot. Everyone's talking about it. It's called Choppers, with lots of motorcycle-gang types with tattoos and leather jackets, drinking, doping, and raising hell for local color. Let's go there."

Alex frowned. "That's probably a bad idea. We're both pretty dressed up to be going to that kind of place, Caitlin. We should probably wait until we're wearing something that will allow us to blend in a little better."

"Oh, come on!" Caitlin giggled. "A big guy like you worried about us getting picked on? Besides, I was told that they have bouncers to handle any trouble that comes up. Don't be such a fucking wuss. Do you know where it is? This is your town, you know, and you said *anywhere*, remember?"

Alex raised his hands in surrender. "Choppers it is, Caitlin. I know it. When we finish up here, we'll go slumming."

New York

Downtown

CHOPPERS was jammed and loud. Smoke curled around cheap lamps hanging from an ancient, bulging ceiling, and the sounds of Ernest Tubbs blared from huge speakers mounted high in two corners above a tiny dance floor. Groups of young men and women in jeans mingled with tattooed men in cutoff, black tee-shirts and leather vests, but mostly the groups were of their own. The smell of stale sweat competed with the essence of *Happy* perfume and the pungent stench of marijuana.

Alex and Caitlin slipped into a booth just as another couple left it. A large-breasted waitress, going to fat, in shorts and a fitted body shirt came to take their order. "I'll have a beer, Sam Adams," Caitlin said.

"Me, too," Alex said.

There was a strange medley of people on the dance floor. Bikers in leather were dancing close with preppy young women with barrettes in their hair. A few of the women were trying to pull their hips away from their sweaty, bearded, unwashed dance partners, most of whom had both hands on the girls' buttocks, pulling them into their erections. But a few of the other women were grinding their hips back to their dance partner, enjoying the danger and the forbidden fruit.

A huge, bearded man walked up to their table, his body odor preceding him. His belly pushed an old denim shirt over his belt, which had a wide, silver Harley Davidson buckle, and a sheath knife strapped on the right side, facing back. Thick, black hair covered his arms and curled from his shirt, which was open halfway to his navel. He smiled at Caitlin, showing his yellowed teeth, one with a prominent gold cap.

"My name's Billy. I run this gang. Let's dance," he said, and reached to grasp her hand.

Caitlin pulled her hand from his. "Thank you, but no. I don't dance."

He laughed loudly and reached again for her. "I'll teach you. You're gonna like it."

Caitlin grabbed his little finger and bent it back. "I said I don't want to dance. What part of 'no' don't you understand?"

Billy ripped her hand from his finger. "Listen, bitch," he snarled. "This is my bar. If I want to fuckin' dance with you, you're going to fuckin' dance with me. If I want you to suck my dick, you're going to fuckin' suck my dick and swallow, not spit. Your little fairy boyfriend there don't have shit to say about this. I'm the boss here."

Billy turned to glare and lean menacingly at Alex. "You got the message, pansy?" he said.

Alex watched two bouncers rush across the room, separating to approach Billy from either side. Others were flowing among the crowd, ready to stop budding trouble.

Alex turned his head and stared at him. "Yeah, I got the message, Billy."

Just then the bouncers got to either side of Billy, and grasped his arms. One of them said, "It's time to go, Billy. We've talked about this before."

They started to pull him away when Billy said to Caitlin, "Listen, you snotty cunt. If I ever see you again, and I fuckin' well hope I do, then we're gonna have some fun. You're gonna find out why they call me big Billy!"

"You're an animal!" Caitlin shouted at him. Then she turned to Alex. "As for you—thanks for all your support! Let's get out of here."

Billy crowed loudly as they pulled him away. "No pussy for you tonight, pansy. No head, neither."

Alex stood, tossed a twenty-dollar bill on the table, and followed Caitlin from the bar. As the bouncers hustled Billy out of the bar, several bikers stood staring at Alex and Caitlin, grinning. Another made little kissing sounds as they walked by.

When they got outside, Alex said, "Let's get out of sight and grab a cab." He had her arm and was moving her very quickly down the street when she pulled her arm from his grasp.

"Keep your hands off me, Cuchulain!" she snapped. "You weren't so forceful back there in the bar. I'm not afraid of those people, and I'm not going to run from them. They're animals! God, that was disgusting."

They walked at a slower pace and finally turned the corner.

"Well, are you going to say anything, Cuchulain?" she said.

He waved down a cab and they jumped in. "Let's go back uptown and have a drink somewhere quiet and talk about it," he said as the cab pulled away from the curb. "I know just the place."

"You're sure there are no bad guys there?" O'Connor sneered.

Alex smiled. "I certainly hope not."

A few minutes later they settled into a corner booth at a small wine bar in the West 70s. O'Connor looked intently at him. "So talk to me, Cuchulain. I sort of assumed that you were the type to jump to my defense, whether I needed help or not."

"And you like men who do that?" he said.

She sat back in the booth and took a sip of her wine. "No, for the most part, I detest it. It's just so macho," she said. "Billy scared me. What a fucking pig! I think he scared you, too. He did, didn't he, Cuchulain?"

"Caitlin, of course I was scared," he said. "Billy had a knife and a ton of friends there. I know that this is going to sound like bullshit. I'm sorry about that, but I think it's the truth. Quite simply, there was no need for me to do anything. So I didn't."

She studied him over the rim of her glass. "And you think you could have? Is that body builder look just a bit of narcissism or do you have that much animal in you? I'm pretty damned sure that you don't, but I would have been less sure before watching you tonight. And if you were that much of an animal, I'm not sure that I'd like you."

Alex chuckled. "Ah, the conundrum of civilized behavior. If you deal with animals by using animal behavior against them, are you civilized for protecting the society, whatever it takes, or have you become an animal and consequently not fit to mingle in civilized society? Do we say 'Thank you' and give out a medal and invite him to speak at graduation, or do we keep our would-be hero chained in the back yard like a pit bull, always half afraid that he will turn on us someday?"

O'Connor sat tapping her foot reflexively, studying him. Finally she said, "In your case, I suspect that the argument is academic, but I'll probably never know. I do know that Brooks Elliot would have reacted differently."

He shrugged. "Maybe."

"Well, I'm going to be in New York for another week and a half. Before I go back to California, I'm going back there. Back to that animal farm. I hate this feeling of intimidation that I have right now. I'm going to exorcise it."

"That's probably a bad idea," Cuchulain said, "but it's none of my business. Do you mind if I trail along with you? I didn't get to drink my beer."

Caitlin studied him for a second. "You're welcome, but you may get spanked if you're not careful."

Cuchulain smiled and said, "Sounds kinky. I can't wait."

New York
Mid-town

SEVERAL days later Caitlin walked beside Brooks Elliot from a conference room at Goldman Sachs. Axial was trying to schedule another round of pubic fund raising in a very difficult environment; Brooks Elliot was leading the charge at Goldman. As they stood awaiting the elevator, Caitlin said, "Why don't I buy you lunch? I want to ask you about something."

"Sure!" Elliot said. "Any 'druthers?"

"You pick, I'll buy," Caitlin said.

"Deal. There's a great sushi place that's not too far," he said.

Fifteen minutes later, they sat in a booth at a Japanese restaurant named Hana, each sipping hot miso soup from black lacquer bowls held in two hands. No spoons.

"Okay, what's on your mind, Caitlin?" Brooks said.

"Have you talked to Alex lately?' she said.

Elliot nodded. "I played squash with him yesterday morning, and then we had breakfast. Why?"

"Did you win?"

"Yeah, I won. I usually do," he said

"Why do you usually win?"

"Alex is fairly new to the game. He tends to muscle the ball," he said.

"Did he tell you about taking me to that biker bar the other night?" she said.

"Why don't you just tell me what's on your mind, Caitlin," Elliot said. "You may recall that I don't like to be quizzed about Alex."

She sat for a moment, phrasing in her mind. "I'd just like to get a better handle on him," she said. "I don't know, Brooks. Alex just seems so calm, so cautious. But there seems to be this underlying aura of menace—of ruthlessness. I can't seem to put my finger on it. I thought that I had a beginning handle on him until the other night, but it looks as though I was wrong. He puzzles me enough to make me uncomfortable."

Elliot sat, waiting.

"You've known me too long," she said. O'Connor gave a faint smile and shrugged her shoulders almost imperceptibly. "But let's just say that I'm very curious. He says he's interested in me. I'm trying to figure out if I'm interested in him. I just can't get a handle on him. He seems like the kind of guy who would jump up, all macho, and embarrass the shit out of me if anyone said a cross word to me, and you know that I just hate that bullshit. But we were in a nasty situation in a biker bar downtown the other night. I was pretty scared and really pissed, too. I'll spare you the details, but this fat pig was saying some really strong shit to me, and Alex just sat there; he didn't say a word. If the bouncers hadn't shown up, it could have gotten really ugly. Alex didn't defend me; he didn't tell the guy to back off. He just sat there like a wimp. Dumb—and probably terrified. I know *I* was."

She shifted in her chair, thinking.

"Alex is not a coward, Caitlin," Elliot said with an odd smile on his face. "He wouldn't bring dishonor on your warrior clan. It's even possible he could bring something to the table."

"Caitlin, there's something I just don't get here," Elliot said as he gazed at her still, closed face. "This just doesn't sound like the Caitlin O'Connor I know. You could have broken the fat guy's finger, but you didn't. Your father once told me you got a brown belt in judo when you were thirteen and wanted boxing lessons, too. He worried for a while about the way you got violent when you didn't get what you wanted—anger management expense for him, wasn't it?"

O'Connor's eyes flashed and she said, "That shit! He never told me he told you that. Anyway, that anger counselor was dumber than a fence post and tried to look up my skirt all the time. Jesus H. Christ, where do they find those idiots and give them a Ph.D.?"

"Remember me?" Elliot said quietly. "I'm the one who doesn't get distracted easily. Give up on the defensive time warp, and let's continue to discuss your relationship with the lovely and charming patrons at Choppers."

"Oh, fuck you, asshole," Caitlin exploded loudly. The other Hana patrons turned to stare.

"You had never been really afraid before like that, had you? I mean really stark terrified," Elliot said. "You lost your nerve because of it, because that much adrenaline was a new thing, and you had more than one potential assailant, all armed. Now you're trying to rebuild your ego by laying the problem off on Alex. Jesus, Caitlin! I'd forgotten how self-centered you are—how driven by your view of yourself!"

"Up your giggy, Elliot," O'Connor whispered. "Take your tabletop psychoanalysis and put it where the sun don't shine."

"And what would you like to discuss instead, my charming, articulate friend?" Elliot chuckled.

Caitlin leaned forward, her right hand extended toward him, long fingers curling repeatedly back in supplication. "Come on, Elliot—Give! This is not about me, right now. What's the story on Cuchulain? You know I wouldn't ask lightly. This is embarrassing enough without me having to beg."

His mind was racing. She was tough to brush off. "What do you want to know?" he said. "Alex is my best friend, and I've only known him as an adult. He's honest, incredibly bright, even by your standards—a wonderful and loyal friend, and very hard working. There's no one on the planet that I respect more."

"I bare my soul and you give me platitudes—pablum!" she spat, while coolly thinking she never dreamed she would hear that kind of endorsement from Brooks F.T. Elliot, IV, about anyone. Cuchulain suddenly became more interesting to her. She decided to take a different tack.

"Brooks, Brooks—I'm lonely," she said softly. "I'd like to have someone in my life. Someone presentable to take to the occasional charity ball, someone to take a vacation with, someone who just likes me for me and not what my press says I am. You know what it costs me to have this conversation with you; it's just not the kind of thing I do."

"Yeah, I know it's not, Caitlin." Elliot sat for a few moments, sipping green tea, thinking. "Caitlin, you know I want to help, but I'm not going to act as Alex's unauthorized biographer. Okay—if I'm going to answer the question, I'll answer it short and straight or I'll decline to answer and take a pass on not just the subject, but the whole topic area. If you structure and phrase your questions carefully, I'll answer them. Don't ask me anything that you could just as well ask him. Don't game me."

She picked up a piece of raw tuna with her chopsticks, dunked it into a film of soy sauce in a ceramic saucer, and popped it into her mouth. Then she picked up her tea mug. "Okay, here goes," she said, sipping.

"Is he a wimp, or a wuss, or something dressed up like a wolf that isn't a wolf?"

"No," Elliot said.

"Is he a wolf?"

"Pass," he said.

"Does he have the courage of his convictions and the willingness to defend them?"

Brooks smiled. "Maybe more than anyone I've ever met," he said.

"That's interesting," Caitlin said, sitting up a little. "Could be a little scary, though. Do I need to think or worry about that?"

"Yes," he said.

She gazed intently at Elliot. "Tell me about that."

"No, and the broad topic is off the air," he said.

"Is he dangerous?" she said.

"Is he dangerous to you?" His eyebrows rose and he allowed a look of incredulity to flicker across his face. "Absolutely not."

"That wasn't what I meant, and you know it!" she fumed.

Elliot shook his head. "Broad topic's gone. You're winning. I'm giving you more than I said I would. This little interrogation is close to being over."

She held her hands up in surrender. "Okay, Okay. Just a couple more. Do you want to hear the biker story?"

"No. I already heard it from him," he said.

"Really! Tell me what Alex said," she said.

"No. Ask him," he said.

O'Connor was fighting her temper, and losing. "Godammit, Brooks, this just doesn't compute. Why are you being this way? Jesus, remember me? I've known you for more than ten years, and we were sleeping together for three of them. I was a virgin when I met you, for Christ's sake. You're one of my best friends. Why won't you help keep me from being hurt? You've actually managed to hurt my feelings a little, which I didn't think you could do anymore."

Elliot started to speak, then stopped, groping for the right words. "I'm not very comfortable with this conversation," he said. "But, I'm going to give this one more try, because even if you're gaming me with the hurt feelings to get more information, I think you should probably know anyhow. You're a very good friend, and I want to help keep you from getting hurt."

Elliot leaned back in his chair and looked at the ceiling, then said softly, "First, I'm more loyal to him than I am to you, even though I very much like and respect you. You should take that feeling into consideration. I agree with you on the marriage and baby thing—probably wouldn't have worked. I owe you big for that."

"Second, Cuchulain is fully formed, intellectually and emotionally. He's not your intellectual equal, but he's in the neighborhood, and anyway, formed in a far different mold. He's applied intelligence; you are pure." He looked back down and smiled. "God, I could sell tickets to Mensa for a chance to listen in on the two of you if you ever get serious."

"Third, you should avoid putting him into situations where he may have to react violently. The biker bar could have been ugly. He and I play by different rules than most people."

Caitlin looked thoughtful. "I'm going back down there. I just have to, and Cuchulain said he wanted to come along. Maybe I should just go without him," she said.

"You should probably take him, my previous comments notwithstanding. He's useful in places like that. I assume that drinking one beer and sitting for a few minutes in defiance will satisfy this unreasonable compulsion of yours to be the Irish Rambo."

She delicately raised her middle finger to Brooks as she screwed her face into a grimace. He laughed.

"Look, Caitlin. You should give him a chance," he said. "This is a wonderful guy. He'll try to keep from hurting you. He'll try to deal with your ego and your intellect, and they are about equal in size. Dealing with them together is no day at the beach—I've been there."

"Oh, I see. I'm fucked up and he's perfect?"

"Don't you pull that shit with me, Caitlin," Elliot snapped. "You're not perfect and neither is he. What I'm not going to do is go down that road with you—or for you."

Downtown

ALEX and Caitlin were back in Choppers, once again in business clothes in a booth at the corner of the room. Billy was nowhere to be seen, and Caitlin had nearly finished her beer. The nachos proved nearly inedible. Bouncers converged on a bearded drunk who was standing behind a girl with his hands cupped over her breasts, pretending to dance as she fought and scratched at him over her shoulder. Caitlin said, "This is disgusting. I'm done proving whatever I was proving to myself. I'm going to the ladies room. I'll see you outside."

Alex waved for the waitress as Caitlin slid from the booth and walked away. When she finally waddled over, he handed her thirty dollars then turned to walk toward the restrooms and the exit. There was some sort of fuss at the door. As he got closer, it faded to the outside and he walked into the men's room behind a biker in full black leather regalia. When he stepped back into the hallway, Caitlin was not there. He felt a faint tug of alarm. He pushed the door to the women's room partly opened and said loudly, "Caitlin, you okay?" There was no answer. He stepped partway inside. There were two women at the sinks, but no Caitlin. He ducked to look under the toilet stall doors. No feet. He could feel the familiar sensation of adrenaline rushing into his body.

"You looking for a tall blonde in a suit? A looker?" one of the women asked, as she glanced at him in the mirror.

"Yes. You see her?" he said.

"She left a couple of minutes ago with a bunch of bikers," she said. "Didn't seem real happy about it."

Alex spun and raced outside. The street was empty except for one Harley at the curb. Just then the biker from the john hurried out, pulling keys from his pocket and moving to his machine, a cigarette hanging from the corner of his mouth.

Alex walked over to the biker, and just as he looked up, Cuchulain grabbed the man's nose between the knuckles of his index and middle fingers and twisted sharply, breaking it. He dropped his hand and snatched the cigarette from the man's mouth, as he grabbed the front of his shirt and rushed him to the outside wall of the bar and banged his back against the old bricks, hard.

"Where did they take the girl?' Cuchulain demanded.

The biker sprayed blood on him as he spoke. "Fuck you, asshole."

"I don't have a lot of time," Alex snarled. He pushed the lit end of the cigarette into the man's cheek for a second, and the smell of burnt flesh filled the air. When the scream ended, he pushed the cigarette within an eighth-inch of the biker's eye, singeing the eyelashes from the lid. "You'll be blind in ten seconds if you don't tell me, then I'll dig around in the sockets. Believe it."

The biker was suddenly aware that his feet were not touching the ground; that he was being held in the air against the wall with one hand while the other held the cigarette. His cheek felt on fire and urine was burning down his right leg. He quickly blurted the address. Alex slapped him on the forehead with the heel of his hand, bouncing the biker's head against the wall; the cigarette fluttered to the sidewalk.

Cuchulain grabbed the keys from the hand of the falling, unconscious man and jumped onto the motorcycle, kicked it to life and accelerated down the street, necktie flapping wildly behind him.

The cooling motorcycle engines were still ticking when Alex jumped from the bike and ran to the door, just as a roar of approval and laughter went up from inside. A large man in a black t-shirt and dirty jeans stepped in front of him, blocking his way as he stuck a hand in Alex's chest. "Beat it, asshole," he said. "This is a private club."

Cuchulain grabbed the hand with his left, just below the wrist, then gave it a hard snap up and out, breaking the wrist, as he stepped under the raised arm and drove his right elbow down and back into the guard's lower back, just above the belt on his right side, then again. Cuchulain reached down quickly, and pulled the man's thighs back from just above the knees so that his face was driven to the pavement with a resounding thunk. As Cuchulain reached for the door, he snapped a kick into the man's left ear. The door was unlocked and Cuchulain stepped inside. O'Connor was being held in a chair by two men, bare breasts exposed, while Billy, the leader, had his penis out from the fly of his dirty Levi's, four inches from her terrified, furious face.

"Hey, Whoa!" Alex yelled.

The room went quiet as heads snapped to see the intruder. Billy's face lit up in a delighted grin. "Well, if ain't the fuckin' pansy. This is my lucky day! You can referee a gangbang—me first. You know, pick out who gets to fuck her next, make sure no one goes twice before everyone goes once and all that shit. By tomorrow, we'll be starting to wear out, and might even give you a little. But first, I want a little blowjob from Blondie. I sort of promised it to my buddy here," he leered, pulling the foreskin up and back. "If she bites me, I'll just knock her teeth out and try again."

Alex said loudly, "I don't think so. That would be really dumb. There will be cops everywhere, and you guys are in enough trouble already. For what?" He looked around at the gang, assessing them. He quickly settled on a small, wiry man with very still eyes and a telltale easy balance. He knew the type.

Cuchulain eased toward him and spoke again. "I'll tell you what. You guys are supposed to be the baddest asses in New York. What if I arm wrestle two of you at once for the girl? If you win, you keep the girl and no cops. If I win, we walk. It would save you a ton of hassle with the cops. You know that I can't beat two of you, so why not? I gotta do something! Deal?"

Ignoring the others, he looked steadily at the small, quiet man who looked around and then said, "What if we all fuck her, beat the living shit out of you, and toss you both in an alley somewhere? We'll just give you both some pills that Billy bought down in Mexico, where you can't remember shit about what happened lately. What then? Cops? You won't remember enough to make a decent witness." The room was quiet as the other bikers turned to look at Alex.

"No, slick. You get me," Alex said coldly.

The small man felt a surge of recognition and imminent danger. The quiet eyes moved over Cuchulain again, assessing him, noting the familiar combat balance, feeling himself sink involuntarily into a defensive posture as cold hostility oozed from Cuchulain's eyes. The flesh on the outside edges of Cuchulain's eyes began to bunch and extend, giving him the facial cast of a hooded cobra. Breath whistled loudly from his nostrils. The small man pulled up his right sleeve and bared a veined, muscular forearm. The distinctive beer can logo of the Navy's Seals was tattooed on the inner arm, starting to fade, but unmistakable.

"I used to be in the Navy. The name's Dodd. Do I know you?"

Alex smiled coldly. "I need something from my right pocket, Okay?"

Dodd reached behind his vest and swung out a small, stainless steel automatic. He clicked the safety off, thumbed the hammer back and pointed the pistol directly at Alex's navel and said. "Do it very slowly."

Cuchulain reached slowly into his right trouser pocket and pulled out a half-dollar coin. He offered it to the small man.

Dodd nodded in recognition, lowered the pistol and said, "No. I heard about this. I just gotta see it."

Alex held the half-dollar in front of him, at eye height, showing it to the crowd. Then he positioned his thumb on the bottom of the coin and his middle and index finger on the top. He began to squeeze. As he increased the pressure, veins swelled across his hand and the skin pad between his thumb and forefinger humped slowly up like a ragged tumor. The room was still, except for the noise of Cuchulain's breathing.

The coin began to bend, then slowly fold.

Cuchulain's hand was now quivering visibly, and his forearm had swollen to stretch tight his suit jacket sleeve. Then the coin folded in half.

"Jeeesus Christ!" one of the bikers exclaimed softly.

Cuchulain casually flipped the folded coin at Dodd' right shoulder and shifted his weight toward him. The pistol came back up as Dodd snatched the coin out of the air with his left hand. "Nice try." he said. "But I still got it. And I still got you. But I know who you are."

Alex waited.

Dodd said, "I'm tempted. You know we can't just let you go. What happens if we just waste you now? No fuss. You know I got you, don't you? And there's twenty of us."

Cuchulain nodded. "You have me. I might not even get you. But I probably would. Probably Billy, too, and three or four others when I take your gun. For sure I wouldn't get all of you. "

Dodd smiled faintly. "And?"

"And you get everyone here dead. Fast. No cops. No jury. Just dead. Probably more than a bit of pain for you if it's convenient. But dead."

"By?" Dodd asked.

Cuchulain smiled. Now he had Dodd. "The Horse, Jerome Masterson, lives in town here," he said. "You know about him and me, and the folks that the two of us know well. Lieutenant Elliot is here, too. He owes me from a Middle East operation. You just might know him."

Dodd shifted, as memory rushed in. "Yeah, Lebanon. You saved his ass. I missed that one. Lieutenant Elliot, huh? He ain't no prize; he's meaner than a fuckin' cottonmouth." He looked around at the gang. They were getting restless and stealing glances at Caitlin's bare breasts, thinking about their turns.

He said softly to Cuchulain, "Okay, I'm in. But I don't think they're going to buy it—won't believe me. We may have to kill some—probably will. Shit!" He raised his eyebrows in a question.

"Try to sell us walking. If it won't go, sell the arm wrestling. Lacking that, I'll take the Colt from the guy behind you and we'll nail eight or ten.

After I kill Billy; go to one knee and work from the right. Head shots. Killing a few more should end it, and the cops will be here by then. That should end it. I'll handle the mess. Anyone looking for you?"

"The cops in a few cities have my prints and would like to find me; same with DEA," Dodd said. "You sure about the arm wrestling? There's some big fuckers here, and I don't want the shooting to start."

Cuchulain nodded, "Sell it."

Dodd shifted back slightly, turning to the group, keeping his right arm hanging down and slightly behind him.

"Listen up, guys!" he said. "I know about this guy. A lot of Seals say that he's the baddest motherfucker that ever lived, and you guys know that there's a bunch of mean motherfuckers among us. He is truly a badass."

Alex stepped back a little, as he chose his target if the balloon went up. He'd need a gun and shifted slightly toward a fat, bearded man with the checkered wooden grips of a Colt .45 automatic sticking up from his belt. The hammer was down and the thumb safety on; Alex would have the gun and take out his throat before the man could ever get his gun into action.

Dodd said, "Our lives won't be worth a shit if we don't let him and her go. Trust me on that. And if we kill him, ten or fifteen bodaciously bad guys are coming for us. Gloves off. They wouldn't dream of using their fists if they could easier shoot or knife you in the back. They'll have machine guns, explosives, sniper rifles—all that shit. It won't be pretty, and none of us will live through it. For sloppy sevenths on a piece of ass? And can you imagine the fucking cops? They're already like flies on shit around here!"

Billy bellowed, "That's bullshit! I told her what I was going to do and I'm gonna do it! This is prime pussy, and that pansy don't look so bad to me. If I wasn't fucked up from spilling my bike the other day, I'd take him myself. You don't run this fuckin' gang, Dodd, I do!"

Dodd sighed as some of the men nodded at Billy's speech. "Look, Billy, there's a bunch of us that don't want to see the cops or the feds up close," he said. "You're left handed. Why don't you arm wrestle him for it? You're messed up for a fight, but there's nothing wrong with your left arm. Besides, no one has ever beaten you but Bubba, and no one beats Bubba. We're getting enough shit from the cops already. It wouldn't be good for business."

Billy looked startled, and then the ends of his lips curled up in a cruel, wolfish smile. "Fuck that! He said he wants two at once, and I want the girl. He gets Bubba and Kevin while me and one-eye take a rest so's we have lots of energy for later. Whichever one slams the pansy's arm down first gets seconds on the pussy after me. The loser gets the second blow job."

Dodd took control quickly. "Deal!" he said. "Let's get a table cleared and some chairs over here."

Alex jerked his tie down and unbuttoned the top three buttons on his shirt, giving him access to the throwing knife that always hung at his back, just below his collar. If things went bad, Billy would find himself with it buried in his throat. Cuchulain pulled his jacket off and threw it over a chair backed to the wall and stood, casually rolling his shirtsleeves, waiting and assessing the crowd for the ones who could be trouble. Caitlin watched him, her eyes wide and her jaw hanging slack, oblivious of her naked breasts.

Alex moved his chair across the wall to the table and waited. Bubba and Kevin brought out chairs and sat down, grinning at Cuchulain. Bubba had long, shaggy hair and a ragged beard, tangled with the remnants of the past few days' meals. He was well over six feet and enormously fat, probably weighing upwards of three hundred pounds. He put a huge arm on the table, hawked his throat and spat a brownish wad of phlegm on Alex's shirt, just splattering the edge of his tie. There was a large tattoo on the inside of Bubba's huge forearm that spelled out "Eat Shit!" in Old English letters. Kevin was a bodybuilder, and a big one. He had acne and his hair was sparse, but the steroids had given him enviable bulk.

Alex dropped into the chair and put his upper arms on the table, with his veined and pulsing forearms vertical and shoulder width apart. Then he began to focus his energy. He felt his local awareness fade as he focused his conscious being into a core of energy just beneath his navel, feeling as if each molecule of his being was rushing to one central repository, then waiting to be dispatched. The sound of his breath whistled even louder through his nose.

Dodd said, "Okay. Get them lined up, and I'm going to count to three. On three, go for it."

Alex was barely aware as Kevin and Bubba lined up. As they each clasped a hand and bore down with their grip, Cuchulain was only peripherally aware that he was countering their force. He heard Dodd at a distance, say, "One, two …" Cuchulain released his energy just before Dodd said three, driving every ounce of his being into his hands in a single, furious contraction. He felt both their hands collapse, then yield under his sudden onslaught; the sound of snapping bones could be heard in the room. Alex slammed both their hands across his chest to the table and stood, then casually grabbed Bubba by the front of his hair and smashed his face into the table, twice. It had taken less than ten seconds. He folded his jacket over his arm.

"I think we will be leaving now, gentlemen," he said, and turned toward Caitlin.

You cheated," one biker yelled. "You went before three!"

"Sit down, asshole," Cuchulain said coldly. "You go on three and I'll go on six. Then I'll rip your arm off at the shoulder."

"Fuck you," the biker yelled. "Why don't you just get the hell out of here?"

Alex nodded and walked swiftly toward Caitlin. The gang was momentarily stunned by the vision of Kevin and Bubba still at the table, each holding a mangled hand, moaning softly as the swelling started and blood began to pool around Bubba's twitching face.

"Bullshit!" Billy yelled as he stepped in front of Cuchulain, pulling his fist back. Cuchulain stepped in quickly and used his huge neck to slam his forehead into Billy's nose and eyes; he felt nose and cheekbones collapse and eye sockets crack and crumble an instant later. The web of his left hand slammed into Billy's Adam's apple and his thumb closed on the carotid artery, shutting off the blood supply to his brain. Cuchulain drove his right hand deep into Billy's crotch, squeezing his penis and testicles through his jeans. He began to rip, focusing on delivering all the power that he could generate. The sound of denim tearing pierced the silent room. As Alex felt resistance there collapse, he began to twist as he squeezed, feeling flesh and tendons ripping and releasing. As Billy lost consciousness, Cuchulain bent his knees to lower him to the floor, his head up as he watched the gang. When he stood, he was holding Billy's pistol. The snap of the safety being released by Cuchulain's right thumb was eerily loud in the room. He worked the slide on the automatic once, and a cartridge tumbled noisily across the dirty floor. He turned and reached for Caitlin, looking coldly at the two men holding her, who stepped back quickly. Cuchulain draped his jacket over her shoulders and led her to the door. He nodded at Dodd just before he stepped out and pulled the door closed.

Outside, Cuchulain stepped hard on the inert guard's neck as he grabbed Caitlin's arm and guided her. He engaged the safety on Billy's pistol and slid it behind his belt at the small of his back. They were almost at a run as they left the alley and moved down the street and around the corner, Cuchulain waving to an approaching cab with its "on duty" light on. He opened the door and pushed her inside, almost roughly, then moved in beside her. He gave the cabbie his home address, then put his arm around Caitlin. She was already shaking, and her teeth were beginning to chatter.

"Just take it easy," he said. "It's over now. We're going to my place."

"No, I want to go back to my room. I want to be alone!"

Cuchulain shook his head and turned to her on the ragged seat. "Listen to me, Caitlin. This is the worst possible time for you to be alone. You could go into shock. Someone has to keep an eye on you, and that's going to be me. We're going to my place."

"I am in no mood for romance, Cuchulain. Okay?" she chattered.

"I promise," he said.

They took the elevator to his apartment. It was sparsely but expensively furnished, with the look of a place done by a decorator and seldom touched since. The exception was two floor-to-ceiling bookcases full of volumes and a small desk that held a dual computer setup with neatly stacked papers around it. A large oil painting on the living room wall depicted a group of fishermen in a traditional boat, pulling in nets at sunrise under the shaded mass of Gibraltar. On the stand beside a reclining reading chair was a worn leather-bound copy of the Quran with a yellowed ivory bookmark placed partway through.

Cuchulain led her to the couch and said, "I'll get some blankets and make some tea. Tea's good in this situation. Maybe a drink later."

She wrapped her arms around herself, shivering. "A drink now! A big drink!"

He walked quickly to the bedroom and came back with two wool blankets and a towel. He wrapped the blankets around her, tucking them tight, then smoothed the towel across her lap, pushing a little dent in the middle. Caitlin seemed a little startled and curious by the towel, but said nothing.

"I'll get the drinks," Alex said.

He came back with two glasses of cognac and the bottle. "Sip this," he said, handing her one glass with a light portion of cognac poured into it. He sat beside her and sipped on his own glass, waiting for her to give him a hint as to how to distract her from the evening's events.

Caitlin tipped up her glass and drained it, then shuddered. "Oh, my God, Alex. I'm still terrified," she said, shaking. "I've never been that afraid before, or that furious. I'm also sorry that I didn't kick that asshole in the balls as we walked out! That was just awful! I hate that those animals exist."

"They've been around since the beginning, Caitlin. Society just doesn't let them out that often, at least in this country," Alex said, happy that she had picked a topic familiar to him. "More of them were in Nazi Germany, Kosovo, and Bosnia-Herzegovina lately than elsewhere, but they're always around. There's still a bunch in the Middle East."

"With all of our technology and power, why can't we just get rid of people like that?" Caitlin fumed.

"I've thought a lot about that," Alex said. "I don't know of a politician, alive or dead, that could be trusted with the power to accomplish that, if even we could do it. Politicians are, by my definition, megalomaniacs to some degree, and most of them care only about money and votes. Those bikers tonight were one form of villain, but religious fanatics are worse, because they think that they can both interpret and enforce the word and the will of God—to their personal benefit of course. I think we should just kill the leaders of those sociopaths, one by one. Their followers will disappear with no piper to follow."

Caitlin snorted. "I don't think they know the first thing about God, or what she thinks!" she said, throwing up suddenly, and barely catching the foul mass in the towel on her lap.

'Sorry," she said. "That came from nowhere. Gross!"

Cuchulain held his hands in front of her so that she could see them shaking. "It's part of the adrenaline depletion," he said. "Try to relax and take your mind away from tonight. It will make things seem more normal, and you'll recover faster. It happens to everyone."

"This is what happens when you're scared, and I was scared, too," he said.

He sat for a few seconds sipping his drink, then started to push the conversation back to something distracting. "I sometimes have nightmares about Torquemada returning in modern form," he said. "People should study the Spanish Inquisition to see what happens when vast power is granted to religious fanatics. It's a shame no one killed him early."

'So, if you've thought about this a lot, what's the right answer?" she asked, studying him, still shaking.

"Darned if I know," he chuckled. "I guess if I've reached any tentative conclusion at all, it's that we should worry about our own country first, and then the others—and pick off the bad guys' leaders, one at a time. Without us the world could once again become a real cesspool—and quickly. It's happening slowly anyhow, it seems to me."

The images of the evening suddenly came back to Caitlin. She turned quickly to Cuchulain, the blanket falling from her shoulders. She pulled his jacket around her ripped blouse. "When you came through that door, I was so proud of you for coming in there to defend me from those animals, but

I knew that you were going to be hurt very badly, if not killed," she said. "I don't even want to think about all of those fucking vermin above me, humping and pumping, one after the other. How did you know what to do? Your behavior seemed so bizarre, but it worked!"

He sat for a second and took another sip of his cognac. "Bizarre behavior freaks people out and limits what they think they can do. I stunned them with it until I lucked out enough to find a guy who knew me a little; my face change helps to create bizarre when I'm excited."

Caitlin sat silent for several moments, wrapping the blanket more tightly around her shoulders, still shivering. "Yes, you looked like a fucking snake, and I hate snakes! But how did he know you? Who are you that he said, and I quote, 'He is the baddest motherfucker in the whole world?'"

Alex sat silent for awhile, then said, "I was an active Marine for quite a while—eight years, in fact. I told you about it, briefly. I was good at it. Dodd had been a Navy Seal, and he just knew me, or knew about me. I have unusually strong hands, as you saw, and that kind of word gets around."

She sat thinking for a while longer, as the shivering subsided. She took the bottle from the table and poured another full glass of cognac and drank half of it. "I thought that I was going to be humiliated and debased. I was terrified—I was consumed with fury! I wanted so badly to kill them, but had no way to do it. They are such a bunch of worthless pigs! And then you came in—and I was afraid for you."

"But I didn't need to be, did I Alex?" Caitlin said. "That reptilian little man was afraid of you, wasn't he? You had it under control, didn't you?"

Alex sighed, and said, "No, Caitlin. I didn't have it under control. I just worked with what I had, and I got lucky. But thank you for being afraid for me. It could have gotten very ugly, very quickly."

"And that little man wasn't afraid of you?" she said.

"He was wary, not afraid," Alex said. "He had heard about me when he was a Seal. Because of what he had heard, he believed what I told him, and didn't like the odds."

"Jesus Christ!" she said. "You told him that Brooks Elliot and some horse person would kill them all if they didn't let us go. And he believed you! Was it true?"

Alex gave the shrug she had seen before. "Who knows? They probably would have tried, and I can't imagine that a bunch of hoods like that would have stood much of a chance against them. Dodd knew that."

"Who the hell are you, Cuchulain? You force your way into my life, and I think that you're a nice, good-natured guy with a great body and a good mind, who happens to own a bunch of my stock. And God, I was worried that you were a fucking wimp! You're clearly a lot more than that, and a lot of what you seem to be is disturbing to me. I didn't even know that people like you existed; you were like an animal, and your face got really spooky—not that I wasn't glad to have you there tonight, but God, you're not what I thought. You were probably some kind of killer or something, trained by the government, and Brooks was probably one, too. Again, who the hell are you?"

And how did you get this way? she asked herself.

Twenty Years Earlier
Audley, South Carolina

NOOOOO! Cuchulain's mind screamed. *He's such a butthole.*
Alex was sprawled on the porch swing of his parent's house, thumbing through a hot rod magazine and enjoying the first warm day of spring in Audley. The window to the living room was open behind him, and he heard his mother and his older sister, Elena, walk into the room, deep into conversation. Elena said, "His name is Junior Harris, and he's the captain of the football team! He's supposed to pick me up at six-thirty. We're going a little early to help with the decorations in the gym." They started to jabber excitedly about what Elena was going to wear.

Alex thought that Junior Harris was maybe the biggest asshole in the entire high school, and worse, he was fairly sure that someone had said that Harris had a regular girlfriend. Harris and Elena were seniors at Audley High. As a sophomore, Alex didn't run in their circles.

Without giving the situation more thought, Alex rolled from the swing and walked into the living room. "Elena," he said, "you just can't go out with that jerk. He brags all over school that no girl has ever turned him down, and that they all beg him to go to bed with them. He's just using you."

"Mother!" Elena cried. "Will you tell this brat to mind his own business? I'm just going on a date with a popular, good-looking guy. I'm not going to bed with him or anyone else."

Alex's mother turned to him, and spoke in her formal, Spanish-accented

English. "I think that you are perhaps exaggerating, Alex, and your language is not appropriate. The Harris boy comes from a very nice family, and I am sure that he knows Elena is a nice girl. Let us not hear any more about these kinds of rumors, when the young man is not here to defend himself. It is not proper."

Alex looked at the determined expression on his mother's face and knew that he couldn't make her share his concerns. He walked to the stairs and started up to his room. Over his shoulder he said, "I sure hope you're right, Mom."

Two days later, in the early evening, he heard a car pulling up to the front of their house, and walked to his bedroom window to look. He saw Harris stop in front of the house in his father's Cadillac, and then heard him beep the horn for Elena. *What a jerk!* Alex thought. *Harris can't even get out of the car to walk up and meet Mom and Dad.* He saw Elena run down the walk and get into the car. Suddenly, it occurred to him that the dance didn't start for nearly two hours.

On an impulse, Alex ran downstairs and jumped onto his bike, pedaling furiously in pursuit of the car. As he rounded the corner by the big poplar, Alex saw the Cadillac pulling from a stop sign several blocks down the street. He was gaining on it. As the car approached the high school, it stopped for another stop sign, and a young man ran from the corner and jumped into the back seat. The Cadillac turned away from the high school, accelerating toward the area above town where most high school students with cars went to "make out." It was a small oval pasture on a hill above the river, about two miles from town. Alex turned his bike toward it. His thigh muscles were on fire as he pedaled up the steep hill below the parking area and finally crested it. The blue and chrome tail fins of the Cadillac were sticking out from behind a tree. Alex slowed to jump from his bike, and pushed it to rest on its side beside a large bush. He moved behind forsythia, heavy with golden blossoms, and began to sneak forward. If everything was okay and he got caught, he'd never hear the end of it from Elena, and his mom wouldn't be very happy either, which was worse. The Cadillac was quiet, and the only car in the pasture.

He sneaked closer, feeling like a pervert, but determined to make sure that Elena was okay. When he was finally close enough to hear the hum of conversation from the Cadillac, he could hear Elena yelling at someone but couldn't make out what she was saying.

Suddenly the passenger door burst open and Elena jumped out of the car. At the same time the back door came open, and Harris's best friend and fellow football jock, Billy Ray Sutter, jumped out and grabbed Elena, wrapping his big hands around her biceps from behind and pulling her back against his chest. Harris got out of the car and walked quickly around it. He smiled as he saw Billy Ray holding her, reaching for his zipper and pulling it down as he stood in front of her. He reached up and began to unbutton the front of her dress, then suddenly ripped it open and tore her simple bra apart, suddenly exposing her substantial breasts. "Jesus Christ, Billy Ray! Look at the tits on her!' Harris exclaimed. He reached up and fondled one breast and then the other. Elena was struggling against Sutter's grip and trying to kick Harris. Elena screamed and Harris slapped her hard once, then twice. "Get her on her knees Billy Ray, so she can't kick at me. Once she's down there, the little spic might as well suck me off." Sutter grinned and forced her to her knees from behind as he held her.

Alex burst from the bushes in a rage, running toward Harris, screaming. Both men were frozen in surprise when Alex's shoulder hit the outside of Harris's right knee in a driving tackle, causing it to collapse to the inside with an audible tearing sound. Harris screamed in agony as he fell to the ground, rolling and holding his knee.

Alex rolled to his feet and turned for Billy Ray, who had released Elena and was raising his hands. Alex went at him with a howl, reaching for his face, as Billy Ray hit him in the stomach hard, once with each fist. The wind went out of Alex as he felt his hands close on Billy Ray's face. He curled his fingers down reflexively and felt a soft spot under his right hand as the pain began to take him. He dug his fingernails into it, then twisted and pulled as he fell to the ground. He was rewarded by a rending scream of anguish from Billy Ray.

Alex was on his hands and knees, still trying to catch his breath, when

Elena started to pull him to his feet. "C'mon, Alex," she whispered. "We gotta get out of here before they can get after us." Both of her assailants were on the ground, moaning and whimpering.

"You take my bike. I'll run," Alex said, struggling to his feet. As Elena ran for the bicycle, Alex began to jog painfully down the hill.

An hour later, Alex's mother was still in the bedroom with Elena and his father was on the phone yelling at someone when the sheriff's car came to the house and slid to a stop, emergency lights flashing red against the shingles of the modest house. The neighbors rushed to their porches, excited for a break in the routine of small-town days. The county sheriff and one deputy walked to the door and pounded on it. Alex's father, Mick Cuchulain, rolled his wheelchair to the door and opened it.

"We have a warrant for the arrest of Alex Cuchulain," the sheriff said loudly.

Mick looked at him for a second. "I don't think I'm going to like this. What are the charges?"

The sheriff flushed. "Your two brats crippled both the Harris and the Sutter boys tonight, Cuchulain. He's under arrest for assault and battery, criminal maiming, attempted robbery, and attempted murder. We may take your daughter as an accomplice."

Mick's face flushed crimson as he shouted, "This is total bullshit, Sheriff. Those boys tried to rape my daughter and force her to blow them besides. My son defends her, and now you're going to throw him in jail? What the hell kind of scumbag sheriff are you, anyway?"

The sheriff flushed even more. "I ain't got any room in my jail for a cripple, Cuchulain, so you'd better shut your fuckin' mouth or I'll ship you down to Columbia for disturbing the peace. I got a warrant here for your boy, so you'd better get him out here."

Alex, who had been listening from inside, stepped to the door. The sheriff said, "Cuff him, Denton," and the deputy stepped forward, reaching for the handcuffs in his belt pouch. Mick Cuchulain punched the deputy in the stomach from his wheelchair, then reached for his gun. The sheriff grabbed his gun from its holster, and stuck it into Cuchulain's face, cocking it.

"I don't mind shootin' a cripple, Cuchulain. It'd save me a lot of trouble." He nodded to the deputy, "Put the goddamned cuffs on the kid, Denton."

As the sheriff drove away with Alex and Denton in the back seat of the cruiser, Mick worked to quiet his rage. He wheeled his chair inside and went to the phone, dialing directory assistance in Washington, D.C. After twenty minutes, he managed to reach a staffer working late in the office of Laurence Grail, senior Senator from the Commonwealth of Pennsylvania and Chairman of the Senate Intelligence Committee. It took another twenty minutes to convince the staffer that the senator might indeed be willing to talk to someone from South Carolina with no political connections. It was of great assistance when, late in the conversation, the staffer found the list of "put through immediately" names that was distributed to all staffers. "You don't happen to be Michael P. Cuchulain, do you, Sir?" the staffer asked with new-found respect in his voice.

"I am," said Cuchulain, "and, as I said before, I need to speak to the Senator immediately!"

"He's at a State Dinner at the White House, Mr. Cuchulain. They won't interrupt, so the best I can do is to contact him when he leaves. That will be at eleven or so. Is that too late?"

"There is no time too late. Please ask him to call me; tell him that it's very important to me."

At 11:15 that evening, the staffer reached Senator Grail in his car. He apologized for the lateness, then passed on the message. Interestingly, the Senator said, "There is no time too late for Mick Cuchulain. Ever. Give me the number." He wrote it down and broke the connection, squinted at the faintly-lit keypad on the clunky wireless car phone and punched in the numbers.

The staffer was deeply puzzled, as he tried to remember anyone named Cuchulain who had that kind of pull with Senator Grail.

The phone rang at Michael P. Cuchulain's house.

Northern Virginia

O N Saturday morning at 0630, Randall Moreau, the Deputy Director of Operations, the DDO, of the United States Central Intelligence Agency was walking up the driveway of his McLean, Virginia home in his pajamas and bathrobe, carrying the rumpled Washington Post and New York Times that had been thrown by the paperboy into the tall hedge beside the garage. His bare feet were chilled, causing him to relish the thought of his first cup of coffee and his only uninterrupted newspaper time of the week. He was fighting mild feelings of misanthropy when his phone rang, making it quite likely that the emotion would again prove justified. He snatched the phone off the hook in the kitchen and snarled, "This better be good!"

"It's Larry Grail. How about buying me a cup of coffee? Now," the distinguished sounding voice said.

Moreau recovered quickly. "Sure, Senator. Anything for a neighbor," he said mildly. "I just got it made. I'll see you here in ten minutes. Don't slam the door and draw attention to us, or the neighbors will start running for their air raid shelters. In fact, bring your tennis racket."

He changed into tennis clothes and was standing just outside the kitchen door as a car pulled up. Grail stepped out, dressed in tennis whites with a sweater draped elegantly around his shoulders, looking both athletic and presidential. There had been talk of him running. The two men walked into the kitchen, making small talk.

They sat at the kitchen table with steaming coffee in front of them, waiting for the bagels to toast. The DDO sat quietly, waiting. After a few moments, Grail looked at him and said, "I'm going to tell you a story that you may have heard. This could be a career enhancing opportunity for you, so listen carefully."

"In 1972, I was a Marine lieutenant in Vietnam, lying in a filthy rice paddy with blood pouring out of multiple wounds and mortar fire screaming in all around me. I knew that it was over for me, when someone picked me up and ran off the paddy with me over his shoulder. I got hit with shrapnel a couple of times more, and I could feel more of it hitting him. He took a heavy shot just as he dropped me. I got a Silver Star, some scars, and a Senate seat. He got the Medal of Honor and a wheelchair. His name is Mick Cuchulain, and he lives in Audley, South Carolina."

"His son is in trouble down there—in jail. Mick says that he is being railroaded, but I don't give a rat's ass if he is or not; I want you to look into it. If the kid is okay, fix it and fix it right. If he's a no-good, call me, and I'll send someone good down there to defend him. "

Moreau looked at him mildly, "You know we can't operate in the States, Senator."

Grail looked at him coldly. "I gave some thought concerning who could best handle this problem," he said. "Let's skip the horseshit, because I want this handled beginning today, with action down there within a day or two. If you get it right, I owe you big time. I know it's against current law, and I don't really give a shit. Do you want the job, or not?"

Moreau smiled faintly at Grail. "I'll take care of it, Senator. Do you have the particulars?"

Senator Grail handed him a hand-written sheet of paper, folded. Then he stood.

Moreau stood. They shook hands. Grail walked out to his car and drove off.

Walking back to the kitchen table, feeling smug and almost whistling, Moreau held the paper between his knuckles to keep from smudging the finger prints on it. A handwritten paper, complete with fingerprints, from the chairman of the Senate Intelligence Committee was almost as good as a recording, and having a big favor coming from Grail was better—it could get him the director's job. He thought he'd reconsider submitting his retirement papers. He poured a fresh cup of coffee and put his feet up on the table, reading over the memo from Grail and thinking. After fifteen minutes, he picked up the telephone and dialed a local number. When it answered, the voice said only, "Mac."

"I need to see you at my place, soon," said Moreau.

There was a pause. "Okay—thirty minutes."

A little later, Moreau walked MacMillan into the kitchen and waved him to a chair. He told MacMillan the story—all of it—so that he would understand the importance of this mission. Moreau knew that he would owe him a big one if he pulled it off, but it was important enough that he dare not use anyone but MacMillan; he had an uncanny way of doing the right thing at the right time, and he was mean. He was a little disturbed that Mac seemed happy to have the job.

Audley, South Carolina

THE sheriff's office, the jail, and the county courthouse shared a three-story brick building in the middle of Audley, on the corner of Lee and Jackson streets. It was a squat red-brick cube with a faded asbestos shingle roof, sitting dull and devoid of imagination in the mid-day sun. Its double hung windows were open in many offices; others had small air conditioners jutting from them, roaring in vain at the unseasonable South Carolina heat.

An almost new, plain black Chevrolet pulled to the curb in front of the building. It was an official car, with several antennae waving their importance. A middle-aged man got out of it, locked the doors and walked toward the building. He was big, square and thick, with the walk of a much lighter man. His toes pointed in slightly and his gait was light, almost dainty, with hips thrust slightly forward in his stance. His face was lined and rugged, the nose broken at some point and poorly set. An old scar ran from the corner of his left eye to the base of the earlobe. He wore a once expensive sport coat, and neatly-pressed gray slacks falling to brilliantly shined black oxfords.

He opened the door marked *County Sheriff* and walked up to a female deputy who was eating a chocolate-covered donut with colorful sprinkles and drinking from a large paper cup with "Big Sips" emblazoned in red on its side. She looked up as he stopped in front of her. She wolfed the last bite of donut, smearing her chin, and said, "He'p ya?"

He reached inside his jacket and pulled out a small folder, flipped it open a little officiously, and held the picture ID with its Department of Justice

Seal in front of her face. "Inspector Francis, FBI. I have an appointment with Sheriff Huntley."

"Yes, Sir! We been expectin' ya. Y'all follow me, Sir." The expanse of uniform trousers undulating in front of him convinced the inspector that he had not surprised her in her first dietetic indiscretion. She stopped and knocked loudly on a closed, glass-topped door with gold letters that read: *Buford J. Huntley, Sheriff.* "Inspector Francis to see you, Sheriff."

The door opened quickly and the sheriff reached to shake his hand and lead him inside, waving him to a chair in front of the desk. Huntley was wearing a short-sleeved white shirt, the buttons stretched at the waist over a large stomach; large rings of perspiration stained his shirt beneath the underarms. His polyester navy-blue tie, embroidered with the logo of the National Sheriff's Association, stopped several inches short of his large silver belt buckle. Huntley was wearing a belt holster with the black plastic grips of a nickel-plated, large caliber Smith & Wesson automatic sticking up from it. His badge was just in front of the pistol, pinned to a leather holder on his belt. He had a crew cut no more than half an inch long and a broad, fleshy face that squeezed his eyes into a slightly porcine look. Huntley was a big man, probably six-two and weighed at least 260. Francis guessed that he was a former high school football hero, and had worked himself up the ranks of the sheriff's department and into the favor of the powers-that-be in Audley.

Francis again reached into his pocket, and handed his credentials to Huntley. The sheriff studied them for a second and handed them back.

"We don't see many FBI folks down this way, Inspector. Got us a nice peaceful little county here and don't often have the need. What brings you down our way and what can we do to he'p you?"

"Sheriff, we have information that you are holding a minor named Cuchulain in your facility, and I'd like to inquire as to the charges and have a few words with him—in your presence, of course."

The sheriff looked surprised and a little wary. "I thought you FBI folks just chased bank robbers and shit, Inspector." He thought for a second or two then said, "I reckon a little professional law enforcement courtesy cain't hurt none, though. The Cuchulain kid is a vicious troublemaker. He almost blinded one of our finest young men, just a senior in high school and ruined the knee of another fine young man in a robbery attempt outside of town. Just jumped them poor boys before they even had a chance to say a word, and hurt them real bad. Vicious little shit, that Cuchulain."

"So—We're going to try him as an adult and charge him with attempted murder, criminal maiming, attempted robbery, and assault and battery. I reckon he'll get thirty years or so—and society will be better off without him."

Francis was quiet for a few seconds, and then said, "Any witnesses, other than the boys who were hurt?"

"Ah, the kid's big sister claimed that she was on a date with one of the boys," Huntley said. "She says that these guys started to feel her up, so she yelled and her brother came running out of nowhere to defend her, but you know how often brothers and sisters will lie about that shit. Besides, we checked her story, and the boy who she said was her date already has a steady girlfriend—a girl from a real nice family. We figger that she was maybe looking for a little action, or working a scam with the kid brother."

"Is the Cuchulain family bad?"

The sheriff leaned back in his chair and looked up at the ceiling, then sighed. "They ain't good. His old lady is a greaser who teaches at the local community college, Spanish probably, and his old man is a cripple. He's from down the road a piece—used to be hell on wheels in a fight before he joined the Marines and got shot up in 'Nam. Got a bunch of medals over there, but the asshole won't even join in on the 4th of July parade, he's so stuck up. He was in this jail a couple of times, before my day."

Francis nodded, grimacing. "A bad war. You spend any time over there, Sheriff?"

Huntley looked away from Francis and said, "Naw. I got my knee tore up playing football, and was 4F. I tried to join the Marines, but they wouldn't take me. It was a big disappointment to me, I'll tell ya, Inspector."

"Okay," Francis said. "Let's have a look at Cuchulain."

Huntley picked up the phone and gave instructions. A few minutes later the door opened and a large deputy pushed Alex Cuchulain into the room. His hands were cuffed behind his back.

"Take off the cuffs," Francis instructed and the deputy complied, after a nod from the sheriff.

To Cuchulain, Francis said, "Take off your shirt." Alex pulled his T-shirt over his head. There were some small bruises beneath his rib cage.

"Turn around." Cuchulain turned, and some vague, almost smudged bruises showed just above his hips, low down on the right and left side on his back. Francis looked at the sheriff, and raised one eyebrow questioningly.

The sheriff looked a little embarrassed. "Them boys he attacked were right popular, Inspector, and one of them almost lost an eye. My deputies got a little carried away with him. He ain't hurt bad, though, and nothing shows. I stopped it soon's I found out it was going on."

"Hold out your hands, Cuchulain," Francis said.

Cuchulain held out his hands. When the cuffs were removed, they left a thin but conspicuous line of scabs oozing pus around his wrists.

Francis looked at Huntley again, and said. "Brave deputies." The deputy standing by the door flushed, and looked down.

"Young man, my name is Robert Francis. I am with the FBI, and I must ask you a few questions. It is in your interest to answer truthfully and to the best of your ability. I know that you have been beaten, threatened, and that you are afraid. On the other hand, you have nothing to lose by answering my questions and may even help yourself. First, what made you think your sister was in danger and caused you to attack the two young men?"

Alex looked at Francis coldly and a little scornfully. "Sir, one of them had my sister on her knees in the dirt with her arm bent up behind her back, and the other one was trying to force his dick into her mouth, he said. "She was fighting and crying. Somehow, I thought she might be in trouble."

Francis looked at him calmly. "What was the date of the second young man doing while this went on?"

"There wasn't any other date. Harris picked my sister up at our house, all dressed up in a suit and driving his daddy's Cadillac. They drove off to the high school for the big dance, and I followed on my bike, because I didn't think he was going to really take her there, him being a big shot in the school and all. When he got near the high school, he stopped at the corner; his buddy Billy Ray Sutter ran over, jumped into the car and they took off. They went up to where the kids go to park and make out, but everyone else was at home getting ready for the dance. Besides, it was still light. By the time I got up there on my bike, they were at it. I just jumped off my bike and went after them."

"What made you follow them? Do you always follow your sister when she goes out on a date?"

"Junior Harris has a reputation. He's always bragging about doing it to girls that tried to change their mind at the last minute. I just decided to make sure that they were really going to the dance, and that Harris was really going to be seen with Elena. I didn't think that he would want to be seen with a greaser's kid."

"Did the sheriff inform you of the charges to be filed against you and that you were to be tried as an adult?"

"The sheriff informed me that they were going to ship me off to the state prison for twenty-five or thirty years, or until I had sucked every black cock and been fucked in the ass by every nigger in the prison system. He told me that he was real sorry he didn't have any niggers in the jail right now, or he would have had one break me in, so it didn't hurt so much when ten or twelve of them fucked my ass bloody the first night. He told me that I would swallow so much nigger cum that my hair would turn kinky." Cuchulain's voice rose as he spoke. He glared at the sheriff, his breath whistling through his nostrils. Suddenly he stopped, as he realized that he had probably shot his mouth off enough to get another beating. He was already pissing blood.

The deputy turned red, and pulled back his big fist. "You shut your lying mouth, you little cocksucker, or I'll beat your face in right now."

Cuchulain's face went still as he dropped into a crouch and spun, ready to go after the deputy. "Watch out, asshole," he snarled. "You're supposed to put the cuffs back on me before you start pounding on me again."

"Stop it, Denton," the sheriff roared. "You just stand there and keep your insubordinate fucking mouth shut."

The deputy settled back, embarrassed and angry. He glanced at Francis, then looked back again. Francis was still leaning back casually in his chair, but his face was pale and his eyes were weird and piercing, like those on a serial killer that the deputy had once interviewed at the state prison. The deputy felt a sudden chill and a strange, unreasonable fear.

"Why don't you take him back for now, Deputy? I may want to ask him a few more questions a little later, so keep him handy," Francis said. The sheriff nodded at the deputy, who snapped the cuffs back onto Cuchulain and shoved him through the door.

"That was one strange fuckin' interrogation, Inspector. I don't believe I've ever seen a law enforcement officer conduct an interview quite like that. Let me have another look at those credentials, Mr. FBI Inspector. We checked with Washington once when you said you was coming down, but I believe I'd better have a chat with your supervisor and find out just what the fuck is goin' on." The sheriff's face was flushed, and he was leaning forward in his chair with his hand out.

Francis reached in his pocket and handed his ID wallet to the sheriff. The sheriff spun in his chair reaching for the phone as he opened the little wallet. He glanced at Francis's photo and read the name. He stopped suddenly. "What the fuck is this? Now it says you're DEA, and not FBI?" He spun the back to face Francis, who was just finishing screwing a professional silencer onto a Beretta 9mm pistol. Francis looked at him calmly, letting the silenced pistol stare directly at the end of Huntley's nose. He reached into his pocket and flipped the FBI credentials, open, in front of Huntley, where they lay side by side with the DEA identity. Francis's picture was on both.

"You'll never know quite who or what I am, Huntley. I am what's known in the trade as a brick, thrown all the way from Washington. I've killed men in Europe, Asia, and one in Greenland—or maybe it was two—all for kind and gentle Uncle Sam. With a little work, you could be next. You and the shit-bag politicians that run this town have royally pissed off some very powerful people. I can put a bullet right between your piggy little eyes right now, walk out of here and tomorrow's paper will say you committed suicide after you found out that you were being charged with false imprisonment, forcible sodomy, and whatever else I feel like writing down."

Huntley's forehead was beaded now, veins of sweat beginning to run down his face. He was unable to take his eyes from the unwavering black bore of the Beretta's silencer. He could see the vents drilled in the fat tube, designed to silence the escaping gasses. It occurred to him that he had never before seen a real factory-made silencer.

"You're going to kill me over a fuckin' kid?" Huntley croaked.

Francis looked at him coldly and let his finger begin to tighten on the trigger. Huntley saw in his eyes the same cold, merciless ferocity that the deputy had seen, and felt his bladder release, sending urine scalding down his right leg. The acrid odor was unmistakable in the humid office.

"You know that old cripple? The kid's old man? The guy that married a greaser? His name is Mick Cuchulain, and he's a pretty famous guy in the Marine Corps. He got that chair in Vietnam, doing his job. He did that job better than almost anyone could, so we the people of the United States of America gave him the Congressional Medal of Honor, and he's spending the rest of his life in a wheelchair, trying to keep his pride on a government pension and an extra fifty bucks a month for the Medal."

"As a further reward for Mick Cuchulain's courage, a couple of local pretty boys with powerful daddies decide to rape and sodomize his daughter, and Audley's scumbag leaders decide to prosecute a pretty courageous sixteen year old kid for using his head and coming very violently to his sister's defense. Who can blame these powerful daddies? The Cuchulain kid hurt their kids, so he'll have to pay. He'll have to get butt-fucked for twenty years to show everyone that it doesn't pay to mess with the big guys in Audley. No matter that these spoiled brats might force almost anyone's attractive daughter to suck their cocks some night when the pretty boys get bored."

"Are you having trouble understanding why I like this particular job, Huntley?" Francis said. "Do you still not understand how much I'd just love to blow your worthless ass away? You and every one of those deputies that kicked the shit out of a hand-cuffed Medal of Honor winner's sixteen-year-old son?"

The urine was burning Huntley's leg, and the ammonia stench filled the room. Huntley's white shirt was soaked; the hair on his chest and bloated stomach showed through the fabric. The hostility that oozed from Francis terrified him.

"What are you going to do, kill us all?" Huntley asked in a shaken voice.

Francis stood up casually. The silencer dipped, coughed, then moved and coughed twice again; ejected casings bounced on the green linoleum floor. A thin ribbon of smoke wafted up from the holes along the silencer and fumes of cordite competed with the stale urine stench. Sure he was dying, Huntley looked down to see where he had been hit. There was a small black hole in the chair an inch from his stained crotch, and two more in the chair, just beside each knee.

Francis eased back down into his chair, the Beretta again casually pointed at Huntley. "If anything happens to that kid, you're dead. If he gets hits by a car, if he commits suicide, gets killed in a wreck, maybe even if he falls and breaks his wrist. You're not dead right away, though. First, I'm going to cripple you, just like Mick, except that I'm going to blow your balls off, too. Look down at those holes in your chair again. I could have just as easily put those rounds into each knee and into your balls. A couple of more into your elbows and we have what I would call a nice start. Maybe I'll gouge your eyes out."

Looking at the sheriff, a wide, delighted grin lit up Francis' face. "Jesus, Huntley, I would just love to do it, because I hate your fucking scumbag guts. It makes me all tingly, like a kid on Christmas morning, just thinking about it. I think I'll do it somewhere where they won't find you for awhile. My colleagues in the Irish Republican Army say that being kneecapped is the worst pain in the world. The elbows and balls are a little bonus just for me, because I think that they might smart almost as much as your knees. I'll come back and kill you real slowly a few years later, after I get to watch you suffer a bit."

Huntley nearly fainted. He didn't know that it was possible for anyone to be this scared.

"Alas, Huntley, I'm just going to have to wait. Maybe the kid will have a heart attack."

Francis' face grew cold and hard again. "Here's the way it's going to be."

"First, get a doctor in here and get the kid cleaned up," Francis said. "I don't want the wrists infected, and I want his kidneys checked for damage. Don't hold out any information on me, or I'll hurt you."

"Second, put him in a cell alone and put a guard you trust outside the cell. Your continuing virility and mobility depend on him suffering no further emotional or physical damage."

"Third, you will not discuss our meeting today with anyone, including your sponsors and your family. You will soon get a call from your sponsors in Audley, ordering you to release the Cuchulain boy at 1800 hours today and to drop all charges against him. You will do so without comments or questions. You will tolerate no questioning by your staff."

"Fourth, you will go to the Cuchulain house and make a formal apology to Mick Cuchulain and his family. You will now and in the future address him as Mr. Cuchulain and show his family the same courtesy. I expect you to grovel—to crawl. Any requests made to you by any of the Cuchulain family will be treated as if they came from me. Any trouble calls received by your office involving the Cuchulain household, the Cuchulain neighborhood, or a Cuchulain family member will be responded to with alacrity. Any arrests or possible arrests will be reported immediately by you—and not one of your staff—to a number that I will provide to you. It is operational twenty-four hours per day. You will open the conversation by saying that the subject is Michael P. Cuchulain, and by the way, it is pronounced koo-HULL-an. See that everyone gets it right."

"Fifth, when I leave here you will gather your deputies and instruct them as to the future handling of the Cuchulain boy. Don't fuck it up. You will also instruct all the deputies involved in the beating of the Cuchulain boy to go to Jim-Bob's bar tonight at around nine. They are to go unarmed and out of uniform. One of them is to pick a fight with me and get me outside into the parking lot, and then all of them are to beat the living shit out of me to teach me a lesson for being a smart-ass. The deputy, Denton that was in here with the kid should probably be the one to pick the fight, since I don't think he likes me. If I get hurt, which isn't too likely, you are to call the number I gave you, using the Cuchulain ID. Tell them that Mr. Francis has been injured in a fight. Expect a couple of young and very large men to show up within twenty-four hours, to give it another try at Jim-Bob's. They will be bad-asses, not old pussies like me. "

Francis grinned that grin again, and Huntley shivered, the cold urine chilling his leg. He for sure did not want to meet a badass if Francis was a pussy.

"Here's the phone number and a sanitized summary of your instructions. Do you have any questions?" Huntley shook his head, and reached for the paper.

Francis stood, unscrewed the silencer and dropped it into his pocket. The Beretta then disappeared almost magically under his jacket and behind his back.

As Francis walked around the desk toward him, Huntley let go a passing thought about reaching for his weapon. He stood to move to the door, when he sensed a flash of motion and a terrible shooting pain in his groin. Francis had driven his hand into Huntley's crotch, encasing his penis and testicles in his grip. He was squeezing hard, their faces an inch apart. Huntley's eyes were popping and he tried to scream, but only a high croaking sound came from his mouth. The veins in his forehead were bulging, and pain was shooting into nerves at the back of his skull. His eyes rolled back as he started to lose consciousness. Then the pressure suddenly lessened a little, but searing pain continued to flare into his legs and stomach. Francis slapped Huntley in the face with his left hand, snapping him back to full consciousness. From a distance of three inches, Francis breathed into his face, "If you fuck any of this up, scumbag, I will come back here on my own time to play with you a little bit."

Francis turned and opened the door. "I'll find my own way out Sheriff, and thanks for the little chat." He strolled past the deputy, who was working on another chocolate-covered doughnut. "The sheriff asked not to be disturbed for fifteen minutes, deputy," he said over his shoulder as he walked out, wiping damp hands on his pocket handkerchief. She nodded, chewing.

In the office, Huntley was bent over his wastebasket, puking the last of his lunch. He was spent—his adrenaline long since exhausted, his whole body shaking uncontrollably, the pain in his testicles now reduced to a massive, throbbing ache. He found himself unable to move. As the stench assaulted his face, he resolved over and over again, almost as a mantra, to never again see the man who called himself Francis, whatever it took.

MacMillan drove toward Audley High School, whistling softly and a bit pleased with himself. He thought the whole visit with the sheriff had gone rather well, if he did say so himself. The Cuchulain kid had been scared and hurt some, but showed balls. He'd seen men twice his age with far less poise. Cuchulain seemed like a good kid, but a little further investigation should give him a better sense of how to proceed. The DDO had been very specific about making sure that this whole affair be handled as competently and completely as possible. "No wonder," he mused, "It's not every day that the DDO gets to have major owesies on the chair of the Senate Intelligence Committee."

A little later, Mac walked from the principal's office and presented his Department of Education credentials to Mr. Webb, the wrestling coach. The coach was in his mid-thirties, fit and compact, sitting in sweats before his spring practice session began.

"Alex is a good one, Mr. Francis. I just can't believe that he got into this trouble; it's just not like him. He's one of the most self-controlled kids for his age that I've seen. I tried to go to bat for him this morning, but the principal told me to mind my own business." Webb shrugged and looked down. "I have a wife and two kids."

"Anyhow, I lost a pretty sure shot at an all-state wrestler," Webb said. "Cuchulain is a natural; he's fast, smart, and unnaturally strong. You see those guys once in a while, those strong ones. They're just born that way, and get even stronger if they work at it. I lost to a guy in the NCAA regionals who was that way."

The coach leaned over a little, thinking back. "He was four pounds lighter than me, and twice as strong. I just couldn't believe how strong he was. I think my skills were a little better than his, but I'd work toward a move, find it, and then he'd just hold me back when he shouldn't have been able to. Weird. He made All-American. A lot of it was just because he was so damned strong for his size."

"Cuchulain's like that, except he's big," Webb said. "That frame of his will support a lot of weight. He's smart, too—real smart. You don't have to show him anything twice, and he has a spatial sense of wrestling that is pretty rare in a boy his age. You sorta gotta know where the other guy is and what he's going to do while the two of you are spinning around in three dimensions. I think it's like that fighter pilot stuff that you read about. I have some of that, but Cuchulain's got it in spades."

Webb stood up, paced a few steps and walked back. "I may get myself in trouble saying this, Mr. Francis, but it's just too damned bad that this happened. Those assholes that he hurt were just that—assholes. Chickenshit, no good, spoiled-brat assholes." He sat back down. "Cuchulain's dad used to come in his wheelchair to watch him wrestle. Poor guy is a war hero in a wheelchair, but he was really proud of his kid. I'm not quite sure why you're here, but if you can do anything to make things a little easier for Alex, I'd appreciate it."

Mac stood up. 'We'll work on that, Coach. I think we might be able to help him out." He turned and walked away from the coach, who looked both puzzled and delighted. As Webb watched the way he walked, it struck

65

him that Mr. Francis seemed a lot different than anyone else he had met from the US Department of Education.

The math teacher was small, slight with a moustache and a slightly effeminate air. "The principal said you had a few questions for me, Mr. Francis. What may I do for you?"

MacMillan thought for a second and said, "You were one of the few teachers who gave Alex Cuchulain an A, Dr. Olsen. Tell me how that happened."

Olsen paused, and then sighed. "I probably shouldn't have. The rules in this high school are that if a student doesn't do his homework assignments, he may get no higher than a B. Most teachers here will give a C in this circumstance. Alex Cuchulain seldom turned in a completed assignment for me. He seldom paid attention in class. Once, during class, I walked behind his aisle during my lecture and found him near the end of a differential calculus book that he must have taken from my library shelf over there, apparently reading it like a novel."

"After that, I paid more attention to him," Olsen said. "I would call on him to answer questions that others in the class, good students, could not answer correctly. Invariably, he would ask me to repeat the question and give me the correct answer, obviously solving it on the fly. I don't mind telling you that it was quite disconcerting for me, but also fascinating."

"Later, I didn't bother with the algebra questions. However, on three or four separate occasions I asked him a question on differential calculus. The procedure was the same. He would ask me to repeat the question, then solve it on the fly. He was so removed from the class that he didn't even realize that I was not asking something that the class had studied. You must understand, Mr. Francis, that a student like that comes along only once or twice in a teacher's career. It was particularly frustrating to me that I did not have the opportunity to nurture his development, but I have forty students in each of my five classes. To fail to help develop a mind like that is wrong. To give that student a grade lower than an A would have been criminal."

Dr. Olsen straightened and pushed his glasses up his narrow nose.

Looking Mac in the eyes, he said, "I realize that my views may not be consistent with yours or those of the Department of Education, but I stand by them."

Mac stood and smiled. "For what it's worth, Dr. Olsen, I think you did just fine. Thanks for your time." He turned and walked from the office and out of the school to his car. He started the car, turned on the air conditioning, and consulted his map for a route to the Cuchulain residence. After a moment, he looked out of the window at nothing and organized his thoughts. A few minutes later, he put the car into gear and drove off. He was thinking that this was the most interesting assignment he had been given for quite some time. It also occurred to him that he couldn't let Moreau know that, because if the senator owed the DDO a big one, then the DDO owed Mac one of similar size. He liked that.

Mac knocked on the Cuchulain's door. It was answered by a slim woman in her mid-forties with fading beauty and a mass of thick, shining silver-streaked black hair piled casually on her head. She looked tired.

"Mrs. Cuchulain? My name is MacMillan. I work for the United States Government, and I would like to speak to you and your husband about your son, Alex."

With a puzzled look, Maria invited him into the living room where Mick Cuchulain sat in his wheelchair by an open window, reading a book. He looked up.

"Mick, this gentleman wants to talk to us about Alex. He says he's from the US government," she said.

Cuchulain looked at Mac for a second and said, "The only thing I want to talk to the US government about is when my son will be out of jail."

"The answer to that, Mr. Cuchulain, is 1800 hours today. All charges will be dropped and you will receive an apology from the sheriff's department. The people in Audley who caused this to happen will suffer severe setbacks in their careers. You and your family will be treated by county officials with the respect you deserve. If there is anything further with regard to this matter that needs to be resolved, we will resolve it." Mac stood, almost at attention, when he delivered this message, looking Cuchulain directly in the eye. He waited as Cuchulain's wife ran to him and began to sob in joy as she wrapped her arms around him.

After a few moments, Cuchulain looked up at Mac. "I'm tremendously relieved and pleased that you've done what you have, sir. Please express my gratitude to the Senator. My only worry now is what to do with a sixteen-year-old kid who everyone in town thinks is a criminal. You probably don't know how to change that, and it's going to be a problem."

"Mr. Cuchulain, we'll do what we can to help," MacMillan said. "As you know, there are no answers that will change the past, but I may have some ideas that could help in dealing with the future.

Cuchulain studied Mac for a long while and finally said, "Well, if it ain't Mac MacMillan! I always wondered what the hell happened to you. You just disappear one day and no one ever hears from you again. The scuttlebutt was that you went off to be a spook, since the old man wouldn't talk about it. I suspect that you are now a very senior spook, based on the rapidity of your results today."

MacMillan grinned and said, "I'm the same guy Mick, and Jesus Christ, I'm glad to see you. If I'd known, I'd have done this all by myself, even if you hadn't called the Senator. Of course, there would be a bunch of dead guys around, so it's probably better this way.'

Maria walked off to the kitchen, delighted to see Mick more animated than he had been in years. She was even more delighted that Alex would soon be free and at home. Her father would be pleased that the matter had been resolved; his fury at the story had concerned but not surprised her. She had difficulty convincing her father that it would be hard for Bedouin assassins to hide in Audley and break into the jail, so it was good for town tranquility that Alex was free.

Cuchulain Residence

A LEX arrived at home at 6:15 that evening, transported in an Audley police cruiser driven by Sheriff Huntley. He walked up the broken and heaving concrete walk to the house, looking tired and worn. His mother rushed to the door to hug him, tears streaming down her face, and said, "My son, my heart, you have been through hell!"

Alex held her, saying, "Mom, I've just been in jail for a while. It was just a mistake. Sheriff Huntley told me it was a mistake."

He walked into the house and over to his father, then leaned over and hugged him. "I'm glad you're out, Son. We should talk about it sometime," Mick said.

"I'd like that, Dad," Alex said. "It was spooky and a little weird."

Mick looked behind Alex to the chair in the corner, and nodded to Alex. Alex turned and looked to see MacMillan sitting quietly in the chair. He smiled slightly and nodded.

"Alex, this is an old friend of mine, Mac MacMillan," Mick said.

"You probably know, Dad, but this is also Inspector Francis from the FBI. He was at the jail today, talking to me." Alex looked at MacMillan. "Sheriff Huntley told me three times on the way over here that if I saw you, I was to tell you that he had done everything you wanted and treated me real nice, too."

"Why, that was right neighborly of him, don't you think, Mick?" Mac smiled.

"Yeah, he's a real prince," Mick said with a snort. "What about the mayor and Old Man Harris?"

MacMillan thought for a second about letting Mick and Alex in on all of it, then decided. "The mayor seems to have fallen temporarily in love with his assistant, a fact that is documented in several very nice eight-by-ten glossies that were taken Sunday night. I've been told that he seemed more interested in the voters and his wife not getting an opportunity to share these little photo ops than in seeing his son's injury avenged. The senior senator from South Carolina also called him and offered some high-volume counseling about his future. Our powerful and esteemed factory owner is in a little more trouble. It seems that one of his former Chief Financial Officers is upset with him over the loss of his job, and was pleased to share, several weeks ago, with our colleagues at the Internal Revenue Service the existence of a second set of books—and their location. There are four or five IRS agents out there now. I see a criminal indictment in his future, which was a little more than we had hoped for."

Mac grinned at Mick and said, "Remind me never to piss you off."

Mick laughed, then seeing the puzzled look on Alex's face, told him the whole story.

When Maria called them to dinner, Mac said. "We should talk later about what Alex does from here. He may not be too popular with the home-folks after this fiasco."

"Ah, you're probably right," Mick sighed. "We'll discuss it after dinner. Maria will sit in, too. Elena, our daughter, is out tonight, so we'll not worry about her, right now."

Later, Mick sat with his chair against the porch rail, while Alex and Mac settled into the cushions of the hanging swing. The sounds of dishes rattling came from the kitchen. "Okay, Mac. It's your show for now. Maria said to start without her. It's 'Men's talk,'" she says. "What's on your mind?"

Mac was quiet, then said, "We can be sure that nothing official around Audley causes any trouble for you or your family, Mick. Small-town attitudes being what they are though, I suspect Alex isn't going to be terribly well received around here from now on. There's not much we can do about that."

"Any ideas?" Mick said.

"I was thinking about getting him into the Corps, Mick. He's sixteen, and will be okay if you sign a permission form for him. Four years in the Corps would cause everyone around here to forget about this mess, and could be a real benefit for Alex. It's a pretty good life, all things considered."

Several moments went by, then Mick said to Alex, "You aren't exactly setting the world on fire in school here, son, and Mac's right about the way the people here will treat you. The Corps is not an easy life, but I found it to be a good one." He looked down at his chair and added, "Mostly. It will be your decision, Alex. Take as much time as you need to think it over. I'll back you whatever you decide to do."

Alex looked at his father and then at Mac. "I want out of Audley. I almost got railroaded into state prison by those folks, and the people of this town let it happen to me—turned their heads, or worse. I was lucky you had contacts to get me out of it, but I don't want to see them, and I don't want to be around them. I don't know what else I would do, so I guess the Marine Corps is as good a place as any. I don't like school much anyhow. When do I go?"

Mac stood up and stretched. "I'll have to make a couple of phone calls. My guess is that we can have you out of here sometime tomorrow, on a bus to Parris Island. I'll go downtown in the morning and get the paperwork from the local Corps recruiter."

"Sound okay to you, Son?" Mick asked quietly. "I'll talk to your mom and sister tonight."

"I guess it's fine with me, Pop." Alex stood. "I'm exhausted. I can't say I slept much in jail." He walked into the house and up the stairs.

The two men sat quietly for several minutes, then Mick said, "Have them lean on him a little down there, Mac. He has potential, but wasn't on his way to anyplace good. He's done a half-assed job in school and nothing seems to really interest him except wrestling. His tests say that he is bright, really bright, but we've not found a way to get him going. Keep my name out of it if you can."

Mac sat in the fading light, looking out into the quiet street where flickering lights began to greet the gathering twilight. He nodded and glanced at his watch, "I'll get back to you tomorrow," he said. Excusing himself, he told Mick he had a few remaining items to clean up in Audley. Mac walked slowly down the walk to the now dusty Chevrolet, eased himself into the seat and drove off to his meeting at Jim-Bob's.

US Marine Corps Recruiting Depot Parris Island, South Carolina

A LEX got off the bus at Parris Island after the short ride from the town of Beaufort. Sergeants in uniform were yelling, "Move, move, move!" and, "Fall in, fall in now, you stupid shitbirds," as young men piled out of the bus and attempted to form a line. As he stood in what he thought was a pretty good line, Alex was worried. All of the men on the bus were older than he was—some a lot older. They had the marks of heavy beards on their faces, and several had tattoos. Their talk was of pot and poon-tang; Alex had never experienced either one.

A sergeant stood in front of their group, flat-brimmed Smokey hat tilted down, shading his eyes. His uniform seemed to fit him perfectly, each crease sharp and straight. The button line of his khaki shirt, the edge of his brilliantly shined belt buckle, and the flap of the fly on his trousers were perfectly aligned. The shine on his black shoes seemed bottomless. He glared at them, seeming to pick each recruit individually. He opened his mouth, and shouted, "HRAAAT HACE—HORWAARD HAAARCH!" There was confusion as some recruits executed a right face and others stood without a clue, looking around them.

After several more hours of screaming by the sergeants, and even more confusion by the new recruits, each ended up standing by a bunk and a foot locker in a barracks with arms full of new clothes and gear, and haircuts that cost them only fifty cents and took less than forty-five seconds. Just as Cuchulain had sorted through his new clothes and laid them on his new bunk, someone started yelling, "FALL IN! FALL IN, YOU HOPELESS SHITBIRDS!" As his fellow recruits ran for the door, Alex followed, wondering what was next. He was already wishing he was back in class at Audley High, where he at least had some idea of what to do.

They formed up in lines as they had all day. The platoon lines were still ragged, but an improvement over the efforts at the bus. A tall, muscular black sergeant stood in front of the platoon. He too was immaculate, as he paced back and forth in front of the assembled platoon. He walked through the ranks, looking at each man and shaking his head sadly, yet sternly. He had not spoken a word.

He moved back to the front of the platoon, spread his feet apart, clasped his hands behind his back, and said, "My name is Jackson, Sergeant Jackson. I will be your drill sergeant for the next twelve weeks. It is my job to turn you from your present sorry state into United States Marines. I don't think it can be done—not be me, not by anyone. You are the sorriest bunch of fat, weak, sloppy, stupid, no-good bunch of shitbirds it has ever been my misfortune to encounter. You are the worst I have seen in my twelve years as a United States Marine. Since I am a non-commissioned officer in the United States Marine Corps, it is often my job to accomplish the impossible, and I will therefore spend a few weeks with you before admitting to the Marine Corps that there is no hope for you—that you are untrainable, and that we are wasting the government's money. We will then send you back to your families and friends in disgrace, as you deserve."

"You will address me as Sergeant Jackson or Sergeant at all times."

"You will obey my orders without question. None of you is qualified to question my orders. If I say "shit," I expect you to say 'Yes, Sergeant' and then squat and strain. Is that clear?"

A few voices said timidly, "Yes, Sergeant."

Sergeant Jackson's voice roared, "IS THAT CLEAR, SHITBIRDS?"

"YES, SERGEANT!" they roared in unison.

Jackson shook his head sadly. "I AM THE MEANEST MOTHERFUCKER ANY OF YOU WILL EVER ENCOUNTER. IS THAT CLEAR, SHITBIRDS?" he roared.

"YES, SERGEANT!"

Jackson paced back in forth in front of the platoon standing erect, hands again behind his back. Each of the recruits felt singled out by his glare. "YOU DON'T BELIEVE ME! YOU DON'T BELIEVE I AM THE MEANEST MOTHERFUCKER IN THE WHOLE WORLD. IF EVEN ONE OF YOU THINKS HE CAN WHIP ME IN A FAIR FIGHT OR A DIRTY ONE, TAKE ONE STEP FORWARD."

No one moved. Jackson roared again, "YOU ARE ATTEMPTING TO BE UNITED STATES MARINES. YOU ARE SUPPOSED TO BE BAD ASSES. IF EVEN ONE OF YOU THINKS HE CAN WHIP ME, HE'D BETTER TAKE ONE STEP FORWARD!"

After a few seconds, one man in the second row stepped forward.

Jackson spun and pointed at him. "You, shitbird! Front and center, on the DOUBLE!" The young man raced to the front of the platoon and stood in front of Sergeant Jackson in an exaggerated position of attention.

Jackson stood nose to nose with him for a second, then realized that he was looking up. The recruit stood at least six feet four, with a neck nearly the size of Jackson's head. Each of the muscles in his neck was visible, but partially obscured by the enormous trapezius muscles running up each side. Veins were visible above the collar of his T-shirt, as thick cords wrapping themselves up and around his neck. Jackson again put his hands behind his back, and strode off for two steps then spun, glaring at the new recruit. "What is your name, shitbird?"

"Magnusson, Eric J, Sergeant," the young man yelled, looking straight ahead.

Jackson snuck a look at Magnusson, Eric J. His T-shirt was stretched by a massive chest, and his lats pushed his veined and distended biceps away from his body. His thighs stretched the legs of his shorts, the definition of the quadriceps apparent. He weighed at least two hundred twenty pounds, perhaps much more. No fat.

"And just why do you think you can whip my ass, shitbird Magnusson?" Jackson asked loudly.

Magnusson looked uncomfortable.

"WHY, SHITBIRD MAGNUSSON?" Jackson roared.

Looking straight ahead, Magnusson said loudly, "Sergeant, I have a third degree black belt in Judo, a second degree black belt in karate, and I was All-American as a heavy-weight wrestler at the University of Iowa."

'SHITBIRD MAGNUSSON, HABOUUT HACE," Jackson yelled.

Magnusson, his face a spectacular shade of magenta, spun and faced the platoon.

Jackson walked up to stand beside him, broke into a wicked grin, and roared at the platoon, "IS THERE ANYONE HERE THAT THINKS HE CAN WHIP *BOTH* ME AND MY NEW PLATOON SERGEANT MAGNUSSON?"

Alex smiled to himself and decided that he was going to stick with the Marine Corps, no matter what they threw at him. The Marine Corps was adaptable; they could take a joke!

Parris Island

TWELVE weeks later, MacMillan drove his rental car to the gate, still unable, after some twenty-odd years, to avoid an inspection look at the Marine guard. He was flawless. His trousers fell without a wrinkle around the knife-edge crease, and his shoes showed the results of quiet hours spent working black Kiwi into leather with a dampened, discarded T-shirt. MacMillan's distorted image was reflected in the gleaming brass buckle that showed no trace of the misty oxidation that drives drill instructors into fits of profane rage. Mac handed his credentials to the Marine, who looked briefly at the papers, checked a notation on the clipboard hanging from the whitewashed wall of the guard shack, and picked up the phone.

"Mr. MacMillan is here, Gunny," He said, then listened for a second. "Right, Gunny," and hung up.

"Gunnery Sergeant Crouch is in Building T-21, Mr. MacMillan. He is expecting you and says that you know the way. Is that correct, Sir?"

MacMillan smiled tiredly, "Son, you and I know that Gunnery Sergeants are always right. Especially Master Gunnery Sergeants."

The guard showed a blazing, recruiting poster smile. "Yes, Sir, Mr. MacMillan! I thought you were one of us. Semper Fi!"

As Mac slipped the car into drive and eased away from the gate, he remembered wistfully a young Lance Corporal MacMillan with the same enthusiasm and zest for life. The passing years had somehow eroded his enthusiasm and corroded his perspective.

In front of Building T-21, Mac parked the rental car in the space marked

Visitor, eased himself out of the seat and walked toward the door. A young Marine recruit burst from the door, slowed suddenly at the sight of Mac's face, then sped up when he realized that Mac was in civilian clothes and required no military greeting. As he ran by, he shouted "Semper Fi, Sir!" just in case, because the guy had a face as beat up and mean as the Gunny's.

Mac opened the door. The reflected sun on the shined brass doorknob contrasted with countless layers of paint on the old pine door, its grain long since buried beneath a compulsion for order and neatness.

A tall, thick Marine stood grinning at him. He was wearing Khakis, with the three upper chevrons and three lower rockers of Master Gunnery Sergeant's stripes on the sleeve, and five rows of ribbons running above the left shirt pocket. Most of them were "I was there" ribbons, signifying that he had been in a particular combat theater or war zone when the ribbons were awarded to all who served there. The top two rows were different; the silver star, the bronze star, and the purple heart with oak leaf clusters were in one row, and the dark-blue ribbon with the single, centered, vertical white bar of the nation's second highest award for bravery under fire, the Navy Cross, stood alone in the middle of the top row. They shook hands and each threw his left arm over the shoulder of the other and gripped.

"It's great to see you, Jerry! You look well," Mac said. "I might even let you buy me a cup of coffee."

They moved into Crouch's office and sat in two armless steel chairs with olive-drab padded seats and back.

They talked for a short while about which of their mutual friends they had seen recently, then Mac asked him, "How's the Cuchulain kid doing, Jerry?"

"He's going to be a good Marine, Mac. I had Jackson leaning on him hard, the first couple of weeks like you asked. Jackson was starting to bitch about it, and he's not much of a bitcher. He really likes the kid. I think he's right. The kid's got big potential as a Marine."

"Tell me about it."

"I suspect that you know most of it, but I'll go back. He's freaky strong for his size, and he ain't small. You remember that little kid Jimenez back in LeJeune? The one they took for the power lifting team? Cuchulain is like him, except he hides it. He is also no little kid anymore; I'd guess he's up to 190 or so."

MacMillan thought for a second. "The kid isn't even seventeen yet. What else? He show any balls, Jerry?"

Gunny grinned, and then chuckled. "The word is that he's got a lot of balls. Jackson says he's the envy of Parris Island, since he's supposedly hung like Secretariat, with balls to match. He was taking a fair amount of shit about it from a guy in his platoon, a big New Yorker named Steiner, and you know how obnoxious New Yorkers can be when they work at it. This guy was calling him ox-nuts, donkey dick and shit like that, sometimes yelling it across the chow hall. He said he was going to sell tickets to see Cuchulain in the shower. A few of the other guys started to pick it up."

"A couple of weeks ago, Cuchulain told the guy from New York that his name was Alex, or Cuchulain and he didn't want to hear any other names or any more shit coming at him. One thing led to another and they went behind the barracks with a crowd to watch. The big guy took a swing, and as far as Jackson can figure it from the barracks talk, Cuchulain broke his left forearm while he was taking him down. Then Cuchulain got a shoulder under the big guy's right arm from behind and just drove the arm up until he had separated his right shoulder. He also took his fucking time about it to make a point. The word Jackson got was that he was looking at the crowd while he hauled that arm up from behind and ruined it."

Gunny sighed. "Anyway, the New Yorker is screaming like a gut-shot Comanche for three or four seconds, then 'pop,' and the guy passes out." The kid stands up and says, 'My name is Cuchulain, but you guys are my friends so you can call me Alex if you want, or Cooch.' The whole thing lasts maybe thirty seconds. And he walks into the barracks. I'll tell you, sixteen or not, Mac, that boy is one cold sonofabitch. And everyone is very careful to call him Cooch now."

"Jesus Christ, Jerry. I didn't ask you to teach him that shit," Mac said.

"We didn't. He's buddied up with some fucking Mormon giant named Magnusson. Our animals in hand-to-hand combat instruction say that he may be the baddest dude in the whole world. The good news is that our guys are learning a lot from Magnusson—and so is Cuchulain. Cuchulain is too young to drink and the Mormon doesn't, so they spend all their liberty time in the gym, wrestling and working out. We already have orders to detail Magnusson to the training squad to get ready to compete in the next Olympics. His old man is a judo instructor back in Bumfuck, Iowa or somewhere, plus he made All-American as a wrestler at Iowa as a sophomore. He just got back from his two-year Mormon mission in Okinawa, and seems to have learned a bit there as well."

MacMillan leaned back. "About Cuchulain. What else? Weapons? Team player?"

"He's a terrific rifle shot; he can run okay—great stamina," Jerry said. "He's pretty good in the woods, and better in open terrain; somehow the kid learned to fucking vanish in the open. Great team player, always willing to help someone out. He's a good Marine. He's so under control it's scary—for a kid that age. Jackson, when he was leaning on him hard in the early days, said that he could never get a flicker of emotion out of him. He'd have him knee deep in a trench at 0200, digging a hole or filling it back in, wearing nothing but skivvies in the pouring rain. He'd dig just fast enough to keep Jackson off his ass. Jackson said he had him digging for three hours one night, trying to get him to say he'd quit, and never even got an inkling that the kid was thinking about it. Oh yeah, he speaks fluent Spanish and Arabic, but you probably already knew that. "

"I guess I should have known that, but I didn't think of it," Mac mused. "Could be a handy set of skills."

"His IQ is off the charts, too. The Corps could use him and a lot more like him, Mac." Gunny sighed, with his big scarred hands wrapped around his hot coffee mug. He waited.

Mac was silent for a second, deciding, then said, "By the way, he's Mick Cuchulain's kid."

Gunny's eyes widened. "No shit?" he said. "I sure as hell am glad that I didn't know that when I had Jackson giving him all that crap. I'm not sure I could have lived with myself. Jesus—Mick Cuchulain's kid!"

"Yeah, that's why I didn't tell you, plus Mick asked me not involve his name," Mac said. "His mom is that Arab school teacher from Algeciras, near Rota, that Mick married. Remember, she was the mayor's girlfriend, and the Spanish police were thinking about lynching Mick?"

"Goddammit, Mac! Steiner was on his way to being a good Marine. Now he's messed up, maybe for good. Jackson was working on his smart mouth and he was coming around. He would have stayed in the Corps, I think," Crouch said.

Jerry sat for awhile, thinking. Mac took a sip or two of his coffee, and watched a platoon of recruits shuffle by, singing a Jody chant. Mac couldn't make out the words, but he knew the song. Just as they were passing out of sight, he heard the drill sergeant, who was running easily beside, with a t-shirt as blackened by sweat as any of them. "HUT, TWO, THREE, FOUR," he sang out. The assembled platoon sang back with gusto, "HUT, TWO, THREE, FOUR." The other chants sang of Jody and of his fortunes and misfortunes with women and life. *I've always liked that high*, Mac thought. *Your heart is pumping hard, your buddies are all beside you, unhurt, and life is good for now. Most of the time, that's enough.*

The voices faded and just a whiff of dust drifted after the platoon, when Jerry said, "Mac, I wish you had told me that he was Mick's kid. I knew Mick; he was a *warrior*. I could maybe have saved Steiner for the Corps if I had known I had Mick's kid. Mick was slow to anger, but God, when he went for it, it was zipper down, balls out and forget about tomorrow. So—I think I lost the Corps a pretty good recruit in Steiner. You should have told me."

"Ah, shit," Mac said quietly. "You're right, Jerry. I didn't connect the dots. Sorry. Cuchulain as nasty as his old man was?"

"You never know nasties until they have been under fire," Crouch said. "But Jackson said that the kid is spooky when he is stoked; his face gets all weird and you can hear him breathe through his nose. He said Cuchulain looked at Steiner like he was prey."

Mac sighed, and said, "Just like Mick. Remember what they called Mick's nose breathing – 'The Wind of Death'? If he turned on a civilian, someone else had to take the fight before Mick really hurt him. Jeez, I'm sorry Jerry; I really screwed this one up."

"That you did," Crouch said, nodding. "It was putting a pit bull in with a bunch of Dobermans and Rottweilers in training. Steiner had no idea what was coming."

"Yeah. I'm going to take Cuchulain, Jerry," Mac said. "You'll have the orders by graduation. I think I'll keep him busier than you will. If he can't cut it, I'll send him back to you."

"Oh, he'll cut it, Mac. He'll cut it just fine. He reminds me a lot of you before you got old and frail," Crouch said with a little grin. "But you wouldn't have been in his league physically, as strong as you were; he's a bit of a freak that way. On the other hand, you were probably everyday meaner," Crouch said. "Did you think about OCS for him? Or one of the service academies? Mick's medal will get him in."

Mac nodded. "Maybe later," he said. "They make round pegs to fit round holes in the service academies—with a hammer if they need it. I'm not sure that's right for him yet."

Jerry shrugged. It was no longer his business. "I'll tell him," he said.

Mac sighed. "Let's go get dinner and talk about young women and old scotch. I'm buying. I'll tell you about Mick."

South Carolina

MACMILLAN drove north on Interstate 95 with Alex in the passenger seat. It was the morning after Alex's graduation from basic training.

They were silent for awhile, then MacMillan said, "I heard you fucked up that guy up pretty good behind the barracks. Why didn't you just discourage him, instead of practically tearing his arm off?"

"I didn't know how to discourage him and no one at Parris Island is afraid of a sixteen year old kid. I did what I knew how to do."

Mac looked at him. "At least they knew that you were a bad ass."

"I don't want to be known as a bad ass. I just don't want anyone ridiculing me. I particularly don't want anyone drawing attention to me."

Mac considered the word "ridiculing" and smiled to himself. He would have said "fucking with me" because that's the way Marines said things. Ridiculing sounded better, somewhat to his surprise. Cuchulain had grown up a lot in a short time; Mick would be proud of him.

"If you use the martial arts or physical skills that others don't have, you are going to draw attention to yourself," Mac said. "Why spend all that time with that Mormon guy, if you don't like that stuff?' "

"His name is Eric Magnusson, and he's a good guy," Alex said, a little coldly. "I didn't say I didn't like it, I just said that I don't want to draw attention to myself. In fact, I like it a lot."

Mac smiled. "How did you feel after you separated that guy's shoulder and broke his arm?" he said. "Did you feel a little sick to your stomach? Were your hands shaking?"

Cuchulain was quiet for a few seconds. "I didn't feel anything, except that I felt pretty sure that he'd watch his mouth in the future. He'd been riding me a lot. I really didn't like him. I knew I was hurting him. I wanted to hurt him. I liked hurting him, at the time. My hands didn't shake 'til later."

It was a quiet ride for awhile through the North Carolina countryside. Mac decided that he really liked this kid, and he wondered if that was a feeling he could indulge.

They talked about the Marine Corps, and a little about the new training that was coming up at the "Farm" near Williamsburg, where Mac and the rest of the CIA's management prepared their new recruits for field work. Mac had offered to get him some leave—to go back home and show off his Marine uniform a bit—to be proud for the home town folks and his parents. Cuchulain's only response was that he'd go back sometime later.

"I'm a little scared that you're putting me into something that I can't handle," Alex said, after a while. "I'm only sixteen. What do I need to know that I don't know now, Mr. MacMillan? Something that will give me the kind of edge Eric Magnusson gave me?"

Mac was silent for awhile, thinking back over his years as a Marine and as a covert operator—recalling his years as a specialist in mayhem and violence, and about Gunny Crouch's comments.

Mac turned a little in his seat and lifted his right hand toward Alex and said, "Hold your hand against mine."

Cuchulain, hesitated, then turned in his seat and held his hand against Mac's, palm to palm, with fingers pointed at the sky. His young fingers were long and thick, extending a full joint beyond the thick, scarred digits of the aging warrior. Alex's skin was smooth and unwrinkled, looking almost child-like but for its expanse.

"Now grip my hand in a shake, and increase the pressure to resist me. If it starts to hurt, tell me to stop. If I tell you to stop, stop." They clasped hands and Mac, still watching the road, steadily increased his pressure. The tendons running up his wrist began to distend and his fingers began to hump and bulge with the pressure. The small ridge on his hand between his fore-finger and thumb swelled like a tiny bicep. He could feel the kid responding, the long fingers wrapping down around his, the muscles in his palm and hand keeping pace. When Mac had reached the limit of his pressure, he told Alex to squeeze harder. There was a little more pressure from Alex, and then it leveled. Mac let him hold it for a few seconds, tiring as Cuchulain strained for more pressure, and then told him to stop.

"Hand strength," Mac said. "I knew a guy once who had unbelievably strong hands, and they were quite a formidable asset. It helped his climbing, his rappelling, and his fighting. He knew that anything he grabbed, he could hold. He got out of fights by grabbing people—their hands, their elbows, the back of their necks, their balls—most of all their balls—and squeezing. He killed a sentry near the Ho Chi Minh Trail in Laos one night by squeezing the back of his neck somehow, when we got surprised—I knew for sure that the four of us would be dead if he yelled. The sentry had just opened his mouth when this guy just reached out and grabbed the sentry's trigger hand with one hand and the back of his neck with the other and squeezed. I could hear bones breaking in both places. It was spooky. Not a sound—and it only took about ten seconds. The guy was dead when he hit the ground like a sack of rice. Then we got on with business." He was quiet for a few seconds. "And nobody ridiculed him."

"There is a guy at the Farm where you're going for training who knows about pressure points, kill points, and other things that combine well with a hand-strength program. If you think you want to develop that skill, I'll have him work with you a little. You're one of those people who have muscle fibers that can do more work than most people's can, so you could probably develop very, very strong hands. It's nothing to be overly proud of—it's just like being able to run fast. You're born with it. Still, it can be useful, it can be developed. This guy I told you about, he mostly just squeezed things like rubber balls and springs. He had a valve spring from an old junker, with a little steel plate welded on the top and bottom. He'd squeeze that thing a thousand times a day—carried it around in his pocket like a rabbit's foot."

Cuchulain was silent for a while. Then he said, "I'll give it a try."

Mac drove in silence for another fifteen minutes. "You know anything about women, Cuchulain?"

"I've never even been laid, Mr. MacMillan. Except for my mother and sister, I've never been around women much. I'm planning to learn though, and soon."

Mac smiled. "I know it's hard for you to believe now, but the getting laid part will take care of itself. You'll help yourself a lot if you always behave as a gentleman around women—hell, around men for that matter. There's no downside, and after a while it's a habit. Don't go talking about women you've slept with, open doors for all women, especially the ones who aren't beautiful, and always be polite; it's amazing how many guys screw that up and screw themselves in the process. It's not sissy bullshit; it's basically respecting people whether they're strong or whether they're weak, until they give a reason to act differently. If you want it, I'll send you a book—an etiquette book for men that pretty much covers what to do. There's not much risk to it, since civilization has worked these rules out over the centuries and they are pretty well accepted."

"I'd like that," Alex said.

"Another thing worth thinking about is what you do with information about yourself," Mac said. "For the most part, you shouldn't let people know how you think, what you know, or what you have. Information is power. If you don't pass any information out some other guy will tell you his life story, just to fill up the silence. For example, you're already pretty much of a bad ass. As big as you are, with what you learned from Magnusson and what the Corps taught you, there aren't a hell of a lot of guys who could handle you in a fight. Don't flaunt it, and try not to let it get around too much. None of the really bad asses I've met was easy to get into a fight; you gotta learn to walk away when it's not important or you'll be fighting every guy around who wants to make a reputation, and there's a lot of those assholes out there. Sooner or later you'll hurt the wrong person badly and land right back in jail. On the other hand, if you have to get in a fight, get it over with as quickly and mercilessly as you can; you never know when the other guy has a gun or has a chickenshit buddy with one."

Mac looked over at Alex and grinned. "It's bad karma to bring strong hands to a gunfight, Alex."

Alex chucked and they were silent for awhile. "You married, Mr. MacMillan?"

"No. And call me Mac." After a few more moments, he said, "There was a woman in Hue, in Viet Nam, a long time ago. She was French—a doctor. She worked in a hospital there, and wouldn't leave when it got nasty; too many patients needed her." He watched the traffic. "The Viet Cong didn't like the French much."

Mac drove on, thinking: *Jesus Christ, Mac. That's more than you've talked to anyone about personal things for twenty years. Just shut up and let the kid enjoy the ride.*

The Farm
Williamsburg, Virginia

ALEX stood in the shower and turned the dial on the water from warm to cold. The September heat in Williamsburg was oppressive, with the humidity nearly as high as the ninety-five degree temperature, but the small room and bath he shared were more than tolerable. It had been another difficult, taxing day at the Central Intelligence Agency training facility on the large, wooded parcel known as The Farm. It had been three months of drills and lessons that he had never even dreamed existed. There was martial arts six days a week; for him, two-hour sessions. The first hour was traditional matt judo taught by a Korean master. It was a different form of wrestling than what he knew, and far more lethal. The second hour was drill, featuring seventy-two different forms, or sets of motion, that someone, somewhere, had defined as the most effective responses to the most common physical attacks, including those with knives and clubs; Alex thought he might have done each of those forms a thousand times until he really didn't think about them anymore, but just reacted. The other five men and one woman in his training group took only the forms, and stayed only a few weeks. They were older, with other responsibilities, and their skills needed to be good, but not great. Alex had not revealed his age to them; he wasn't asked to mingle socially. Alex became a loner.

There were classes on explosives, locksmithing, weapons, and tactics—all with drills. He worked with a strength coach two hours a day, and once a week a sort of weird guy came in and worked on strengthening Alex's hands, developing both strength and technique. His hands were thicker now than before, and heavily calloused. He was now getting two weeks off. His body felt good, but his mind was ready for a break.

Audley, South Carolina

CUCHULAIN drove the small car that he had borrowed from Mac down Route 20 into Audley. The town looked different somehow, and smaller. There was the Exxon station where he once thought he'd like to work. It operated as a kind of town center, busy with pickup trucks being filled and old men in worn baseball hats, gabbing and gossiping. Women sat and rocked on the porches of homes along the highway, watching for any little news and discussing, once again, everything old. It dawned on Alex that this was their life; they had little else to do. He was glad that fate had taken this existence from him—and a bit sad too. This life of sheltered Americans, content enough if not exactly happy, was likely closed to him forever. He had seen that there was more, much more.

People walking on his street turned when he drove down, curious about the unfamiliar car. When he stopped in front of his parents' house, he felt a curious hesitation when he started getting out of the car. He had been in trouble here, and his father had bailed him out. Their letters had been loving and encouraging, asking him to visit. He knew he couldn't stay, even though he was not yet eighteen. He looked up at the house. His father was sitting quietly in his wheelchair on the porch, smiling and watching him, a worn blanket covering his shriveled legs. His mother stood behind, holding the arms of the chair. Alex grabbed his bag and went up the cracked, broken walk to them. He shook his father's hand and squatted to hug him, then stood and picked his mother into the air, kissing her on both cheeks.

Alex's mother, tears glistening in her eyes said, "Oh, how wonderful you look, Alex, all tanned and grown. I wish you had worn your uniform so that I could walk down Main Street with you at noon."

He carried his bag through the house. The sofa was worn and faded. The stairs still creaked the groaning gremlins impersonation that had scared him so much as a small child, in his bed. Alex grasped the doorknob to his room and lifted slightly, to pick the warped door off the floor, out of habit. His room was clean, but otherwise untouched. The faded posters on the wall, the now tarnished wresting trophy and his collection of dated hot rod magazines all had awaited his return.

At a sound, he turned to the door. Elena stood quietly, and then ran to him to be picked up, whirled around, and kissed resoundingly on each cheek. She pushed back and said, "Look at you, you've grown a foot. I am soooo glad to see you, Alex! I am dying to talk to you, but get unpacked and freshen up. We didn't know when you would arrive, so I have a friend from work coming over in a few minutes, but we can talk after that."

He hung the few clothes he had brought in the closet. His Marine dress uniform had been worn only once, at graduation when the pictures were taken. It hung in his locker at the Farm, still covered by the plastic from the cleaners. All he had was six sets of combat fatigues in various camouflage patterns and boots, hats and arctic gear, hanging neatly in a wall locker somewhere near Williamsburg. He wasn't even sure he was still a Marine, but suspected that he was. In any case, he was drawing sergeant's pay, which was not too bad for a kid who had turned seventeen not long ago.

He stripped off his travel clothes, wrapped a towel around his waist and walked down the hall to shower. He pushed the slightly mildewed shower curtain back and turned on the hot water, knowing it would be at least 45 seconds before the aging water heater in the basement could send warm water up the clanking pipes. He looked at himself in the mirror above the old porcelain sink. He hadn't really looked at himself in a mirror, other than to shave twice a day, in nearly a year. He knew he was about 45 pounds heavier—202 or so, and an inch taller at six feet two, but seeing the veined, sinewy musculature in his arms and upper body and the ridges on his flat stomach startled him a little. He smiled to himself and thought, *I may not want to be known as a bad ass, but I sure do look like one.* He flexed one bicep for the mirror and grinned at himself. *In fact, Alex my man, I think you actually are a bad ass.* He stepped gingerly into the steaming water and began to shower, humming the Marine Corps hymn and feeling pleased about life.

Alex pulled on a pair of gray cotton workout shorts and an old T-shirt, then dug in his bag for the two bottles of wine that Mac had bought for him to bring; one was a rioja from Spain for his Mom and the other a vintage port that Mac assured Alex his father would like. Alex padded barefoot down the stairs. He could hear his sister talking to someone on the porch swing as he walked past the partially open window into the kitchen. His father was reading the paper; he folded it and laid it down as he saw Alex. His mother was at the sink, peeling potatoes, and humming one of her old Bedouin love songs; she smiled at him, and then winked.

Mick looked at Alex fondly and said, "You've put on some size, son. You look like you could play linebacker for the Falcons. The Corps must agree with you. Are you happy with it so far?"

Alex thought about telling his father where he was really working, then immediately decided against it. The people at the Farm were nuts about security, and Alex liked it there. If they wanted him to know, they'd tell him. "I like it for now, Dad. It's exciting. I like the money, and I'm learning a lot about life and people that I probably wouldn't have learned here. Besides, I got my GED, so I am now officially a high school graduate."

"Now how could that be, Alex?" his mother said from the sink. "You would just have finished your sophomore year here."

"And you weren't exactly on your way to being valedictorian," Mick added with a chuckle. Maria shot Alex a quick wink to take the sting from the words.

"You just gotta have a little faith, Mom," he grinned. "They give you a test. When I passed, they gave me a piece of paper that says the United States of America affirms and attests that Alejandro Mohammed Cuchulain has received the equivalent of a satisfactorily completed high school education. Heck, even most colleges accept it."

Mick groaned a little in his chair, and shifted. "He's right, Maria. They even had that when I was in the Corps." He turned to Alex. "I fade a little at this time of day, so I'm going to take a nap before dinner. Let's spend a little time after dinner, when I'm at my best." He turned his chair with a little grimace and pushed it toward the bedroom.

"That'd be great, Dad." Alex looked at his mother, and raised one eyebrow.

She watched Mick as he rolled into the bedroom and closed the door, then said softly, "He's not doing too well, Alex. The doctor says that his lungs are beginning to fail and fill. He doesn't think it will go very well." Tears began to roll down her cheeks as she leaned into his arms. "Oh Alex, I have missed you so! I am so happy that you have come home to see us. Come sit with me for a few moments. Have you had a chance to keep up with your Spanish and Arabic while you were becoming a high school graduate?"

Alex had spent many of his summers visiting relatives in Spain and staying with his Mother's father, in North Africa, who paid for the trips each year. Alex's language skills in Arabic were a little better, or maybe just deeper, than his Spanish, because his grandfather liked to sit and talk, while his friends in Spain liked to fish, wrestle, and avoid contact with adults at all costs. Grandfather Kufdani had no sons, and just one grandson. Alex was called Mohammed, his middle name.

Abu Kufdani was apparently well off, because Alex was never without motivated tutors when an appropriate opportunity arose, whether math, Arabic language, or some form of violence prized by the Bedouin. Kufdani was a Bedouin elder who traded goods in North Africa, Europe, and around the whole area. He lived primarily in a big house on a hill in the kasbah suburb of Tangier, Morocco near the old citadel. When Alex visited, they would spend a week at this house, then four weeks at a traditional Bedouin tent camp in the South of Morocco, a desert. The last week before he traveled to Spain to visit with his mother's sisters and their girls, Alex would sit and talk with his grandfather each evening and learn from the various tutors during the day. He didn't like the tutor part so much, but it was part of the agenda his grandfather defined, so it was okay. It was the time in the desert that Alex liked best. He had learned to shoot a rifle and ride camels; he had learned about the desert and how to live in it, and a friend, Achmed, had taught him to hide, even almost vanish in the desert. There was always someone near to teach him how to do things best. His grandfather had bragged in the evenings around the fire about Mick Cuchulain, his father, and had said about Alex, "This is the son of a great American warrior, and my last living male issue. He will be a great Bedouin warrior."

There was a dinner each night cooked on an open fire by the women. After dinner, the men gathered to talk and tell stories. Men arrived in trucks and cars, often with their families, with tales of trade and politics around North Africa and Arabia; the information network of commerce was played out around the fire. They left and others arrived, seemingly without end, and certainly without much notice, although they were seen long before arrival. Alex marveled at their different accents, yet he could understand them all. He played a game with his grandfather where he guessed the region of the accent; when he got it right he got sweet dates and approving smiles. Alex had playmates everywhere and the games were different and fun.

Alex grinned at Maria and said in Spanish, "Mom, I take lessons three times a week, with native speakers." And then he spoke in Arabic, "I listen to news tapes in both, daily. I don't have a television. Is that enough?"

"I'm glad," his mother replied in Arabic. "You don't need a televison. You need to remember who you are. You're accents are quite good, but I'm surprised that you have the time for it."

She leaned toward Alex and said softly, "As you learn more, you will find that Islam is a beautiful religion wrapped around a philosophy that can be quite unattractive when interpreted by some. That conflict is how my sisters and I came to live in Spain when our Mother died; it was for freedom of thought and action as a woman. My father has sent you a present to help you understand the real Islam. It is on your nightstand; treasure it. There is also a smaller package. We will talk of this again as you mature."

Alex said, "Yeah, I know you and Islam, Mom." He then stood as Maria did. She turned to the refrigerator. Alex grinned to himself and thought, "*Mom never was one to use two words when one would do.*" He went up the stairs to his room and saw two formally wrapped packages on his nightstand; each was bound in white paper. Alex ripped the paper from the larger package and saw that it was an old, leather-bound edition of the Quran, Islam's holy book, the gold lettering on the spine and cover nearly worn away from use. The second gift was an old, yellowed ivory cylinder, engraved with images and Arabic lettering; with it was a note from his grandfather that said in Arabic, *For your friends when they are not.* He heard his mother walking down the hall outside his bedroom door.

"Mom," he called. "Do you have a second?"

Maria walked into the room as he held the ivory cylinder up. "Any idea what this is?" he said.

Maria slowly nodded and smiled. "I do," she said. "It is the identification device for a senior member of the Yahia tribe of Bedouin. Your grandfather honors you. Treasure this; it may be handy sometime, and it is a great honor to be so chosen by a Bedouin elder. It places you high up in the Bedouin hierarchy, and marks you as a thoughtful and honorable man. As you know, the tenets of the Bedouin life are honor, generosity, and hospitality. It's something to live up to. "

"Huh," Alex grunted and handed her the note. "I can translate the Arabic, but I don't get it. What's with the *friends* thing?"

Maria smiled slightly; a smile he hadn't seen. She took the cylinder from Alex's hand and made a motion on its base with her hand; a thin blade leapt from its top. "Your grandfather has become a cynic in his old age," she said. "Friends who betray a friend have no place in his life. It's a Bedouin thing."

Later, he walked onto the porch, smelling the promise of fall mingling with the scent of his mother's cooking. Songbirds quarreled as they fluttered in the gnarled, splayed old magnolia in Widow Lee's yard. He felt a rush of nostalgia, not so much wishing he was back to his old existence, as knowing that he could never return. He had changed; Audley hadn't.

He turned to the swing as his sister spoke, introducing him to her friend Linda. At twenty-five, she was seven years older than Elena. Linda was a big woman—at least 5'9" with 25 or 30 extra pounds on a large frame. She had an even featured, attractive face with large greenish eyes and straight white teeth between full, painted lips. Her looks were marred by heavy makeup, apparently hastily applied, and an ellipse of loose flesh that hung beneath her jawbone. She had enormous breasts that pushed out and up from a thin sundress; white bra straps were partially visible under the calico. A slight roll stretched the dress at the waistline, which flared into substantial hips. Her lower legs appeared to be her best feature, showing slim calves and ankles beneath her hem. She held his hand as they were introduced, being obvious about her slow gaze from his face down across his shoulders and chest, pausing for a second at his groin and then moving down his legs. He felt his face flush and the blood began to rush to his groin.

"You call this a *little* brother, Elena? I think he is absolutely gorgeous. I can't believe he is only seventeen, and already a Marine." She reached and squeezed his bicep, moving closer. Her touch felt strangely hot. He could smell cheap perfume and stale cigarettes on her breath.

"It's nice to meet you, Linda. I don't want to interrupt your talk with Elena, and I gotta go inside and get dressed for dinner," Alex stammered, his face flushed purple, as he stepped back from her touch. He saw her eyes drop to his crotch, then widen as she saw his newly stretched and tented shorts. He walked quickly—almost ran—into the house and up the stairs to his room. He closed the door and spun the flimsy key in the lock, then grabbed some tissues and pulled off his shorts, his erection almost painful. He wrapped his fist around it and began to pump furiously. After a few moments, as his erection slowly drooped and his pulse began to drop, he slumped back onto the bed, spent and depressed. He thought that he and Eric Magnusson were the only two guys in his platoon at boot camp who had never been laid—and he wasn't sure about Eric.

Linda was laughing as she sat back down on the swing beside Elena. "That's some little brother you have there, Elena. I can't believe he is only seventeen!"

"He's a good kid," Elena said. "Now we just need to make sure that some scheming woman doesn't decide that she wants a cute Marine for a husband, and goes after that the old fashioned way. Mom's a bit worried about that, too. Alex is pretty naïve, or he was when he left here a few months ago."

"He just needs to spend some time with an experienced woman, teaching him the ropes," Linda said with a slight smile. "Maybe it will be easier for him to avoid that kind of trap, when life is not such a mystery."

"Oh, no," Elena said. "You keep your claws off my little brother!"

"Hey, no problem," Linda said with a shrug. "He's a bit young for me that way, but I could use some muscle to help me do some things around the house while I have time off from work. Alex appears to have plenty of muscle, and can probably use the money."

Linda glanced at her watch, then stood up from the swing and said, "Gotta run, my sweet. My ex will have the kids back in a few minutes. He's taking them to Myrtle Beach for two weeks tomorrow, and I have to get them ready. The cheap shit never took me to the beach for even a week." She hurried down the steps to her car, and called over her shoulder, "See you soon."

Audley

DINNER was a great change from "dining" at the Farm. His Mom had made stuffed pork chops, mashed potatoes, creamed corn and a pecan pie for dessert. They drank the wine Alex brought, and talked long into the evening. He showed his father the Quran that Abu Kufdani had sent, and all admired that quality of the ancient binding. They talked of Christ and God, and about Mohammed and Allah.

When Alex and Mick were alone later, sipping on the port Alex had brought, Mick said quietly, "Are you working for MacMillan now?"

Alex nodded, a little uncomfortable with where this discussion might go.

"That figures, I guess. Your hair is a little too long for the Corps. 'Nuff said about that. Maybe it's good," Mick said with a whimsical grin. "That bunch has always been nuts about security. The good news is that they spend so much money training their people that they hate to lose them; it's hard for them to make their numbers work if they lose too many expensively trained workers. That makes working for them a bit safer than being a Gunny in a line combat unit. Even if I'm just a cynic, there is no downside to that view for you and for me. I imagine you'll find time to read and study as well; use it."

"I've heard that training cost argument, and I've already been reading and studying a bit. More to come, I hope." Alex said, as he leaned forward in his chair. "You're still a legend in the Corps, Pop. Your name is on every glory wall I saw at Parris Island. Any advice for me? Anything that you've learned, that would give me an edge? What does a Marine with the Medal have to tell his son about combat and life?"

"There are a few very simple rules I think you should follow," Mick said quietly. "Some may not make sense for a while." He raised his right hand and extended three fingers, then folded the first one down and said, "The most important rule is ARF, *Always Retaliate First*. Don't hesitate and wait for the bad guy to start the fight. End it before it starts, and err on the side of being too violent."

Mick folded the second finger down and said, "When you're in combat, everyone on the other side is the enemy. If they brought their women and kids to the battlefield, they've made them the enemy. Kill them all, first chance. The first corollary to the *Kill Them All* rule is don't leave witnesses behind. If witnesses don't shoot you in the back, they'll find a way to make your life miserable by talking to others."

The third finger folded down Mick said, "Finally, be ready mentally and physically. Work at it. Be better, stronger, faster, and nastier than anyone else."

Alex looked a little troubled as he considered his father's words, then shrugged and nodded. He'd think more about it later. "Tell me a little more, Pop," he said. "Be a little more specific, with maybe some examples."

"It all sounds a little harsh I guess," Mick said. "Most of us who have that little blue ribbon with the five white stars are dead, but I'm not yet, so I looked into things a little by reading a lot to supplement what I learned in the Corps. I've had a lot of time to do that, unfortunately. I've learned that wars have been going on for a few thousand years to no good effect, except to protect those at home from some real or imagined threat. On the imagined threat, I've learned that some number of politicians everywhere tend to feather their own nests on the bodies of patriots. I've searched desperately for a better political system than ours and found none, as Churchill predicted. But what does one do with all of that philosophical bullshit that tends to send kids off to get killed to get an extra few votes or the favor of their leaders, and then ties the kids' hands with rules of engagement that the bleeding hearts demand? I'd say be very careful when dealing with politicians, and avoid them when you can. Do your job quietly and well, and of course, never volunteer. A lot of what combat troops do is worthwhile for our society, so it has to be done—and right now. Other times the reason for the combat is stupid. You don't get to make that decision. That's the way our systems works, but I think my few rules add to the chances for your survival and for your buddies' too."

Mick shifted a bit in his chair and looked off into space for a while, then said, "Anyway, back to thinking and expanding a little on the three rules. When you're out there in the middle of a fire fight, there is no time to ponder a philosophy of life. You must have made up your mind, long before the first shot is fired, what you are willing to do, and why. Then just do it. A half-second hesitation on coming back on the trigger or driving a knife home can be fatal to you—or maybe worse—make you responsible for getting your buddies killed. That's the easy part. I think the hardest thing is dealing with civilians in a combat op; you hesitate to kill a kid who may be a threat, and then he pops a grenade or blows himself up and your whole crew with him. Civilians are part of the problem, and they shouldn't be there maybe, but civilians get killed in every war. If they are there and with the defined targets, they're targets; there is no time to sort out the good from the bad. Don't let anyone stab or shoot your back—kill them all. Kill them all before they can kill you. The bleeding hearts here who worry about civilians and how nice we should be to them have never been shot at by a kid or a woman—or lost a son to them."

"And always be in the best physical shape you can be. Exceed your own expectations. Physical exhaustion can kill you by forcing bad decisions in that draining, panting fog. Be sharp, alert, and able to function; that takes preparation and forethought. If you have to sprint for a hundred yards, then drop and shoot, you should not be out of breath and unable to function, but that's not a decision you can make at that moment. You have to be physically ready, early and always. There are times when you need to be able to kill with your hands or using other physical skills, but if you can shoot or knife a bad guy, don't punch him or do a cute spin move and kick his head in. He probably has a buddy a half-second away who will kill you while you're sucking your bleeding knuckles instead of spinning with the slack out of your trigger to search for him, the next one. MacMillan will make sure that you learn and use the mental preparation needed, I'd imagine. He was a helluva warrior."

"In Vietnam, the NVA and the VC would sometimes cut off the balls of a captured GI, stuff them in his mouth and let him choke to death on them, then drop him where he'd be found. It wasn't to punish him, I'd guess, but probably done on an order to send a fear message to their enemy—to make him less effective. That cruelty had a political purpose, and that is the kind of thinking you will face from the other side. They won't hesitate to march an army of kids in front of them in an assault, or to clear a minefield the hard way with them if they'll gain an advantage from your unwillingness to shoot a child or a woman."

"Jeez, Dad!" Alex said. "That's tough to think about. What the heck?"

Mick shifted in his chair and grimaced a little. "I guess I'm saying the nobility concept is bullshit when things are very busy and lethal—don't be noble in combat; the enemy will take advantage of you if they find that most of what you worry about is this concept of nobility. Figure it out before you get dead, sort of by accident, while you worry about the meaning of life for the innocent women and children in the combat zone, as folks are shooting at you. Think things through. Survive. Kill the enemy efficiently and without conscience. You should also never brag or fess up to anything; keeping your mouth shut is almost always the best way to act. If there are no witnesses to a situation, tell the simple lie that works best. But don't confuse a combat op with politics, and avoid politicians.

Mick and Alex were both silent for awhile. Finally Mick said, "I guess that's the big picture the way I see it after all of this time. You'll have to figure things out as they happen."

Alex nodded, considering.

Mick said, "I'm fading. Think about what I say. We'll talk again some-

Audley
Dawn

ALEX awoke at 0500 from force of habit. There was only a hint of dawn in the sky, and not even the birds were awake. There was no sound in the house when he went into the kitchen, drank a quart of milk from the refrigerator, tossed the carton into the trash and walked into the street, wearing his running shoes, an old red and gold Marine Corps T-shirt that stretched tight across his chest and back, and the gray cotton workout shorts—this time with a jock under them.

He started out at the six-minute mile pace that he had been using every day for more than four months. At first he looked around the neighborhood, trying to figure out what was different than when he left, almost a year ago. When he came up with the answer—not much—he let his mind begin to wander. He reflected a little on what he had learned at the Farm, so much disciplined violence and so much skill training, all so he could do a good job at killing people for Uncle Sam. He was pretty sure that he didn't want to stay with this life for too long, but had no idea how he would get out of it or what he wanted to do. Mac had told him that he could have an appointment to any of the service academies, because his Dad had the Medal, but he didn't think he'd do too well in the academic structure of a service academy, and he wasn't sure he wanted to be an officer.

He let his mind wander to Linda, and the way she looked. The fact that she was fat turned him off a little, and he thought that she wore too much makeup. He also thought that he did not really give a rat's ass about any of that; he was clearly going to work his butt off to see if she would let him bang her brains out, however you did that. He thought, for some reason, that she might. He thought for a while as he ran about her enormous boobs and then about her big butt, and planned his approach to convince her to sleep with him. It did not occur to him to think about whether he or Linda would be in control of the tactical situation.

After an hour of steady running, Alex moved smoothly down the street toward his family's house. His cropped hair was matted wet against his head, his shirt soaked, and the shorts streaked with sweat. He felt good. He was thinking about where he could find a decent place to work out, when it occurred to him that the gym at the high school was pretty good, and that Coach Webb might arrange for him to use it. He picked up his pace and turned at the big sycamore on the corner, away from his home, hoping to catch the coach before school. It was only a couple of miles; he should be there by 0630 at the latest.

The school hadn't changed much either, Alex noticed as he slowed near the door to the gym. The door was ajar, and he went inside. He could hear, coming from the weight room, the distinctive clang of a weight stack coming together. The coach was just standing up from the seat on the lat pull-down machine when he looked up and saw Alex walk in. "Can I help you, son?" he said. Alex looked at him and grinned. "Well, if ain't Alex Cuchulain," Webb said in amazement. "I thought you were off in the Marine Corps or something. You're looking good though; put on a little weight, it looks like. Been working out? Doing any wrestling?'

"I'm just here on leave for two weeks, coach," Alex said. "I've been doing some working out, but haven't done any wrestling for four months or so. I did a little in Parris Island and got to like it a lot—you were right about that. I thought maybe you'd let me use the gym while I'm home, for old-time's sake."

"Sure Cuchulain, no problem. I'll be done here in ten or fifteen minutes, and then I'll spot for you. How much time do you need?"

Alex thought for a second and looked around the room at the equipment. "I guess about forty minutes," he said.

"I don't have a class until ten. Do you wanna wrestle a few falls when you're done?" The coach grinned. "I'll take it easy on you. I just want to find out if you learned anything about wrestling from those jarheads. What do you weigh now, about 180? I'm about 172 or so."

"Coach, I got some real bad news for you," Alex said mockingly in a semi-stern voice, "I'm about 202 right now, and the man don't live that can give me thirty pounds on a wrestling mat and think about winning even a single fall. You being an old man and all, I would have taken it a little bit easy on you, but you've disparaged the image of the United States Marine Corps, and I'm gonna have to punish you a little."

Webb grinned at him. "Well, you just get your blocks or something, sonny, while I finish up here. I will then give you a hand with your puny weights prior to commencing wrestling classes for the United States Marine Corps' finest."

Cuchulain walked to the pull-up bar, reached up, and hung for a minute or so, twisting this way and that, stretching his lats and back. He then started to pull himself up slowly until his chin was over the bar, and then lowered himself even more slowly until his arms were again fully extended. The next repetition was pulled until the back of his neck touched, and again lowered slowly. After each set of two, Alex moved his hands a little wider on the bar. When his hands were three feet or so apart, he began to move them slowly back together with each set.

The coach watched in awe as he went over thirty repetitions, still showing no sign of strain or stress in his face. He knew that he was probably watching the strongest person he had ever met. He was sick with the thought of how much ass Audley High School could have kicked if he had been able to keep Cuchulain. He was also beginning to suspect that he had his work cut out for him on the mat.

Later, they worked Cuchulain quickly through the weights, each exercise a casual demonstration that Webb was witnessing a very rare physical phenomenon. There was no way that a 200 pound man should be able to lift this much weight, Webb thought, let alone a seventeen-year-old kid.

They walked from the weight room to the wrestling mat in the corner of the gym. "You take the top first, coach," Cuchulain said, and Webb went to his hands and knees with Alex beside him. When the coach said "Go!" Cuchulain vanished under him in the wrestling move known as a "switch," spinning fast to the right under Webb to reach behind his right shoulder and under with his right hand, getting his palm on the back of Webb's left inner thigh, with his long fingers reaching across the hamstring. He squeezed hard, and with his back arched, leaned against the grip as he ran on his heels to get behind Webb, at the same time forcing the coach's shoulder to the mat with the leverage. When he was behind, he drove his arm between Webb's leg and grabbed his right bicep near the shoulder, squeezed to immobilize it, then rolled him up and over until his shoulders were flat upon the mat. His body weight kept Webb there as he struggled, and then relaxed in submission.

After the first pin, Cuchulain allowed the pace to slow, working at whatever level the coach chose. Webb was amazed at how much Cuchulain had learned about wrestling over the past year. He knew that someone had been teaching him, because moves like Cuchulain had did not come instinctively. As they worked, the coach found himself enjoying wrestling for the first time in a long time. He was also miserable, because he didn't think there was a college wrestler in the East who could touch Cuchulain at his weight, and he would only be a junior at Audley! Twenty minutes later he called it off, exhausted, but content. Cuchulain was on his knees, relaxed, drenched with sweat, but breathing normally.

They walked back across the gym toward the outside door. "Thanks Coach! I appreciate the workout and the use of the gym. Is it okay if I come back a couple of more times?"

"No problem," the coach said. "Any time. If you get time, come by in the afternoons from four 'til six and give some pointers to my kids. I'd appreciate it. They might like advice better coming from you, particularly after a fall or two with you."

Later, Alex walked into the living room of his parents' house, freshly showered and wearing clean shorts and a T-shirt. His mother and Elena were sitting together talking, while his father casually watched a Winston Cup race. His mother looked up and said, "Linda called and asked if you would mind helping her move some furniture today. She'll pay you, of course. I told her that you'll call. The number is by the phone."

Alex shrugged, and then walked to the phone feeling a distinct stirring in his crotch. He dialed Linda and told her he'd be happy to give her a hand. She asked him to come over as soon as he could, so he told his mother that he would be back a little later and walked out of the house. Elena gave him a strange look, almost as if she was going to laugh, or maybe cry. He found Linda's small house after only one wrong turn, parked by a broken curb, and moved easily from the small car. Whistling to himself, he bounded up the steps two at a time, then walked up to the open door and rang the doorbell. Linda was wearing a white shirt with the top four buttons open, the shirttail out, and a pair of jeans. She was clearly braless, her breasts swaying as she walked across the room to him. The nipples painted little circles on the thin cotton.

What the heck do I do now? Alex wondered to himself, as he felt himself stir and swell. *Maybe if I work my ass off, I'll get lucky.* He walked into the house behind her, watching her buttocks undulate beneath her jeans and feeling optimistic. The small living room was cluttered with magazines stacked on the end tables and old clothes strewn about.

"What can I do to help you, Linda?" he asked.

She walked to the kitchen and pointed to the open cabinet doors under the sink. A large, rusty pipe wrench was lying on the floor of the cabinet. "The drain pipe is loose and leaking under there, Alex, and I'm not strong enough to tighten it. We'll get to the furniture later."

Alex picked up the wrench and got onto his back under the sink. Linda got on her hands and knees and looked inside, then leaned forward and put one palm on his thigh, pointing to the pipe with the other. Alex could feel the heat of her hand on his leg as he put the wrench on the pipe and tightened it; his erection felt like it was going to burst from his shorts. As he started to slide out from beneath the cabinet his crotch came under her hand, as if by accident. There was a little squeeze.

"Oh, I'm so sorry, Alex," she said, moving her hand away. "That was an accident!"

Alex came to his feet and sat the wrench on the counter. Linda was on her knees in front of him, looking up. His excitement was obvious and pounding against his shorts, just in front of her face.

She looked up at him, and then at his throbbing crotch. "Are you all right, Alex? I didn't hurt you or anything did I?" She reached for his shorts and clasped her hand around him. "Do you mind if I check? Your mother would be furious with me if I hurt you," Linda said with a soft voice.

"Your face is all flushed, Alex. Slip out of those shorts until I make sure that everything down there is okay," Linda said, still on her knees, but smiling at him in anything but a motherly manner.

Alex watched her face while he worked his shorts and jock down, then stepped out of them. Linda reached up with one hand, then two.

"It's all swollen, Alex. Is there anything I can do for you to make it better?" she asked in a coy whisper. "Here, let's keep you from getting a chill." She stood and took off her blouse, wrapping it around his shoulders, then reached again for him and leaned forward to whisper hotly in his ear, "By the way, Alex, you seem more than adequately up for things." Alex looked at her massive breasts, then down at her hand.

"Nooo!" he groaned, then felt himself release across her hand onto her bare stomach and to the floor. As she felt it, Linda leaned forward and put her tongue into his ear

"Let's go into the bedroom so that you can lie down. I'm sure that you'll feel better after that." Linda said, as she led him into the bedroom and pulled the covers down on the king-sized bed. She walked to the bathroom and came back with a warm, wet towel and began to clean around his groin, leaning down with her mouth close to him as she worked.

After a few seconds Linda said, "Maybe a little mouth to mouth will help," as she looked up to him with a grin.

He watched as she lowered her head to him, looking at him with those big greenish eyes. He felt himself leaping to readiness.

Linda stood, pulled her jeans off and dropped them to the floor and said, "Get on top of me, Alex. Now!"

Alex thought to himself, *Yes! I'm finally going to get laid!* He knelt, oblivious to anything but his need to be inside her. She reached down with one hand to guide him. "Easy now with that thing!" she whispered to him. He felt the rush of another orgasm beginning, so he drove himself forward. Linda's eyes rolled back into her head and she made strange mewing sounds, her mouth wide open. It was easier now for Alex. He could feel his orgasm rising further, urgently. Sweat poured from his face. Linda's eyes were wide as she tried to push him back with her hand on his stomach. He was oblivious, driven by his need. Pain and pleasure mixed for her, but she knew that he was nearly finished. With a few final strokes, he began to whither and collapsed, chest heaving, upon her chest.

Linda ran her fingers through his hair, and leaned up to kiss his neck, then pulled his mouth to hers. He stuck his tongue into her mouth, and then moved it rapidly in and out like an amateur well digger. Linda knew she was going to enjoy her role as teacher. She had nearly two weeks to teach him to get it right, and he was already more fun than her ex. After a few moments, she pushed him from her, and got to her feet. "Come on, stud, I'll buy you a Coke," she grinned at him.

Alex, disappointed that it was over so soon, followed her to the kitchen, watching her bare buttocks jiggle. She reached into the refrigerator and pulled out two Cokes, handing him one. She pushed the door shut, then noticed him staring at her breasts with a look of fascination.

"Come on, let's sit on the bed. I'll teach you about breasts," Linda said as she walked back to the bedroom. Alex followed eagerly, happy that it appeared to be intermission and not the end of the game. She sat on the edge of the bed and patted the place beside her. As he sat, she smiled at him, then reached for one heavy breast and lifted it to his lips. He bent over and kissed it, almost chastely. She looked down at him. He was already stirring again. She had forgotten the blessing of being with an adolescent.

She pulled him up to her. "This is the way to kiss, Alex," Linda said. She put her lips gently on his, then began to lick around his lips, exploring the tip of his tongue with hers. She pushed him back onto the bed and rolled up beside him to whisper, "Maybe you'd like to practice what you learned."

Alex rolled to her and put his lips on hers. His tongue slipped out to tease the inside of her lips, then tangle gently with Linda's. She slipped a hand into his hair and murmured, "Uh-huh," and smiled.

Linda pushed gently down on his head. "Slowly and gently is the secret." He did as she asked, moving from one to the other, moving over her as he did.

Linda ran her fingernails lightly up his back, then rumpled his hair and pulled his head up to kiss him. "Take it real nice and slow, Alex. I'm not going anywhere," she whispered. Linda's hands went behind his buttocks.

"Easy now," she said. "Give a girl time to adjust to you. The last time was way too fast."

He began to push forward, telling himself to go slowly.

"Good. You've got the idea now. Kiss me, Alex," Linda murmured a little later. "Kiss me and hold me and keep that pace. Learn control." He kissed her gently for a long time, then moved on to her neck and kissed that. He moved up and nibbled on her earlobe. After several minutes, she felt her orgasm rising, and her hips started to buck a little. Alex increased his pace, but Linda whispered, "No, no. Not yet. Just keep going like you were until I tell you. Later, you'll know when to pick up the pace."

He slowed, trying to follow directions. Her breathing quickened. "Keep up with me now, Alex, but don't get ahead," she whispered, and he kept pace. Suddenly her eyes went wide and Linda moaned, "Oh, my God! Oh, my God! Now!" Linda's neck strained and her jaw clenched as her orgasm peaked, and again quickly, then slowly began to subside. Alex continued until he let go with a groan.

Linda lay for a few minutes, then got up and walked to the shower, as Alex lay on the bed and watched her move. She came out a few minutes later still nude, and toweling her hair. She walked back to the bed, sitting on the edge beside him. She smiled at Alex, and said, "How do you feel? I think I am now a statutory rapist, so you'd better be having fun."

Alex grinned at her. "I feel great! That was fantastic!" Linda rolled onto the bed between his legs, with her head just above his groin. Alex relaxed and watched, until finally she pulled from him. She moved up beside him and began a slow kiss. "Alex, there's something that I'd like you to do for me that makes me feel wonderful."

"Sure," Alex said. "Anything."

She rolled onto her back and pushed his head down onto her stomach. "Kiss me here, on my stomach," she said. He slid down and began to kiss her soft, smooth belly. Linda put her hands into his hair.

"Now just move down a little more, sweetheart," she said, pushing his head down a little further. "Mmmm, that's nice. Now—"

Twelve days later Alex drove his borrowed car out of Audley, whistling happily to himself, heading back to Williamsburg and the Farm. He wasn't sorry to be leaving, but was sure glad he had come home. His mother thought that he must have completely redone Linda's house, with the time he had spent helping her, and Elena couldn't resist giving him little digs each time he came home for dinner.

The Farm

Much Later

ALEX walked from the admin building at the Farm, strolling and shaking his head a little, bemused at the ways things sometimes play out. He was leaving his semi-regular meeting with the Agency's resident psychiatrist there. He had been seeing him for eight years or so. The shrink was known by the regulars as "Barry the Shrink" and had the job of helping the CIA's special-ops warriors deal with the killing and violence they both experienced and caused. There was a little talk that Barry was a pure and impartial shrink and interested in their individual happiness, but more that he was a smart guy who would help them deal with the bad stuff that screwed up their heads. Alex knew that he was Barry's special case; he had been seeing him since he was seventeen years old, a third of his life, and got to observe things as they evolved. Alex had slowly learned to watch and analyze Barry as Barry watched and analyzed him, as they talked. He hadn't taken the drugs Barry prescribed to help him cope, but he had coped. Somehow, Alex had become quite talented at the special operations trade, and Barry had been with him all the way, helping him to reason through why he shouldn't feel too much guilt about the killing and dismembering of sometimes apparently innocent others, albeit with Barry's contracted Agency view. Barry worked for Mac, and there was more than a bit of good logic about the way he led Alex to view his life, but of course Alex had slowly learned to put things in context, and often thought about his father's advice about combat and life. There had been adequate time to study and to take local college courses of choice, albeit with sudden breaks in attendance when the special-ops jobs called. Mac was good about influencing civilian professors to cut Farm students a little slack as long as the work was done at the end; he paid a lot of their bills.

Alex had become one of the government's best electronics and explosives technicians. After attending every school the military and the CIA could provide, and having taken useful college courses nearby, Cuchulain was one of the few men in the world who could blow up one-third of nearly any building, destroying all it enclosed, while maintaining the structural integrity of the remainder of the building. More importantly, he could set it up so that the remaining occupants were troubled merely by severe concussion headaches, rather than suffering the dismemberment and vaporization that troubled the target audience. Among his skills were remotely detonated car bombs, airplane engine explosives that detonated without a trace at a particular altitude or time of day, and such household items as pens or rosary beads that could be blown up with just enough precise force to kill only the persons carrying them. He had designed most of his own devices, and his employers had quickly adopted many of them as their standard.

Alex's operations-partner for the past five years or so had been Jerome Masterson, a career Marine with more than twenty years service. Strangely, despite their age difference, he and Jerome had developed a symbiotic operational relationship, each doing what he did best. On an op, it had become a flowing thing where there was little need for overt communication. Things just happened the way that worked best. He had saved Jerome's ass a few times and Jerome his—all without words; it just flowed. He had decided to wait to see how the flow went this time before telling Jerome about his decision. The conversation with Mac would tell him something about that.

Alex had told Barry that he was ready to get out of the Special-ops business—that he wanted a different life, and soon. This was his notice to Mac, delivered in conversation with Barry. He had little doubt that Barry was already on the phone with Mac, and Alex had his regular Wednesday dinner tonight with Mac. It should be an interesting evening—one that might give him a better hint of where Mac's head was, and how Alex fit into that. Was he just another talented op, or did Mac really have some personal feeling in all of this, given the mission he had? How long was Mac's view of things?

Alex and Mac walked along the groomed lawn after dinner. Mac carried a small bag. They sat on a bench overlooking the James River, as they had for many years, talking but never reporting. Reporting was done elsewhere and more formally, often even under hypnotism for later recall of essential mission details. Mac said, "I talked to Barry today, about thirty milliseconds after you got off his couch, like you'd guess. Hey, you've done your job better than most; bailing from the killing work is not a problem. If you want to skip this mission, we can find someone else, but it is sort of up your alley. You're the best for the job. I'll have to pull both you and Jerome; you're sort of a matched pair."

Mac bent over to open the bag, the quiet of the evening punctuated by the rippling of the river and the discordant background buzz of myriad insects. From it he pulled a 1977 Fonseca port wine, took a fancy corkscrew out of a side pocket in the bag, and began to open the bottle.

"Yeah, that's part of the problem, Mac," Alex said, "I've been doing this for nearly eight years, and we have been active. Folks know me, and know about me. I'm getting more active, not less, and Jerome is part of it. In or out, we are indeed a matched pair."

Mac unscrewed the cork, and then handed the corkscrew to Alex. "Brand new. I can't decide if I like it, but the design is nice. Forget what it's called."

Alex turned it over in his hand. The grips were old, red stained wood and the whole thing was carefully put together. He opened the small knife that was designed to remove the top of the foil bottle capsule, and then closed it again. "Nice piece," he said. "I saw a couple of these in Europe. Has a bumblebee engraved at the base of the blade. I used to call it the bumble bee thing. It's got a name though."

Mac nodded, busily extracting two Riedel port glasses from the bag, and two white Irish linen napkins.

Alex sighed and said, "Barry says I'm starting to get used to being called a wolverine where I just kill everything in sight without much thought and no hesitation. I prefer being called Cooch to being called a wolverine, but that doesn't change why they all want me, nor who I am. I'm a good boomer, and no one dies from a kid shooting them in the back if I'm watching their back. Jerome says he acts as a useful bonus, since he helps keep me alive. Even the dreams and my nightmares are starting to go away. I'm not sure I like what I'm becoming. In fact, I'm damned sure that I don't like who I am becoming. I'm twenty-five years old, for crying out loud."

"You're fine with Jerome, I assume?" Mac asked. "We can get someone else if that's problem."

"Oh yeah, I'm fine with Jerome, and him with me. Jerome is me and I'm him, on a mission. Left hand, right hand. He's wisdom, I'm action, up close maybe. I guess I don't really know, except that it works. He's the most patient man I've met; it's unbelievable. I can't imagine breaking in another partner, or having him break me in. I suspect that he feels the same way."

"Had to check," Mac said. "I don't want to lose you for something I can easily fix, but I understand about the dreams. I don't have those dreams anymore, and I haven't for quite a few years. I think it makes me less of a person now that they're gone—less human," Mac said with a sigh. "You're better than anyone I have, Alex, because of your skills, your lethality enhanced by wolverine instincts—but most of all by how fucking smart you are. How smart you are, is what bothers me. Do you know how fucking smart you are— the tests—that shit?"

"Yeah, as much as I want to know," Alex said, as he accepted a glass filled about halfway. "I've long since figured out that the time of my life that big intellect was fertile ground is past me. It would take me ten years to get a decent Ph.D. Still, I'd guess that I am the smartest assassin active today. Don't quite know what to make of that."

Mac sipped a second time from his glass. "Still a nice port," he said softly.

Alex swirled the thick red wine around his glass, then stuck his substantial nose into the glass and took a long smell. "'Tis," he said, and then took his first sip.

"I guess I'd call myself a patriotic assassin, rather than plain vanilla assassin," Mac said.

"Yeah? You figured out how to rationalize who you are—who we are?" Alex said.

"Yeah," Mac said. "I think we're making a difference in the fight against the dark side. If I have to be an assassin to do that, that's okay. But I gotta do a good job of things if I'm going to pay that price. I'm selfish. Those clumsy, greedy politicians should never get a clean shot at me or mine. I might be willing to die for the idea, but I'm not going to jail for those windbags."

"I've gotten that impression from you over the past five or six years that we've been killing brain cells out here, telling lies, with the best port we can find," Alex said. "I guess I'll rationalize with you, and call myself a patriotic assassin rather than an efficient, cold blooded killer. It sounds better."

"You know what I am hoping you'll decide to do someday, of course," Mac said.

"Yeah, I do, Mac," Alex said. "But I don't think I'm wired for your job; we talked about that kind of thing. You'd be better off with someone who loves to plan right down to the gnat's ass, just the way you do. You tell me what needs to be done and how to do it and I'll make it happen with good applied intelligence, or I'll be the dangle that gets it started. I get no joy from figuring out the how. You love that shit. I love getting in the zone and just letting my training and instincts take over. I love to see a structure disintegrate exactly as I planned, and watch the bodies spinning in the air. The shooting is less fun; it just starts when targets show up and ends when they're down. They're just targets to me. I got over the guilt part before I was twenty years old. I'm a sick puppy, I guess."

"I suppose most would say that about the whole bunch of us here at the Farm," Mac sighed. "But, there's not much resistance to funding our budget. We seem to be a necessary resource to have available, but it often ain't pretty. Even the agency people look at us like we're more than a little strange."

"You think?" Alex laughed. "Just because we're a bunch of stone-cold killers on a twenty-four-hour call alert? Hell, you do the planning for it. They could just get rid of you and it would fall apart in a hurry. Feeling any career pressure, big guy?"

"I'm not," Mac said with a little smile. "Assassins that can plan and execute well seem to be in short supply. The good news is that you may be the most lethal individual on the planet. It's made things easier."

"I'm a boomer and a killer, Mac," Alex said. "I blow shit up and kill people. I'm good at it, but I can't see me doing it for twenty years. It's time for me to move on."

Mac poured a bit more port into Alex's glass and said, "I can't quarrel with your logic and I love you like a son. I'll scratch this mission and have you both discharged with pensions within sixty days. You know what you want to do? If I can help, I will."

"Whoa, whoa!" Alex said, then took another sip of his port. "This is six months to a year's notice, not six hours and giving me a pension at my age would be politically dangerous. This is just when we talk. I haven't even talked at length to Jerome about any of this—not since he finished his degree. It may change. I got no clue what I'm going to do, and that may change as I think it through. I'm just letting you know that the time is coming."

"Okay, that makes my life a little easier," Mac said. "We'll talk more about it, and we're out of port, once again. This is my last bottle."

"It's my turn. I found a six-pack of '63 Dow for only a little less than the price of a house. We'll start on that next," Alex said. "When's the mission brief?"

Mac leaned over, poured a little more of the purple juice into his glass, put the cork back into the bottle, then leaned back and said. "It's tomorrow at 1000, in the secure conference room. Dopers—Thailand, maybe Burma."

Alex took a sip and studied the sly movement of the eddies in the river below. "Jerome's been alerted?" he said.

Mac rolled his neck around to look again at Alex and raised one eyebrow, "Duh," he said.

Alex snorted with amusement just as he was sipping the last of his port, sending wine squirting painfully up his nose.

Rural Thailand

A local warlord and major supplier of raw opium to the world's heroin dealers, together with his major growers and processors, were reportedly planning a strategy meeting on how to increase production. Cuchulain and Jerome Masterson had been inserted into the area to see if a serious crimp could be put into their plans.

Alex and Jerome had been encamped on a jungle hilltop above the crowded compound for five days, waiting for signs that the meeting was still on. Their mission became complicated quickly. During their fourth day of observation, they saw a trio of men carrying some electronic gear into the main house. A quick look through their spotting scope confirmed that the equipment was of the latest security technology, similar to what they themselves had used only eighteen months before.

"Shit! Let's get down there and do our dirty before they get that stuff calibrated tomorrow," Alex said. "We'll just wait until the bad guys show up later to arm it."

Jerome nodded and began to pick up his gear. He had been recruited from the Marine sniper school by Mac several years before. He was a master with many weapons and had the patience to get in place to use them, nearly invisibly if required. "I'll find a spot that covers the main house. It's big enough that they'll stay there, I'd think."

They moved the half mile down the hill at midnight, and at 0300, Alex went to the main house and slipped into the kitchen through a partially open window. Jerome was set up about 100 yards away in a small clearing just up the slope that led to their holding site. Watching Alex through the night vision scope of his rifle, and looking around the compound, Jerome saw no sign of life. He double clicked his radio, to let Alex know that all was still *okay*, and got a quick double click in return.

The house was empty and huge, with at least six bedrooms. Alex moved quickly through the house setting charges where they wouldn't be seen, and placing listening devices that could be activated remotely to avoid—at least for awhile—notice by electronic detection devices. As Alex placed a brick of C5 explosive into the toilet tank of the master bathroom, he felt a soft bag hanging. He cut it loose and dropped it into the flap pocket of his shirt. Alex quickly wired the remaining rooms and moved back to the kitchen window. He double clicked his radio and was chilled by a quick 4-click back: a *stop* signal from Jerome. Somebody, or something, was moving out there. He peered from the window into the courtyard and saw a large yellow dog, nose to the ground, moving toward him, alert. When the dog was fifteen feet from the window, it suddenly rolled over with a whimper and then jerked once. His radio double clicked; Jerome had taken care of the problem with two silenced shots.

Alex slipped through the window and moved quickly to two other buildings, placed a few charges, then ran to the dog, snapped its neck for insurance against having a large wounded dog awaken right next to his throat and threw it over his shoulder. He kicked dirt onto the blood stains to hide them, then began to run toward Jerome. The extra hundred pounds or so of the dog's carcass slowed him only a little, until Jerome stepped out to the trail with his bag and spread a large poncho liner on the ground. Alex dumped the dog's remains onto the cloth and picked up two corners. Jerome grabbed the other two corners and brought all four together to tie them; there was good reason to leave neither the dog nor a blood trail. Alex picked up the bag and loaded it over Jerome's backpack. They moved quickly back to their hide to wait for daylight. Jerome buried the dog and dug another hole to bury their trash when they left. Alex took transmitters from his pack, inserted fresh batteries in them, and checked the trail alarms.

"Good shot on the dog," Alex said as he set up the listening gear and moved the alarm monitors closer to where they were going to sit and wait. They leaned back against a pair of trees, and began to wind down.

"Thanks. It wasn't hard, but you don't want a big pool of blood there for someone to notice, so I took the head shots."

Alex nodded and took a drink of water. "We should be okay. I kicked some dirt over what was there." He nodded at the alarm monitors. "I suspect we'll get plenty of notice if there's an issue."

"I'd be surprised if we hear from them," Jerome said and stared out into space a bit. "I had a dog that looked a little like that once. Great dog. Almost sent me to college."

"Helluva dog, to do that," Alex said. "College can be expensive."

"Yeah," Jerome said. "When I was a teen-ager, I used to do chores for a rich couple that lived on the other side of town. Grass mowing, car washing, hedge clipping, shit like that. Got to know them a little over a couple of years. Then the old man died of a heart attack."

"It like to broke her heart when he died—I'd like some woman to like me that much someday," Jerome said as he settled in for the wait, sitting with his back against the second tree and his legs stuck out in front of him. "Anyhow, the old man bought a yellow Lab; Wilson was his name. Paid a fortune for him, I found out later. Wilson was a national field trial champion, from a long line of them. The old man bought him for a ton of money from the trainer who handled him, after Wilson won the nationals."

"Named him for a basketball?" Alex asked incredulously. "And why pay all that money when you could buy a good pup, cheap, and have someone train it?"

Jerome laughed quietly, remembering. "Named him for a town where they had a summer place; Wilson, Wyoming. And the old man told me, 'I'm too god-damned old to wait for someone to train a dog, and too rich to need to. If I drop a duck, I want to know that my dog will pick him up and bring him to me with no bullshit, and sit still as a stone on his stand until I need him. In fact, I want the best damn bird dog in the U.S. of A. So I bought Wilson.'"

"They hired me to run with Wilson—to exercise him—and I gave him a bath when he got into a skunk or poison oak. The old man got poison oak if he drove near it, he was so sensitive, but that dog was with him all of the time, so he had to be clean. I gave that dog a lot of baths."

Alex chuckled. "Hell, if it was enough to pay for college, you must have damn near drowned him!"

"It was a skosh more complicated than that," Jerome mused. "After the heart attack, the old lady couldn't look at Wilson without thinking of the old man, and starting to cry. After a couple of weeks of that, she asked me if I'd take Wilson, and I said, "Sure!" She gave me all of his papers, a bill of sale, his crate, and all of his food and stuff, and said she was going to put the house on the market and travel a bit. She cried a little when I took Wilson, too."

"When I got home, all excited, my daddy told me that I had to pay the dog's way if I was going to keep him. Him and me, we sat down and tried to figure out how I was going to do that. When Daddy got to reading all of the paperwork, there was a letter from the trainer that asked if the old man would breed him, if he was paid. I don't imagine that the old man ever answered, but I sure did. Got paid $800 bucks a breeding, and Wilson was happier than a hog in slop to help out. That's where I first got interested in accounting, what with keeping track of the stud fees and the costs and all, for the taxes."

Alex laughed and said, "I guess Wilson *would* be happy! And it was enough to pay for college?"

"After three years, I'd saved about two grand, after expenses. Then Wilson got snake bit while he was flushing pheasants for me, ran right through a nest of rattler babies. The vet bills were about two grand, but then we finally had to put him down. Rattler babies are worse than the adults. Bye, bye college money."

"And how was your Dad about that, the losing two grand?" Alex said.

"Not too, happy, but he said that it was my dog and my call," Jerome said softly. "My daddy was a good guy. Back then, I didn't realize how good he was; I guess you never do. Six weeks after Wilson died, I graduated high school and joined the Corps."

They woke at dawn, and settled in to watch the compound. There was soon frenzied activity, as the service people ran about with armloads of blankets, food, and drink for the main house.

By mid-morning, armed outriders in Jeeps and trucks began arriving at the compound, followed by cars with armor and darkened windows. As men emerged from the cars they were met by local women bearing bouquets of flowers, who led them to the main house. By noon, the procession of incoming cars slowed to a trickle, and workers began to carry steaming plates of food to the main house. Guards armed with automatic weapons stood at the perimeter of the compound, looking out into the jungle.

During the afternoon, Jerome patiently reloaded tapes in the recorder as used ones ran out. The recorded conversations would make their way back to Virginia, by high priority air delivery, for translation and intelligence analysis. Alex lay on his stomach and watched through binoculars, alarm alerts in front of him.

Happily, there were no unusual sounds inside the house, and no sign that their little presents had been detected.

As darkness fell, Alex quickly armed the electronic transmitter and set the detonation time for midnight. He then put a small charge on the transmitter and set the fuse for 0200. He pulled a miniature burst transmitter from his vest pocket and keyed the number 5, then hit send. The green LED winked faintly as the message was sent and bounced from a satellite high above them. They had let their minders know that they would be at the pickup LZ in five hours. The brass in turn would point the nuclear carrier Enterprise toward land to get into position to launch the helicopter that would pick them up, as well as launch the fighters that would protect the helicopter.

Alex and Jerome quickly put on their night vision goggles and began the jog to their extraction point, fifteen miles away. The helicopter would be near that clearing for a maximum of ten minutes, but would return for each of the next two mornings at the same time, waiting for the signal to drop down for the pickup. Masterson and Cuchulain had no intention of missing the first pickup.

They reached the clearing with seventy minutes to spare, having spotted only one patrol. The local militia moved noisily, confident that no one would dare to invade their domain. Ten minutes after the patrol was out of earshot, they continued their jog; the trip to the clearing had been uneventful. Cuchulain pulled the transmitter from his pocket and set it to send their *all clear for pickup* message every five minutes. At five minutes before midnight, they heard the whooshing sound of the stealthy Special Operations helicopter dropping to the clearing. Alex re-keyed the transmitter to the *coming in now* signal, and they ran toward the middle of the clearing just as the chopper touched down. In ten seconds, they were feeling the extra weight of the helicopter at maximum climb. A crewman handed them headsets. "Any injuries?" the crewman said.

"Negative," said Masterson, "just get us out of here."

"I just love you fucking spooks," the crewman grinned. "You're where you're supposed to be the first time; you're early—no injuries, no one shoots at us, and no one knows." He sniffed, then grimaced. "Jesus," he grinned, "Didn't you guys ever hear of Right Guard?"

Just then the sky lit up as the villa, several miles to the East, exploded. Chunks of timber could be seen tumbling in the air, and flames shot high into the sky. The crewman stared at the flames for a second, stunned, then grinned even wider. "At least none of the good guys get hurt, but I think you just ruined someone's morning." He got no response from Cuchulain or Masterson.

Two hours later, they were back at the Enterprise, being escorted to their assigned quarters. Their weapons and night gear would be shipped in the diplomatic pouch to the Farm when the carrier next came to port. After five days in the jungle, there had been only two quiet shots fired, and those at a dog.

As Cuchulain stripped the rancid jungle fatigues from his body, he felt the lump of the chamois bag in his pocket. He dropped it into his toilet kit, took a quick shower and rolled into the bed, physically relaxed, but emotionally exhausted now after days of constant danger and maximum alert status. Seven hours later, he and Masterson sat buckled in rear-facing web seats aboard a two-engine prop plane for the flight to Singapore, and felt the slam of an enormous steam piston as it launched their ride down the carrier deck. They were dressed as naval warrant officers and each carried a small bag of personal effects.

It wasn't until they were at the airport in Singapore that Cuchulain remembered the little sack from the villa. He reached into his bag, opened his toilet kit and dug it out. Discarding the plastic wrapping, he opened the throat of the bag and looked inside. Glinting back at him were at least eighty very large, cut diamonds. He had found the escape money of a drug lord. He closed the bag and dropped it back into his toilet kit. A small smile of contentment crept across his face. No one could ever know that he and Masterson had these diamonds, and if they were careful, they could do whatever they chose with them.

"You look like the cat that ate the canary, Cooch," Masterson said. "What's up?"

"I'll tell you on the plane," Alex said. "We have a lot of hours to kill, and they're starting to board."

There was a small crowd boarding the 747 to Honolulu. A group of businessmen went toward business and first class, while a group of twenty-five or thirty American high school students boarded with their teachers. Alex and Jerome had a full row in coach to themselves. As the plane cleared the runway and the wheels came groaning and thumping up into the wheel wells, Alex turned to Jerome and pulled the chamois bag from his toilet kit.

"This is what we took from the general's toilet tank," he said, and dumped four or five of the large stones into Jerome's hand.

"Jesus Christ, Cooch! Are those diamonds?"

"I certainly hope so, but I'm not sure. I think we found the general's scared money," Alex said with a grin.

"What are you going to do with them?" Jerome whispered.

"It's not just me, big guy; it's we! We sure as hell ain't going to turn them in. No one knows we have them, no one knows they even exist, and I'm not planning to tell anyone; I don't do morality. I do believe it's retirement time."

Jerome was quiet for a few seconds, then nodded, "I'm in, but only for enough to buy me a gym somewhere—probably back in New York—and retire. Maybe find a woman. I don't need a lot of money to do that, and I tend to spend whatever I make, which would make me more obvious to the gendarmes than I'd like. How are we going to handle this?"

Cuchulain grinned at him. "I don't know, but I'm sure as hell going to figure it out. When we get back, I'm going to take a month or two off and look into it. They've been after me to use some leave, anyhow."

"Go for it, Cooch. Just don't let them throw my fat ass in jail, and fuck up my retirement. You're smart enough to figure it out, if you work at it. You seem to like all that book shit anyhow. I never saw anybody pick up explosives technology like you did. You knew more in a month than most of us figured out in two years. You were always just sitting there reading those goddamned manuals and books. Learning about diamonds should be a piece of cake."

"I'm going to take it real slow and careful, Jerome. Like I said the other day, Mac knows that we're getting out of the biz, anyhow, and he's fine with that. I have some ideas. Anyhow, I've been in jail, and I'm not going back. I'll figure out some good lawyers early in the process and give you their names. If push comes to shove though, you're not going to help me any by confessing. If anyone reads you your rights, just clam up and wait for your lawyer to get to you. You'll be long retired before anything like that could happen anyhow; just don't let them flutter you after you get out, and you'll be fine. I don't imagine we left any witnesses behind."

Jerome grimaced. "I never did like that lie detector shit, anyhow, so I ain't doin' any fluttering. Once I'm gone they are never going to get me hooked back up to that thing. I'm going to be one permanently-retired spook." He was quiet for a second, and then said, "I think I'm going to miss the action though. I've been playing shoot 'em up for more than twenty years."

Southern Virginia

THE drive from Williamsburg to Charlottesville, Virginia was routine, nearly all good interstate highway. Alex checked into a small, clean motel on the outskirts of the city, near the University of Virginia, and then walked to the campus to register as a special student and pick up his ID. He paid his fees with a check drawn on an account he had opened a week before in Richmond, under the name Frank Santayana. He had also sent for a birth certificate in the same name, since Mr. Santayana was unable to do so as a result of having been in a coma in the Medical College of Virginia hospital for the past two weeks with complications from AIDS. He was not expected to live, nor was he expected to die any time soon. A passport application would be sent shortly after the arrival of Mr. Santayana's birth certificate.

He walked into the University of Virginia main library, and spent an hour getting familiar with its layout. Then he strolled over to the reference librarian, gave her his best smile, and said, "I'd like to find out about investment-quality diamonds. Would you please show me how to use the catalog computer?"

Six weeks later, he returned to Williamsburg knowing far more about investment quality diamonds and their worth than most retail jewelers. He was also delighted to find a passion—one that might keep him interested and gainfully employed for the rest of his life. In the library of the Darden School of Business at Virginia, he had discovered the world of stocks and bonds. More to the point, he had discovered that it was possible to analyze companies' management and products reasonably well and their financial performance quite well, in a way that could allow exceptional financial returns if the analysis proved accurate. The whole concept excited him. He had also figured out how he was going to turn his diamonds into cash, almost legally.

The Old Frog Restaurant

ALEX called Jerome and arranged to have dinner at a small place, near Old Town in Williamsburg. As they were working on coffee and the place began to empty, Cuchulain started.

"Okay, Jerome. Here's the deal. If we sell the diamonds, we have cash," Alex said. "When we put it into the bank or start spending it, we leave a money trail. If we do this, the IRS, sooner or later, is going to want to know where we got it and why we haven't paid taxes on it."

"Shit, Cooch!" Jerome sighed. "I knew it was too good to be true. There goes a quarter of a million bucks."

"Hold on, my pathetic, parsimonious, pessimistic partner," Alex whispered with a wicked leer, rubbing his hands together. "The great Cuchulain has a magical method."

"The great Cuchulain has dip-shit delusions of deification," Jerome snickered.

"Okay, here we go," Alex said. "Listen up and think about what I'm saying, because we can't go hire a consultant to see if we're right, and we ain't exactly gifted planners. You're the one with the accounting degree. I need you to look for holes in the theory."

"First, IRS gets as capital gains taxes some percent of all gains on investments held longer than six months. Virginia gets a little, too. I was thinking about moving us to Texas to avoid the state tax, but it gets messy and it's too visible."

"Cuchulain, my man, we ain't got no gains, remember?" Jerome said.

"Quiet. The great Cuchulain has more."

Jerome nodded, intensely interested in what Alex had found.

"Second, it is very easy to make enormous gains, easily quintupling your money in a few months in the stock market, if you know exactly which stocks are going to go up, and which are going to go down—and by how much."

Jerome nodded and shrugged.

"Third, if you file your tax returns, show a long-term capital gain on them and pay the taxes due on that gain, the IRS knows exactly where you got your cash. You earned it by investing and did your lawful duty by coughing up the tax money; you get to keep the rest."

"And?" Jerome said.

"And, my friend, we sell the diamonds and work up a set of stock transactions from last year to show where we got the money. I still have to check some more, but I don't think the IRS knows how to check on someone giving them too much money, only too little. We'll use a broker in Switzerland to complicate things for them a little. We file the returns, pay the taxes, and put the rest of the money in our pockets."

Jerome was excited. "Son of a bitch, Cooch! You figured it out! How do we beat the income tax?"

"Loyal Americans like us? We don't. That's the way we stay out of sight and out of jail. Hell, it was never our money, anyhow."

Jerome nodded. "Right. Has the Great Cuchulain figured out whether there's going to be enough cash from the diamonds for me to buy a gym, after we sell them and pay the taxes? Or even *how* to sell them?"

Alex grinned. "I'm not quite sure how much a gym costs, Jerome, but I think I've figured out how to sell the diamonds for something between four-and-a-half and eighteen million dollars."

"You get me two hundred grand for a gym and equipment, and the rest of it is yours, my brilliant young friend." Jerome put his hands together, looked up at the sky, and said, "Thank you, Lord."

Cuchulain sobered. "You'll get a quarter million dollars after tax, no less.

Half of what we get if you want it, or I'll just invest for you; tell me later. The biggest diamond buyers are in Amsterdam and Brussels. We'll go with Amsterdam, because there are more dealers there. I have a few names of buyers who are supposed to be honest, but I'm going to need you to cover me. This is too much money for the pros to ignore," he grinned. "Them not knowing that the real pros are the sellers."

He reached into his jacket pocket and handed Jerome a list. "Here's what I think we'll need—to be safe. Look it over."

Jerome whistled through his teeth after a second, and then grinned. "If we can't sell the diamonds, we'll be able to start World War III. I assume you want me to mention my heroic saving awhile back of that SAS major's ass? He retired and now vends these vicious viands of violence."

Alex rolled his eyes and raised his hands in surrender. "I'll need two passport photos from you, dressed in a suit and wearing those photo chromic glasses that get darker as the sun hits them. Put a little of that cotton padding along your upper teeth, inside your cheek. I'll get you a passport. This is not going to be the Alex and Jerome show. I think we'll come back into the US through Canada, just to be safe."

"Walk or ride?" Jerome said.

"Walk, I think. I want to do this only once. Somehow, I don't think US Customs or Immigration is going to find us crossing. We'll buy some gear and rations in Canada. Probably some light weapons, too."

"Buying weapons in Canada is a little risky," Jerome said. "Why don't I just take a little package up to Toronto while you're setting the rest of this up? I have a few little leftovers from what we've been doing. They may come in handy. I might work your list over a little, too, except for the explosives. I'm not busy, because I'm going to put my retirement papers in tomorrow."

"I'm touched by your faith in my planning ability. You're right about Canada, Jerome—dumb thinking on my part—and I need you to keep picking holes in our plans. You're the weapons jock. One thing though—no trademarks. You don't use an Ingram or a .300 Winchester Magnum, and I don't use my own fuses. I don't want Mac or anyone else figuring this one out."

The next day, Alex drove to Washington, easing his way up I95 and thinking about his trip to Europe. He had made an appointment with a lawyer in Washington, one who specialized in white collar crime and tax fraud; he'd gotten a Watergate defendant off. He had found him through some research at the University of Virginia; better yet, he was Irish. Alex crossed the Key Bridge from Virginia into the District and drove down looking for the Four Seasons hotel; the lawyer he wanted had offices just beside it. They called the lawyer "Gentleman John." It made him sound easy to talk to.

Holland

SIX weeks later, Alex and Jerome met in a coffee house in Amsterdam. Jerome had arrived a week earlier. He had picked up his package from the retired SAS major's delivery boy in Rotterdam and checked it out carefully. After driving a small rental car to Amsterdam, Jerome spent three days looking into the security of the offices of three different diamond buyers Alex would meet, and working out the best ways to get away from each location safely and quietly. Each office layout was carefully sketched with as much as was visible from different vantage points. Jerome also created a map showing streets, police schedules, radio frequencies, and the best hiding spots along the way.

Cuchulain studied it all for half an hour. "Let's do it. Guilder's expecting me at 1730, so you have two hours to get set up. I'll try to stall him until after 1800 to let the crowds clear. I got vague hints that this guy is bent, so we'll probably get to make our point tonight."

At 5:35 that afternoon, Cuchulain rang the bell outside a small office building. A tinny voice at the speaker asked him in English to identify himself. He smiled to himself and said, "Frank Santayana."

The door buzzed open and he walked up the stairs to Suite 203. The door was open and a small, aging man waved him in, saying, "Please." There was an old, scarred wooden desk inside and two straight-backed chairs. On one of the chairs sat a very large, middle-aged man. Scar tissue was bunched beneath his eyebrows, tilting them outward, and his lumpy nose wandered partly across his face. "My security advisor, Herr Kohler," the old man smiled. Alex nodded. Herr Kohler simply stared.

"Now, young man, what service may I provide to you? From our telephone conversation, I understood that you have goods to sell. Have you brought to me a sample as we discussed?"

Alex reached into his pocket and dropped a small velvet bag onto the desk. The old man opened it and rolled the diamond inside onto the desk blotter. He pulled a loupe from his pocket and screwed it into his eye, then picked up the diamond with a large pair of tweezers to examine it under the desk lamp. He dropped it into the tray of a small manual scale, and adjusted it before he looked up. "It is slightly flawed," he said, "and the color isn't wonderful. I could give you $12,500 in cash for it, right now."

"I think not," Alex said, picking up the bag and holding it out for the diamond. The greed faded from the man's wizened face, replaced with a look of mild concern. "Perhaps $15,000, because I have a buyer in mind—but not a penny more."

"Just return the diamond, please." Alex stood and turned a little toward Kohler as he came to his feet, still holding out the bag with his left hand. Kohler seemed a little puzzled that Alex did not seem afraid; the old man was increasingly concerned by the aura of relaxed menace surrounding him. He was suddenly chilled as the memory of a visit, long ago, from the SS came back to him.

"Of course, of course," Guilder said hastily. "There's no reason to be rude, young man." He dropped the stone into the bag.

The door was locked at the bottom of the stairs, and Alex had to push the call button again and wait for Herr Guilder to answer. After a moment, the door buzzed and he left. As he walked down the narrow street, he reached into his shirt pocket, put a small speaker into his ear and clicked the transmitter in his pocket twice. The response came instantly. "Negative on the mean looking guy, he's still in the office. The old man is on the phone. No tail. Stall on the corner while I move."

Cuchulain slowed his pace, stopping once to look into a bakery window and again to gaze at some Indonesian art. He heard, "In place" and double clicked his transmitter again. He turned right and walked casually down the street. After several blocks, he heard, "You have a tail. Two walkers, two riders, not trying to close. They're going to ride you home. I'm moving—see you there. Watch your ass." Alex doubled clicked again, maintaining his casual pace. This was the most dangerous time. If four of them came for him now, and if they were pros, he was in trouble without Jerome. After two more blocks, he turned left to walk one more block to his hotel and breathed a sigh of relief.

"The riders have parked and are moving toward the hotel. They're going to take you in the room. I'm moving." Double-click. Alex walked slowly down the street and then through the lobby of the hotel. He stepped into the elevator, just as two men slid in beside him. As he hit the button for 4, he felt a gun at his ribs.

"Just keep moving toward your room, keep your mouth shut and you won't get hurt," the smaller of the two said in English.

"Just don't hurt me," Alex said. "You can have anything you want!" He held down the button on the transmitter as he spoke, to share the conversation with Jerome. As they stepped off the elevator, Alex reached in his pocket for his room key. The gun jammed harder into his ribs. "Easy!" the little man commanded. Alex held his room key up for both to see, and gave them a sickly smile. As he opened the door, the big man pushed him inside and across the room. Alex tucked into a roll and reached for his ankle holster, then yelled "Now!" and the connecting door to the next room burst open. Jerome was on one knee, holding a 12-gauge pump shotgun pointed at the little man's face. He yelled, "Freeze, Motherfuckers!" as Alex rolled up into a combat crouch holding his 9mm Beretta centered on the big man's nose.

The smaller man laid his gun carefully on the floor. "On your face on the floor, hands clasped behind your heads. Now!" Alex said, pointing. Both men went to the floor quickly, and locked their fingers behind their heads. Jerome threw a roll of duct tape and a small bag of plastic ties on the floor, then got on his knees behind a stuffed chair, his shotgun pointed at the door.

Alex moved quickly behind the men, ripped strips of tape from the roll and slapped one across each of their mouths. He grabbed the ties and secured their wrists and ankles, then dragged them away from the door. He picked up the Beretta and stood beside the door, screwing a silencer onto the end of the barrel. Then he looked at Jerome, one eyebrow raised, and said, "Freeze, Motherfuckers?"

"Hey, that's what Danny Glover says in the movies," Jerome said, grinning. "Worked for him. Seemed to work fine for us, too. Universal language, courtesy of Hollywood."

There was a quiet knock at the door. Alex jerked the door open and stuck his Beretta into the face of one man, while he grabbed the tie of the other and yanked him down and into the room, then repeated the move with the other. This took less than five seconds. Alex swung the door shut, clicked the night latch and turned, dropping into a crouch and swinging the silenced Beretta up. Neither man was facing him; both were staring into the bore of Jerome's riot gun.

"Don't move and don't make a sound," Jerome ordered, holding a finger in front of his mouth. Alex quickly secured the ankles and wrists of the newcomers with the plastic ties, then rolled them over and sat them up.

"Okay, who's in charge here?" Alex demanded. When no one answered, Alex tore off two more strips of tape and slapped it, hard, across their mouths.

"Unfortunately, Torch, I think your services will be required." Alex began to unlace the shoe of the original gun wielder, the only one he was sure spoke English. As Alex pulled off the man's shoe, Jerome pulled a tiny propane torch from the nightstand drawer and lit it—the flame a blue hiss in the room. He leered at the man, and said, "I do believe your hiking days are over, my good man, unless my colleague gets a lot of answers to his questions, right now! A little later, I may interfere with your future love life as well." Jerome reached to squeeze his own crotch suggestively, and again tried a leer.

The Dutchman began to shake his head furiously, making noises around the tape. Jerome made himself look disappointed. "Shit! I think he's going to talk before I even get my name written on his foot." He reached up and jerked the tape from the man's mouth, taking some skin and all of a small moustache; tiny droplets of blood formed quickly on his upper lip.

The Dutchman was shaking now, barely able to speak. "There has been a mistake. We have made a mistake."

Alex nodded as he took a small notebook from his pocket, and said, "I don't have a lot of time. I'm going to ask you some questions, and you are going to answer them fully and completely. I know the answers to some of the questions, and if you get one even a little bit wrong, I'm going to tape you back up and let my friend draw pictures on your foot for a long time, just to convince your colleagues that honesty is advisable, and infinitely more comfortable."

"What do you want to know?"

Alex went through his questions and confirmed his research on the best and most honest diamond dealers. Guilder had hired the men through the leading local gangster. Alex took down the man's name and headquarters location. He then sighed and put his notebook away.

"I guess you did okay. We should really kill you, but this isn't our city, and we wouldn't know quite where to throw the bodies. So, you get to be our messenger boys. Tell your boss that he has pissed us off, mightily. There are only eleven of us, but we know you and you don't know us. If you pull any more shit like this stunt tonight, we'll pull this town down around your ears in a very noisy and violent fashion so that the cops won't ever quit hassling you. Our boss is one mean son of a bitch, so he sent us to see if you wanted to be reasonable."

Cuchulain sighed again, then looked thoughtful for a second. "I'm quite concerned, my good man, that your boss won't take our boss seriously. That would be very inconvenient for us—and extremely unhealthy for you and your colleagues."

Jerome reached behind his back and came out with a flat black combat knife. It had a six-inch blade, razor edged on one side and serrated on the other. He squatted in front of the small man, cupping and squeezing his crotch with his left hand. "How 'bout we cut his balls off and mail them to his boss? Or maybe just the left one?"

"We'll save that for the next time, I think," Alex said. "But it does give me an idea." He turned to the man. "We're sending each of gents you back to your employer with a little memento, since you tried to rob me. Tell him that we will try to think of a few things a little more civilized, to act as a more personal message to him from us."

He drove his left hand into the man's crotch and squeezed, hard, for fifteen or twenty seconds. The man collapsed to the floor, nearly unconscious, as vomit trickled from his mouth and his bladder released. Alex moved to the others, ripped the tape from their mouth and repeated the routine. The stench began to fill the room. Jerome quickly cut the ankle ties from each of the men, as Alex wiped his hands clean.

They packed up their gear and moved quickly from the room, exited at the back of the hotel, and jumped into Jerome's rental car. Alex consulted his city map, trying to locate the headquarters building of their recent visitors' boss. When he found it, they drove off to reconnoiter.

It was an old unattached building. Alex stepped out of the car and into the shadows, as Jerome drove off. It was fifteen minutes before he heard, "In place—piece of cake for the front. No direct views of the sides." Cuchulain doubled clicked as he moved quickly to the cars out front, checked the license numbers and reached quickly under each before he moved on. At one, a new Mercedes sedan, he slid under the car for a second, then opened the driver's door, bent down and reached beneath the dash. As he moved away from the cars and back into the shadows, he double clicked again.

"Go a half block, the way I took the car. It's on the left. There are some whiskey bottles on a shelf near where they're sitting. I think I'll do those," Jerome said. Suddenly a front window shattered, followed by the repeated sound of glass breaking every two or three seconds. This went on for fifteen seconds, punctuated by confused shouts of frightened men, and the sound of running.

Alex ran down the street as the glass first broke. At the car, he paused to throw his bag into the trunk, then jumped in the car and started the engine. Looking out, he saw Jerome rappelling down the side of the four-story building, pushing out twice with his legs from the wall. His rifle, with its sleek scope and long, fat cylindrical silencer, was slung on his back. He pulled the rope through its stay on the roof, then coiled it as it dropped. Jerome ran lightly to the car, threw his gear into the trunk, and jumped in beside Alex. They drove off, the evening finally quiet behind them.

"I do like working against amateurs, my man," Jerome grinned. "Much healthier."

"I suspect that we got our point across," Alex smiled.

It was after nine when the four assailants limped slowly into the old building. They looked at the broken window as they went in, then gaped at the destruction in the room. The smell of whiskey was everywhere, and two men were sweeping broken bottles into a pile.

"Where's the boss?" the small man groaned.

"He's in the back," one sweeper said. "What the hell happened to you guys, anyhow?"

They ignored him and limped toward the back room. As they walked in, there was a man in his late sixties, sitting quietly, drinking coffee and looking into space. He was dressed formally, with a starched white shirt and small bow tie—blue, with tiny white polka dots. He looked over at them, saw the tiny droplets of blood oozing from the marks over their mouths where the tape had been, and waited.

"We got set up, boss. The two nastiest, politest pros you ever met. It was over so fast that we didn't even get our hands up. Americans, I think. Boss, I don't think eight of us would have been enough."

The old man looked at them for a second. "Why are you limping like that?"

One of the other men spoke up. "Because one of them—the white one—squeezed our balls almost to jelly for jumping him. Jesus Christ, he was strong."

"He wanted us to tell you that they were to be left alone with their business here. There's supposed to be eleven of them, according to him, who will be pissed off at us if we mess with them any more. He said that, since Amsterdam wasn't his city, he'd rip it down around our ears and have the cops hassling us forever. I'll tell you Boss, eleven's way too many for us. We should get some help from Antwerp or Rotterdam. He said that they were going to send you a personal message—more civilized."

The old man smiled ruefully. "I think they have already been by for a visit. I started my car a few minutes ago. When I hit the starter, an American flag popped up from the dash; it was wired to the starter. Someone shot up the wall of the bar a little earlier, putting one round into each of the bottles at exactly the same height, using a silenced rifle and subsonic rounds. You could put a glass level on the line of the bullet holes."

"I don't think I'd know where to buy a silenced rifle," he said thoughtfully.

The old man stood. His voice firmed and he said, "There is nothing for us to win in this one. They are Americans, so they are not trying to establish themselves in our business in Amsterdam. Clearly, we won't get any diamonds without getting some of our people killed or hurt, and probably attracting the attention of the police to the detriment of our other activities. We are probably outgunned as well. If you can buy a silenced rifle, you can buy plastique, body armor, fuses, and so on. We will stay away from these people, even if we happen to see them on the streets. We will stay away from our traditional activities in the diamond trade for the time being. You will speak of this to no one. Later, we will discuss these matters with Herr Guilder." He walked past the shattered glass to his car and drove away.

Amsterdam,

the following day

AFTER sleeping late, spending a pleasant hour in the gym, and enjoying a fine lunch at the old Grand Amsterdam hotel, Alex and Jerome began to set up again. At 6:00 p.m., Alex walked into the offices of a Herr Joosse. After Alex again provided the diamond, Herr Joosse went through the same routine as had Herr Guilder. He returned the stone to the velvet bag and handed it back to Alex. "A lovely diamond, Mr. Santayana," he said. "As a single purchase, it is worth $200,000 wholesale, perhaps a little more. If I understand your inventory position correctly from our phone conversation, you have a number of similar stones. That puts you in a more favorable position, and will probably add 3 to 5 percent to your realized price, depending on the quality of the stones."

"Bingo!" Alex thought to himself. To Joosse he said, "The quality of all my stones is similar. They range in size from one to just over three carats. I have ninety-one of them."

Joosse leaned back and raised his eyebrows. "That's quite a fortune, young man. In what form will you expect payment?"

"Five hundred thousand dollars in cash, the remainder wired in dollars to a bank in Switzerland. I will provide instructions to you if we reach a deal."

Herr Joosse nodded. "When may I see and value the stones? It will take a few hours for me to make you an offer on them."

Alex said, "I'd like to do it now, if possible."

"You're carrying several million dollars in negotiable diamonds in your pocket? You could be robbed! You must be careful!" Joosse seemed shocked.

"I'm a careful man, Herr Joosse," Cuchulain said coldly, staring at him. "Can we transact our business this evening, or not?"

"Yes," Joosse said. "It will go faster if I may call my assistant in, however. He has departed for the evening, and I must ring him at home. Agreed?"

"Agreed," Alex said. "One person only."

Joosse nodded and picked up the phone and dialed. "Philip, I need you here immediately. Yes. Thank you."

Alex plucked a second velvet bag from his pocket and dropped it onto the desk. Joosse stood and walked through the door behind him. Cuchulain pulled the Beretta from his ankle holster, spun the silencer from his side pocket onto it and slipped it into the soft suede holster at the small of his back. He followed Joosse, screwing the tiny earphone into his ear. He double clicked the transmitter.

"I don't have that window. No one has come into the building. Watch your ass—I'll watch your back."

Double-click.

The room was long and cluttered, lit by the glare of fluorescence. There was a long workbench along one stark wall, with vises mounted to it. Small electronic scales were scattered along its length and square glassine drawer units were stacked against the wall at the back of the workbench. Joosse was reaching inside a cabinet with battered, green double-doors. Cuchulain reached back with his right hand, swinging his jacket clear and resting his hand on his hip, his hand two inches from the butt of the Beretta, the other hand casually stuck into his left trouser pocket. They waited, with Herr Joosse puttering, taking items from cabinets.

"One guy entering the building, in a hurry. Doesn't walk like a hitter. Walks like a damned penguin."

Double-click.

Herr Joosse turned from a cabinet, holding a scale and several instruments

142

in his hand. He started at the sight of Cuchulain, looming menacingly in the doorway. He walked back toward the office, carrying the scale, an instrument that looked like a miniature microscope, two sets of large tweezers and a yellow note pad.

"I think we're ready, Mr. Santayana," ' he said as he sat down and arranged the tools on the desk. "Philip should be here soon."

"I think he's on his way up," Alex smiled.

Joosse looked up, startled, and then noticed the earpiece. He smiled, a little ruefully. "I think that you are not only a cautious, but perhaps a dangerous man as well, Mr. Santayana. My advice seems to be unnecessary."

"I pose no threat to you, Herr Joosse," Alex said, as he moved casually to the wall behind the door. "I merely want to transact my business without interference."

"Try not to upset Philip, if you please," Joosse said. "He is quite talented and loyal, but easily intimidated. I'm a little older."

There was a knock at the door, then it opened. A short man walked in; he was narrow at the shoulders and wide at the hips. He started to speak to Herr Joosse, then noticed Cuchulain standing along the wall. Cuchulain smiled and nodded. Philip did walk like a penguin.

"This is Herr Santayana, Philip. He has a rather large transaction for us to sort and price."

Two hours later, they had finished. Joosse, his aging face showing the strain of the close work and the late hour, looked at the tape on his adding machine, then compared it to the one Philip handed to him. He nodded. "Seventeen million, six hundred, seventy-four thousand US dollars, Mr. Santayana. Do we have a deal?"

"We have a deal. What are the mechanics?" Alex said.

"You may either leave the diamonds with me in a sealed container, with both of us signing over the seal, or you may take them with you, then wait an hour or so while we go over them again. I will have the $500,000 in cash delivered in the morning, just after we open at ten."

Alex nodded and paused, then said. "Let's put them into an envelope, seal, and each of us sign across the seal. Then I will take it with me. In the morning, you can take as long as you'd like to recheck the diamonds."

"Fine. We shall expect you at ten tomorrow morning." Joosse stood, as Philip stared at him. They bagged the diamonds and put them into a padded envelope, then signed. Alex handed him a small envelope containing instructions.

"I'm moving. Turn right out of the building and hang out near the entrance to the second building on your right," Jerome said.

Click-click.

Cuchulain walked out of the building and turned left, then quickly right. An elderly couple was walking their dog, pausing every few seconds as it discovered new opportunities to mark his path. Alex walked casually to the second building, then faded into the shadow of the doorway, still checking the street. He heard a steel door open, then Jerome, wearing a black trench coat, walked from the other side of the building. They moved quickly to the car, where Alex slipped into the driver's seat and started the motor, while Jerome watched the street. Jerome opened his coat and slipped the Heckler and Koch PSG rifle onto the floor of the back seat, then dropped his trench coat over the rifle. As Jerome slipped in, Cuchulain drove briskly to the third of the hotels where Jerome had rented a room for the week, cash in advance, and no questions asked.

"How'd we do?" Jerome asked excitedly.

"A little over fifteen million in the bank," Alex said. "And five hundred grand in cash for pocket money, plus a bit unsold for a rainy day"

Jerome whistled through his teeth. "Far fuckin' out! What's with the 500 grand in cash and the unsold shit?"

Cuchulain grinned in the dark. "I got a little greedy and a bit paranoid. I decided that we'll have enough money after paying taxes that the IRS won't be able to track another 250 apiece if we're careful. Just keep it in cash. Don't put it in a bank and don't go playing the ponies with it. It also struck my always-active paranoia that we can fit a million dollars into a hollowed-out shoe heel if we ever have to run or vanish; that's four diamonds each from our pile."

"Fat chance on the ponies and me," Jerome snorted. "And I like the paranoia thing. A million bucks in cash takes up a lot of space. Four diamonds in a shoe is a nice, concealable liquid touch. Good one!"

East Coast, United States

Later

ALEX spent the next several years at Carnegie Mellon University in Pittsburgh, getting a degree first in electrical engineering, then in computer science, spending much of his time studying. With the credits transferred for the courses he had taken on government money at William and Mary and at the University of Virginia while still working for Mac, Alex was able to earn both degrees in less than three years. His grades were so good that his advisor had suggested that an academic career at a very prestigious institution was within his reach. Alex was restless, not ready to take a job, not wanting to pursue the Ph.D. his advisor was pushing, and not sure why he felt one way or the other. Earlier, Alex had received a rather formal written invitation, forwarded after close examination at the Farm, to come to England to visit with Lord Archibald Alistair, the father of a slain SAS captain with whom Alex had served while on a cross-training assignment with the Britain's elite SAS in Scotland and again on a later mission. Colin Alistair had befriended Cuchulain before he had died; not many had.

Lord Alistair's letter came at a good moment, and triggered Alex's next move. For a time he'd had a sense of something missing from his life. Perhaps, because of having been a "patriotic assassin," Alex longed to be more thoughtful, to consider the deeper side of things.

After consulting with his CMU advisor and an Egyptian friend on the faculty, and having promises of a handful of decent recommendations, he applied to the program in Arabic studies at Oxford. His grandfather would be delighted. There was much he wanted to think about, with academic guidance. It would be at least three months before he would hear from Oxford. Whatever the decision, Alex wanted to spend most of the waiting time in the desert. He'd get to England sooner or later.

Alex had stayed in touch with Mac, often weekly by phone. From time to time, Mac flew to Pittsburgh for dinner and chat. When Alex mentioned his tentative plans for the next several years, Mac suggested a going away gift—a trip to South Dakota to shoot pheasants and spend a little down time together. Alex was enthusiastic.

Alex flew to Minneapolis from New York, and Mac from Dulles. They met and checked in to start the puddle jumper run. The plane had twin turboprops and landed in several small airports before finally reaching Pierre, South Dakota. As they collected their luggage a grizzled man in a camouflage-patterned ball cap and worn plaid wool shirt walked up holding a sign reading, "MacMillan."

"Mr. MacMillan?" he asked.

Mac reached out to shake his hand. "That's me."

"I'm Jason," he said. "Let me help you with your stuff, and I'll drive you to the lodge. You'll have time for a drink before supper."

"Let's do it," Mac said. "This is Alex."

The drive from the airport lasted about thirty minutes. The land was flat and farmed, and the sun cast angled beams across endless fields of wheat and corn. The lodge was fairly elaborate, in a country sense. On the first floor, its log construction held a kitchen open to a large dining area, and just beyond, a huge television for watching the inevitable football games. The upper floor held two rooms; one for poker and cigars and another with a pool table and a second bar. Drinks and wine were included in the price. The taxidermy was extensive; the heads of mule deer, elk, and moose adorned the walls, while tables were graced with dead fox, pheasant, and the occasional coiled, inert rattlesnake. Guest rooms were spread among long wings extending from the public areas.

Dinner was steaks, baked potatoes, carrots, and pecan pie with ice cream; there was unlimited food and wine, and extensive banter among the group of twenty or so other guests. As they settled in near the fire to finish their wine, Alex told Mac that he had decided he would return to the desert for a month or two. He was curious about being a Bedouin as an adult. Mac was quiet for a few moments, and then said, "It could be one hell of an intelligence opportunity for understanding and maybe tracking the Arabs, from what you've told me about the Bedouin gossip network."

"I suppose," Alex said, after a sip of red wine. "But then I'm part Arab. I'll have to see how my grandfather feels about that by asking very gently—philosophically. I sort of guess that he'd be fine about that conduit as long as there were no obvious fingerprints left by us. I'll bring it up. We'll see. It makes sense; he's no fan of radical Islam. If for no other reason, it's bad for business."

The shooting began after a full country breakfast and a ride to the fields with eight excited men in each small bus. A small trailer rolled behind, stacked with aluminum kennels for six dogs and a rack on top with rails to hold dead pheasants. Inside the bus, gun racks bolted to the floor held shotguns, and boxes of shotgun shells were stashed under the seats. One guide talked gun safety on the way to the fields while another drove.

The eight men spread in a line at the base of a corn field that had not been harvested. Around them were fields of corn, sunflower, and sorghum stretching to the horizon. Each field seemed about fifty yards wide and a half-mile or so long. Three dogs, a Labrador and two German Shorthairs, were released from their kennels and immediately began to mark their territory. The other three dogs, still in their kennels, began to bark and howl from the devastation of being excluded from the shooting, at least for now. Electric training collars were strapped to the necks of the first dogs; any disobedience became a sharp, momentary pain in the neck, transmitted from a small box with pointed contacts hanging snug under their necks. The dogs were to run a short distance ahead of the walking line and flush ring-neck pheasant from the corn. The lodge guests would shoot the birds and the dogs would fetch the dead or wounded bird and bring it to its owner, a guide. The head guide said that only pheasant roosters should be shot, to maintain the pheasant population. The penalty for killing a hen was a two-hundred dollar fine, to be paid to the South Dakota Pheasant Conservatory after all the shooters finished razzing and teasing the hen shooting culprit. Pheasant roosters are colorful, with long tails. Guides yell "Hen!" or "Rooster!" when single birds are flushed. In a multiple bird flush, the shooters are on their own while looking down a shotgun barrel for long tails.

They began in a line, walking down the rows of the corn field with the dogs crashing through in front of them. A rooster flushed and was shot before Alex could raise his gun, then another. A group of ten or twelve birds flushed suddenly and Alex shot twice; missing both times. This was a new experience for Alex, who had only ever shot birds in the United Kingdom, and just once, with Colin Alistair, his SAS buddy in Scotland. There, the birds were driven toward the shooters. In the US, the birds flew away as the shooters "walked them up," with the dogs in front. It was a different shot, and in both cases, aiming with shotguns was unlike with rifles and pistols. With a shotgun, the shooter's focus was on the bird and on swinging the gun in the path of the pheasant; with rifle and pistol it was on aligning the gun's sights, with the target in the subconscious mind. And the smooth pull of a pistol trigger was far different from slapping the trigger of a shotgun. Still, the pheasant didn't shoot back; he liked that part.

Alex missed again several times, and twice, Mac killed the bird he missed. Alex focused. Two birds flushed suddenly; he was ready. He mounted his shotgun to his shoulder in a flash and shot, then at the second bird. He fired before any of the others. The first bird dropped without a flutter; the second flew on unharmed. The droppings from the back of that bird announced its fear. There was silence on the line.

"Nice shot on the first bird," the guide beside him said with a grin. "You missed the second one clean. That's good—saved you two hundred bucks." The lab ran up to the guide proudly, holding the pheasant hen gently in his mouth. The guide took it and held it up. "But you owe the kitty for this one."

Mac had a big grin on his face as the rest of the men hooted and hollered at Alex. Alex stood, shaking his head, grinning and feeling stupid. "Oh well, it's a good cause, anyhow. I guess I'll be more careful now," he said.

The men in the line killed fifty or so pheasants that day, and again the next. Alex shot four, including the expensive hen. At noon each day, they rode the bus back to the lodge for a big lunch. Some of the guests drank heavily, and then returned to the corn fields for an afternoon shoot. Alex spent more time watching out for the drinkers than he did the birds. They seemed to shoot fine in spite of the booze—probably an indication of extensive practice in combining the two that helped them, Alex decided. They still made him nervous.

When they were ready to leave, Jason handed Alex and Mac each a box of cleaned, skinned, flash-frozen pheasant. Alex was leaving the country soon, so Mac got a bonus box.

Southern Spain

LEX flew from Kennedy to Madrid and made his way south to Algeciras, near Gibraltar, to join his mother. A week or so later, he boarded the ferry to Tangier, in the north of Morocco, to be with his grandfather. The invitation for an extended visit had been outstanding and much discussed on the telephone for a long time. It was time for Alex to revisit his roots. Although he talked often with his grandfather by phone and made short visits, he missed his time in the desert. He missed his grandfather. He hoped he didn't miss blowing shit up and killing people.

When Alex settled into his room in the big kasbah house he noticed again that the room was his alone. It was kept meticulously clean, but apparently had not been used since his last visit. The view of the harbor from the big bedroom window was sublime. Alex put his "city" clothes away in the closet, then stepped into the huge shower. A few minutes later, he walked from the room dressed in the loose garments of a Bedouin native.

A servant met Alex as he walked into the great hall. "Sheikh Kufdani awaits you. There is tea," he said. Alex followed him into a small room that adjoined Kufdani's bedroom. The walls were hung with Bedouin carpets, and a fire blazed in a corner fireplace despite the moderate temperature. Abu Kufdani rose from an ornate chair and opened his arms. Alex walked quickly to him and they embraced.

"I am so happy to see you!" Sheikh Kufdani exclaimed. "I thought that you would never come; these modern phones are inadequate, and who knows who is listening these days. And you're staying for two months or more! We have much to discuss; most of it will be in the desert, but you are here with me now. Sit, my son."

"I stopped in to see my mother. She is well, as are your other daughters," Alex said, as he settled into an overstuffed leather chair, away from the stifling fire.

"Of course. I am attentive to their needs," Sheikh Kufdani said. "I would be enormously displeased if someone was to cause them difficulty."

Alex nodded and smiled. There were traders of goods, important people, who relied on the goodwill of his grandfather and his trading network in the extended Muslim world. There were many Jews who had been trading in the network for generations; the Bedouin were Semites by blood after all, if not by religion for the past few centuries. Information requested by Sheikh Kufdani was information granted, and a little violence was easily arranged if, even indirectly, requested by him to protect his honor, which would certainly include the welfare of his daughters. The phrase "enormously displeased" when issued by Abu Kufdani brought swift action to cure his displeasure. Alex thought that the daughters' undoubtedly were safer than they would be in the house of the city mayor, or some other seemingly secure places in that city.

In Algeciras earlier that month, Alex had been on a morning jog near his mother's house. He had noticed a watcher, who seemed to have little to do but watch the area around his mother's house. Just after lunch that afternoon when the house was empty, Alex had dug Zeiss binoculars from his bag and settled into a kitchen chair with them, elbows resting on the table. He had a cup of tea and a notebook. He had spent two hours examining the hill where the watcher sat in the shade, idly leaning against an adobe wall. Alex had then looked over a map of the city to orient himself.

Alex had later walked slowly by the watcher, then suddenly leaned down and lifted the man by his biceps and slammed his back into the wall. He had slid down beside the gasping man and reached for the man's left arm. He had tucked the man's elbow into the hollow between Alex's right bicep and forearm, then folded the man's hand down and held it with his right hand

Alex had said in gutter Spanish, "Tell me, my friend. Why are you watching me?"

"I am just a humble worker, resting for a moment," the man had gasped in Arabic accented Spanish.

Alex had switched to Arabic and moved his hand that held the other's back a little, causing a sharp pain in the wrist. "You are very close to dying painfully. I don't like being watched," he said. Alex had quickly found that the man had been hired by a good friend of his grandfather, just to keep an eye on things. The man had a new cell phone and a number to call if there was any trouble. It was innocent, almost, but typical of his grandfather's methods. His grandfather seemed often devious to a fault, then very direct if need be.

Shiekh Kufdani's Residence

"So, what are your plans for the future?" his grandfather said. He gave Alex a little grin. "The legendary Cooch has retired from the business of killing and exploding, apparently. We should discuss that in private sometime. In my tent, rather than in a room with walls—and ears, perhaps."

The old man nodded slightly to Alex in respect and said, "And congratulations on your remarkable academic performance at the Carnegie Mellon. I am quite proud. I have been considering an appropriate and acceptable graduation gift for you. We should discuss this as well."

Alex gazed at his grandfather for more than a minute, bemused; the man worked at being underestimated. "And you know all of this how, grandfather?"

"There is a professor at the Carnegie Mellon named Al-Zarian," Abu Kufdani said. "You have met him?"

"*This is getting to be fun,*" Alex thought. "*He reminds me a little of Mac.*"

"I have," Alex said. "Nice man. But he is Egyptian and not Bedouin. You trust him?"

"Of course not, but a good question," Kufdani said. "He is the son of a business acquaintance of mine. I granted him a scholarship to teach for two years at the Carnegie Mellon as a visiting professor, where he had a good opportunity but not the wherewithal to pursue it. He was happy in return to keep an eye on you and advise me of any need that you may have had. He is also a reasonably adept Islamic scholar. I thought perhaps the two of you could talk from time to time, to keep up your language skills, of course."

"Of course," Alex said, then mused to himself, *I wonder why I'm first seeing this part of him. Ah well, he's on a roll. He'll probably tell you if you shut up for long enough.*

Kufdani continued, "The Cooch matter was just asking a continuing favor of a man well connected in the intelligence business in Spain, once I was able to identify your nickname or *nom de guerre*, or whatever that Cooch title is. That rumor mill was robust when you were active in the CIA. You made quite a reputation among the commandos of the world. The information flow came to an abrupt halt when you left the service."

"That's good," Alex said. "At least about the rumors shutting down. I am not so happy that I was easy to follow in the special operations community."

"Nor was I, but at least at first they resisted," Kufdani said. "I now provide to Spain some selected information about the mechanisms of Arab commerce and its information flow. They in turn mine the grist of the commandos' information rumor mill for me."

"Enough of this," the Sheikh exclaimed. "We should have a drink and prepare for dinner. We leave at first light for the desert. We will talk much more there. Oh, and we have dinner guests."

The guests were two older men. One was a cousin of the Moroccan king, and was the deputy foreign minister. The other was a Bedouin of the Yahia tribe, an Imam and Islamic scholar at the local university who openly held strong Western biases in his teachings. Conversation ranged from Muslim ambitions and conflicts around Arabia to actions of the Western world. Alex was recognized in conversation as an American, yet treated as a Bedouin leader might be, perhaps because no English was spoken after their greetings. Again, Alex sensed the subtle hand of his grandfather, gently nudging pieces around a chess board.

After dinner, they settled into the small meeting room where Alex had joined his grandfather earlier. The Imam was lecturing ponderously to Alex on how the children of Shem, who was in turn the son of the Old Testament Noah of ark fame, begat the Bedouin race. The foreign minister was nodding off, his head snapping up after a long downward drift. Alex found his grandfather watching him, almost idly.

"Tell me, Alex, are you going to stay with me for more than a month or two and assume your rightful place as a Bedouin leader, or do you have other plans?" Abu Kufdani asked. The foreign minister snapped awake and the Imam quieted. Both looked at Alex curiously. This could be an event of great note in the Arab and Bedouin communities, and they were first-hand witnesses. Abu Kufdani controlled vast amounts of the commerce in both the Arab world and Europe and was aging; a named Bedouin successor would be greatly influential and inevitably tested by others, both in Bedouin ways and in the ways of commerce.

"I'm afraid that I'll never be a true desert dweller, grandfather, but I have your Bedouin genes and I love the desert," Alex said. "I have not yet decided what I will do with the rest of my life. I've applied to the Arabic Studies program at Oxford University. If I get in, I'll figure out what's to be next in my life while I learn."

The Imam was scribbling furiously in a notebook when interrupted. "What do you think of my grandson's chances of getting in, my friend?" Kufdani asked.

"I would think they are good, Sheikh Kufdani," the Imam said. "I am not without influence as a scholar. It would be my honor to investigate this for you."

"Marvelous," Kufdani exclaimed, as he smiled fleetingly under his full, gray beard. "I look forward to your report."

"Uh, yes, of course," the Imam stammered. His words had somehow been transported from a small brag into a major commitment. His honor would suffer on bad results. Perhaps the grandson had been to college; he at least spoke well. He planned his approach.

"Thank you. It is a great honor to have an advocate such as you," Alex said to the Imam while his grandfather beamed and nodded. Alex liked his grandfather better all the time; it was a nice complement to the love he had felt for many years. The respect had always been there as well; it was demanded by the Bedouin culture. He supposed there was no need to tell his grandfather that he had already applied to Oxford; apparently his request for help had been granted even before asked. The Imam was hooked, and he knew it.

Tangier

IN the morning they boarded his grandfather's Range Rover, already packed with clothes, goods, and presents, and began the long drive south to the desert. There was a driver, Achmed, who was Alex's age and a best friend of many years. It was Achmed who had taught him how to be invisible in the desert, and they had learned together how to fight with the curved knife of the Bedouin, using wooden replicas. In the passenger seat rode another of his father's retainers, his well-tended rifle adorned with silver fittings and held between his knees; he was a noted hunter and marksman.

They finally reached the camp, where tents were used for sleeping as well as gathering places. They were set in a circle around a huge fire pit in a swept open area. Carpets, woven from goat and camel hair, were the floors of the tents and strewn with elaborate pillows for sitting and sleeping. In some places, several joined tents could be used for private reflection or, more often, for discussion of commerce.

At the dinner fire the first evening, Sheikh Kufdani introduced Alex in a way that left no doubt that he was the chosen successor. After a still moment, there was quiet but animated talk among the gathered men. Some of the young men were unhappy to have a Yankee, perhaps even a Christian, as a leader.

Voices became loud later in the meeting tent as several different conversations broke out. One very large young man stood up and said, "I mean no disrespect, Sheikh Kufdani. But we are Bedouin. Leadership granted is a sign of respect, not of right. We don't know this man with the Christian name, your grandson. He must earn our respect. He must be tested."

"And how must we do that?" Abu Kufdani said with a benevolent nod. "Who is it who will test him, and how?"

"We are warriors. That is our blood and our heritage. Is he strong or weak? Can he fight and kill? What does he know of Islam?" the man demanded.

"It is said of the Bedouin that we and our brothers can defeat our cousins. Then we and our cousins can defeat the world," Sheikh Kufdani said. "We will investigate tomorrow in the ring. I have said for many years that my grandson would be a great Bedouin warrior. Perhaps, as you say, it is time to take the first steps to test my judgment."

Later, as Alex sat with him in his tent, his grandfather said, "Tomorrow, in the ring, you should be as calmly and quickly violent as you can. The man who challenges you, Hussein, is a good man and immensely strong. Try not to hurt him too badly. There are several others who may be more violent and have little to lose with no family to support them. You may have an opportunity to be accepted and have your legend grow in your absence, or be viewed as a Yankee mercenary of no use to the tribe once I am gone. I will sit opposite you, in your field of view."

In the morning a wide ring was swept into the sand. Men, women and children were gathered in a circle around the ring, the women in the rear, pretending to be uninterested. Alex stood in loose garments at one end of the ring while Hussein, his opponent stood at the other.

"There will be no biting or gouging permitted," Kufdani announced loudly. "Kicking will be thought to be a sign of weakness. When one opponent is endangered or unable to continue, he will make a motion of acceptance, or I will decide that the fight is over and so signal."

The Sheikh sat in the chair provided for him. He raised his arm in the air, then dropped it to his waist. "Begin!" he cried.

Hussein moved across the ring cautiously, balanced. His arms in front of him, he watched Alex intensely. Alex was bent from the waist as he moved to the center of the ring, head up, his right hand scraping lightly against the loose dirt. They circled, looking for an opening. Hussein lunged suddenly, both arms wide to hold and crush him. Alex gave way and fell to the ground with his right foot in Hussein's chest as they fell and his hands grasping the insides of Hussein's sleeve. As Hussein's momentum carried him, Alex extended his leg suddenly and the force and speed of Hussein's rush worked against him as he sped in an arc that shortened when Alex pulled in slightly on Hussein's sleeves. Hussein hit hard, but was rolling to his stomach to regain the initiative when Alex was suddenly behind him, pushing one of Hussein's feet up to the knee, then leaning against it to immobilize him. Alex then drove his left arm under Hussein's left shoulder and reached back to grasp the back of the neck with his hand. He squeezed his thumb into the gap between the trapezius and the neck and dug a little. With his right, Alex got his hand under Hussein's right forearm then reached up to grasp the back of his bicep. Hussein was immobilized as Alex shifted his weight to Hussein's back and put his mouth by Hussein's ear.

Hussein struggled, and Alex waited. After a minute or two, the struggling Hussein was losing vigor, and Alex dug his left thumb in again. It was a spot that created great pain; Alex had found it in training a thousand times. "Hussein, my cousin," Alex whispered to his ear. "I am willing to hurt you, but I would rather not. I would rather release you and stand to embrace you as a fellow Bedouin if I have proven my worth in the ring. Nod your head a little if that works for you."

At the slight nod, Alex released his grip and rolled slowly to his feet. Hussein scrambled to stand, and then said loudly, "This is a Bedouin warrior. I embrace him." Alex could smell Hussein's rancid breath and body odor as they embraced. It was wonderful.

"It is over," the sheikh said loudly. "Let us prepare the feast!"

"No!" shouted a voice from the ring. A young man walked across the ring to confront Alex, who glanced at his grandfather. Kufdani frowned beneath his beard and shook his head. The man was perhaps twenty-five, very tall and slim, with traditional Bedouin dress. "Bah," the man said, loudly to the crowd. "So he can wrestle a little. It ended without victory, a sign of weakness. We Muslims are in *Jihad*! What is to stop me from cutting you right now and claiming a victory that you were too weak to claim? You are a weak American. What do you know of mortal combat? What makes you a Bedouin beyond the half-blood of your grandfather?"

He leaned over Alex menacingly and put his hand to the hilt of the curved Bedouin knife stuck in his belt. "I should kill you right now, in the name of Allah!"

Cuchilain heard the words of his father just then: *Always Retaliate First. End it.*

Alex snapped his right hand to the man's chin and his left to the back of his head. He grasped and leaned back to torque his body in a quick snap that ended at this hands. The man fell dead to the ring—neck broken and the knife part way out of its scabbard. There was a gasp, then silence.

Alex stood very still, then said to the crowd, "I have grappled with Hussein. He is a strong and honorable opponent. I have been threatened with knife violence while unarmed in the name of *Jihad*; I know of no such *Jihad* that glories in the killing of an unarmed Yahia cousin. I was given no respect and I responded. I suggest to you that this man threatened the honor of my Bedouin family; I will not tolerate that. We have had enough of this testing for awhile. I spent time with you for many summers as a young man; now you know me as an adult. We have tested honor. It is time for hospitality."

"And will you first speak to us of your life to be as a Bedouin, now that you have been accepted at least a little?" his grandfather asked.

"I will speak from my heart," Alex said. "I will soon be gone to study Islam, and much more, in England. I cannot promise to return for long periods in the desert, but I will return for short periods if accepted for study. In the next few days I will discuss among us my beliefs as they affect us, as you may or not be willing to hear. As our disrespectful cousin said, I am an American. But still, I am a Bedouin. Bedouin lives have changed greatly over recent years. We can no longer support our families as the Nomads of the

Desert, but must find work in the cities and abroad, to support our families and our tribe just as Sheikh Abu Kufdani has done. Still, we return to the desert to be renewed and to visit with our Yahia and other Bedouin tribes. It may be that another is best suited to lead the Yahia—one who is often present among us. You will make that decision and not I, and our sheikh is still active among us. But I will return to be with you when I can, whether as a leader, a tribal elder, or as simply another faithful Yahia Bedouin. For now, I would be among you as a cousin."

The Sheikh stood and said, "The feast awaits."

Conversation broke out as the men discussed the day's excitement. Heads were nodding and there was laughter among them. Two older women pulled a hand cart to the ring and struggled to load the corpse of the fallen *Jihadi* into it, then pulled it away. Everyone else moved to find places around the fire. Alex was surrounded by excited men, shaking his hand and formally welcoming him to the desert, while others congratulated his grandfather.

Much later, Alex again sat with his grandfather. "I did what felt right to me, Grandfather," he said. "That *Jihad* stuff gets my goat."

"Gets your goat." Kufdani said. "I haven't heard that one for years! And I've never heard it about *Jihad*." He gave a short laugh, more like a snort.

"And?" Alex said.

"And I agree with you about *Jihad*," Kufdani said. "I can't find anything in it today that Allah would bless as I read the texts. As far as today's events are concerned, I can't imagine how it could have gone much better. You showed wisdom while engaged in a tub of violence. Marvelous!"

Alex grinned and said, "Well, at least there's no question about whether I'm sufficiently violent to pass as a Bedouin."

"Will the taking of that life bother you in the future?" Kufdani asked.

"Unfortunately not," Alex said. "I got past all of that some time ago. I suppose it should bother me."

"It probably makes you more effective and more rapid to respond," Kufdani said. "And since it works, why worry about it? It keeps you safer as you decide how to spend the remainder of your long life."

"A question to be answered by study, grandfather," Alex said. "But, as you say, I'm pretty well formed as to who I am. I just look for a better way to handle it."

England

DURING his time in the desert, Alex was accepted at Oxford to the College of Oriental Studies. Six weeks had passed since he had applied; it was easy to imagine some help had come from the Imam who came to dinner.

Alex's time at Oxford was unlike than any other period in his adult life. He was encouraged to study subjects that appeared to have no practical value. He discovered first the beauty of learning for its own sake, and was then surprised by the evolving utility of it. Beyond his studies in Islam, he studied what the Brits called Modern History, fascinated by the evolution of the enlightenment beginning in the late seventeenth century. He became a good, if one-sided, friend of Locke and Hobbs as they agreed and disagreed, and followed around the London of earlier times—through his writings—a man named Pepys. He spent some time at the country estate of Lord Alistair, his slain SAS friend's father, who lived alone on a country estate near the village of Binsey, along the river Thames, a short distance from Oxford. The conversation was strained in the early visits, polite and inane. They would smile at each other, and talk of whatever had been in the newspaper that week, or talk of the Dons at Oxford, several of whom Lord Alistair knew well. At first, Alex found the conversation only mildly interesting, but he had liked the son, Colin, and understood the loneliness the old man felt. Later, he became more interested as they got to know each other and the old man opened up with his opinions. They began to laugh together, and argue into the night.

After a few months of frequent weekend visits to the estate, Lord Alistair invited Alex to dine with him at White's, his club in London. During dinner, Lord Alistair was quiet and seemed troubled. They retired to the library after dinner and sat alone in one corner, drinking coffee. Alex sat quiet, waiting. Finally, the old man broke the silence.

"I had only my son and now just his daughter, who lives with her mother and stepfather on the other side of London," Lord Alistair said. "I seldom see her, which certainly upsets me and seems to bother her as well. I have been unable to find much from our government about how my son died, other than honorably. I have been reluctant to demand the information; that's not done. The English establishment is notoriously reticent about that sort of thing. Colin wrote that the two of you were becoming friends, and we met briefly at the pheasant shoot in Scotland several years ago. I have grown to know you well enough to understand the foundation of that friendship. You and Colin, in spite of dramatically different backgrounds and education, had much in common. I believe you would have become closer over the decades. If you have information on how he died, it would be a comfort to me to hear it."

Alex was silent, thinking. The raid near Beirut had been covered briefly in the international press after a formal protest by the government of Lebanon that had been lodged. Both the US and Great Britain had denied involvement, since none of the dead or wounded had been left behind to be identified. He looked at his watch; it was 3:00 p.m. in Washington.

Alex looked at Lord Alistair, who looked old as he waited. "Perhaps I can help, but the decision is not mine. If you will excuse me for a few minutes, Sir, I'll make a phone call."

Lord Alistair looked at him speculatively, then nodded and picked up his coffee.

Alex walked to the phones and called Mac. He had mentioned earlier to Mac that he had become acquainted with Lord Alistair and described the situation cryptically.

Mac was silent for a few seconds and then said, "Hold on for a minute." Alex could hear Mac typing at his computer and murmuring to himself.

Mac picked the phone up with a clatter. "Okay, swear him to secrecy and tell him the story. He's a solid citizen and deserves to hear it. He was quite a decorated tank warrior in World War Two. It's old news to the press anyway."

"Good," Alex said. "Come to visit me sometime and I'll introduce you. I think you'd like him."

Mac laughed, and said, "I just may. I have a buddy over there at Oxford that I want you to meet anyhow. Come to think of it, I think I'll give him a call and ask him to look you up. He was also a helluva warrior in his prime. Good guy. Real smart."

"Sounds good to me, Mac," Alex said. "Thanks."

He walked back to the table, where Lord Alistair was sitting quietly, waiting.

"If we have your vow of secrecy, sir, I may tell you the story."

Alistair nodded and said, "You were there? You seem a bit young for that."

Alex looked steadily at him. "I was there. I had just turned twenty-four. It was my fourteenth such operation."

Lord Alistair raised one brow, leaned back in his chair, picked up his coffee and said, "Of course. Even the cold wars are a young man's game. Go on, Mr. Cuchulain."

Lebanon

The Planning Phase

IT was 1993. US Intelligence had placed Abu Nidal, the international terrorist, in an apartment building at the edge of a small seaside town, Halat, sixteen kilometers North of Beirut. Nidal was risking increased visibility for an important meeting with his key lieutenants. The group reportedly was planning a terrorist operation in the US, with potential results that seemed to make the risk worthwhile. It was an operation that the Joint Intelligence Committee of the United States was desperately anxious to thwart.

Alex had gone into the operation as the outside man, the "boomer." He was the explosives guy whose job was to ensure, at the end of the operation, that nothing remained of the planning operation and planning staff that was in place for Abdul Nidal. The Navy's Seals had the responsibility for the infiltration, the perimeter security, and the stealthy killing that was necessary. Two members of Britain's SAS were attached to the Seal team primarily to demonstrate the UK's commitment to fighting terrorism, and, of course, for the endless cross training.

They had just finished rehearsals near Nellis Air Force base, on a mockup of the target apartment building. During the debrief, Alex had made several comments on what he felt were unnecessary obstructions by friendly movements into established fields of fire. Later, as they sat on the ground in the shade of a truck, waiting for a pickup and transportation to the airfield, the Seal team leader walked up to him. "We really don't need any fucking CIA spooks on this job. Why don't you keep your fucking mouth shut about things you don't know anything about?" The leader was a lieutenant with an Annapolis background, dressing up his file for promotion. He was finishing a three-year tour, but this was his first real operation.

Alex told him, "We work for the same boss. You're the mission commander. If you don't like the rules or think that I can't do the job, just call it off. I just blow shit up. You do your job and I'll do mine." The Seal, a big man, hovered over Alex menacingly. "If you fuck this up, I will personally rip your fucking head off and piss down the stump." Alex stretched his legs out and looked the man in the eye, irritated. "In your dreams, asshole," he said, and closed his eyes. The Seal stretched a big hand out and grabbed Alex by the throat. "I'm talking to you, boy—don't you go fainting on me."

Alex hunched and distended his neck to relieve the heavy pressure on it. He reached up to the seal commander's right hand and gripped it an inch or two below the wrist, his thumb reaching under the man's thumb pad. He squeezed, hard, his hand compressing the base of the thumb pad as his fingers bent the right side of the hand. As Alex felt the bones in the seal's hand start to compress and bow, he spun the hand out and away from his throat, then slid his other hand to the lieutenant's elbow and dug the ends of his fingertips into the nerve socket, causing electric pains to shoot up the seal's arm and into his shoulder, immobilizing him. "God didn't bless you with much in the way of judgment, Lieutenant. I've done thirteen of these little road shows, and if you touch me again, I'll hurt you. If you endanger this mission with any more of this amateur-hour shit, I'll see you replaced. Now just do your job."

As the lieutenant stormed away, Colin Alistair looked at him, raised one eyebrow and said, "I say Cooch, my boy, I don't believe that our fearless leader has heard of you. If he had, one would guess that he would have used something more effective than a one-handed choke. You might be a bit cautious with him in the future."

They had met and become friends several months earlier, while Alex was seconded to the SAS, Britain's equivalent of the Delta Force. The cross training there was surprisingly rigorous, but Alex liked it. He had learned new things, made new friends, and even got a chance to share his arcane knowledge of how to best "blow shit up." Alistair and Alex had spent much of their downtime together, talking and working out. Once, Lord Alistair came to Scotland for a pheasant shoot with them; he had arranged it with a Scot friend.

Alex had looked at him and smiled. "Colin, we know each other well enough by now for both to know that you are quite an accomplished master of understatement, and I am, in fact, the quintessence of caution."

Alistair had given an inelegant snort, and had said, "Yes, quite so. Your livelihood attests to that, of course."

Lebanon

The Action Phase

THEY flew to Athens on a C-141, and then unloaded their gear into a helicopter for the ride to the aircraft carrier USS Midway. The next morning, a launch took them to a sub that had surfaced just minutes earlier. The mission was on.

Late that evening, they rode from the surfaced sub in inflatable Zodiacs with muffled outboard engines to a beach in the far outskirts North of Beirut near Halat, an uneventful trip. The main party had a two-hour wait, in defensive positions, as the specialty team members moved into place and midnight passed. Listening devices revealed that only four contiguous apartments in the target building were occupied. No one had yet matched Nidal's voice with the voiceprints stored electronically in the devices. Several of his key lieutenants had been identified by voice print—which was all it took to make it a go. Killing the mission planning, the mission planners, and therefore the mission, was paramount.

At 0130, the telephone wires for the entire complex were cut, and they moved in quickly. Alex placed his explosives around the outside of the building in three or four minutes and fused them for remote detonation, with a half-hour automatic override in case he got hit. He was moving up the stairs past the rear Seal on guard when he heard the clacking of bolts moving on their slides on silenced Heckler and Koch MP5-SD3 nine millimeter submachine guns and the distinctive coughing sounds of rounds being "tapped" out three at a time. He ran up and placed his inside charges, finishing just as he heard the distinctive sound of a burst from an AK-47, then several pistol shots, followed by more concentrated AK-47 fire.

Cuchulain heard a voice yelling "Charlie 47. Back to the boat. There's nobody here but bad guys and junior shooters. We got the plan papers. Blow the whole thing."

Since the validation code, Charlie 47, was right, Alex threw his nearly empty explosives sack under the stairs, near a charge he had set. There was no need to carry it out, since he was going to blow the whole building. Aesthetic considerations were pointless. He pulled his Beretta from its holster and began to run toward the boat, passing several groups of two men, each pair supporting or carrying a third, wounded man. Cuchulain had activated the small infra-red lights on the chest and back of his vest to keep from being dropped by the escape shooter, who was on his stomach seventy five meters out. The shooter was equipped with a telescopic night sight and an accurized M-14 7.62 mm rifle, loaded with mercury tipped rounds that insured no further resistance after a hit. As Cuchulain ran, he scattered small antipersonnel grenades fused for five minutes before activation; he could disarm them remotely but could not change their timing. Five minutes was usually more than enough. As soon as everyone had passed, the escape shooter would pick up and run back to the boat. Being last to clear was a dangerous job; Alex's grenades would help slow the pursuit. Someone was on the roof of a second building with a machine gun, starting to fire wildly. Alex dropped beside the escape shooter, and said, "Boomer," to alert him he was the explosives man. He pulled the transmitter from his vest, and fused the building to blow in fifteen minutes, just in case he got hit. He waited, instinctively worming his way into the sand to get below the small mound in front of him to avoid fire. Alex wanted to blow the building as soon as possible after the Seals had cleared, to eliminate the hostile fire coming at them from at least that building, and also to shake up shooters from the other building.

Men began to pour from the apartment building beside the target, the distinctive sound of their AK-47s loud as they ran, shooting wildly. A steady flow of fire from the escape shooter was dropping many of them as they emerged, the "snick, snick" of his magazine changes so fast that it seemed as one sound. Dirt kicked up in the mound in front of Cuchulain's face, and he heard the Seal beside him grunt. "I'm hit, can't shoot," he groaned.

"Damn!" Cuchulain said as he reached across the Seal and picked up the rifle, rolled left to tuck the stock into his shoulder then rolled back right, put his cheekbone on the stock and looked into the night scope. He picked some near targets and shot until they fell to give him a bit of a feel for the M-14, then started to shoot the bright green figures as they ran from the building. His magazine changes were slow as he dug fresh ammunition from the vest of the wounded shooter. He saw the last of the spottable infra-reds pass his sights, and yelled "Wounded shooter!" as the man ran by.

The Seal paused and yelled, "I'm hit too. I'll send help," then stumbled on.

Alex flicked his transmitter and the building went up in two blasts, the first caving in the four walls to collapse the roof, the second raising the roof again and exploding it into jagged shards that ripped into those nearby. Men flew into the air at the second blast, and many others fell to the ground around it with the concussion. Cuchulain had mixed thermite into the charges to ensure that anything that could burn, would. The thermite sparkled in the dark sky. Cuchulain put six quick rounds into the machine gunners, then flipped the selector switch on the M-14 to full-automatic and quickly emptied the magazine at the crowd. Some of them returned fire wildly as they dropped to the ground. Alex rolled over and grabbed six fragmentation grenades from his vest, two at a time from their pockets. He had fused them all, with timers designed to be set with a quarter, half, or full turn of the grenade top. He took two, gave them a full turn and tossed them beside him onto the path. He quickly threw two, with a half turn, part way down the path and threw the quarter-turn pair as far as he could. He reached into his vest again, took a large flat parcel from it and put it under the stock of the M-14, pressing it down and flicking a small switch. Cuchulain bent, picked up the Seal with a fireman's carry, turned and started to run, leaving the weapon behind.

The Seal was a heavy man, and Alex realized that he had neglected to take the extra magazines from the Seal's vest; he could feel the man's blood pumping into his shirt. He was tiring fast as he cleared the underbrush and ran into the sand toward the Zodiacs. Again his father's words came to him, *Be in the best possible physical condition*, and Alex thanked him one more time for the advice. The wounded Seal who was to send the help was still stumbling along; Alex passed him. Two Seals were pushing a Zodiac into the surf while the others knelt with their weapons at their shoulders facing toward Alex when he yelled, "Hey! Charlie 47. Wounded."

Four of the kneeling Seals broke toward him running. Alex could hear the sound of their safeties being engaged as they swung their weapons over their shoulders. Two grabbed the Seal from his back, then ran back and dumped him into a Zodiac just before Cuchulain rolled in. The others carried the stumbling man back. A corpsman cut away the clothes of the wounded and started to work to stabilize them. As the hushed outboard kicked in and shot them over the surf, a ragged series of small explosions could be heard as the first of the antipersonnel explosives initiated. Two explosions came from the shore, followed by two, and a final two, each punctuated by screams of pain and fear and wild fire from AK-47s. A few moments later, there was a much larger explosion, and Cuchulain, lying heaving and exhausted in the bottom of the Zodiac, grinned. The big booby trap under the M-14 had been found.

As he rested on a spare bunk on the sub, Cuchulain sensed someone walking up to him. He opened his eyes. A Seal, white bandages wrapped tightly around his right shoulder and back, stood watching him from a lined, pale, haggard face. Cuchulain grinned at him. "It looks like you'll live. I would have been mightily pissed to carry a guy as big as you that far and find out that he was dead. You were bleeding like a stuck pig."

"My name is Brooks Elliot," the Seal said, sticking out his left hand. "I owe you, big time. They nicked an artery and you got me out fast enough that I didn't bleed out."

Alex smiled and reached up to take his hand and shake it. "They call me Cooch. Buy me a San Miguel sometime, and we're even. You'd have done the same for me." He closed his eyes and heard the Seal walk slowly away, then his eyes popped open. "Hey, I saved a bunch of your loaded magazines for you for next time!"

Elliot turned around, laughing. "Yeah, I heard. No wonder you're tired. Our bozos weighed that damned vest. Thirteen pounds."

Later, Cuchulain walked to the surgery and sat down beside it waiting. After a few minutes, the surgeon walked out with arms bloodied to the elbow. He tore off his green cotton skull cap and threw it against the wall with a splat. "I hate those fucking AK-47s," he screamed at no one.

Alex looked up. "Who'd we lose, Doc?"

"It was Morgan and that SAS Captain."

"Alistair? Shit!" Alex said.

London

Whites Club

LORD Alistair sat silent for several minutes as Alex sipped his coffee and waited.

Finally, Alistair shifted in his chair and nodded. "Thank you. This is a great comfort to me. There are things worth dying for, even in the absence of personal threat. Unfortunately, our societies must deal violently with those who understand nothing else, or we would perish at the hands of barbarians. It has been forever so. Your studies of history should help bring it all into perspective for you. It may have been your George Santayana who said that 'those who cannot remember the past are condemned to repeat it.'"

He sat for several minutes, gazing off into space. Alex was silent, respecting the old man's grief and rationalization.

Lord Alistair shifted in his chair again and said, "You have much experience of violence, Mr. Cuchulain. Violence tends to corrode the soul. I am glad that you are at Oxford. What you can learn is to put what you have done in perspective, and perhaps mitigate the corrosion. We English comfort ourselves with a veneer of civilization that masks and perhaps rationalizes a thousand years of war after war, where our best and brightest are killed to perpetuate our society.

You are, like it or not, Mr. Cuchulain, a warrior. Society values warriors greatly when they are required for the collective survival of the common good. When the conflict wanes and victory is won or perceived, society, particularly young societies such as yours in America, would like to put you away. They would like to treat you as a bloodhound, useful only if the madman gets out of his cage. They despise your skills, seeing only the ability to end life quickly and efficiently, rather than your protective ability to help the society adapt and innovate without barbaric interference. Older societies, such as ours and those in Europe, have longer memories as a result of a thousand years of armed strife, and the brutal occupation of our countries by the victors, who by traditional right feel free to amuse themselves with our women and confiscate our property. You colonists have never been through this set of experiences, and think that they are a relic of the past. We in Europe see no reason to believe that ten thousand years of tradition has been obliterated as the result of the death of Hitler and Tojo. Only warriors have the quickness of action, the resoluteness of purpose, and the zeal to mobilize the populace in the face of great danger. For those reasons and many more, we in England quietly value our warriors, and honor them for the long term."

Lord Alistair studied Alex for signs of either boredom or interest. He found Alex watching him intently, waiting.

Alistair smiled at Alex and said, "You are kind to indulge an old man's ramblings. I would call you Alex, if I may."

Alex looked at him and smiled. "Of course, Sir."

Early in his second year at Oxford, Alex ran into Brooks Elliot, the Seal he had carried away from the firefight in Lebanon several years earlier. Elliot was there on a Rhodes scholarship, having served his time in the Navy before exercising the fellowship. They spent some time together, then more as the friendship deepened past the social reticence natural to them both. Mac's friend had contacted Alex; he turned out to be a former SAS officer, now on the Oxford faculty. He invited Cuchulain to dinner several times. Later, Alex introduced Brooks to him, and later still introduced the two of them to Lord Alistair. Over time, an easy relationship developed among the four of them. Many evenings they would talk late over a glass or two of vintage port, their conversations wandering easily from philosophy to history to ancient or modern weapons and their impact on society. Usually, the major's wife, a concert pianist, rehearsed for her performances in the parlor behind them. On weekends sometimes, they would go to Lord Alistair's estate to shoot woodcock or pheasant, then talk over dinner long into the evening. Intellectual male camaraderie that was not framed in a background of violence was an entirely new experience for Alex. He found it stimulating as well as personally broadening, and resolved to figure out what else he was missing in life. He had long since come to the somewhat disturbing conclusion that he had never had the adolescence that he had heard others describe with nostalgia many times; a period of questioning, of doing whatever seemed as if would be fun or interesting, of casual flirting and dating, of arguing into the night about the existence of God.

Alex bought a good camera and took a photography course in the town of Oxford; the university would not dream of offering such frivolity. On weekends he sometimes strolled through the streets and museums of London, observing and taking photographs. He sat in Hyde Park from time to time, listening to the speakers at the Corner. When the crazier ones stood up to speak, he tried to imagine himself in their shoes and occasionally joined them for a pint at the local pub as the day wore on, listening and asking questions. He tried to learn to paint and was hilariously unsuccessful by the measure of his friends' reaction to his early efforts. Brooks Elliot taught him to play squash, and he learned to love the game. He was unsuccessful at golf, and not amused by the failure; it was on its surface such a simple game.

When he finished at Oxford, he shouldered a pack and wandered through England and Wales for a few weeks, then crossed into Ireland. He thought about looking up his Cuchulain relatives, then decided to leave that for another time and flew to Paris from Dublin.

He met a Danish woman while he stood studying a painting at the Louvre, and they were together for several weeks as they wandered through the South of France, sleeping at inexpensive pensions and walking among the vineyards. She teased him about being an exercise addict while he marveled at her ability to eat enormous quantities without gaining weight. She threw

New York City,
the present day

IT was late on a blustery Friday afternoon. Pedestrians hunched against the wind as snowflakes rushed at grey buildings, twirling up at the last moment. The financial markets had closed for the day. Cuchulain was sitting in a tattered booth in Sam's Deli, on the ground floor of the building that housed his office. The cracked, crimson, vinyl bench sagged with his weight. The ancient pattern on the table top had been rubbed nearly invisible by countless Clorox-soaked cleaning cloths. He was nursing a cup of coffee and chewing on a nearly perfectly toasted cinnamon raisin bagel. He smiled to himself, glad that Sam lacked interior-design skills or ambition; he could always find his booth free at this time of day.

Alex felt his cell phone begin to vibrate, and quickly plucked it from his jacket pocket to answer. "Cuchulain," he said.

"Alex, it's Caitlin."

"Hey!" he answered. "All settled into sunny California and over your biker fantasy?"

"More like a nightmare than a fantasy," she snorted. "And how is the baddest motherfucker in the whole world? Kill anyone today? "

"Nope, but the day is young, to paraphrase Jack Palance," he said. "And this is New York. But it's so cold here that I'm afraid to go out, so my chances are slim."

"Well, this is your big chance to better your weather. My date for a big charity dinner dance for the magnet schools here just flaked out on me. It's next week. Any chance that you'll be out this way and willing to escort a jilted physicist, to help her save just a little face? I simply can't miss this one."

"You tell me when and where, and I'll be there." he said.

"Super! I'll e-mail you the details," she said. "Oh, shit! It's black tie! I hope you have a fucking tuxedo."

"Relax, Caitlin," he said. "I actually do own a tux. Send me the details and I'll let you know when I arrive and where I'm staying. Where is the dance?"

"It's at the Menlo Circus Club in Menlo Park," Caitlin said.

"Great! I'll probably stay at the Stanford Court in Palo Alto, but I'll let you know," Alex said.

"Okay. Gotta run," she said. The phone went dead.

As Alex looked quizzically at his cell phone, he saw Sam grinning at him from the doorway to the kitchen, with a damp dish towel draped over his scrawny shoulder. "It's about time you found a woman, Cuchulain. I was getting concerned about your virility."

Alex swung out of the booth and attempted to look haughty. "I'm just very selective, Sam. You know, you just have to wait for them to come to you."

Washington, DC

THE 737-400 banked steeply, as it followed the curves of the Potomac River, south toward the District of Columbia. Cuchulain looked over the wing to see workers at their desks in an office in a Rosslyn high-rise, just up the river from Washington's Reagan airport. He could hear the whine of the flaps coming down to their landing position followed by the bump of wheels striking the runway. The flight attendants immediately began pleading with passengers to stay in their seats "until the captain turns the seat belt light off," to little avail. The passenger complement of New Yorkers, bureaucrats, and politicians didn't lend itself to being controlled, unless a real or virtual pistol was being held to its collective head.

The plane lurched to a stop at the gate, and the fasten seat belt light was switched off, accompanied by its usual, annoying clang. The Delta Airlines shuttle from New York to Washington had been packed, as usual. As Alex stood and pulled his bag from the overhead bin, a pleasant-looking woman in her early fifties rammed an elbow into his ribs and stepped on his toe as she jostled to leave the plane first, then race for a cab. She turned and glared at him as someone behind gave a push, bumping him against her back. The door opened and the crowd surged forward. As he walked through the jet way and entered the terminal building, he looked for someone who looked as if he might work for Mac. To his surprise, he saw Mac himself leaning against a concrete pole just outside security, a toothpick hanging from the corner of his grinning mouth, his short gray hair long enough finally to show a part on the left side, above a scar.

Alex felt a rare rush of affection and emotion. Since his father had died, Mac was as close to being both a father and best friend to him as he could imagine. They shook hands, grinning at each other, then turned without speaking and walked out of the terminal to the short-term parking lot. Using a remote, Mac popped open the trunk of a top-down, bright blue Shelby Mustang convertible, then motioned for Alex to throw his bag and briefcase into it. Both men took off their suit jackets and put them, folded at the shoulders, over the bag.

"Whoa, Mac! What kind of government wheels are these?" Alex whistled. "You've gone uptown on me since I saw you last!"

Mac grinned and slammed the trunk. "Nothing but the best for Uncle Sam's prodigal son. I always wanted one of these, so I bought one last week. With you managing my savings, there's enough extra that I could buy a Rolls Royce Corniche without feeling any pain. Besides, this frivolous filly fits my semi-retired image. You're my first passenger, but I did put the top down last Sunday and drove down to Annapolis to watch the sailboats. I think I've entered my second adolescence— or maybe just my first, since I was a Marine at eighteen. Let's just drive around for awhile … I enjoy this thing, and nobody can listen to us here."

Mac pulled the car into gear, swung around the parked cars, and pulled out of the airport.

"You're sure about that?" Alex said. "I have increasingly less interest in sharing our extra-legal homicidal adventures with our politically sensitive law-enforcement brethren. Particularly with Feds who have no sense of humor and a hook or crook promotion agenda."

"Watch this!" Mac laughed, and flicked two green buttons beneath the radio. The buttons turned to red and blinked for thirty seconds or so, then one returned to solid green and the second began a slow blink.

"Your protégé Lev Epstein outdid himself on this one. The first run looks for bugs along every spectrum, and if it finds none, the second creates white noise to foil anything the first missed."

Alex looked chagrined. "I should have thought of that! Ah well, I knew the first time I talked to Lev that he was a lot smarter than me."

Mac smiled. "He's the best! He has a sense of larceny in his heart that warms me. The Mossad trains them well."

Alex loosened his tie and unbuttoned his collar button, enjoying the crisp air of Washington's fall. As they drove up the George Washington Parkway, a slight breeze blew leaves across the road. The glory of fall foliage was a few weeks past, and most of the leaves were now a flat, dull orange.

They drove for awhile, silent, each thinking about different parts of the past.

"How's your love life, stud? You're getting to the age that you should be settling down and having a few kids," Mac said quietly.

"Yeah, *stud*. More like *steer*. I'm lucky to get laid about once a month, maybe less, but it has been better lately. I had a nice date on Friday and another on Saturday. The Saturday date was better, but they were both good. Before these two, it was mostly older women I've known for a while who know exactly what they want, and for the most part know exactly what I want. Most of them even want to buy me dinner first. Love ain't a part of that picture. No kidding, Mac. I think they were starting to pass me around. Jeez!"

"What, you can't find younger women who like you?"

"In New York? I can find a new bimbo every night, but what do I need with bimbos? I can't find anybody who has anything to say after the morning orange juice. I'd sure like to find someone who's fun after the sex. At least with the older women the sex is better than good and nobody is bullshitting anyone about what is going on. So we don't talk much. That's okay. I lie less if I don't talk. You can put that on my tombstone."

They drove a while longer, silent, exiting the Parkway down Route 123 past the entrance to the CIA and then veering right through Langley and then McLean toward Great Falls.

Mac turned to look at him and seemed mildly concerned. "I think that you've taken my advice of the past a little too seriously, my friend. I once told you that to open yourself up was to give the other guy advantage, that you should be quiet and let others open up to you to your own advantage. That's true for our profession, but probably less true for our social lives right now. Not that I mean you should talk, or even hint, about our extracurricular activities, but I suspect that we have to open up a little personally if anything worthwhile is going to happen."

Alex shrugged, then turned to look at Mac. "How about you, Mac? You finally found someone you like?"

Mac sighed. "Maybe. There's a professor at George Washington—an Air force widow. I've just decided that no one worth having will let you see them, if you don't let them see you, in the spiritual sense. I'm having an easier time with women I find attractive when I open up a little personally. But of course, I can't open up too much. My ninth-ranked national security job lets me justify a little paranoia—makes me mysterious, too. Some women like that."

"I'm willing to open up a bit when I get some good vibes, but that hasn't happened much lately," Alex said. "My personal philosophy of life as manifested by our little homicidal efforts would turn most reasonably intelligent women off immediately. That woman in the biker bar that I told you about seemed to think that I was a bit disturbing, and Dodd didn't help much with his little speech there."

"It's good thing that you didn't take Jerome. He'd have splashed Dodd when he reached for the gun, and you two would have had to take the place apart. Then she really wouldn't have liked you!" Mac shook his head a little and chuckled. "The serial-killer business just ain't what it used to be!"

"Did you look into Dodd?" Alex said.

"Yeah, he got tossed from the Navy. He was dealing some coke," Mac said. "Nothing for us there. Brooks says those bikers are scarcer around New York than a watch shopper at Tiffany's. Billy's still in intensive care; you seemed to have interfered with his future love life."

"Pity," Alex said. "Billy getting any visitors?"

"Nary a single one," Mac said with a little grin.

"Go figure," Alex said. "Even sick scumbags don't like working for sick scumbags."

"Uh, huh." Mac was quiet for a second, then said, "First, there is no loyalty among scumbags; witness Billy's visitor list. Unless, of course, there is religion involved and manipulated. Second, if you take out the scumbags' leadership they dissolve into individual dumb scumbags."

"So we let the local law pick them up when they screw up," Alex said. "Works for me."

"Dodd?" Mac asked.

"Don't bother looking for Dodd, unless he acts up and we see him do it," Alex said. "Dodd gets it; he knew who I was and who I knew. He came over to me very quickly after the half-dollar gig."

"Well, you are a charming, convincing guy," Mac said with a little chuckle.

Alex grinned. "True."

MacMillan drove across a bridge over the beltway—the highway that defines the political geography of Washington, and looked down at the bumper-to-bumper traffic. "At least we're not down there, and our lives ain't boring."

Alex looked down and laughed, "I think we live some version of the old Chinese curse. We certainly live in interesting times! Of course, most of it is by our choice."

"Do you think it beats a couple of brats and a fat wife who bitches every day about money?" Mac asked.

"Probably," Alex laughed. "But you and I both know that there are a lot better family-building choices out there than that."

"Oh, ho!" Mac exclaimed, turning his head with eyebrows raised to look at Alex. "Do I hear the faint sound of the romance bugler sounding the charge?"

Alex laughed. "I liked the woman from the biker bar a lot, but I wouldn't be surprised if she runs the next time I see her. The good news is that Brooks doesn't think she will, and he has known her pretty well for a long time. I've talked with her by phone a few times, and she seems to be dealing with the whole scene well, and even with a bit of humor."

"Caitlin O'Connor," Mac nodded. "There's nothing in Uncle's files that would make me think she's a danger to us, and she has a slew of security clearances. And God, what a looker! And how does it feel to be around someone smarter than you? Is it obvious when you're with her?"

Alex was still for nearly a minute, looking out the window at the passing scenery of Great Falls National Park. "It's most obvious when anything quantitative is being discussed. She does complex algebra in milliseconds, and draws conclusions from several disparate problems that it would take me hours to synthesize and apply to the overall problem," he said. "I sure as hell wouldn't want to compete with her in an advanced calculus class. But so far, she hasn't tried to bully me with it, so it doesn't bother me. If we had similar educations and experiences, it might. She also has a giant ego, and constructs conversation games to exercise and protect it; I guess that's okay with me. She's not the nicest woman I ever met, but I find the whole package immensely attractive. She's invited me out to Northern California for a benefit next week."

"So, you'll get a chance to see her again in a couple of days," Mac said. "That worked out well."

Alex smiled. "What's up? Does our new el presidente want us to shut up the Christian right in the Republican Party?"

"We ain't got enough ordnance to do that, Alex," Mac laughed. "But there is a problem out there that he wants us to handle. I told him I'd look into it."

"Did the cowboy convince the president that we were useful, or did someone else?" Alex said.

Mac chuckled and said, "A little of both, I think. The president hinted that he got a call from a predecessor, where we were discussed in some detail. Senator Elliot dropped by as well, I think, just to chat."

Mac pulled off into a dirt parking area and put the Mustang into park, then turned a little in his seat, looking at Alex. "I don't give a rat's ass for the old president as a person, Alex, or the new one." Mac said. "Politicians mostly care about two things—money and votes. They'd give us up in a heartbeat, if it benefitted them. That said, I do care a lot about having the only society that really works in this world and trying to protect it. If things weren't bad here, we wouldn't be given the resources that we have. We wouldn't have access to the databases, we couldn't get the staff or equipment we need, and we consequently couldn't make a difference. At least both of these presidents recognize the problem and have given us the power under presidential protection—fragile and unreliable protection though it may be—to go out and touch bad guys that the Constitution won't allow us to touch legally. The new president appears to have some balls, and he is very quick. I like him so far. Are you still in or do you want out?"

Alex sighed. "I'm in as long as you keep us away from any gigs but the ones that only we can do. I just hate to see the whole system fail because of a relatively few scumbags that the law can't touch. I'm willing to touch them, and take the risk that goes with the effort. But you already knew that, Mac. We're still the patriotic assassins."

"Yeah, I did, and we are, so let's get to it," Mac said. "We have a group of Colombian druggies who have corrupted some key players in Silicon Valley."

Alex interrupted. "I hope I'm not risking a murder charge, among others, to protect a bunch of computer nerds from design piracy!"

Mac erupted. "Will you shut the fuck up until I'm done talking? I'm in this thing as deep as you, maybe deeper, and I ain't going to do any wet work, super-secret presidentially-sponsored spook outfit or not, that doesn't involve serious national security issues that I understand. As usual, you can hear the story and decide whether you want to play or not."

Cuchulain looked chagrined. "Sorry, Mac. Tell me the story."

"Yeah, and maybe I shouldn't have jumped down your throat," Mac said. "I'm just a little up-tight about this one. It's within the US."

Mac glanced down at the still blinking green light on the dash. "'The computer jocks on contract to DARPA in Silicon Valley have figured out how to use radar to beat the stealthiness of the F-117, and probably even its successors. They're using a centrally-controlled network of five geograph-ically-dispersed radar dishes. Basically, the five different radar images come in to the central computer server over fiber-optic lines. They've been digi-tized by the computer workstation integrated with each of the dishes. The digital images are compared, to look for anomalies that can't be accounted for by the difference in geographical perspective. The central server then goes through comparisons of speed, altitude, and direction to see if those three parameters are within the flight capabilities of a tactical aircraft or cruise missile, or whatever it's set up for. If it gets a match, it turns out that pinpoint high-powered radar searches are much more efficient at spotting stealth hardware than broad-based sky sweeping searches, and it goes into pinpoint mode. The main computer takes the radar data, chooses a spot in the sky, and directs the ground-to-air weapons systems to fire at it. In a test at Nellis a couple of months ago, they shot down six of nine stealth drones beyond a half-mile envelope around their targets, three of them with conventional ack-ack that was just being fired at a directed point in the sky."

Alex whistled softly through his teeth and was silent for a few seconds, thinking about Mac's revelation. "I guess I'm not too surprised. The concept makes sense. Computer power for the buck grows at an unbelievable rate over time, so it's probably already cost-effective if we need to deploy it, and will get a lot better. Better yet, the components don't have to be miniaturized, because weight and size isn't much of a problem in a ground-based tactical system; that would keep the cost down. For less than a million dollars, you can get more scientific computer power in a box the size of a file cabinet today than all of General Motors had twenty years ago. In an application like this, it would be easy to build specialized chips to do the math calcula-tions and probably the comparisons. Not having to translate the software to machine instructions would speed things up dramatically."

Alex looked out the window for a second, no longer seeing the landscape. "I'll tell you though Mac," he said, "from what I've read, the bad guys are at least ten years from having the manufacturing technology alone to build stealth aircraft, let alone the computer and software to make it effective."

Mac chuckled grimly and said, "You are a quick study, Son. Sometimes I wonder what that mind of yours would have produced if things had worked out differently, and you had ended up at Caltech at seventeen instead of in the Marine Corps. But now, put your thinking cap on backwards and tell me another way to look at the problem, given that the bad guys aren't going to able to build stealth hardware for quite a while. Think about why the powers that be have approached me about using our specialized, wholly unconstitutional set of services. What could possibly make them quit shitting their pants about our mere existence and their knowledge of it, and actually want to put us back to work, breaking the law for them?'

Mac pulled the Mustang back onto the road and turned right on a narrow country trail called Great Falls Road, falling in behind the heavy commuting traffic of Mercedes, Porches, and BMW sedans on their way to estates nestled behind the trees. Horses grazed behind freshly whitewashed fences, and from time to time, there was a glimpse of a private riding ring and hard-hatted, high-booted riders jumping low obstacles. Alex resumed his sightless gaze out the side window, missing the high-priced pastoral scenery.

Finally, he looked over at Mac, eyes wide, and said, "You gotta be joking, Mac! Someone grabbed it? No, that's not it, is it? It's that someone is trying to grab it! Man, we could kiss our ability to blast Iraq at will, or anyone else, good-bye if they get hold of this thing! Any ability we have to act as the world's policemen without serious US casualties will vanish."

"Bingo!" Mac snorted. "Give the man an exploding cigar of his own design."

Alex shifted in his seat to look directly at Mac. "Man, that would be a real hit with DOD and the Congress! What do they have invested in all of that stealth technology? Fifteen billion, maybe twenty billion bucks in R&D alone? I gotta assume that the Arabs, the Chinese, and our faithful allies, the Japanese, would love to get access to it. Anyone else? What's the story?"

"We think it's the Arabs and the Chinese, for starters," Mac said. "Maybe someone else. We don't know a lot yet. We got lucky on this one. A project leader Ph.D. working on this effort developed a nasty coke habit that he was having trouble supporting. He was approached by his dealer to meet with his boss, with a little free nose candy as an inducement to do it. The meet was with a Latino guy, Colombian as it turns out, who said he was willing to deal him all the coke he could use for the rest of his life, in return for access to the stealth detection radar plans, two sets of the specialized circuits, and the software. This guy was smart enough to figure out what his life expectancy would be if he pulled this grab off, so he called his older brother to help him blow the whistle. His brother, who is also a Ph.D., works in the company as a Middle East analyst. I knew him a little from his briefings when I was there. Good guy. Anyhow, he goes to the DDO, the DDO hotfoots it to the director, and the director calls the president, all in the course of two hours, from what I was told. I got called in two days later, after they decided that this kind of caper was likely to become a parade if they let the first one succeed. Almost as bad would be splashing this mess all over the papers and then having the bad guys at the top never get indicted or get off, if they do as usual."

Alex nodded. "So it's ours? Give it to the boys who skip newspapers, lawyers, and indictments, and just allow us to present the invoice to the piper?"

"Yeah, but we don't know how much time we have," Mac said. "We have Lev Epstein setting up as much electronic surveillance as he can, as fast as he can. We have a little already, but they have damn good counter-measure gear, and they use it. They just don't know Epstein like we know Epstein. NSA is working on the phone traffic, but there is a ton of Spanish language voice traffic out there, and the recognition software they use to sort out the Colombian accents is slow. NSA has the varsity on it, so we should know more in a week or so, and we should have more keywords for them to use for subsequent runs of the voice data. DEA gave us a voice print of the guy we think is their head honcho, but we haven't gotten anything on it yet from NSA."

"What do you want me to do?" Alex said.

"We need more inside info than we have," Mac said. "I need you out there as the access dangle to see if they'll bring you in, at least a little, and I need you to have a decent cover. DEA is in on this only at the very top, and only because they have so much information on the druggies and their organizational structure. FBI, CIA, and everyone else is out; they haven't even been briefed. I don't want DEA or anyone else knowing who you are, where you're from, or anything else about you. You should go in as a Hispanic and speak English with an accent, probably Puerto Rican, using your good friend Paco; he knows how to dress rough and play rough. When you shave, comb your hair, lose your accent, and slip into your Brioni, you should be invisible for our purposes. I have a full set of backup ID for you in the glove compartment. Can you adjust your schedule to make it fit?"

Alex nodded. "I always have a reason to be in Silicon Valley, with so many public companies there. Caitlin invited me to the benefit event soon; that's a bonus."

Mac slowed the car and pulled into the gravel parking lot of a white stucco, one-story restaurant. The small sign by the door read *L'Auberge Chez Francois*. "Good. I'd like you to catch the buyers and the sellers together if you can, or at least let me know where they are. We want to send a message to the buyers' governments, Arabs, Chinese, or whatever, that we know they were here, know what they were doing, and that diplomatic immunity is inoperative in this kind of situation. If you need some combat support setting things up, and you probably will, you should probably use Elliot and Jerome. You guys seem to live in each other's heads during an operation. Elliot is coming down tomorrow to help me put the plan together. Page me if you need them sooner. Make sure that you're ready, on very short notice, to destroy at least the Colombian side and any goodies that we find out they've received. The big, lesson-teaching show would be nice, but we can't take any chances on letting that stealth stuff get out of the country and sending our message to the bad guys."

"You'll get my goodies to me at my California hotel?" Alex said. "I'm going to leave New York tomorrow right after work."

Mac rested his big, battered hand on the steering wheel, allowing the car to idle into a parking space. "Yeah, we'll get a box to you with the usual weapons, explosives, and another set of ID matching these. The Paco ID is already set. We'll throw in some magazines and letters from San Juan, too. We'll update the computer files every four hours with anything we get, and encrypt it with the software Epstein wrote for us. You can pluck it off whenever you need it. Anything else, you need?"

Cuchulain laughed and pushed open the door. "Probably, but I can't think of it right now. Let's eat. I'm starving. I love this place, and I have to get back to the city tonight. You're buying."

"The kid makes a zillion million a year, and I gotta buy every dammed time I see him," Mac grumbled as he popped the trunk and tossed Alex's suit coat to him. "You'd think he'd have a little more respect for our tax dollar."

As they walked to the door, Mac slapped Alex on the back. "Jeez, kid, it's really great to see you!"

New York

CUCHULAIN'S car pulled up to a five-story brownstone on East 68th Street, just before eleven that evening. He told the driver that he would catch a cab home. Alex went up the steps, tapped the doorbell twice, and ran an electronic card down a reader placed beside the door. The door buzzed and he pushed his way in.

"I'm in the den," Brooks Elliot called from upstairs.

Alex took the steps two at a time and walked into the small, cluttered den. There was a large desk covered with papers and two computers, a Dell PC and a Sun workstation—standing on cabinets at either end. There was a fire blazing, and a bank of security monitors above it showing the front door and other sensitive spots. Alex flopped into one of the leather chairs in front of the desk, and threw a big leg over its arm.

"I'm going to California tomorrow. I'll be in Palo Alto Tuesday and Wednesday night. I have decent cover."

Elliot made a note, then looked up and said, "Great! I'll spend another day with Mac to go over things, and I'm going to go through the DEA files. I think I found us a way to get a little ways into the big doper in San Jose—the one who is buying the plans—and I've identified most of the network they use. I think we should trash the whole network to maximize the hassle and expense for the big daddy in Columbia. You may get a shot at the local Kahuna if things break right with you as a dangle. Mac is going to try to arrange a stonger message for the guys in Columbia. I talked to my father; he's fine with things and will provide whatever cover he can, on a screw up."

Elliot's father, Brooks F. T. Elliot the third, was a senior member on the Senate Intelligence Committee and the Chair of the Senate Armed Services Committee. He had served briefly in the Marine Corps with MacMillan. Senator Elliot was a key member in a group that routinely subverted the laws of the United States, and elsewhere, to deal violently with national security problems not easily solved with legal means. His son, Brooks, was the chief planner, and Alex the chief operator. Mac originated and ran the missions. With each change of administration, there was a period when the new president got oriented to the job; Mac was always introduced as the chief national security fixer, working for the National Security Advisor. When a need arose for the group's services, it was strongly suggested to the president that he bring Mac in to help deal with the problem. When the problem went away, the president was told, "Don't ask." It had only once been necessary for Senator Elliot to meet with a president to discuss his culpability in whatever "problem solving" was going on, and to mention that Senator Elliot had even more culpability, and thus would fight viciously to protect himself.

"Jerome is going out Sunday to recon the area and provide a little support if you screw things up early," Brooks said with a grin. "Screw it up later, and you're on your own."

"Here's what we have so far," Brooks said. "And I got pizza."

Two hours later, Alex was standing on the corner of Second Avenue and East 68th, waving for a cab. Elliot was still hard at work, eating the last of the pizza.

John F. Kennedy Airport, Queens

THE following afternoon, Alex was at JFK for his flight to San Francisco. As he walked from the jet way into the first class section, he was pleased to see that he had gotten a Boeing 757 configured for overseas flight. The first-class seats were larger than the ones built for domestic flights, and very comfortable.

The flight attendant came to offer him a drink, then lingered to flirt when she noticed that he wasn't wearing a ring. He smiled and declined the drink, then talked to her for a few minutes. She was taking a break from college to see the world, using her vacation time and the free tickets the airline provided to her for her travel adventures, while earning tuition money. Alex thought she might be twenty-two years old—fresh, attractive, and full of zest for life. He leaned the seat back and smiled to himself as he closed his eyes and thought back through his somewhat different twenties and the financial preparation for his college years. He and Jerome had taken a rather less conventional approach to providing for their future.

The flight was uneventful, and the drive from SFO to Palo Alto, down US 101, slow, crowded, and boring.

On Wednesday morning, Alex dialed into Mac's secure line to review plans. He received a package from a delivery service, a box with a small battered duffle bag full of worn clothes, scuffed shoes, and a small package of semi-permanent tattoos. On Wednesday afternoon, he took a two-hour nap.

Just after seven on Wednesday evening, Alex walked from his room at the Stanford Court hotel, wearing a Brioni tux and a conservatively ruffled

Brioni dress shirt. He had spotted some Barbara Heinrich shirt studs and cufflinks several months before at Bergdorf's and bought them; this was their virgin evening. He chuckled to himself at the memory of trying to rent a tux when he first got to New York. He had always been able to buy blazers and slacks with a minimum of tailoring. On a tip from Mac, he had semi-custom shirts from the Custom Shop. When he had walked into the rental store, the old man at the counter had glanced at him, and then looked back skeptically. "I hope you're not looking to rent a tux, young man," he said.

Alex had been puzzled. "That's what I had in mind. Is there a problem?"

"Do you happen to know what size you are?" the old man had said.

"Sure," Alex had said. "I wear a size fifty-six-long jacket, and a nineteen-and-a-half shirt with thirty-six-inch sleeves. My slacks are thirty-four waist and thirty-four-inch inseam," Alex had said.

The old man had chuckled. "Except for the slacks, those aren't what you'd call popular sizes, son, particularly in one package. My fifty-six coats have trousers with a forty-six-inch waist standard, and I don't have a shirt in stock with more than an eighteen-inch neck." He had looked at Alex for a second. "When is your big tux event, young fellow?"

"Next week," Alex had said, looking a little concerned.

"I'll tell you what I'm going to do, Son. I'll mix and match from what I have to get you into a tux that looks like it's all the same color and comes close to fitting, and I'll order a new shirt for you. It'll take three days, and that'll be $72.50, in advance. Shoes aren't a problem. As soon as you get some money put together, you go out and have a tux made, and some suits, too. You can't make it in the Big Apple in a sports coat and a pair of slacks. And you're just too damned big in the upper body to wear off-the-rack clothes, if they have to match."

Even though the "tux event" had been successful, Alex had taken the old man's advice. After some expensive trial and error, he had found a combination of vendors that suited him.

Alex had hired a sedan from a limo service, and slid from its back seat in front of Caitlin's small house on a side street in Palo Alto. As she opened her door, he handed her a dozen long stemmed roses. "You're such a sweetheart, Alex," she said, stretching up to kiss him on the cheek. "Let me put these in a vase and put my jewelry on. I'll get my coat."

Alex stood in the foyer, gazing into Caitlin's living room. She had done a spectacular job in its decoration. The professional low voltage lighting highlighted a Chinese tapestry on the wall and several vases on small lacquered tables. The modern couch and two stuffed chairs were upholstered with soft, grey leather, and rested in muted light on a magnificent oriental rug. At each end of the couch was a glass-topped table with red lacquered legs and a small lamp with an intricately patterned ceramic base.

Caitlin came into the room carrying her coat. She wore a floor-length sheath in black silk, with an open seam to mid thigh on one side, allowing her leg to peek through. She wore an extraordinary diamond and pearl necklace with matching earrings. The necklace was made up of a number of different pearls of various sizes that were set into crescent moons that fell around her neck. Each small crescent was different, with small black pearls graduated around one, and small white pearls in the next; there was a fiery, white diamond at the center of each. The ear rings were dangles, with a single crescent falling an inch or so beneath each ear. The center diamond on each of the earrings was larger than those on the necklace, perhaps a carat or more, and brilliantly white.

"That's absolutely marvelous jewelry! You must have hit the lottery. They are spectacular!" Alex exclaimed.

Caitlin spun around holding her arms out. "My grandmother bought them for me when I got the Macarthur award. It's quite handy to have at least one rich grandparent."

"This executive life agrees with you. You look spectacular, Caitlin! No one will ever guess that you had to pick up a guy by phone, in a deli named Sam's, with only six days notice," Cuchulain chuckled, holding her coat for her.

At the benefit, Alex had a better time than he expected. Caitlin's friends at her table were a combination of professors and business executives.

Most were cordial and some of them interesting. He learned a little about university and high-tech things because he asked, and drinking people talk. The talk flowed around politics, university life, and deals. He was mildly amused to find that he knew, only recently, quite a bit more than most about the intricacies of international politics and the geo-politics of the South American drug dealers, which happened to be the current hot topic. Some of the women flirted mildly, and one asked him what he did. When he answered, she laughed. "That's comforting. With those hands, I thought maybe you were a stone mason."

Caitlin was light when she danced, making him feel more competent than he was, since the government had not chosen to provide him with ballroom dancing lessons. In heels, she was tall enough to rest her chin on his shoulder, and moved her pelvis to weld it against him. As they danced, her hips moved to the music. He enjoyed himself more than he had in quite some time.

Later, as they stood outside her front door, she leaned against him and said, "Well, Alex, you certainly pulled that one off. The folks at the table were really puzzling it out tonight. First, I leave the office in a huff at one-thirty on a Friday without a date, and then I show up at eight on Wednesday with a huge, good-looking guy who just charms everyone right off their feet." With a wicked grin she said, "From the looks you were getting, I'd say that a few of those female barracuda would like to charm you right out of your pants, too." As Cuchulain smiled at her, she moved closer to murmur, "You are a wonderful dancer. Are you a good kisser, too?"

She tangled her hands in his hair, then ran her tongue across his lips and kissed him. Her tongue darted into his mouth, teasing. She pulled away. "Would you like to come in for a drink, Alex?" she said. "You'd better say yes!"

Alex waved the car away and they walked into her little house. Caitlin took his coat, and waved him to the living room. "Have a seat. I'll be with you in a minute."

After several minutes, he turned as he heard her say from the door, "Are you going to sit there all night, or would you like to have a drink with me?"

She was standing, nude, leaning against the doorway, wearing only the necklace and earrings. She had an open bottle of wine in her hand, and two glasses in the other, one a quarter full. The soft light kissed her body, hips flaring in a shadow under a tiny waist. She was almost hairless, with muscular legs—swimmer's legs. She had large pointed breasts with tiny nipples budding from them, and a tight, flat stomach.

Alex stood and turned, studying her. "I'm overcome with thirst and hunger. Caitlin, you look good enough to eat," he grinned.

She took a sip of her wine and winked at him over the rim, then said with a throaty chuckle, "Don't take me there."

When he reached the door he flexed his knees and picked her up. As he stood, one arm went around his neck, and she moved her face against his to suck on his lower lip, pulling a little of it between her teeth, gnawing gently.

Alex carried her into the bedroom. There were small candles on the nightstands and the bed was turned back. Caitlin shifted in his arms, and he allowed her to swing her feet to the floor. She walked past the ice bucket on the nightstand, poured some wine into a glass, handed it to him, and then said, "You seem a little over dressed. Would you mind terribly if I worked on that?"

Alex couldn't take his eyes from the impact of the spectacular jewelry on her naked body. He pulled his tux jacket from his shoulders and folded it over a chair. "Now that seems like a wonderful idea!" he said, and turned to her.

Caitlin stood in front of him, her breasts drawing his attention. She was concentrating, the tiny tip of her tongue sticking from the corner of her mouth. She pulled his bow tie open and began to work the studs from his dress shirt. When she had his shirt open, she pushed his braces aside and pulled the shirt from his waist. Caitlin was startled for a moment at his muscularity, his definition more like a gymnast than a money manager, and she marveled at the various puckers and zippers on his skin and fantasized about their origin.

"I assume that these are merit badges earned on the way to becoming the baddest motherfucker in the whole world," she said, and stuck her tongue into a particularly nasty circular scar, high up on his left chest.

"More like zigging when I should have been zagging," he laughed.

Enjoying herself, she leaned over to his chest and licked one nipple, then the other before she leaned back to nibble the first one gently. She stood to work the shirt from his back, pressing one of her nipples and then the other to his lips. He licked each one, then sucked it gently, making no effort to lead her.

She stood up. "Why don't you do the rest of this while I go to do girl things? I'll be right back."

Alex quickly removed his shoes and socks, then stood and folded his trousers over the chair, careful to preserve the crease. T-shirt and boxer shorts followed, also carefully folded. He eased into the king-sized bed and pulled a soft percale sheet to his waist. Caitlin came back into the room and quickly slipped under the sheet. She pushed her hand into his hair and kissed him softly, then with more attention. Her tongue darted into his mouth and flirted with his, quickly becoming more searching and aggressive in his mouth and along the inside of his lips. "You're a good kisser, too," she said. He smiled at her and waited.

"I think I'll just be the aggressor tonight. Do you mind?" she murmured into his ear, reaching for him.

"Marvelous," he said. "I'm all yours."

As she kissed him again, her hand slowly slid down his stomach and under the sheet. He felt her hand close around him, exploring.

She snuggled against him, her hand more active now. He could feel her breath warm in his ear when she whispered, "Jesus, Alex! I didn't know you cared *this* much!"

"You can always get a rain check," he murmured to her.

"Oh, I don't *think* so," she breathed into his ear, with a tiny giggle. "Besides, I've always wanted a pony."

Alex felt her move and then the dewy whisper of her breath on his chest, moving down slowly, licking and teasing as her hand fondled him, stroking. Then the sheet moved away and he felt the first faint tickle of a tongue.

In the morning, Alex was out of bed early, found the spare bedroom and showered. There was a disposable razor and toothbrush in the medicine cabinet. He made coffee, found the San Francisco Chronicle and the Wall Street Journal on the front porch and was sitting, reading, at the breakfast counter in boxer shorts and a T-shirt, when Caitlin stumbled into the kitchen, rubbing her eyes, wearing only a long t-shirt. "I figured that was you rustling around out here. Christ, it's still dark. You fucking Marines have no civility."

He laughed. "The early bird gets the worm, and all of that. It's almost nine o'clock in New York. Still, you look good at this time of day."

"Thanks," Caitlin said. "You know, back at Princeton, you'd be known as the Head Master. How about a kinky encore?"

Alex smiled and said, "I'm almost afraid to ask what you mean by kinky, but I think I'm up for it."

Caitlin snuggled to his neck and reached for his thigh to run her finger nails to his crotch, then explored a little. She whispered in his ear, "Indeed you are."

Silicon Valley

ALEX was having lunch at the Stanford Park Hotel, while a man named Francisco Leon stood looking out the window of his office on the top floor of an office building in Menlo Park. His office was furnished expensively in chrome and black leather furniture over a thick, white, wool carpet. He was tall, nearly six feet, and slim. He wore tailored gray wool slacks and an Italian silk shirt with the top three buttons open. An elaborate crucifix hung in his thick, black chest hair. His long hair was slicked straight back, black and shiny.

Francisco was mildly amused and even a little smug as he looked over the offices below him, filled with software programmers, hardware engineers, marketers, executives, and thousands of minions laboring seventy or eighty hours a week to fulfill the American dream of riches and early retirement. Many of them had succeeded, and many more would follow. A large majority of the others made more than enough with the products of Francisco's company, Oro Distribution, to allow them to relax. Oro's products shared advantages with those of the software companies. Product costs were low, prices were high, and demand for both seemed insatiable. Distribution was the key to both enterprises.

In the case of Oro's products, the distribution was done by low-skilled entrepreneurs who had no office expenses, no overhead, no research and development costs, and no general and administrative expenses. A particularly skilled distributor could earn five or six hundred dollars per day, tax free. Francisco had several hundred of these distributors working in Silicon Valley.

This network was managed by loyal Colombians in six offices dispersed across the peninsula. These workers brought to Oro a daily profit—also tax free of course—of about fifty thousand dollars in cash, seven days a week. This income tended to rise, week after week, as consumers became incapable of controlling their desire. The steady influx of new clientele was a planned bonus.

Francisco was a bit bored with the business of cocaine distribution. Two years ago his father, who controlled the worldwide business from Colombia, had sent Francisco to the United States to take over the lucrative Silicon Valley franchise from his elder brother, Alfredo. In his youth, Francisco's family had been poor. When food had been scarce, Alfredo always got first choice, and a bit more of it. When life improved, both his Francisco and Alfredo were treated well, even if differently. Francisco's lesser role as the second son was clear, and traditional. Even now, Uncle Felipe, his father's younger brother had less. His father had an enormous villa and a large staff of bodyguards and servants; Felipe ran one of the distribution centers in Columbia with a nice living, but not much more. *I can raise my place,* Francisco vowed to himself. *I will make myself the favorite son, my way. With money for stealing gringo defense secrets, I can make Oro Distribution a world-wide player. The Yankees call it vertical integration, leveraging one product set to build a newer, more lucrative one. I'll just call it Fuck the Gringo.*

Francisco was given a free hand and a checkbook to set up his operation, and he was determined to outshine his brother in business. He brought with him from Columbia a group of subordinate managers who exercised strict and somewhat ruthless control of the distribution. They were under his supervision, and they fully protected him from any exposure to the law enforcement authorities. When one of his managers would get arrested, Francisco would pay all expenses for the best legal defense money could buy. Ordinarily, it would buy far better talent than the government's own over-worked and underpaid professionals. In the event that his man would get convicted and sent to an American prison, Francisco and his father would provide generously for the man's family in Columbia and ensure that the rather large community of Colombians ensconced in American prisons would welcome and protect the new arrival.

So far, only one of his Colombian associates had chosen to cooperate with the authorities. But he had suffered sudden and severe memory loss when pictures of the eldest of his four teenaged daughters were smuggled into his hands. One of the photos showed the girl being raped by one man while having her mouth sodomized by another, with a long line of men in clear focus waiting their turn, fondling themselves. Francisco had directed the photographer himself and was quite proud of the quality and sharpness of the image. He almost wished that he had pictures made when he had personally deflowered and then sodomized her, but his father had a strict rule against photos of the family ever being available.

Francisco turned to his senior manager, who was standing patiently in front of the desk. "What is the status of our pet project, Alberto?" he asked in Spanish.

"We hope to have a full set of plans and several of the special electrical boards within the month, *Jefe*," Alberto said.

Francisco exploded. "The month? Our customers are planning to be here in less than one week. I told you to have everything ready by next week."

Alberto flushed. "One of our consumers has resisted, and he is one of the key targets for this project. I cannot kill him or even beat him badly; his colleagues might alert the gringo authorities. He is too visible and too important. We have strengthened the product that we provide to him and have begun to mix what the gringos call crack into it. It is unbelievably addictive, according to our chemists back home. I am confident that he cannot hold out much longer."

"We are businessmen, Alberto. We are expected and paid to keep our word," Francisco said. "This is even more important when we are dealing with new customers who have no desire for our primary product and who have no more compunction than we do to use violence when frustrated. The Arabs and the Chinese are not weaklings like the Americans. Besides, the twenty-million-dollar payment they offer is more profit than we make in many months of selling directly to the consumer." Francisco paced back to the window, then turned and said, "Find someone to abuse. And make it messy on his mind, not on his body, to shock our weak Northern cousin. Make it ugly. It should be someone known to our recalcitrant consumer, perhaps precious to him. A little object lesson on what could happen to him, or those he holds dear, should move things along."

Alberto looked thoughtful, then said, "*Si, Jefe*. That is an excellent idea. It will be done."

"That will be all, Alberto," Francisco said.

As Alberto turned to leave, Francisco said, "I will be displeased if you fail me. Oh, and send that new girl into me. The young redhead. Tiffany?"

Alberto smiled and nodded. "*Si,* Tiffany. She has a smart mouth, but a big appetite for the product. I think she is a little strung out today, since she has no money for a purchase. She is quite beautiful."

Francisco looked into Alberto's eyes and said, "Later, she could be yours. Do not fail me. Do not fail me, Alberto."

Alberto looked directly at Francisco and said, "My life is your life, *Jefe*. I will not fail you."

Francisco sat at his desk and thought through the situation. His father had warned him against this venture, saying that the Americans would not tolerate that kind of interference in their national security affairs. Francisco smiled. He knew better than his father and his arrogant brother how weak the Americans had become, and how their stupid laws allowed him to operate with total impunity. If he were successful with this first venture, he thought he could get an extra fifty million dollars per year, pure profit, by selling gringo defense secrets to foreigners. He'd like to see his brother's face when he found out that Francisco had become the new favorite son with his father.

There was a knock at the door, and Francisco said, "Enter."

The door opened and the young girl named Tiffany came through. She was small, almost tiny, five feet or a little less, beautiful and young—perhaps nineteen. She wore a white polo shirt, and khaki shorts. Her hair was dark red, thick, straight, and parted in the middle. It fell to her shoulders on either side of her face, framing high, delicate cheekbones and the perfectly symmetrical lines of her jaw and chin. She wore too much eye makeup and bright red lipstick. Large, nearly green eyes were accented by a scattering of freckles on her cheeks and across her thin nose. Her legs were slightly tanned below the shorts that reached to mid-thigh. A tiny waist rose to a swelling, almost out of proportion bust line. The nipples on her breasts pushed out from the polo shirt, announcing that she neither needed nor wore a bra. She walked across the room, confident, and smiled at Francisco.

"You called?"

"Yes, my dear," Francisco smiled in return. "How have you been? I have seen so little of you. Is there anything you need? Is there anything I can do for you?"

Tiffany walked to the black leather couch and sprawled upon it. Her poise was slipping a little, as she wetted her lips with her tongue and wiped her nose discreetly. She was unable to maintain the pose, and began to move around on the couch irritably, licking her lips and clasping her hands randomly. Her nose began running again and she brought a tissue to it.

"I'm fine, Frank," she said. "But, you know, Alberto has been stingy with the coke recently. It's not that I need it, but I really like it, and Alberto hasn't had much to give me lately since I ran out of money. If you'll just trust me for the money for a few days, I'll get it to you."

Francisco smiled, leaned back and said, "I know, my dear, but there is a shortage of the product right now, and we don't have enough even for our paying customers. I think that I have the only supply in the area. It is wonderful stuff, but I'm afraid that I have only enough for me and for a woman who is coming in to be with me tonight. Alberto has told me that he would like to have something for you, but I am afraid that it is impossible, at least for the next several weeks. We both know that you don't really need this stuff, so why don't you just take a few weeks off and Alberto will call you when we get a new supply? It won't be longer than a month, I assure you."

Tiffany's face tried to conceal the panic that was welling up in her. "I suppose that would be okay," she said. "Listen, Frank. Tell me about the woman that you're meeting. Maybe I can help out with whatever you need."

Francisco shook his head ruefully, and said, "Tiffany, my dear. She is going to provide services to me of the type that you are much too young to understand. She is a call girl."

She looked down at the floor, then glanced up quickly, a look of determination on her face. "I've always found you to be very attractive, Frank. Maybe I could take her place just this once. I'm not a virgin, you know. I've been with a few guys."

"Tiffany, Tiffany," Frank sighed. "You are so young that you couldn't know much about men. Men have needs that young women don't know how to serve—basic needs. You don't want to know about these things."

"I know more than you think," she said.

Francisco stared at her for a second, then reached into his desk drawer and brought out a glassine package and dropped it on the desk top. "That is enough blow to last you for a month. Are you telling me that you would like to work for it? That you will do whatever I ask for as long as I wish?"

Tiffany stared for several moments at the fat package and whispered, "Yes."

Francisco smiled and said, "I'll give it a try, but only once. Stand up and take all of your clothes off, very slowly."

Tiffany hesitated, then stood and slowly pulled her polo shirt loose from her shorts and drew it above her head. Her breasts stood out against her narrow torso, the size of large cantaloupes with small and very pale aureoles and thick nipples standing out from them. She reached to unbutton her shorts and dropped them to the floor. She wore no underwear and the thatch of her pubis was a thick, dark red.

She stood nude and proud, and smiled at Francisco, her legs quivering only a little. "How am I doing?" she said.

He walked to her, stopping a few inches in front of her. Her reached up to one breast and fondled it, as if weighing it. He tilted up her head and looked into her eyes as he grasped the other breast. His fingers moved to each of her nipples and squeezed gently, then much harder. Her pride gave way to pain. She pushed his hands away.

"You have a great body. Biggest tits I've ever seen on a girl as small as you. But you're a long way from the coke, and I'm getting bored." Francisco walked over to the window, looking down. He smiled to himself. This was the part he enjoyed most about dealing with the arrogant Anglos; their pain, humiliation, domination, and ultimate submission. It added spice to an already enjoyable experience. He really should get a camera.

Tiffany panicked, oblivious of her nakedness. "What do you want? I'll do anything you want. Tell me what turns you on."

"Okay, Tiffany, I'm going to take it easy on you until you mess up. I am going to tell you exactly what to do, because you don't know shit. The first time you mess up and don't do exactly what I say—and do it with tender enthusiasm—I don't want to see you again, ever. Go get your coke elsewhere, clear? If you don't get it right, you are history."

Tiffany stood with her head bowed and hands clasped in front of her, her breasts pushing out between her arms. Her eyes filled and she whispered, "What do you want me to do?"

Francisco turned from the window and walked to the high leather chair. He sat on it and swiveled toward her, his legs pushing straight out and spread a little. His hips were slid forward to the edge of the seat. He put his hands behind his head and said, "First, get on your knees. Then crawl to me and put your head in my lap."

She slowly fell to her knees and began to move to him, her head still bowed. When she reached him, she put her head in his lap and was still.

Francisco savored the fantasy of Tiffany's father, maybe a little chubby with a bushy red mustache, an engineer, standing mute across the room and watching his little Anglo princess about to perform. He reached to her tousled hair and stroked it gently, smoothing it. He picked up her head and looked into her eyes and smiled. "This is a start, my innocent one."

"You know what to do," Francisco said.

She dropped her eyes to his fly and began to pull down on the zipper. She looked up at Francisco, who was watching her intently.

"Now, my dear, we will see if you have any creativity," he said. "Do the very best you can. Think of it as something on the path to the cocaine. Act as if you need me to be pleased, as much as you need the coke." Tiffany shuddered slightly, then looked back down. She pulled back a little and Francisco wrapped his fingers in her hair, twisting. "Never, never pull away," he said.

Closing her eyes, Tiffany lowered her mouth to him and began. After a short, active interval, Francisco pushed both hands into her hair and pulled her mouth onto him, forcing her mouth open and shoving himself into it, pumping, gagging her until his spasms began to erupt a few seconds later. Tiffany tried to put the humiliation out of her mind. She wanted to sink her teeth into him so that his spasms were those of pain. She tried to think only of the coolness of the snow in her nose. She wanted its sharpness, its ecstasy; what she felt instead was a foul, viscous mass that made her both retch and swallow.

"Swallow, bitch, swallow," he groaned. "And look at me!"

Tiffany looked up at Francisco as she tried to swallow.

"How did I do, Frank?" she asked, after a moment. "Do I get the coke?"

"That is what is known as a good start, Tiffany," he smiled. "You are still a long way from being done."

Francisco stood, removed his clothes and stood close, with his flaccid, sticky penis in front of her face. He reached down casually with his forefinger, scraped a hanging strand from her chin, wiped it inside her lower lip and said, "Get back to work, Tiffany."

Tiffany looked at him. Tears trickled slowly down her cheeks as she reached for him and leaned forward to begin again. When Francisco again felt capable, he pushed her from him and onto her hands and knees. He dropped to his knees behind her and positioned himself as he pushed her knees apart.

He pushed her head to the carpet. "You must watch me, Tiffany, always watch me."

She looked back and saw him stroking himself. He entered her with a lunge, and began to thrust rapidly. A few long moments later, he withdrew and shifted. Tiffany felt a sharp, strange push back there and recognized the imminent loss of her only remaining virginity; her final shred of dignity. There was a spontaneous moan, not from Francisco, but from with Tiffany. She pleaded.

"My dear, I would be pleased to stop if you'd like, but there will be no cocaine for you. Not tonight—not ever," Francisco said, as he pulled back from her. "Would you like me to stop?"

She could only say, "No." And it began.

She laid her head against the carpet and tried to relax through the pain as her forehead skidded back and forth on the rough carpet. Suddenly he groaned and pulled her hips back so that she was tightly welded against him and she could feel his spasms begin. He reached for her breasts and squeezed both of them, hard.

Tiffany screamed again, new pain obliterating the old. He released her then, and slowly pulled from her. Tiffany lay with her head against the carpet, still exposed to him as she heard him get up and walk to the powder room. She heard water running, then the sound of him urinating. A few moments later, he walked back to her and kicked her in the ribs.

"Get up, bitch, and get out of here," Francisco said, and threw her clothes onto her still raised hips.

He walked to the desk and threw the packet of cocaine at her, hitting her on the cheek. Tiffany got slowly to her feet and began to dress. She felt on fire, physically and emotionally. She was so sore that the thin cotton polo shirt hurt her bruised and swollen breasts. She pushed the cocaine into the pocket of her shorts and limped toward the door, her thighs sticky and clinging to her shorts.

"Get out! Get out before I give you to my soldiers." Francisco screamed.

San Jose, California

EL Tecolete is a small tavern, located in the worst section of San Jose. It caters to Latino laborers who work in produce and construction. There is just one large room, smoky, with a crude bar along one wall and several booths along another. There is no ladies' room. A few whiskey bottles stand ignored and dusty behind the bar, largely untouched, on shelves made of crude planks.

The open middle of the room was crowded with men, talking in small clusters, roughly dressed and still dirty from the day's work. Beer was the drink of the day, every day. The place was loud, with men jammed three-deep at the bar, yelling at the bartender for *cerveza*. Spanish was the only language heard.

Cuchulain sat alone in a small booth at the back of the crowded room, nursing a beer. Dried sweat matted his hair. A soiled blue bandanna was tied around his head. Sweat had dried on his cheekbones, highlighting the shadows beneath them in the dull, harsh light, and salt crystals set a pale path in the furrow of the scar on his face. Without the two-day growth of beard on his face, he would have looked more Native American than Hispanic. He wore a tattered denim shirt with two buttons missing at the top, exposing a thatch of matted chest hair and a primitive crucifix hanging from a thin gold chain. Shirtsleeves rolled halfway to the elbows exposed wide wrists above gnarled, calloused hands and an intricate, tangled pattern of veins tracking up from the wrists. Cooch wore jeans faded nearly white and torn just below the right knee. Scuffed, steel-toed work boots, one crossed over the other, stuck out beneath his booth.

Cuchulain earlier had walked onto a construction site in North San Jose and easily found work, loading bricks from a flat bed truck onto a wheelbarrow, then wheeling them a few hundred yards to masons who were laying a wall. No one had asked him for a social security number nor had him fill out employment forms. When he had been asked for his name, he had said, "Paco." One name was enough. The work was physically hard and tedious. On his breaks, Cooch joined casually in the talk of his fellow workers about soccer, women, and working in the US. Except for the union men working in masonry and electrician jobs, the workers all seemed to be Mexican, who picked up on his accent and chatted with Paco about life in Puerto Rico. No English was spoken. The burly foreman, Enrico, had paid him forty dollars in cash at the end of the day. As he was paid, the foreman had asked—almost ordered—him to come by for a drink after work, at El Tecolete, a few blocks from the site.

At the bar, conversation paused, then resumed, but at a lower pitch as men parted for the foreman. Enrico gazed around the room at the bar and the booths, nodding occasionally, then spotted Alex in the corner. The foreman was a big man, six feet or so, and wide. His stomach bulged over his beltline, but he moved with the easy grace of an athlete, balanced on his feet and carrying his weight well. Two men walked just behind him. One was short and very thin with a narrow mustache, slitted eyes and a knife scar running for several inches from his left eye down a cheek among pitted remains of either old acne or healed smallpox. The other man was very large. His eyebrows and cheekbones had the ragged, humped tissue of a boxer. The top of his head was lumpy and shiny—bald with a greasy half donut of black hair that wrapped his ears and fell to his shoulders in a long, tangled shower. His failed personal hygiene was evident by the collar of a once-white shirt.

"Ah, my friend, there you are!" Enrico boomed. Several men in the crowd looked at Alex, then leaned to whisper to their friends.

The foreman slid into the booth across from Alex, the thin man quietly beside him, hands beneath the table. The larger man thumped in beside Alex, crowding him. Alex turned his head and looked at him coldly, causing the big man to give him a wide smile, exposing one stained gold tooth in front along with the rest of his ragged, decaying teeth that were yellowed to the shade of late summer wheat. His rancid breath was no surprise.

The foreman smiled easily and leaned across the table to him. "So, *Chico*, how did you like the job today? Good money, easy work, and no taxes for the gringos, eh?"

Alex looked at him coldly. "It was hard work and bad money, but I like the no taxes and I need the job. It'll do until I find what I'm looking for."

The foreman's face darkened and the smile vanished. "Ah. Another pretty boy smart mouth who doesn't like to work! Maybe you want to work in the gringo men's store and be a fancy boy, eh? You can get all dressed up in fancy clothes and say 'Yes, Sar, No, Sar' before you go into the back room and let them line up to fuck your ass! Is that what you want? If it is, my associates and I would be glad to fuck your ass bloody, *cabron*!"

He shifted and leaned his bulk back, then smiled again, coldly. "I neglected to tell you that there is one small tax, *Amigo*. You owe me twenty dollars for first-day work processing. It's the paperwork, you know. Then five dollars a day for insurance, to keep you from getting hurt. It is not much, and you can give me the twenty dollars, now."

Alex rested his elbows on the table, and put his chin lightly on his folded hands. He turned slowly to look at the man beside him, then at the thin man across the table. Both looked at him expectantly, smiling coldly. The room grew quiet, with much of the crowd watching, nudging and whispering to each other. Cooch looked finally at the foreman, the flesh around his eyes bunching and his breathing audible in the room. The face of Alex's father flashed in his mind and his words of advice: *The most important rule is ARF, "Always Retaliate First."' Don't hesitate and wait for the bad guy to start the fight. End it before it starts, and err on the side of being too violent.*

"And if I don't?"

The foreman's face flushed, then he leaned forward and said softly, "If you don't, my associates here will …"

He stopped speaking abruptly, as Alex drove his left elbow back into the face of his seatmate, feeling the nose give way just before a cheekbone collapsed. He then drove his hand across to the thin man, the web between his thumb and forefingers driving into the larynx as his long fingers probed for the porous bone structure just behind the jaw and the ear. He squeezed hard and felt bones crackle and fold. The thin man's eyes widened from the pain as he gasped for air from the throat blow, then passed out.

Alex immediately drove the elbow back into the other cheekbone of his seatmate, breaking it as well, then clasped his hands and raised them in the air triumphantly. The three separate moves had taken less than five seconds.

"*Caramba*! One handed, yet! I will receive applause now," he announced loudly. Alex smiled a wide, evil smile to the crowd and nodded his head in half a bow. He could hear a few hands come together tentatively in a terrified parody of applause. "*Si, Si! Gracias, Amigos!*" Alex said loudly, nodding and smiling like a flamenco guitarist.

He resumed his icy stare at the foreman. "It was rude of me to interrupt you, *Senor*, but your fat friend had his hand on my thigh, and I am not a fancy boy. His little girlfriend over there seems to have had a knife. It's on the floor now." He leaned forward and whispered to the foreman, "You will find this hard to believe, I know, but there are people—strong people—who would have fear in their hearts for themselves and for their families if I thought they had called me a fancy boy."

Sweat beaded the foreman's face, and his mouth moved but no sound came out. Alex continued his cold stare, waiting. The room was still, the only sound gurgling and moaning from the burly man beside Alex trying to breathe through his pain, as viscous ribbons of blood fell and spread across his chest. The thin man's forehead still rested on the table. Finally, the foreman stammered, "There has been a mistake. I have made a terrible mistake. My apologies, *Senor*."

Alex shook his head sadly. "*Senor*, you have offended me. I come to you in peace to do honest work for honest pay with you as my leader, my benefactor, my *Jefe* even—and you betray my trust. You threaten me. You call me a fancy boy. In front of all my new friends here, you talk about doing things to my virgin ass that are clearly forbidden by the Church. Just as the Inquisition of our forefathers brought heretics to the faith, I know in my soul that it is my job to counsel you as to the path to salvation. I think I will have to introduce you to Lola, my fat friend."

Cuchulain put his right forearm on the table, palm up, and pulled his sleeve above the elbow. Among the distended veins of his forearm was an old, obviously amateur, tattoo of a Spanish dancer with a flowing multi-colored skirt. As Enrico looked down at it, Alex's left hand snaked out and with the large knuckles of his middle finger and forefinger grasped the skin of Enrico's upper lip, just below the center of his nose, and squeezed. When the foreman reached up to pull his hand away, Alex squeezed much harder, paralyzing him with the pain. He eased back and pulled the foreman's head down to look at the tattoo. The pain forced tears down Enrico's cheeks.

Alex opened his right hand on the table and said, "Put your left hand, palm up, into this hand and I will release your lip."

As foreman put his hand into Alex's, Alex closed his fingers around it, then released the foreman's nose. Many in the crowd crept forward. The foreman was not a favorite among them, and several had suffered beatings for one offense or another at his direction.

The foreman was becoming increasingly terrified, sure that he had met the devil. "What … What are you going to do?" he stammered, now afraid to resist. He had forgotten completely about his employees, lying bleeding in the booth with him.

"Lola is going to dance for you, and you are going to watch. You see, my fat friend, Lola is a magic tattoo. When you see her dance, you will ask forgiveness for all your sins, and then go and sin no more."

Alex grinned wildly, allowing his eyes to widen and dance, leering at the foreman. "Okay, *Jefe*, here we go! Watch Lola closely as she dances!" Alex started singing in a loud, off-key voice, "Whatever Lola wants, Lola gets …"

He sang and began to squeeze the foreman's hand. As the pain grew, the foreman grabbed for his left hand with his right, but Alex caught it in the air and slammed it hard, down onto the table, then held it there, increasing the pressure on Enrico's left hand. As he squeezed harder, his muscles flexed and moved, causing the tattoo to writhe almost like a cartoon on his arm. Lola's hips and slim feminine torso swayed as Alex manipulated his grip, the muscles rippling in his forearm.

The foreman let out a long, sustained howl of pain, head back and mouth open. The small bones in his hand could be heard snapping. Others gave way, as his hand gave up resistance. Enrico passed out with a sigh, slumping forward slightly, his chin on his chest.

Alex ignored him, continuing to squeeze and break for a few seconds, laughing merrily, and glaring wide-eyed and wildly at the silent crowd that had gathered closer. He pointed at the tattoo and shouted, "Look at her go! Isn't that fantastic?" He started again, loudly and off key. "Whatever Lola wants ..." then stopped suddenly, Enrico's hand mashed and pulpy in his grasp.

Alex pushed the hand away and turned to face the crowd. He held his right forearm high like a posing bodybuilder and made the tattoo dance once more, his huge forearm working the muscles in it. He forced himself to giggle. "Anyone want to dance?' he said in a high pitch as he leered at the crowd. Alex lowered his forearm and slowly turned to the flaccid, bloodied men in the booth beside him, raising his hands as if he just discovered them, looking up wide-eyed in a gruesome parody of surprise. The room was still. The bartender stood slack-jawed at the front of the crowd, holding a sawed-off pool cue limply at his side.

Alex turned and pushed the big man beside him hard, off the seat and to the floor, then bent over him to run his hands over his clothes. He then reached for the thin man, grabbed him by the hair and shirt and jerked him cruelly to the floor. This time Alex came up with a SigSauer 9mm pistol, which he showed to the crowd as he raised his eyebrows in mock surprise. He pulled the slide back, ejected the magazine and examined the weapon.

Apparently satisfied, he released the slide, reseated the clip with a snap and slipped the weapon under the waistband of his jeans and pulled his shirttail out to cover it. With his toe, he reached under the table, slid out a knife and kicked it toward the small man, shaking his head in mock sorrow. Finally, he reached for Enrico and pulled him out of the booth, stacking him on the other two and going through his clothes. He fished out a fat money clip and leafed through it. He stuck several hundred-dollar bills from the wad into his pocket. The remainder he tossed casually on the floor in front of the crowd, then turned to them. He was cold now, no longer gay and laughing. There was no resistance coming from any corner of the room.

"*Compadres*, I put before you payment as thanks for not talking to the police about Lola or me," he said, pointing to the money clip. He raised his right forearm and allowed the dancer to writhe for them again. "This will be the payment if you betray me to them, or to anyone else. Lola will be very unhappy. She could take your manhood."

Alex walked to the door. The silent crowd parted. Several men crossed themselves as he walked by. He walked through the door, then moved quickly to his right against the wall and waited. The crowd could be heard growing more animated, but no one came out. He moved briskly down the street for several blocks, then turned suddenly left, and ran down an alley. Midway, he waited several minutes, his back pressed to a shallow doorway, the SigSauer now in his hand with a round chambered and his thumb on the hammer, but no one entered the alley from either side. He thumbed the safety on, stuffed the pistol back in his waistband and trotted to the end of the alley, then turned right, walking calmly. In the next block he stopped in the shadow of a wall, and quickly dialed a public telephone.

"Mac."

Alex sighed. "It's done, Mac. I did the Lola gig like we planned. It was a little hairy, but not too bad. There were no heavies there. You're sure that the Paco legend is still clean?"

"It's in place, Alex. There are a lot of people around and about who

217

remember Lola and Paco, and you always just disappear. If someone asks in-depth, they'll hear stories that will curl their hair. Any collateral damage?"

"If no one has a heart attack, no one should die, but there's an opportunity for a talented orthopod and probably a face surgeon. Not that I care, but that's the way it worked it out. Listen, I'm clean now, but I hope I'll get some visitors tomorrow at work, if we dangled this right."

Mac said crisply, "Elliot is briefed and moving, and Epstein is full bore. Jerome is out there and has found a place. The warnings have been sent to Colombia about the dangers of this kind of operation. Stay on the East side of any obstacles at the construction site."

"Roger East. I'm gone," Alex said, and hung up, searching the area. There was no one on the street.

He walked back to his rooming house, and went up the stairs to his room.

San Jose

ALEX awoke before dawn, very hungry, and still feeling the adrenalin depletion. A gym would have been perfect, but Paco would never have used one. He eased into a yoga position, losing his thoughts to a little bit of everything and not very much of anything. Most of his troubles just seemed to float away if he didn't dwell on them, gently pushed out of his semi-consciousness. Finally, Alex rose and walked to the wall of the tawdry room and rolled himself into a handstand, heels supported against the wall. He relaxed again for a moment, focusing, then walked on his hands to the middle of the floor, legs together, toes pointing and arched gracefully over his back. He concentrated, then brought himself to his fingertips, rocking from side to side to provide ease and a moment of lift when he did not have the strength to push himself up directly. Once Alex had settled onto his fingertips, he was reinvigorated. It was relaxing. It felt good. His mind was again free to ruminate and consider options. The strain was gone, if only temporarily, and his inner life was good; no thoughts of sex or danger could wander into his little cyst of peace. He slowly bent his arms and lowered his body to the floor, still supporting himself on his fingertips, feet floating arched above his back, then he even more slowly pushed himself back up. He stopped. And then he did it again. He never counted the repetitions; that would have been cheating and useless. Rather, he felt his ability to relax into the exercise begin to diminish. Then he devolved into weakness. The progress, or progressive failure, of moving from tangential meditation to serious, traditional Western exercise evolved over a period of perhaps five minutes.

As the repetitions became more difficult, Alex found himself fading from the ability to react in a meditative sense to the strain. His mind became increasingly more focused on the increasing pain of doing the next repetition than on any pleasure in the sense of the world flowing around him. Finally Alex was entirely focused on performing the last repetition, until he collapsed in a sweating ball upon the stained carpet of his rented room. The smell of past cats and long spent passion offended him in his exhaustion, and destroyed the last possible vestige of who he thought he would like to be in a perfect life.

With a long sigh of luxuriant self-pity, Alex began to stretch. An aging instructor at the Farm had converted him to a stretching regimen, but not into the complete yoga routine that was being favored; that took four hours. A good stretching routine took Alex, who was quite limber, about an hour.

Finally, Alex stood and moved to the small sink. He grabbed an old white towel nearly translucent with age, wrapped it around his waist and headed down the hall to the communal bathroom. He remained concentrated on his "Paco" persona. He held a second towel balled in his hand, which concealed his toiletry items and the Sig-Sauer.

He walked onto the job site a little early. Enrico was not present. His co-workers parted as he walked by and averted their eyes, perhaps to avoid his curse. No one appeared ready to work, a possibility that Cuchulain had not anticipated.

"What am I supposed to do now?" Cuchulain thought. *"Tell them that Lola said they should work hard?"*

Just then, one of the older workers approached him hesitantly and asked, "Should we go to work?"

Alex decided that he had to respond to the man, and to seize the opportunity to expand the legend of Paco that he and Mac had developed over the years.

"*Compadres*, gather around," he shouted, standing on the raised fork of a tractor that was facing east.

The workers quickly gathered around him.

"I bring to you words of wisdom that you will not like, but you will hear the ring of truth in what I say. I am a simple man, very strong as you know, but not a worthy leader for you. My mind and body are not a force like the stream, flowing and finding its way. I am rather like the pestilence, lying dormant until disturbed. If not disturbed, I am the least of you and happy. If disturbed as I was last evening, as I sense many of you know, I become a different person. I know much of violence. I, in a sense, may be the Prince of Violence. When my mind fades under pressure, I become another person, a violent but not evil person."

"The foreman has not come to work today, because I hurt him badly, and his people as well. I did not plan to do that. I did not do it for you, but if one man like me can bring three of those vermin down without trouble, what can four of you do if you strike without warning? Yes! I struck without warning and humiliated the three of them! Where is it written that we must give them warning? They give us none, but rather come to our huts in the dead of night with more power than even the wives of your neighbors will allow to be challenged. Never, never, give them the battle ground! You are many and they are few. Yes, my friends, I am saying that you should deal violently with them before they deal violently with you. Your wives will counsel you to stay back for the sake of your family. Bah! So your daughters can suck the cocks of unwashed brutes? While your sons watch your *cojones* shrivel in the land of "it's just not worth it?" Ask yourself what I have that you do not. Do you want to know what my edge is? It is simple. No one lives forever, and I won't be humiliated in the meantime. If you try, I will strike without warning. Always without warning."

The crowd of construction workers roared in approval, waving their hands and calling, "*Bravo, bravo!*"

Alex held his hands up for silence. "No, no, my friends. Listen to me. It is at your great peril that you misunderstand me. I am a killer, not a god. I am not Pancho Villa, I am just Paco from San Juan. I am just one, strange, voice of reason. I do not suggest that you offend the legal authorities with your actions. I also do not suggest that you stand alone against the powers of the devil and his henchmen."

An older man, perhaps a grandfather, walked up and said to Alex, "What shall we do then?"

Alex spun and walked away from his stance, then slowly returned. "Father, I do not know."

The man stood for a second, and then said, "What would you do?"

Alex looked around at the workers and said loudly, "I do not have children. I have little to lose. A wise Anglo named Bacon once said that having wife and child gives hostages to fortune; it limits your choices as to how you may live. That said, each of you still must ask yourselves how you wish to live your life."

"The pain of death comes quickly. The pain of submission comes with time, exquisitely painfully. It becomes the hopeless pain of seeing your children suffer as a result of your weakness and cowardice."

"People fear me. They think that I am an agent of the devil. This is not true. No one can say that I have intentionally hurt an innocent person. True, God has given me strength, great strength, and I have used it. Some of you saw that last night. God has blessed me to do that. Each of you can be equally blessed by God, by using the brain that God gave you."

Alex gazed over the small crowd; they in turn looked raptly back. "Look, let's get this straight, because we have to get to work. I'm not going to last here too long, because the police are going to be looking for me. I have also have provoked trouble elsewhere. I ask you not to betray me to the police."

Alex raised his voice. "The law was originally designed to protect the community, the masses, so that we may do our work without worrying about the safety of our loved ones. Lately, the law hasn't done too well at protecting our community. We have protection people, we have bums, and we have misfits making things hard for us. Clearly, the gringo law is not going to protect us fully, but we must let them do the best they can and allow them very much room for error. Some of our brothers and sisters work for the police and are trying their best to make it work for all of us.

But, when one of you has to use his knife to deal as a matter of honor with these scumbags we face, you should close ranks when the police or the man's associates come to ask questions. He was fishing with you, he was playing cards with you, he was with your mother; get your stories right. Try not to be stupid; wash blood from your weapons with gasoline. Think about these things in advance, and plan, plan, plan. That, my friends, is what separates us from the monkeys. When I am gone, as I shall be soon, talk about this among you, and plan."

"Okay, let's go to work!" Alex said.

There was a murmur of cautious approval from the assembled men as they moved to their work stations, talking excitedly.

Menlo Park, California

A few miles away, in a second floor office in the Menlo Park office building of Oro Distribution, Alberto Diaz was completing his daily meeting with Jesus, his manager of the San Jose drug dealers. They were from the same village, Alberto a few years older. The cash receipts had checked out properly, and he had told Jesus where he could find his supply of product for the day, handing the keys for a rental car to him. The car was in long-term parking at the San Jose Airport, and the cocaine was in the trunk. The car had been rented by one of their gringo customers, whose payment was a generous free sample. As he stood to go, Jesus turned to Alberto.

"I suppose you heard about the wild man at El Tecolete last night, Alberto?" he said.

Alberto looked up from his notebook. "No. Something exciting?"

"You know that fat Mexican guy, Enrico Comperte? The foreman who runs the protection racket with the construction workers around San Jose? Well, he tried to shake down a new laborer in the bar last night and got his ass handed to him. He ended up with one of his hands crushed to a pulp. He's in the hospital, waiting for them to operate on his hand."

"Really?" Alberto said. "The guy stomp him or what? And where were his two bodyguards? He never goes anywhere without them, and I hear that the skinny one is the fastest thing with a knife that ever was. And he's supposed to be not bad with a gun, either."

Jesus chuckled. "They're in worse shape than Comperte! This guy smashed them up somehow, really bad, before he started on Comperte. The word is that this guy, a Puerto Rican from his accent, is a crazy man and stronger than is believable. There's all sorts of wild talk about a tattoo, and a woman named Lola. It's so hard to figure out that I left. It's none of our business."

Alberto thought for a second, then said. "Find this man, Jesus. Talk to him a little, and tell me what you think. Hint that you may want to hire him to sell our product for you, and let him know what it pays. I want to know more about him. Is he crazy? Is he stupid? Is he dangerous or just lucky? And send someone to get the details of this business at El Tecolete last night. I wish to know what happened."

Jesus looked at Alberto for a second, surprised. Then he shrugged and said, "*Sí*, Alberto. It shall be as you wish. I will do it today."

Later, at the construction site, the food truck had just pulled away after servicing the workers on their lunch break. Alex sat alone in the shade on the running board of a rusty, yellow dump truck on the East side of the construction site with two tacos and a quart of bottled water, eating.

A man walked around the end of the truck, looking around, then spotted him and approached. The man was of medium height, and thin, probably in his early thirties, wearing expensive black slacks and a blue silk shirt, open at the neck. His hair was greased and combed back, but well trimmed. He wore reflective sunglasses and walked with confidence.

Alex laid the greasy paper holding his tacos onto the running board and stood up, turning to face him. At six-three, he towered over the visitor.

"Please, please, continue with your lunch," Jesus said, stopping a few feet from Alex.

"I know you have only a few moments to eat, and I would not keep you from it. I have just come to chat. I have heard that you are a man of action, a decisive man, and I wish only to speak with you for a moment."

"What do you wish from a humble man like me, *Senor*?" Alex said, still standing and balanced in front of the man.

"First, let's sit," Jesus said with a smile, removing his sunglasses and slipping them into his shirt pocket.

"Please." Alex gestured to his right, waiting for the man to sit. He sat down next to him, close, then looked over at him. "You don't seem like the gringo police, Senor, but if they come around this truck looking for me, you will be the first to die."

Jesus laughed easily. "If they come around this truck, I may die of shock before you have a chance to kill me. I am a businessman from Colombia, spending just a few years here to better provide for my family back home."

"I recognize the accent," Alex commented. "What do you want of me?"

"I just want to get to know you a little," Jesus said. "You are much discussed around the barrio this morning, because of your activities last night. You are from Puerto Rico, no?"

Alex turned his head to face him. "I have been to Puerto Rico. I have been many places. I come to this place to live in peace, where no one knows me. I mean no offense, but I do not want to know you, and I do not want you to know me."

"It is okay, my friend," Jesus said. "Perhaps you would like a job that pays far more than this one? One better suited for your skills. I could help you with this. I have a friend in business here who might hire you."

Alex looked into his eyes coldly, and said, "And what would I do in this better job? What would I have to do and how much does it pay?"

Jesus looked back at him calmly. "It pays many hundreds of dollars per day, if you are good at it, and don't allow your customers to steal from you. It is not legal, of course, but also not hard work. My friend has a product that many desire, often above all else. You would provide it to them and make sure that you are paid the proper price."

Alex relaxed visibly and leaned back against the door of the truck. "Ah yes, the *coca*, the white powder of dreams. This is a good business. A very good business, and I could certainly use the money. Unfortunately, it brings one to the attention of the authorities, the police and gringo drug enforcers. I am tempted, but I cannot stand that kind of attention, just now, nor do you want what that attention would bring to you and your friend when they identified me. I came here to be invisible. It is important that I do so."

Jesus hesitated, and then stood, Alex coming smoothly up beside him, still close. "It was just a thought. I will leave you to your work and your invisibility," Jesus said. He had walked to the end of the truck when Alex spoke.

"*Senor*, I have spoken to you truthfully and treated you with respect. If you betray me to the police, I will come for you and cause you great pain. Your protectors will be as if they are smoke."

Jesus stared at the scruffy man looming by the truck door. He was tempted to tell this shabby peasant who he was threatening, but hesitated. There was no benefit in doing so, and he felt oddly chilled and threatened in the man's presence. He merely acknowledged the threat with a curt nod and walked quickly from the construction site to his car, willing himself not to look back.

Jerome Masterson pulled his eye away from the six power sniper scope and rolled his neck to loosen it. He was 247 yards from the dump truck, in a room located in a cheap rooming house. From several special cloth banners he had tied onto construction equipment early that morning, he happened to know that there was a three-knot wind, quartering from the West across the site. Knowing the exact range and the wind allowed him to be confident that he could put a bullet into an area about the size of a quarter every 1.5 seconds or so until his 30-round magazine was empty. The Heckler and Koch PSG-1 sniper rifle cost Uncle Sam about $11,000, but it was the best sniper rifle in the world. Jerome thought of himself as an insurance man, with a policy where body armor wouldn't prevent collection.

Menlo Park, California

SEVERAL hours later, Jesus was back before Alberto.

"He turned me down," Jesus said. "He said that he would like to have the money, but was afraid of how visible he would be to the authorities. It would be bad for us and bad for him if he is discovered, he said. I think he understands our business and has much experience of violence. Comperte is so terrified of him that I expect he will never again work in protection. He actually babbled when I questioned him about this man. He thinks that this peasant is the devil. I have never seen such a thing! And there is a woman named Lola of whom he is also terrified. I do not know who she is or where he met her."

Alberto smiled. "It probably doesn't matter. If we need her, we will find her."

Alberto turned in his chair and looked out the window, then turned back. "Is this peasant a man to fear, Jesus?"

Nodding, Jesus gathered his thoughts. "He is very big and is extraordinarily muscular, particularly in his upper body. He moves very well. I think that neither of us, nor even the two of us together, would last ten seconds in a fight with him. Still, that alone would not be a problem; there are many paths available to us. It's really that he has such an air of menace about him that it feels like you are sitting beside a hungry jaguar. This is a very dangerous man, Alberto. I sense that he knows much about weapons and death, like some of the specialists that we use from time to time. It is my advice that we do not bother him, or that we kill him now."

Alberto smiled and leaned back. "Jesus, such timidity does not become you. I would like to meet this man whom you think is so dangerous. Go to him and tell him that I would like to meet him, and offer him one hundred dollars to come to me this evening for a chat."

Jesus nodded and walked from the room.

The Offices of Oro Distribution

AS the streets of Menlo Park faded into the shadows of the low hills to the West, Jesus escorted Alex into Alberto's office. Two young men, each with a silenced 9mm Beretta in his hand, stood on either side of Alberto's desk, eyes fixed on Alex.

"That will be all, Jesus," Alberto said. Jesus turned to the door with a nod and walked out.

"Search him," Alberto directed. The two men walked to Alex, one standing back a little, in a combat crouch, his Beretta raised to Alex's face. The other motioned him to put his hands up, tucking his Beretta into the waistband behind his back. As Alex stood with his arms raised, the body-guard expertly patted him down for a weapon, finding nothing. Alex stood with his eyes fixed on those of Alberto, his face cold and impassive. When the body guards had moved back to their stations, Alex did not move, still staring coldly at Alberto.

"Please be seated, Senor," Alberto said. "I have heard much about you today, and am pleased to make your acquaintance. I am Alberto."

Alex continued to stare coldly at Alberto, then sat in the chair, clasping his hands lightly behind his neck, elbows forward and relaxed. "I am Paco. What it is you wish of me?"

"I am looking for a man of violence for a small job that pays very well. It seems that you are such a man," Alberto said.

"You are mistaken. I am but a humble peasant who does not wish to be disturbed. You are disturbing me, *Senor*," Paco said.

Alberto laughed, scornfully. "You say that when either of my associates here would shoot you through the heart at a nod of my head? Incredible!"

Alex turned his head to look at one, then the other of the bodyguards. "I think not," he shrugged.

As Alberto turned to one of the bodyguards, Alex dropped his hand down the back of his shirt neck, pulled a flat throwing knife from the sheath that was hanging there, and in one motion threw it at the second guard, hitting him squarely in the throat, then leaped from the chair at the first, just as he was bringing his Beretta up. He grabbed the hand raising the Beretta with one hand and with the other drove his extended, flattened knuckles into the guard's larynx, crushing it.

Alberto was half out of his chair when Alex sat down, holding the Beretta. With a languid, almost bored, motion, he waved Alberto back to his chair with the pistol, then unscrewed the silencer. After inspecting it and giving it a nod of approval, he dropped it into his shirt pocket. He pressed the magazine release on the side of the Beretta, and allowed the magazine to drop into his hand. He pulled back on the slide and caught the chambered round as it was ejected, then pushed it into the top of the magazine. He pulled back on the slide and allowed it to lock. He looked down into the chamber, then again released the slide and worked it back and forth on its rails several times. With a faint, cold smile Paco pointed the pistol at Alberto and pulled the trigger, causing a loud click as the hammer fell on an empty chamber. He pushed the magazine back up into the butt of the pistol until it engaged with an audible click, worked the slide again to chamber a round, and engaged the safety.

Still looking at Alberto, and shaking his head sadly, Alex said, "The weapons are dirty and the trigger pull is ragged and fouled. Watch the bodyguards of the American president sometime on the television. They never look at the president—only at the crowd where the danger lies. When these men looked at you they lost nearly a full second of reaction time."

The liquid sounds escaping from the dying guards were loud and demanded attention. Alberto forced himself not to look at them.

"I don't deal well with pressure, *Senor*. It makes me violent, but then again there are those that think that I am by nature a violent man. But now that I am feeling violent, it is also true that I have a great need for money to help me avoid further difficulties in my life. Tell me what is that you wish me to do, and how much you will pay me to do it. When I have had some time, a day perhaps, to find out who you are and whether I can trust you, I will give you my answer."

Alberto looked at him, slumped easily into the chair, relaxed. The noises had stopped as the bodyguards died, but the stench from their voided bowels and bladders was becoming oppressive.

"And how do I check *you* out, my violent friend?" Alberto said.

Alex leaned forward, pulling his right sleeve up to expose the tattoo. He flexed his forearm and caused her to dance for a second, and said. "She is Lola. I am called Paco. It should be enough." He gestured to the bodies on either side of the desk. "And, perhaps a small payment for the demonstration? Would a thousand dollars be too much? And you also owe me one hundred dollars for the meeting."

Alberto, comfortable again, laughed. "That seems a reasonable sum." He reached into his desk, noting the Beretta coming up and Paco's thumb releasing the safety. He slowly removed a stack of one hundred dollar bills, and counted eleven of them onto the desk. He replaced the stack in the drawer, then closed it, picked up the bills, and handed them to Alex.

Alberto folded his arms on the desk and began to speak. "We wish to cause great fear in one individual, such that he will convince his older brother to provide a service to us. The older brother is too important for us to convince directly and has so far refused to help us. Both of these men are consumers of our product, and have a need for it, but they need something more in the way of motivation. You are to provide that motivation. For this we will pay you ten thousand dollars."

Alex stood. "I do not wish to offend you, *Senor*. There are many who would do this task for the amount you offer, or less. But I have standard fees, if you will, and a certain reputation. I will kill a man for $50,000 if he is ordinary; not a politician or one with priority access to the machinery of government to pursue me. For an official or a law enforcement officer, my fee is $250,000. There is no sum for which I would kill a prominent national figure such as the gringo president, since escape from such a mission is unlikely. I prefer to kill, because there are no witnesses. But as I said, I need money. I will do this job for $50,000 if you choose. If you would like to find another, less expensive, person to do this, I will understand. It is business. But if you choose another, do not betray me to the authorities nor attempt to blame me for the task."

He walked across the room to the bodyguard with the knife handle protruding from his throat, stepped casually on his face and pulled the knife out. He wiped the blood from the knife on the shirt of the corpse and reached behind his head to replace it in its sheath. He walked to the door and turned. "Whoever trains your bodyguards should look for a throwing knife suspended below the collar in the back. It would make your life safer. But if you betray me, nothing will protect your life. Later, perhaps I will train some bodyguards for you. For a fee. I will come back here tomorrow after my work, unless I hear differently from you."

As he walked out of the building, he moved quickly into the shadows. Screwing the silencer back onto the Beretta, he waited, but no one came out. After a few minutes, he walked quickly down the street. Ten minutes later, he was at a pay phone in the shadows beside a 7-11.

"Mac."

"We got lucky. I think I just met the number two guy for the area; he matches the DEA description. He has an office in Menlo Park, in the same building the DEA gave us for the boss. I think his will be a lot easier to bug, so we should have a team on that ASAP. I'm going back there tomorrow. He wants me to scare someone for him with no marks, so I'll need a safe interrogation room. A basement somewhere would be good, a garage where I can stash a car without being seen would be better. Things are moving faster than we thought. And Mac …?"

"Yeah, Alex?"

"Any chance that you get someone else to do the scare routine? I really hate that shit, and it's getting worse. I had nightmares about it for a month the last time. I just hate those nightmares," Alex said.

"Yeah, I remember," Mac said, and then was silent for a second. "Sorry, Alex. I should have anticipated this and had someone out there, but I didn't. Like you said, things are moving pretty fast. I guess you're stuck with it this time. Last time, I promise—even if I have to do it myself."

"Ah shit, I guess the prize is worth the game. That's why we're risking all this anyhow. It wouldn't be good to bring in an outsider—just adds to the exposure," Alex said.

Mac sighed, and said, "I'm glad to see your paranoia is alive and well. We'll get on it. Anything else before I hand you over to the recorder?"

"They're going to check me out today. I gave them Paco and Lola. See if NSA can find out who they contact, and maybe we can catch an Interpol bad guy, too. Here comes the memory dump."

Alex talked steadily and quickly, describing in detail the building and the rooms, furniture, office equipment, computers, and staffing of the office where he had met with Alberto. He described Jesus and Alberto in detail, then abruptly hung up. Fifteen minutes later, he was brushing his teeth at the tiny sink in his room.

Washington, DC

MAC turned from the phone as the recorder stored Alex's details, and put his feet up on his desk, pondering. He hated that they were operating within the US; all sorts of political problems could arise from getting caught doing that. But letting the druggies mess successfully with national security could lead nowhere but nasty places. They had vast pools of cash and the powerful addiction of their consumers to enable a new business. Somehow they had to be convinced that they shouldn't be tugging on Superman's cape, as the old Chicago rock singer, Jim Croce maybe, used to sing about. Ten minutes later he picked up the phone and dialed.

"Office of the National Security Advisor," a woman answered.

"Shirley. It's MacMillan," he said. "I need thirty minutes with the boss, soon."

"Hold on a second," she said. After a few moments she returned to the phone and said, "Forty minutes. His office."

"Roger that," Mac said. He hung up the phone, pulled his file from the secure filing cabinet, and slammed the drawer, locking it. He picked up a pen and began to organize his thoughts on a yellow legal pad.

Thirty-five minutes later, Mac walked into the ornate office waiting room and plopped into a chair, nodding at the assistant, who smiled as she picked up her intercom phone and spoke into it. After a few moments the National Security Advisor, Cyrus Miller, opened the door and said with a grin, "Well, look what the cat drug in. Are we being invaded, or to what do I own the honor of a surprise personal visit? Come on in, Mac."

Miller was a big man, dressed in a suit that was getting a little baggy on him; the seventeen-hour days and no time to work out were taking their toll. He sat down in an upholstered chair in front of a small round table positioned to the side of his cluttered desk, as Mac eased himself into a similar chair facing him.

"What's on your mind, Mac?' Miller said.

"It's about that cocaine bunch chasing DARPA secrets out West that I'm working on," Mac said. "I think there's more to be done there than my little band can do; much more than we discussed earlier.

"Oh?" Miller said as he sat a little straighter. "How so?"

"We have the DARPA radar thing under control, I think. We're on the druggies and have figured out how they are doing things and identified the top of their organization. They'll probably go down tomorrow or the next day. We'll splash the leadership, foul their distribution operation, and cause the baddies back in Colombia some consternation as a result, but I think we're missing the chance to make a much bigger point with them and their clients about messing in our national security sandbox."

Mac leaned forward and said, "I think our objectives should be two-fold."

"First," he said, "What we really should do is throw a big wrench into any thoughts the Colombians and their ilk have of using their drug cash to enable a shortcut to the Middle East and its potential cocaine consumers, as well as making their European supply system bigger and better by leveraging the Muslim network. To me, if they make that work, it's not a stretch to see the druggies start to use their distribution network to start moving weapons of mass destruction around in North America in return for that Muslim help in getting into Europe and the Middle East with their drugs. It's a way for them to get a double win and a lot more money. At least so far, they can't see much risk to implementing that strategy, and the money would be good. It's time to cause them to have an attitude adjustment about their risk."

"Second," Mac said, "the Chinese and obvious others would love to replicate our military advantage without spending the vast R&D money that we've spent. They'd rather steal our stuff and work from there. We believe that many of China's top defense electronics scientists are in play for us, as a result of this druggie venture. We've identified six of the ten that got aboard that yacht in Puerto Vallarta as big names. Their CVs are in the briefing doc. There are also two flag officers that lead the electronics efforts within the Chinese defense system. These are not folks that they can afford to lose, so there are eleven bodyguards protecting twelve ranking Chinese. It looks to me like the Chinese see a big opportunity here, and see the risk to their players as acceptable—given the US wimpiness that we have given them reason to count on. As discussed, the yacht's owner and four of the Arabs on board are known Al-Qaeda supporters."

"Well, on the first topic, the business of leveraging an illicit distribution network," the National Security Advisor said. "We've certainly had conversations *ad nauseum* about the three prongs of weapons of mass destruction getting out of control, and it seems to me that your worries could entail at least two of the three, radiological and biological cargoes, being moved by the druggies. Chemical attacks involve a lot of weight, like blowing up a train or a refinery. Our job there may just be a matter of figuring out how to minimize damage after a chemical attack, broadly, and I have people worrying about that; we think it is just planning for the downwind scenario of something like a chlorine explosion. But, I'd love to see us send a credible message that would give everyone second thoughts about the risks of enabling the movement of the first two. What do you have in mind?"

"Well, hell, I want to kill all of the players stealing Defense secrets, for sure," Mac said. "That's what I do for Uncle, and avoid expensive trials as a result—and this is too good to pass up. It sure looks like a free lunch for us. But while I do that, we should want their assessment of risk in a caper like this to make the caper unattractive and consequently unacceptable. That's the key to this op. Let's try to make it just a business assessment for them; here's the risk and here's the potential reward. It's just business."

"Your blood lust is widely appreciated, Mac, and not a surprise," Miller said, chuckling. "As you say, the bigger part of this is the message we send, but if we can cripple the Chinese's defense brain trust for a while without negative geo-political impact, I just might kiss you. I assume that you also have a way for the homefolk in Colombia to think new thoughts about risk."

"Yeah, I do," Mac said, "And I'll show you the part to kiss when it's time, and when we have time to draw a crowd in Macy's window. But more about that later. First, let me summarize the macro-situation that the dumb-shit Colombian druggie in San Jose or wherever just served up, by maybe setting back the Chinese electronic warfare efforts for years. We can hit this ball out of the park. The Chinese and the others have no business off our West Coast in a yacht that is receiving allegedly stolen defense secrets. We're not supposed to know they are there, so they'll have trouble with any public accusations, but they'll know it was us, of course. They've obviously decided that the potential reward of gaining our secrets justifies their risk in sending their big brains abroad. That is the key bet. The Chinese would lose too much face in defending why their men were there if there were no proof that they were. I think that they would just suck it up, and reassess this objective with that long view they have. With a little luck, they'll also execute the mission planner and his crowd, if this works for us. The Arabs are just looking for another way to stick it to us. Killing some of the major Saudi sponsors of terrorism is a wonderful bonus."

"I'll need more access to DOD assets than we discussed earlier," Mac continued. He pushed the op file across the table to Miller and said with a worried frown of his face, "The Man gave me a problem to solve, and I think we'll solve it quickly. Expansion of this mission to a violent global *riposte* is not the kind of thing that I can easily talk to the Man about. That's well beyond my pay grade."

"I'll talk to the Man if it comes to that, and it well may," Miller said. "Tell me what you have in mind. I'm liking this already. I keep forgetting what a devious sumbitch you are."

Silicon Valley

THE following evening, Alex became Paco once more and returned to Menlo Park to meet with Alberto. He was searched before entering Alberto's office, the bodyguards rough and hostile. They took the ceramic knife from its sheath behind his neck, then allowed him to enter.

Albert rose from his desk and offered his hand. "Paco, *Amigo*. Be seated."

Alex sat in the same chair as the night before, but no bodyguards were present. He relaxed into the chair, crossing his right boot to rest on his left knee, his hands resting comfortably on his knee, a short reach from the handle of the throwing knife resting in its boot sheath. He watched Alberto without expression.

"So, *Amigo*, Interpol says that you are perhaps a dangerous man," Alberto said, looking at a single sheet of thermal paper, still curved a little a little after rolling from a facsimile machine. "Contract assassin, no photo, no political ties known. 6'2 to 6'4, 100 to 110 kilos. Tattoo right forearm, female dancer with name Lola inscribed beneath. Expert in small arms, martial arts. Rumored to have extraordinary physical strength. Said to favor throwing knife and explosives. Believed born in Puerto Rico, 1964 to 1970. Believed to have worked for the Syrian, Iraqi, Libyan, French, and Thai governments. Rumored to have done extensive private work as well. No warrants. Detain for questioning."

Alex looked steadily at him. "I have read it. I also killed the man who gave them the description—slowly."

Alberto smiled and said, "You have a contract, Senor. We have a bit of time pressure, so when can you begin?"

"I can begin when you give me the information I need, and twenty-five thousand dollars in clean cash. I will collect the remainder when I have completed the job."

Alberto reached into his desk and pulled a sealed, thick white envelope from it. He handed it to Alex who leaned up and stuffed it into the hip pocket of his faded jeans. Alberto reached for another single sheet of paper, with several photos attached. "This is your target, with his girlfriend. His home address, work address, automobile information, phone numbers, places frequented, and all of that are on the sheet," he said, looking down at it. "He is expected to be in the bar noted at eleven o'clock tonight to meet with our distributor to make a purchase. I am led to be confident that he will be there. Any questions?"

Alex shrugged. "This girl, she is a customer?"

"She led us to him and to his brother. We rewarded her, as is our custom, with several free samples of our product for this referral. She claims that he is madly in love with her. Why?" Alberto said.

Alex shrugged again. "Leverage. Exactly what do you want me to have this man say to his brother, and should I give him any other help with the message? A broken finger perhaps, or a broken nose?"

Alberto smiled. "Nothing that would be visible, please, but you may be creative if you wish. No marks. The state of mind that your foreman, Comperte, exhibited after your encounter would probably be useful, but use your judgment. If he doesn't perform, you don't get paid. Do you speak English?"

Alex looked coldly at him as he stood. "Of course. I will return for my money when I have finished. I may be gone for as much as thirty-six hours. It is more difficult to achieve the mental state you want me to achieve without demonstrating the pain of failure."

This time it was Alberto who shrugged. "Use the girl. We have no further need of her. As I mentioned, we are under time pressure. Move as quickly as possible," Alberto said, not rising.

Alex nodded as he walked out, holding his hand out to the guard for his knife. Slipping it into the sheath behind his neck, he walked to the elevator. He walked back to the rooming house, threw his few possessions into the worn gym bag, and left the building, stopping to tell his landlady that he was leaving. Earlier, Alex had broken the firing pin of the Sig-Sauer and tossed it into a storm sewer.

After several Big Macs, a large order of fries, and two large cokes for dinner, Alex shaved and rinsed his hair in the Men's room of a McDonald's. He changed into a pair of worn blue twill pants, and a blue cotton shirt, clean, but wrinkled from being in his the bag. He brushed the mud from his work shoes, and ignored the stares of the other patrons. Outside, he boarded a bus that advertised "San Jose via Camino Real," and walked to the back. He sat on the outside corner of the back bench seat, watching the traffic go by, on the alert for anyone who seemed too curious about the passengers on the bus. After ten minutes and several stops, no one had so much as looked up from a passing car, and he was the only passenger left. As the bus entered the northern border of Palo Alto, Alex pulled the call cord and got off at the next stop. He slowly walked a few blocks in the darkness to a mall. He walked around the mall for awhile, checking the patrons, and then selected a pay phone in a nearly deserted passage leading to the rest rooms. He dialed the number.

"Mac."

"I'm out for now. I'm going to the hotel. I'll scan what he gave me and send it to you. I'm hired. Unless you tell me different, I'll start tonight," Alex said.

"Good," Mac said. "We're making progress. Epstein got Alberto's office wired last night, and we're getting good information on their operation. There's nothing about our little problem, but I think that they have that compartmentalized to Alberto and his boss, Francisco Peron. We're getting a few cryptic remarks among them that imply we're on the right track. It's all encrypted now and ready for you to pick up. I'm getting optimistic. You need to meet with the DEA guy sometime soon, though. They can't figure out who we are, and how we got enough pull to take over their playpen, even for a week or two. They're pushing the national security advisor pretty hard."

Alex thought for a second. "Where's the DEA jock?"

"The head guy for the area is in an office building up by the airport, but you don't want to go there. He's happy to come to you. We checked him out, and he's okay. He's one of their stars. Ex-Marine, too."

"Okay, I'll meet him outside the bookstore at Stanford tomorrow morning at eight. No recorder. Have him reading a copy of the latest Foreign Affairs and wearing a Stanford Business School sweatshirt over a blue cotton dress shirt. I'll be in green Nike warm-ups over a white T-shirt and wearing a 49ers logo baseball hat. He's Izzy and I'm Cameron."

"Done. Anything else?" Mac said.

"I'll let you know after I go through the files and the transcripts. Make sure the cleaned-up originals of voice from the surveillance are appended to the file."

"They're there. Talk to you later," Mac said, hanging up.

Alex walked quickly to the Stanford Court Hotel, then entered the lobby behind a small tour group. He walked up the stairs to the second floor and turned right, reaching into his pocket for the key that he had been hidden earlier in a compartment in the bottom of his gym bag. He hung the *Do Not Disturb* sign on the door handle, then walked to the closet and picked up his suitcase. Sitting it on the bed, Alex checked each lock carefully for signs of tampering, but found nothing. He spun the combination dial on each, twice. He heard a comforting beep as the locks popped open from their special security niche. He pulled his NEC laptop PC from the bag and walked to the desk, connecting one end of a cable to the port for the modem on the PC and the other to the data port on the hotel wall. Sitting down, he accessed an internet site from the PC that gave him a high-speed link into the computer in Washington. After entering his encryption code, he initiated the download from that computer to his laptop, then walked to the shower. The download was complete by the time he walked back into the bedroom ten minutes later. He read through it quickly, then again, more slowly. Cuchulain sat for several minutes, thinking. He then brought the voice segment of the file back to memory, and listened to the conversations in Colombian-accented Spanish played through the tinny speakers on the PC. He selected several to listen through a second time, then set a program to begin writing repeatedly over the record with a random combination of characters that would make it nearly impossible for anyone to recreate the files.

Alex walked to his bag, selected a number of items, and stuck them into the now emptied gym bag. He put on a pair of clean boxer shorts, then slipped back into the narrow, flat nylon harness that wrapped around his shoulders to hold his knife. He walked to the bathroom with a small black leather bag from the case. He stood in front of the mirror, extending a chrome arm from the wall and fastened his hair with hair pins. He then picked up a small jar, unscrewed the shiny black cap, and began to apply makeup to his face. When he had finished with the various jars and pencils, his face was gray and lined. Two small scars stood faded and pink, one over the left eye and the other running in a semicircle from his left ear to his jawbone. The bullet furrow beneath his right cheekbone had vanished in favor of a large, unsightly mole with a long black hair. Alex next dipped a small brush into another jar and then pulled it through his hair. In a matter of minutes, his hair was a dull gray, with random strands of black dispersed throughout; the battle against age clearly had been lost.

Satisfied, took a pair of black cotton trousers and a faded, dark gray cotton dress shirt with a button-down collar from his bag. He put on a pair of black, ribbed socks and nicely shined, but worn, black wingtip shoes. A digital watch completed the picture. After locking the bag and returning it to the closet, he tied a loose knot in a faded striped tie to complete the image he wanted. Finally, Alex picked up his small bag and left the room, checking that the sign was in place. He double locked the door with his room key.

He concentrated on his walk, slowing, as he gingerly stepped down the stairs to exit the hotel. His shoulders were a little stooped, and he looked around at his surroundings hesitantly as he walked into the restaurant, then turned confusedly and walked out its door. Cuchulain had an image of who he was and was working to ingrain it in his behavior. Increasingly, he found these character changes enervating. He handed his parking ticket with a dollar bill to the attendant beside the hotel.

After several minutes, the huge Lincoln Town Car from Hertz slid to a stop in front of him. The young attendant jumped from the car, holding the driver's side door for him to enter.

"Yes, thank you. You're very kind," Alex said, as he lowered himself into the car and slowly adjusted the seat. He put the car in gear and drove slowly away.

The parking attendant grabbed another ticket from a restaurant patron, and dashed for the car. He hoped for a better tip this time.

Alex drove through the lot of the night club, looking for the license plate of his target, or his target's girlfriend. When he spotted it, there were no parking slots nearby. He drove around the lot, finally finding a spot where he could watch his target's car while he sat. Because it was early, he walked slowly to the club and in the front door, as if looking for a public phone. A young, stylishly dressed hostess wearing a short shirt and a tight, nearly sheer, white silk top walked up to him.

"Welcome!" she trilled. "Like, you know, we're rilly full right now, but if you wanna wait, we'll find a place for you. It might, like, be a while, ya know?"

Alex looked around uncertainly. "I think that I should perhaps just use the men's room and then move on to a place that is a little less busy. I can't stand for a long while anymore."

"Yeah, I know," she said. "My granddad has like the same problem, Nice seeing you though."

"Yes, quite," Alex said, as he moved slowly toward the rest rooms, spotting a phone near the men's room door.

He stood by the phone, puzzled and frail, as several patrons bumped by him to rid themselves of the remnants of cheap chardonnay. Finally, he picked it up and dialed.

"Mac."

"I listened to the voice tape twice. I think they're going to use a boat, like you guessed. That's the only way that they can get the heavy weapons scientists from both countries here on the sly. They'll have to have computers to check the plans and chips, without going through customs and raising some flags. Get the names and alert customs anyhow, but I don't think they'll take the chance. The file shows a Bertram 48 named Snow White, and the head guy joked in one of the recordings about using a gringo fairy tale to finish shoving it up our ass. We gotta bet they will use it. I need Elliot here yesterday! And tell him to bring that titanium zinger that I designed, and some more goodies. We might be able to do some serious Fourth of July here!"

"Boy, you sure do move fast, but I hear you. This ain't a business for the faint of heart. All that you want and more, Sweetheart, will be on its way to arrive before the dawn. It's gonna take one of Uncle's expensive airplanes to get it there, but what the hell. We're probably toast if this doesn't work anyhow, maybe even literally," Mac said. "I'll have the Navy look around for a yacht that looks fishy."

Alex snorted quietly. "Yeah, yeah. I love you too, Sweetheart. Duty calls."

He hung up and moved hesitantly toward the door, walking down the steps gingerly and making his way to his car. A few minutes later a slot opened up beside his target's car. Alex started the Lincoln and moved quickly into it, then settled back to wait.

He put a jazz station on the radio and waited, thinking at one point that Earl Klugh's Finger-painting performance was the perfect way to pass a quiet evening, but not with the speakers that came in a Lincoln. Thirty minutes— or maybe forty—passed before he saw his target, the girlfriend, and a large, dark-skinned man come out and walk through the first row of cars. There was a huddle, a fast moving of hands, and then the group separated. His target and the girlfriend moved toward the car, heads together and laughing.

Alex opened his trunk, and looked inside. As his target moved to his car, Alex said, "Excuse me, young fellow, but could you give me a hand here?"

As he moved toward Alex, he said, "Jesus Christ, Granddad. Can't you old farts figure out anything?" His girlfriend giggled, and said. "Fuck 'im. We gotta blow, baby." She doubled over laughing at her double entendre.

Alex grabbed his target's neck as he came around the trunk, and pressed his fingertips into the carotid artery, shutting off the blood flow to the brain. A moment's struggle, and then the young man faded into unconsciousness, slumping to the ground. Glancing around the lot, and then at the young lady already sitting in the seat fixing her face in the visor mirror, Cuchulain dumped the young man unceremoniously into the trunk and then said timorously, "Excuse me young lady, but your friend appears to have fallen into my trunk."

"Jeeesus Christ!" She jumped from the seat and came around the car. Seeing her boyfriend slumped inside the trunk, she hurried over to look, an expression of faint concern on her face. As she approached the Lincoln, Alex reached up to her neck and repeated his earlier action. When she dropped, he picked her up and loaded her on top of her boyfriend. He reached into the corner of the trunk and pulled out his small bag. He took a small vial of clear liquid and a single hypodermic syringe from it. After scanning the lot, he held the vial up, tapped it several times with his fingernail and then inserted the syringe needle into it. He pulled several ccs of the clear fluid into the syringe and then injected each of his captives. He pushed the trunk lid down until the self-closer engaged, then walked slowly to the open driver's door. Alex drove off.

He guided the Town Car down the ramp beneath the nearly finished apartment building. There was a small concrete building at the end of the parking pad. It was obviously designed to be a maintenance shack, but was unused so far, for lack of tenants. Alex parked the Lincoln and got out to check the building. The door was unlocked, and the light went on when he flipped the switch beside the door. Taped beside the door was a key. Alex tried it, then looked around the room. There were two sturdy wicker chairs bolted to the floor, and four steel eye bolts protruding from fresh concrete, each pair about twenty-four inches apart and thirty-six inches from the other set. An odd assortment of items sat on a table in the middle of the room: several rolls of duct tape, a tiny and modern piezo-lit blow torch, a wooden block holding a bunch of "never sharpen" knives, several pair of handcuffs, a small Maglite flashlight, several oranges and apples, a fresh can of tennis balls, a small chamber pot, a box of tissues, and a box of rubber surgical gloves. An electric soldering iron sat alone on the floor by an outlet, unplugged, with a bright orange extension cord coiled beside it.

Cuchulain walked quickly out the door and opened the trunk of the Lincoln. He grasped the man by one arm and pulled him out of the trunk, draping him over his shoulder. Inside, he dumped him onto the floor. Turning, he walked outside again and got the woman. He then pulled the door of the room closed, checking to see that no light escaped, and got into the car, driving it deep into the corner of the covered parking lot. Alex got out and checked around the deserted lot, then walked briskly back to the small room. He walked to the table, pulled on a pair of the rubber gloves, and picked up the largest of the knives. He then turned to one chair and cut a ragged hole in the middle of its seat, trimming the sharp ends. He grabbed the man by the hair and belt, lifted his inert body onto the chair, then bent over and removed his shoes and socks. He threw them into one corner among the construction debris. Quickly, he tore off his shirt and trousers and roughly pulled the jockey shorts from him. He picked up the flashlight and moved it over the arms and legs of his target, looking for the telltale track marks of heroin addiction. There were none. Alex positioned the man onto the chair, then put his forearms along the arms of the chair and taped them down at the wrist with several wraps of duct tape. He bent the legs at the knee, brought the calves to the chair legs and taped them at the ankle.

He moved quickly to the woman and tore her clothes off as well, binding her to another chair in a similar fashion. His inspection for track marks revealed a long line of punctures on the veins running down the inside of her thighs, along with several on the veins of her feet.

Alex took a cotton balaclava from his bag and pulled it over his head, positioning the eye, nose, and mouth holes for comfort. Walking to the corner, he slumped down and waited, thinking about the problem he faced. His stomach was sour, as he reviewed the nauseating task in front of him. It was one thing to learn it in a classroom; it was another to actually implement it. Alex had taught it. He looked at his watch; it was nearly midnight.

Within ten minutes, the young man stirred. Alex pushed himself up from his slumped position and studied him, alert for signs of awareness. The young man was of medium height and slim, almost skinny. He looked to be in his early thirties, but was probably younger. There were small dark bags beneath his eyes, accented by a sallow, unhealthy complexion. He had long, tousled blonde hair and an attractive, almost effeminate face. His chest was flabby, the pectorals hanging slightly down and compressing his tiny nipples to a frown. A roll of flesh sagged around his stomach, his penis and testicles out of sight, hanging out of sight below the hole Alex had cut into the seat of the chair.

He turned to look for the first time at the woman. She was slim, with surprisingly good muscle tone. Her auburn hair was stylishly cut and her makeup applied with careless excess. She had small, perfectly formed breasts, marred only be what appeared to be a love bite above the nipple of one. A small waist swelled into substantial hips, with long tanned legs. She had no tan lines. At one time she had probably been beautiful.

The young man opened his eyes, dazed, and looked around the small room. He tried to move, found his bindings, and then sensed his nakedness. Fear began to blossom in his eyes when he saw Alex in the balaclava. He struggled futilely against the tape. Alex stood and walked over, gathering himself. "So, *Gringo*, you are awake. Did you have a nice rest?"

Wide eyed, the young man began to scream. "Help me, somebody help me!"

The young lady stirred and opened her eyes, still groggy. She looked around the small room, and then at the piled assortment on the table. She lifted her eyes and saw Alex looming above her, his balaclava making him seem ominous and impersonal. She also began to scream.

Alex walked back to his corner and sat down, waiting and looking at them in turn. When they began to become hoarse, he stood again and walked to them. They quieted and watched him apprehensively. He walked to the woman and fondled her breast, tracing the love bite.

"Let her alone, you filthy pig!" the young man screamed.

Alex turned to him as if surprised. "Yes, of course. I was just curious. I have no interest in young women—or any women for that matter," he said with a strong Hispanic accent.

He walked slowly to the young man and tucked a finger under his chin, tickling it. "But I like boys. And what is your name, my pretty one?"

"His name is Brian, and mine is Kelly. What do you want?" the girl asked in a quavering voice.

Alex could see Brian's face go slack with fear and apprehension. His mouth worked, but no sound emerged.

Alex reached under the man's armpits and probed, then squeezed one tendon over another abruptly. The young man threw his head backed in pain, and screamed repeatedly, while his girlfriend watched, slack-jawed. Alex walked back to his corner and sat down, waiting. After several minutes, the screaming slowed, then fell to a whimper, as the tendons finally slid back into place. Sweat poured from Brian's face onto his chest, and his eyes were wide with fear.

"You have both been given to me as playthings by my leaders. They would like you to provide a service for them." He looked at Brian. "They want you to convince your brother that he should cooperate with them— and quickly. I understand that they have had a disagreement about this matter. I am to convince you to go to your brother and persuade him to cooperate. If you do, you are to be released with a generous amount of the coca as a reward. I will be given a small payment."

"Good luck! I wouldn't piss on you if you were on fire," the young man snarled.

Alex allowed his voice to light up. "Good, good! If you don't do what they want, or if you fail, you two belong to me for as long as you last!" He giggled in a high-pitched voice. "I had the last two for almost three weeks before they died. I had such a wonderful time! It was selfish of them to die; I think perhaps that I should have sold the girl instead. It was probably the blood loss that killed them, but I think I know how to keep that from happening this time. You two will be with me for a month, perhaps even two!"

Alex undressed quickly, nude except for his balaclava, putting his clothes in the corner. He turned and walked between the captives. Their eyes went to his massive, muscled upper body, and then fell to his groin. He did some bodybuilding poses for them and then fondled his penis, whirling it like a limp rope in front of them. He giggled in a high-pitched voice. "I am beautiful, eh, my sweet? All the boys love me!" he said to Brian. "I think you will see and feel much of my body before we are done. Maybe you would like a little love with me now?"

"Fuck you!" Brian shouted, his face chalk white and showing his terror.

"Ah no, my little *paloma*, fuck you! Over and over and over again!" Alex waved his penis in front of Brian's face, then danced a little step, turning to the girl.

"He is not cooperating!" Alex said to her. "You must talk to him. You must convince him that my love for him is pure! I must have him. I think he is a virgin. I love virgins."

She looked at him, eyes wide. "How would I do that?"

Alex grabbed the roll of duct tape and threw it furiously against the wall. "Does he love you?" he demanded.

She was silent, nodding.

"Perhaps if I were to use you as a boy? It would not be so much fun for me, but I could close my eyes and pretend. It would take a very long time for me to be satisfied with you, and you would feel some pain, but only for a short time. He is so beautiful." Alex sulked a little. "I want him to want me."

"God, Brian! Do something! Do whatever he wants!" she wailed.

"Wait, wait!" Alex said. "I will show you a wonderful trick.' He walked to the table and picked up the can of tennis balls and opened it, the vacuum releasing with a hiss. He turned to them with one tennis ball in each hand. "Watch!" Cuchulain said, as he bounced the tennis balls lightly in his hands. "Think of us as lovers, Brian. Our very first time, but you are too much like a man and not enough like a boy. It interferes with my happiness, so I reach down to fondle your manhood and *pop!*" Alex squeezed both tennis balls sharply and they exploded with a loud noise, showering Brian with yellow rubber shards.

Alex gave a loud, high-pitched giggle and began to dance around the room. He snatched the oranges from the table, and exploded them over Kelly's nude body with a squeeze, then grabbed the apples and did the same to Brian.

"Squeeze, squeeze, pop, pop!" Alex giggled as he danced. "You're on the bottom and I'm on top."

"Jesus!" Brian whispered, finding the man's insanity to be numbingly terrifying.

"So, can we have a little love together now, my sweet?" Alex cooed. "You will be very happy after the pain has gone."

"Look, if I can get my brother to do what you want, will you let us go?" Brian said quickly, consumed in a panic.

Alex stamped his foot. "It is not fair! You should want me *now*, and *then* do what my leaders want! I must have you. I must have you now!"

Kelly cried out, suddenly hopeful. "You said that your bosses told you to get Brian to have his brother do something for them, to cooperate with them. If he's able to do that, you have to let us go!"

Alex slumped his shoulders a little and whined, "I don't see why you can't do what I want *and* what my leaders want as well."

Brian's face brightened with hope. "I can do it! I can get my brother to cooperate with your leaders! Just give me a chance. Oh, Jesus, just give me a chance."

"This gives me such great sadness, my sweet. You are making a mistake. We could have been so happy together, at least for a while," Alex said as he walked to the corner, picked up his clothes, and dressed. He then walked to the table and picked a boning knife from the block. He sat down in front of Brian, and then reached under the chair and grasped Brian's penis and testicles in his hand, pulling them down a little and holding the boning knife up with the other. "Perhaps it would be better for you without these, or maybe I should just give them a nice squeeze, like the apples, just to remind you that I still have Kelly?"

"No!" Brian screamed.

Alex stood again and looked at Brian. "I will release you, but I will keep the woman. If you go to the police, if you betray me, all of my friends and I will use this woman badly before I kill her, and then we will find you, I promise. My leaders will be very unhappy, and you have perhaps heard that we Colombians will follow someone to the ends of the earth to avenge a betrayal. I will be the avenger of that betrayal, if it takes a week, a month, or a year to find you. You will suffer. I will take your manhood and make you my woman. Then when I tire of you, I will kill you slowly."

"You won't touch her if I get my brother to help you?" Brian asked desperately.

With a sigh, Alex said softly. "It is not permitted. My leaders are businessmen and men of their word. Unfortunately, it is not my decision."

Alex turned and walked to his bag and brought out a cellular telephone and a piece of paper and said, "I will release you now to dress yourself. When you are dressed, I will blindfold you and take you back to your car at the bar where I first met you, and you will be released. You will contact your brother, and within twelve hours you will contact me on my telephone, using this number, advising me of your success. You will call only at five minutes before the hour until five minutes after, so the authorities cannot find my location and interfere with the beginnings of my revenge on you, if you fail me." He held the piece of paper in the air, then put it into Brian's trouser pocket. He picked up the boning knife and cut the duct tape holding Brian to the chair, and waited while Brian dressed, frantically.

"Please Brian, if you love me, don't fuck this up!" Kelly wailed.

Early morning traffic was light, as Alex drove back to the deserted bar. He loaded Brian, still blindfolded, into the driver's side of their car, then said, "Do not move for five minutes to look at me or my car. It is stolen, in any case. When I get your call, I will release the woman where she can get to a phone. Do not fail me, and do not betray me."

Alex moved quickly to the Lincoln and drove off, watching his mirror to see if Brian, or anyone else, followed. There was no one.

A few minutes later, he parked down the street from the Stanford Court and resumed his slow, nearly painful walk into the lobby and up the stairs. He entered his room and quickly undressed, removed his makeup, and showered, then fell into bed. He lay there for several hours, trying to clear his mind and achieve a state of relaxation. It proved impossible.

Palo Alto, California

At seven, he rose and pulled from his bag his workout clothes and a small fanny pack to hold the phone. He dressed quickly in an outfit that included a 49ers baseball cap and large mirrored sunglasses. He walked from the hotel and began to run. At seven-fifty, he turned into the Stanford University campus and ran toward the bookstore, slowing to a jog and then a walk as he neared it. There were a few joggers out, and several students hurrying to their 8:00 classes. A man in a Stanford sweatshirt with a blue collar peeking from it sat on a bench nearby, reading a copy of Foreign Affairs. Alex walked toward him, pulling the hotel towel from around his neck and wiping the sweat from his face. As he passed the man, he turned suddenly and said, "Hey, Izzy. How are you?" The man looked startled for a second, then stood and said, "Cameron! I haven't seen you for a while."

"Let's walk and talk for awhile," Alex said, still moving.

Izzy hurried to catch up, and then fell into step beside him.

Cuchulain looked around for any listeners, then said, "I'll make this quick. The Colombians are deep into a national security matter, and we're going to take a few of them out. We need you to take credit for breaking up the ring, and to roll up the lower-level managers and dealers, all at once. Tell them that they have been deserted by their superiors. When no lawyers show up, and I suspect that they won't, they'll start to believe you, and you can probably turn a few. We may be able to find their big stash, and let you know if they have turned any of your boys. I'll let you know of any extras like that, and you can add them to your glory. Give me a number, and I'll try to give you three or four hours notice to get your team in place, then I'll let you know when to execute."

"Jesus Christ! Who the hell do you think you are?" Izzy exploded. "I think I'm going to have a casual meet with a fellow fed to find out why you're playing in my sandbox, and you start giving me orders! I need to know who you are, what the fuck you think you're doing, who authorized you to be here, and most importantly, exactly what the hell is going on."

Cuchulain nodded, then shrugged and said, "It's the usual national security bullshit. Everything is compartmentalized and you don't have the proverbial "need to know." As a fellow jarhead, I'll give it to you straight. The dopers are into some heavy national security stuff and looking as if they want to get in even deeper, just for the money. If you push us too hard, you'll probably end up as the DEA training officer liaison in Toule, Greenland. If you just treat me as an information source, you could get a career boosting, front page mega-bust out of this. In either case, you have complete deniability and no exposure. This meeting never happened, and this whole thing will be done in a week or less. The bonus for you is that the bad-guy leadership will be toast, and your job will be one hell of a lot easier if we pull it off."

"What's the catch?" Izzy said.

"The catch is that we never had this meeting, and you know nothing about me or anything of the national security aspect that I mentioned. Whatever happens, happens. You don't tell your boss, you don't tell your wife, you don't tell anyone. You take all of the glory and forget all about us forevermore, because it's best for our country that way. We vanish."

Izzy shrugged. "It's not clear to me that you can do anything that we can't, but I'll buy the national security thing. God knows I heard it often enough in the Corps. Besides, my boss told me that you guys seem to have unbelievable political clout, and that I should watch my ass with you."

"It all will be clear in a few days. I suspect that you'll also understand why we don't want any publicity," Alex said, as he stopped and turned to Izzy. "How about that phone number?"

Izzy pulled a business card from his pocket and wrote a phone number on it. "It's my private cell. Someone is on it twenty-four hours." He handed it to Cuchulain who glanced at the card, then nodded, not taking it.

"See you around, Izzy," Cuchulain said as he turned and jogged away.

Izzy watched Alex as he increased his speed to a run, then shook his head and walked toward the parking lot. He had some planning to do.

A block from the Stanford Court, Alex slowed and stopped at a pay phone.

"Mac."

"Izzy's on board. Is Brooks here with the goodies?"

Mac gave him a phone number. "He's waiting, and has a set of fairy-tale plans."

"Good. I'll call him now. Our pigeon is off and running, and his soul mate is still stashed. Get her out if things turn to shit. She can see and the lights are on. She's a junkie. If you can get a babysitter in with her, it would be good," Alex said.

"Done. We provided a good set of fake chips and plans for the kid to pick up. Stay in touch." Mac hung up.

Alex made contact with Elliot and arranged to meet him at the hotel in an hour, then jogged back, just another fitness buff out for some exercise before work.

He had showered and dressed when the knock came. When he saw Elliot through the security viewer, he opened the door and stepped aside. Elliot was dressed in the quintessential preppie outfit; gray wool slacks, a blue, button-down cotton shirt, rep tie, blue blazer, and Bass Weejuns. No socks. He carried a Land's End canvas briefcase and a set of rolled plans tucked under his arm. He could have easily passed as the architect of choice for the rich and famous.

They shook hands quickly, and slapped shoulders with the other hand, like brothers.

Elliot walked to the bed and spread the plans for the Bertram fishing yacht across it. "The boat is pretty much standard from what I've learned from its interior-decoration people. I walked by it. Believe it or not, there's not even a guard on board!"

They spent several hours going over the plans and making decisions, Alex drawing on the plans from time to time. They were interrupted only once by a call to Alex's cell phone. He looked at his watch. Five before the hour. He picked it up from the dresser and said, "*Si*, my pretty one. Is it done?"

Brian's voice sounded weak. "Yeah, he said he would get what they want to them today after work. We want ten full pounds as the reward. Let Kelly go, now!"

"I am so disappointed! But perhaps you are lying to me, and I will come for you later. The reward of ten pounds will not be a problem, but of course I cannot release the woman until my leaders tell me that your brother has completed your end of the bargain. I am to talk to them early this evening. If all is well, I will release her then. Call me at nine o'clock this evening, not before. If I am not occupied with my leaders, I will answer. Otherwise, call me once each hour." Alex disconnected.

"Jeez, Alex. You almost scare me. You think he's going to come through?" Elliot said.

"Hell, Brooks, I scare myself! It's disgusting to be into that mindset, but I think he'll come through. I have this weird Paco shit down so well that I can guess when it's going to work."

Elliot stood and stretched his back. "I think we know what we have to do, and I think I understand your placements. Let's do it right now, in broad daylight. I have some clothes. We'll both carry the goodies in and I'll go on board to get things ready while you keep watch, then you go in to place the fuses and goodies while I watch. Jerome has a good cover spot if it gets nasty. I'll come back in to put it all back."

Alex laughed and shook his head. "You always did have big balls, Brooks. I guess I'm more alert now than I will be tonight, so let's get to it. I'm going to need you to cover me tonight, anyhow."

They walked down the stairs to the street, and got into a gray Ford panel truck. They drove to a dock near the San Francisco airport. Wearing gray coveralls and official looking badges hanging from clips on the pockets, they walked past the office of the marina and down a dock to the yacht "Snow White." Alex and Elliot each carried a heavy satchel. When they reached the boat, they gently laid the satchels on the dock. Elliot jumped on the stern deck and walked to the cabin door. He pulled a slim black nylon parcel from his pocket and bent over the door for a second, then opened it and went below. Alex walked fifty yards or so, then bent over the piling next to an abandoned sail boat and pretended to be engaged in his work. He watched the entrance to the dock as he listened to the whine of a power drill removing the screws holding Snow White's lower deck in place. Fifty minutes later, he saw Elliot carry one satchel inside, then the other. Another thirty minutes went by, then Elliot came out of the boat and walked to Alex. "All yours, Genius," Elliot said as he sat down beside him.

Alex stood and moved casually but quickly to the boat and went inside. Below, he moved along the spars that supported the boat, that normally were hidden by the deck that had been removed at the perimeter by Elliot. He taped packets of C-6 plastic explosive along the hull. They were connected with white detonation cord taped among them, and through fresh holes drilled through the spars and connecting each set of packets. At the bow, a metal device shaped like the breastbone of a chicken pointed outward. Each arm was about three feet long and recently screwed into place by Elliot from the plans they had drawn. Large, shaped, lumps of explosive were arranged in metal pockets along the arms Alex moved quickly among the packets, removing his custom fuses from the satchel and setting them into the explosive and along the white cord, cutting it here and there. He stood for a second, checking his work, then walked quickly off the boat and back to Elliot.

"Let's get the hell out of here, Brooks. We're pushing our luck," Alex said, as he sat down.

Elliot moved back to the boat. In a few seconds, the sound of the electric drill came again as Elliot replaced the deck, covering their handiwork.

Fifteen minutes later, he was re-locking the door to the cabin. He stepped from the boat, carrying both satchels. They drove from the marina, looking for a place to have lunch.

At six o'clock, Brooks knocked lightly on Alex's door. Alex, in a pair of slacks and a sport shirt opened the door, then turned and walked into the bathroom. He splashed some water in his face. "Let's call Mac," he said. They walked together to a pay phone.

"Mac."

"We're all set with the fairy tale. What's going on with you?"

"It's coming together," Mac said. "It's working out as you thought. We found the boat that they're probably going to meet. It's a 180-foot mega-yacht, owned by a Saudi businessman who's been sponsoring terrorists for awhile. It's been hanging around offshore for a couple of days, doing nothing. No one has seen the top bunch of China's defense scientists in the period since the yacht left Cabo San Lucas, but we do know that they got to Cabo. Your boys are getting the goods from the brother this evening at six, and it sounds like they will take it out to the ship tomorrow morning, leaving the marina around nine. They're pretty cryptic, so it's tough to be sure."

"We'll just do the best we can," Alex said. "I'll put the instant go and the arm and trigger radio codes for our little present in your computer tonight, plus the DEA guy's cell contact. I'm going to go in and get my money from Alberto tomorrow sometime, hopefully in the morning if he's not going along on the cruise. Brooks and Jerome are going to cover me."

"I don't think Alberto will go," Mac said. "It will be the boss and four or five bodyguards, plus the boat driver that they use for at-sea pickups, as far as we can tell. And you watch your ass in there with Alberto. Jerome can't find a good angle into that office. If you get a chance to put the window shades up, do it."

Alex and Brooks got into the panel truck and drove by the office building in Menlo Park, then discussed the best way to have Elliot cover Alex when he visited Alberto in the morning. Elliot dropped Alex at the Stanford Court, where he went to his room and downloaded the latest voice files on Mac's computer. He reviewed the computer files, and then set the erase program. Cuchulain lay down on the bed and tried to relax, thinking. The morning meeting with Alberto could be a problem, but there was no way to avoid it.

As it got dark, Alex drove his Lincoln back to the interrogation room, after stopping at a McDonald's. He speed-dialed a number on his cell phone and a man answered, " One, one." Alex responded, "Nine, nine. Coming in."

The voice responded, "I'm out of here. All routine." The phone disconnected.

The parking lot was still deserted when Alex pulled up to the block shed. He took the balaclava from the Lincoln's glove box and pulled it over his head, then unlocked the door. He walked to Kelly, carrying a bag he'd picked up from McDonald's. The girl looked up hopefully, then her eyes widened with fear. He took a boning knife from the block and cut the duct tape binding Kelly's arms. She rubbed her arms where she had been bound.

"Eat." Alex threw the bag into her lap. She tore it open with hands trembling, and tore the paper from a sandwich, stuffing half of it into her mouth. Cuchulain sat a large Coke in a paper cup beside her on the arm of the chair, and stuck a straw into it. She grabbed and drained most of it while still chewing.

As Cuchulain sat and watched her devour the food, he finished three Big Macs, an order of large fries, and two large Cokes.

She looked at him. "I have to go to the bathroom. I've had to go for a long time, but I really have to go now. That person that was here never said a word—never answered me."

He picked the chamber pot from the table, together with a pack of Kleenex. After handing them to her, he cut the tape around her legs and pointed to the corner.

Kelly tried to stand, but fell to the floor. She lay for a moment, weeping softly, then struggled to her feet and limped to the corner with the chamber pot and the paper. Alex turned his head.

"Now what? Did Brian do what you wanted?" she asked after a few moments.

Still not looking at her, he said, "I do not know, but I think so. He says that he has. Put your clothes on, and I will release you tonight."

He could hear her begin to weep again, and it sickened him. She walked to her clothes and dressed. Then he could hear her rooting in her purse and he looked around. She had found a small packet of cocaine and had her nose down in it. She snorted and sneezed.

"Sit down," he said, and pointed to the chair. She sat, a look of health and confidence flooding her face. He walked to Kelly and put a blindfold on her, then quickly put a wrap of the tape around her ankles. He walked from the room, pulled the balaclava from his face and stuffed it into his pocket, then walked to the Lincoln and drove to the door. Alex put Kelly in the trunk again, tossed her purse and a knife beside her and drove off, stopping at a pay phone at the side of a darkened bank office a few minutes later. He reached into the trunk, pulled her out and stood her beside the phone, her purse and the knife beside her, wiped clean.

"Your purse and a knife to cut the tape are beside you. You may call for someone to pick you up. Do not go to the police or try to see my car as I leave, or I will come for you."

Menlo Park

WHEN Alex walked into Alberto's office the next morning, he immediately knew he was in trouble. Four bodyguards were spread across the room, with two Uzi's and two Berettas between them. All weapons were pointed at Alex. He stopped, and said, "I have done as you wished. I am here for my twenty-five thousand dollars."

Alberto smiled coldly. "You have done as I wished, but you have treated me with much disrespect."

He turned to the guards. "Search him, then tie him. Search him well."

They took the knife from his neck and the silenced Beretta from his waistband, then tied his hands behind him and his feet together.

Alberto walked to Alex and hit him in the face with his fist, breaking his nose, then stepped back and kicked him in the balls. As Alex doubled over in pain, Alberto picked up his knee into his nose, crushing it even further. Alex fell to the floor, trying to cover up as he felt a number of shoes kicking him and the painful snick of ribs breaking. Finally they picked him up and threw him into Alberto's office. Alex lay on the floor in his vomit, as blood streamed from his nose to paint bright scarlet ribbons on his jaw.

"We will be back for you to play with you for a long time, and then we will leave your tortured carcass for others to see, so that they know our power," Alberto said. "Right now we have to wait for my *Jefe*, who wishes to meet you, but I assure you *Amigo*, you will wish that you had not met him. He is not a nice person like I am. With your disrespect, you have made him unhappy. Much more unhappy than you have made me."

With another vicious kick to Alex's groin, Alberto walked from the room and closed the door.

The pain came in waves, confusing him. Alex tried to focus. Finally giving himself up to the pain, he began to work through it. He worked his hands down from his back and over his buttocks, feeling the broken ribs grinding and accepting the pain. He rolled onto his back and the pain came again, stronger, almost intolerable. He waited, then slowly moved his hands down across his thighs to his knees, waiting for the pain, and when it came, accepting it, waiting for it to again become tolerable. After he adjusted to a new threshold of pain, he moved on, finally bringing his hands to his ankles. With a sigh and renewed vigor, he pulled up the pant leg on his jeans and worked the throwing knife from his boot, then began to saw through the ropes binding his hands. As they released, the pressure on his ribs subsided and he felt an urge to lie back and rest, just for a minute. The absence of severe pain was serene.

Alex cut the ropes on his feet and struggled slowly to his feet, then stood, woozy, waiting for his head to clear. Alex's nostrils were now swollen shut, and blood was pushing down his throat. For some reason that infuriated him; he nurtured that fury. He spat thick wads of blood, then bent and pulled the knife from his other boot and prepared himself, thinking about the layout of the outer room and where the bodyguards would be positioned, knowing that he didn't throw left-handed very well. Killing two or three of them and getting killed himself would be far better than letting them slaughter him slowly. Where the hell was Elliot?

He swayed on his feet, gathering himself, trying to decide how long to wait, but prepared to attack if the door opened. Suddenly he heard the distinctive clatter of a silenced automatic rifle ejecting spent casings in the outer room, firing in the distinctive three-tap pattern of a Navy Seal in a hurry. Alex threw open the door and pulled his arm back to throw. He saw Elliot in his preppie outfit, dropping to one knee and swinging to cover him, his face and hair aged with makeup as Alex's had been earlier.

"Whoa! It's your old buddy Alex, a little the worse for wear," Alex croaked thickly as he dropped his hand.

Elliot swung back to cover the only man remaining standing, who had his hands held above his head. "Jesus Christ, Alex! Looks like they fucked you up pretty good."

"It turns out they didn't like old Paco after all, Brooks. They were just warming me up for the boss. Just don't shoot the last guy over there. We need to talk to him, a lot. That's the number two man."

Alberto was in the corner with his hands up, unharmed. He was gaining confidence quickly as he said, "You have not shown me a warrant. You gave us no warning. You broke into our property illegally. I wish to talk to my lawyers, immediately! I will have your jobs for this!"

"Shut up, pal. I got some bad news for you," Elliot said as he moved toward him. "We're your worst fucking nightmare. We have all the technology of the United States working for us, and none of the rules. If you want to live to see morning, you're going to talk to us. You see, you have pissed off Uncle Sam. Worse yet, I think you have royally pissed off old Paco."

Alex moved carefully among the bodyguards, looking for anyone who might live. All four were on their way out.

He looked at Brooks, and asked, "What about upstairs?"

"I took them out first, like we said. There were only three. Jerome got one of them and Lev another. Looks like that was a painful call down here; I guess we should have taken these guys out first."

Alex nodded slowly, carefully. "I'm not going to be worth a shit for awhile. I got four or five broken ribs, and maybe some kidney damage. I think someone might have hit me once or twice on the sniffer, too, one more time. You need to shoot him up and we'll get out of here. I'm supposed to see Caitlin tonight, so you might want to give her a call."

"Turn around," Elliot said to Alberto. Alberto, getting scared now, complied. Handing his Ingram to Alex, Elliot dug an auto-syringe from his pocket, pulled the cap from it and slapped it against Alberto's thigh.

"I'll watch him, you look around," Alex said. "There should be some pocket change in the top drawer of the desk in the other office. I don't know where the big money is."

Elliot pulled a garbage bag and a pair of rubber gloves from his jacket pocket and walked into the other office. Cuchulain could hear drawers being dumped as he watched Alberto slowly fade into a groggy semi-consciousness.

"I took the pocket money from the top drawer; maybe seventy-five grand," Elliot said. "There's another big wad of cash in bundles in the file drawer. We'll leave that for the Feds. There's some other stuff and a pound or two of coke—but nothing big— and a bunch of paperwork, bank receipts, and stuff that should make the narcs happy. There's a small wall safe, but it's locked. Is that your puke in there on the floor?"

Alex nodded and said, "Yeah, it is."

Brooks shrugged. "I poked around a little. The good news is that there's no dark blood in it, so there's no big rush to get help for you. Sure couldn't tell it by looking at you."

"Sure couldn't tell it by the way I feel, either. When the adrenaline wears off, I'm going to be a hurtin' puppy." Alex groaned. "I'll call the Feds."

He rang the number that Izzy had given him. A secretary answered, and Alex said, "Lemme talk to Izzy. This here's Cameron."

After a few seconds, Izzy came on the line. "This is Izzy."

"I assume that you have caller ID. If you don't, I'll read it off to you. You should get a warrant for the place at this number, and for the boss's place upstairs. We'll lock up. You can go in as soon as you want, and you might want one man around quickly to watch that no one else goes in. Keep this phone around so that I can reach you as I get more. It's pretty messy here. You may want to bring a couple of locals with you and some of those cute rubber body bags—and some air freshener."

"Oh, great! My good friend Cameron leaves me a mess. We have the number. You sound weird. Are you hit?" Izzy asked, sounding more curious than concerned.

"I'll be okay," Alex said. "Stay by the phone."

It was late morning when they took Alberto to the elevator, sagging between their arms and mumbling from the drug, as they held him upright. The elevator was empty as they entered and dropped to the garage. Elliot bent and threw Alberto over his shoulder in a fireman's carry, and handed the car keys to Alex. "Stand still," he said. "I gotta do a check. He reached up to Alex's face and pulled both eyelids open, and looked in his eyes. He pressed his index finger against his carotid artery and looked at the seconds clicking by on his digital watch. "Have you pissed yet?" he asked Alex, who shook his head negatively.

"Can you drive?" Elliott said.

Alex nodded and moved slowly behind him toward the rented car.

With Alberto in the trunk, Alex drove once more to the small room beneath the apartments and stopped in front of it, handing Elliot the key from where he had stashed it in the ashtray. Elliot opened the glove box and popped the trunk release, then moved quickly from the car and got Alberto from the trunk. As Brooks carried him through the door, Alex drove the car to the other side and parked it. He picked up Elliot's small bag from the seat, then worked himself out of the car and moved slowly toward the room. The secondary effects of the beating were appearing, now that the adrenaline rush had faded. His face throbbed steadily, with occasional sharp pains radiating out from his nose. His ribs hurt when he walked, and were excruciating if he moved suddenly. His kidneys and his groin were on fire, and his eyes were starting to swell shut. He knew he would be pissing blood at best, and hoped that he didn't need surgery.

Cuchulain walked into the room and closed the door behind him, then dropped the small bag beside him. Elliot had stripped Alberto and was taping his legs to the chair. Alex walked to the other wicker chair and sat down painfully.

Elliot pulled a small kit from his bag and laid it on the table to open it. In it were several syringes and five or six small vials. He pulled some fluid into one syringe then walked to the chair and injected it into Alberto's thigh. After a few seconds, Alberto began to become more alert. As he waited,

Elliot took a small digital recorder from the bag, pushed the "Play" and "Record" buttons simultaneously and laid it on the table. He sat on the floor with a legal pad on his lap.

"Alberto! Alberto!" Elliot, said trying to get his attention. He reached out and took a little of the skin on Alberto's thigh and pinched, then twisted it.

Alberto reacted to the simple pain and opened his eyes, now becoming alert. He looked around the room, first at Elliot, then at Alex, and finally at the assortment of items on the table. His eyes widened, and he said, "If you release me, I will pay you more money than you have ever seen. If you don't, my people will pursue you to the ends of the earth."

Alex stirred, and said in a phlegmy, constricted, almost hoarse voice, "He's a liar. You can't trust him. If you let him go, he'll kill us both. Cut his nuts off before we go any further. Feed them to him."

Elliot sighed. "Okay," he said. "I'll do it, but the boss wants him to talk to us. We gotta let him go if he does, with or without his nuts." He stood, walked to the table and pulled on a pair of rubber gloves, sat a small blow-torch on the floor near Alberto's legs, then pulled a butcher knife from the block. "I hope this fucker doesn't have AIDS or something."

He walked back to Alberto's chair and sat on the floor, reached with his gloved hand and grabbed the penis and testicles with his left hand and stretched them down, then looked at Alex. "Pecker, too?"

Alex nodded. "Pecker, too. It will give things he eats a little extra spice."

Elliot leaned forward, looking under the chair, still pulling on the penis and testicles. He reached under the chair with the knife in his right hand, a look of resolute disgust on his face.

"Wait! Wait!" Alberto said loudly, almost screaming. "What is it you want from me? I will tell you what you want. You cannot do this!"

"Cut him! Cut him!" Alex croaked. "Make him a *castrato* and send him back to the barrio to be the local *maricon*!"

"No! I will talk to you!" Alberto said, his face frozen with fear.

"Ah, shit, Paco. The boss will go apeshit if we cut him up when he says he'll talk. Let's see what he has to say."

"No! I will do it, and slowly." Alex said, as he struggled from his chair. "Give me the knife! He can talk to us later."

Elliot held the knife away from him. "You just sit down, Paco. If he doesn't talk, you can have him for as long as you want him."

Alex slumped back into his chair, and was silent for a moment. Then he said, "You could let me blind him! It won't hurt him so badly. It would make me feel better until I geld him later."

Alberto was trembling, looking from man to man during this dialog. Perspiration was pouring from him.

Elliot looked disconsolate. "I'd like to, Paco, but I'm sorry. I promise you five minutes with him the first time he lies to us; just don't kill him."

Alex snorted through the blood, spat on the floor and said, "When you give him to me, he will die, but not for a week. Maybe two. He will have no eyes, then no genitals, then no ears, no fingers, no toes, but he will not die. He will live in a world of endless pain."

Alberto's bladder released. "What do you want? Ask me, and I will tell you!"

Alex cried, "No! That is what his boss Francisco said this morning, and then he lied to us."

Elliot rolled his eyes and said, "Yeah, and then you killed him. Man, was the boss pissed at me over that! You gotta quit killing people before I tell you it's okay."

Alex sulked in his chair. "I squeezed him harder than I thought; I didn't mean to kill him just then. But I know that this turd will lie to you, as he did to me. You must promise to give him to me for longer than five minutes if he lies to you. An hour, just one hour."

Elliot stood and walked to the table. He picked up the small torch and lit it, and then he nodded and extinguished it. "Okay, Godammit Paco, but use the torch to cauterize so that he doesn't bleed to death. One hour, no more, and leave his eyes 'til last! Agreed?"

Alex sat for a moment, then shrugged painfully and nodded, slumping down into the chair. "Agreed. I want him to watch me."

All hope Alberto had of rescue had vanished when he heard that Francisco was dead. Worse, Francisco's father might kill Alberto when he found out. He resolved to talk his way out of this by telling at least some of the truth. He was to be released if he cooperated. He could get his revenge later.

Elliot picked up the notebook and turned on the recorder. "Okay, Alberto, let's see if we can catch you in a lie. First, tell us the names of the DEA people who are working for you and how you pay them."

After an hour, Elliot loaded another syringe and injected it into Alberto's thigh. He started again with the same set of questions, checking the answers as Alberto answered groggily, but readily. Cuchulain dozed, and once walked to the chamber pot. Elliot stood quickly and moved beside Cuchulain as he voided, watching the stream.

An hour later, Elliot turned the recorder off, and stood. He walked to the table and picked up another syringe, then loaded it from a different vial. He walked to Alberto, and emptied it into his other thigh. After a second or two, he helped Alex up and supported him as they walked to the car.

A few blocks down the road, Elliot pulled into a gas station with a pay phone and got out. He dialed.

"Mac."

"Elliot. Everything they have is on the boat, on its way. Need some clean up at the interview room; it wasn't too messy, but his body probably shouldn't be found with all that Mossad truth juice in it. We've identified some local turncoats, a big pile of product, cash routing and distribution, and the hierarchy and players at their end, including two bent congressmen. We have bank codes for maybe a million or two. Plus a little cash. Do you want to give it all to DEA here?

Mac was silent for a second. "No. Give them local turncoats, product, and the bank codes. Put the cash in our bribe pot. I'll smooth the waters here with the rest."

"They pounded Alex pretty good. No concussion, pulse is a little high, and he's pissing a fair amount of blood. No old blood in his early vomit. Nose is smashed and maybe one cheekbone. Some broken ribs for sure. No sign of shock. He needs to go to a hospital. He's walking though."

He could hear Mac rustling papers, then, "Take him to Stanford. We have a guy there. There should be an alternate set of ID for both of you in your bag. Use those if anyone asks. We'll handle the billing side and I'll arrange security."

Elliot said, "Right. We'll be there in less than thirty minutes. Set it up. I'll send the interrogation file when I get to my PC. "

He hung up and handed the phone to Alex, who dialed Izzy.

Izzy answered.

Alex said, "Your number three guy there, Morris, is bent, and so are two of your field guys, Gordon Large and Phillip Fellini. Large appears to be the leader. We have the bank routing for their payments. There is fifty pounds or so of product in a self-storage unit in San Jose, and there's a million or two in the bank that we can get you to. There's some other information, national, going back to your big boss in DC. Give me a fax number, and I'll get this stuff to you."

Izzy gave him the fax number and said, "What about Leon and Diaz? They are the ones we really want. If we don't get them, they'll be back in business in three days."

"Leon and Diaz aren't going back into business. Watch for their replacements coming in from Colombia," Alex said.

Izzy chuckled cynically. "So much for due process. They must have really pissed someone off."

Alex hung up the phone and struggled back into the car.

Elliot put the car into gear and drove North on El Camino Real. Looking at Alex, he said. "Here's your big chance. You've been admitted to Stanford Medical School."

"Yeah, whoopee." Alex groaned, as he shifted in the seat. "All thanks to their affirmative action program." He reached into Elliot's bag and took out a small bottle of nail polish remover and a rag. He wet the rag and rubbed Lola from his arm.

As Brooks and Alex pulled into the emergency ward lot at Stanford University hospital, a Bertram 48 Sport Fisherman approached a magnificent white yacht flying the colors of Saudi Arabia and floating just beyond the twelve-mile limit. Crewmen in white coveralls waited, with lines in their hands. As the Bertram slowed, Francisco stood on the bow and raised both hands to the sky in victory, relishing the thought of telling his father and brother of his victory over the gringos. A small group of men standing on the stern of the yacht, several in traditional Arab headdress and the others, smaller, in Mao style suits, raised their arms in response to Francisco's jubilation. As the distance between the Bertram and the yacht closed, the small microprocessor within Cuchulain's titanium device received a signal. The device had been accepting input from five tiny sonar-type pulsars that had automatically activated forty minutes after the Bertram left the pier. It sensed the proximity of a large metal mass and, when the distance between the Bertram and the yacht closed to within five feet and the point of the titanium "spear" was positioned to maximize penetration, it closed several circuits.

A sheet of white flame leaped from the bow of the Bertram and blew a ten foot hole in the side of the mega yacht; after a moment's hesitation, water began to pour in. A second explosion vaporized the remainder of the Bertram and launched a wave of burning diesel fuel across the deck of the now sinking yacht. In two minutes, an oil slick and flotsam were the only signs that two boats had floated there. At 7843 meters away and closing at 3 knots, the attack submarine USS Razorfish was 60 feet beneath the surface of the calm Pacific, its periscope just above the surface and focused on Snow White as it approached the large motor yacht. Razorfish had been following Snow White since she cleared the Golden Gate Bridge; the Saudi yacht couldn't run fast enough to elude the Razorfish, if it came to that.

Suddenly, Commander Charles Lightfoot pulled his rugged face from the worn padding around the periscope's eyepiece. The Razorfish's captain reached for his handkerchief and wiped the sweat from the periscope, then from his face, mopping his brow.

"Down scope. Close the outer doors. Secure the torpedoes. Battle stations stand down. Take her to 300 and go to course 350. All ahead two-thirds."

"I'm getting too old for this shit!" he said to his exec, Lieutenant Jered Washington. "You have the conn." He walked to the video recorder and popped the disc from it.

"Great White Father want heap clear evidence," he said as he walked away, waving the disc in the air. "Cheap at the price as long as it wasn't us that had to do it!"

Six thousand miles away and six hours later, a flight of four F-117 Stealth bombers separated from refueling from a KC-135 tanker, 34,000 feet above the Caribbean Sea. Each engaged its mission computer and turned toward the South American mainland. Several hours later, fourteen of the largest cocaine warehouses in Colombia were smoking rubble, and the home of one Felipe Peron, the uncle, was destroyed. No one on the ground had seen or heard a thing, until the explosions started. The F117's were again snuggled, one by one, drinking from the KC-135 before they turned to head back to Missouri.

In Saudi Arabia, two men were arrested and seven others killed resisting arrest. They were the second and third echelon of the terrorist financing arm that funded the operations of several Al-Qaeda groups. They had been unable to reach their leader when informers disclosed government plans to raid their offices.

Stanford Medical Center

BROOKS Elliot and Jerome Masterson sat beside a small table in the corner, idly playing backgammon, a large, green canvas bag gaping open at their feet.

"Well, there goes another one," Jerome said. "You suppose we're making any difference or just shoveling shit against the tide?"

"Well, except for the dopers, Cooch is taking most of the damage. I'm just as pretty as I always was," Brooks said.

A huge hand moved from beneath the bed sheet across the sterile room, and came upright. The middle finger extended slowly from it.

"On the other hand, I think Mac will get the word around that there's a big price for tugging on Superman's cape," Brooks said. "Maybe we're helping the tide to go out, just a skosh."

Jerome sighed and nodded. "We've been doing this for awhile. I bet I've I killed a hundred folks or more."

"Bother you?" Brooks said.

"Nah, I actually sort of like it." Jerome said with a smile. "It keeps the blood flowing; it ain't boring. And I really dislike the folks we're killing, and who they are. And, I like it that we can tell Mac 'No'."

"Bother you much, Brooks?" Jerome said. "You do it up close and personal; you can see their eyes. They're just targets to me."

"I don't get any joy from looking into their eyes while they die hating me, and I think it corrodes our souls when we do it this way, but I think we make a positive difference. I've always wanted to make a difference. I suppose it makes me feel special." Brooks said quietly.

"Hell, asshole, you were born rich. Gotta find some way to feel good about life, I guess," Jerome said, with a snort. "Works for me, being what Cooch calls a patriotic assassin."

Brooks nodded, then came smoothly to his feet as there was a quiet knock on the door. He moved to it as Jerome slid a short barreled pump shotgun from the open bag, and went to one knee.

"Yes?" Elliot said to the door as he stood to the side of it, back from Jerome's line of fire. The barrel of a Kimber .45 caliber pistol came from beneath the bed sheet.

"It's Caitlin. Your gorilla minder out here said that I'm on the visitor list."

Elliot flipped the lock and opened the door. "Careful, he's sensitive," Brooks said, nodding at the large young man grinning at them, "Try not to hurt his feelings."

Caitlin walked in just as Jerome was slipping the shotgun back into the bag. "Gee, you must be the Horse!" she said to him with one raised eyebrow and a half smile. "Did I miss the party?"

"We're just cautious. Someone has been picking on Alex here. I'm Jerome Masterson," he said with a smile as he stood and put his hand out.

"Alex says nice things about you, like 'You'll kill anyone who is mean to him,'" she said. "Nice friend to have."

"How about giving a girl a little privacy, boys?" she asked, turning to Alex as he sat propped up on the hospital bed. Brooks and Jerome moved to the hall outside the door.

"Goodness gracious, Alex. It appears that you are not really the baddest motherfucker in the whole world," Caitlin said with a smile and a wink. "Those are really spectacular colors on your face—a veritable rainbow. I can't wait to see your nose when they unveil it from beneath that bandage pile."

Alex gave a little snort and a groan. "It hurts when I laugh; he got a couple of ribs, too. He was bigger than me, and he didn't fight fair, and

Jerome didn't even get around to hurting him. Anyway, how's chances for a rain check on that date last night?"

"I guess so, when you can move again, and that other stuff. At least you're not boring!" she said. "Besides, you weren't all that pretty to begin with."

Washington, DC

IN the old Executive Office Building, just to the North of the White House on Pennsylvania Avenue, Mac put his feet up on his desk and stared blankly out his window. *"All in all, a decent outcome,"* he mused. *"Watching the ripples from the Arabs, the Chinese, and of course, the Columbians will be fascinating. NSA should have the first of it before long. I wonder how many of China's top scientists were on that yacht."*

The red phone on the corner of the Government Issue desk rang, and he reached to pick it up. "MacMillan," he barked.

"The president has ten minutes and would like to see you in the Oval office," said Neil Gomez, the head of the Secret Service detail on duty.

"On my way," Mac said, as he rose. "Two minutes."

The president looked up from his desk as Mac was ushered into the Oval Office, waved Mac to a chair and asked the secret service agent standing to the left of the door to give them some privacy. The agent went to the door and left the room.

"Well, that was fast, exciting, and, no, I don't want to know the details," the president said. "But it seemed to be effective, even if massively illegal— and it dealt with a particularly dangerous problem with a bit more creativity than I dared hope. You seem to be a tool that I didn't anticipate; I just hate that I seem to need you. When all of this blew up I asked the National Security Advisor about you. He advised me of your idea for a somewhat more forceful message than I had considered. He's a fan of yours, but of course also a former Marine. He told me that you have access to more ground-level intelligence than nearly any of us, that you have an unusual ability to synthesize disparate data, and are consequently extremely valuable to me, and us. Comment? "

"That's what I think I bring to your table, Mr. President," Mac said. "Most of what I conclude does not involve anything illegal on its surface, even though sometimes immediate violent action seems the best solution to a given problem. I just try to chew on disparate facts that have not yet been scrubbed by the politicians, provided by contacts that I have developed over the years and have always protected—and then I draw tentative conclusions from them and chew on that some more. When I need to advise you on a relevant problem, I think I bring a more immediate and nuanced set of observations and conclusions to the table than may be appropriate for a policy discussion. That gives more perspective, perhaps, than might otherwise be available."

"The real problem for me is how to keep you from going off half-cocked to solve some problem that the country does not have, to the public ruination of us all," the president said. "You may be dangerous to the country. I understand that you were offered the DDO position at the CIA several times, and turned it down, even after having *acted* in the job—effectively *done* the job I'm told—while a successor was being considered. Compared to being DDO, you're hiding in the bushes here with a much less visible job, and a lot less prestige. Why?"

"I know from experience what sort of person does the DDO job best, and it's an important job. I'm not that person. I'm too blunt, I don't have many bureaucratic skills, and I think I'm best used in a more informal role," Mac said. "I don't much like lots of meetings and formal dinners, and I have little ambition beyond doing this job well and maybe someday teaching. But you are right about the danger I represent, Mr. President. I consider that in everything I do."

"And what do you conclude, once you synthesize those concerns?"

Mac was silent for a moment and shifted in his chair as he framed his response. "You are the commander-in-chief. You command the military, and with it you command the national security apparatus; your command is absolute. That situation is fundamental to being an American, a bedrock of who we are. You'll never have to worry about a military coup. I am a former Marine, which means, above all, that you don't have to worry about me going off half-cocked. I serve at your pleasure."

The president nodded. "I suppose that's at least some sort of specific answer to my specific question. I'll keep you around, at least for now, since you have been surprisingly useful recently. You are free to sit in on Cabinet meetings and so on, if you choose, as an observer. I'll let you know if I want you in a particular meeting, and perhaps why. If you have something to say, err on the side of letting me know privately if your conclusions are likely to involve these special skills that you've just demonstrated. You are dismissed."

"Yes, Sir," Mac said as he stood to attention. He turned and walked briskly from the room.

Read on for an excerpt from

A Patriot and An Assassin,

coming soon from Royal Wulff Publishing

Southwest Texas

THE afternoon shadows from the pool house stretched up the gravel path from the pool toward the huge, log-framed ranch house. Alex Cuchulian walked beside his friend, Brooks Elliot, talking idly about the travails of the economy and the housing bust. The t-shirts they wore were wrinkled and newly dry, and there were damp circles at the waists of their swim trunks. Behind them walked two women, their dates. One was the ranch owner's daughter and their host, LuAnn Clemens, a tall, slender brunette with a long, printed t-shirt covering her to mid-thigh.

The other woman, Caitlin O'Connor, was a little taller, blond, and well-muscled, with a swimmer's body wrapped in a long tie-skirt below her bikini top. The hair on both women was slicked back and still wet from the pool. Each carried a bath towel wrapped casually around her neck.

A sharp snap sounded just behind Alex. He turned his head just as a sharp pain hit his wet bathing suit, accompanied by another snap.

"Ow!" Alex yelled and turned to see LuAnn pulling her towel back and Caitlin's towel snapping just past him as she pulled back on the other end. Both women were grinning and giggling.

As LuAnn's towel snaked out again, Alex snatched the end just before it unraveled, and gave it a pull. LuAnn sprawled forward and fell on the sharp gravel, letting out a loud yelp.

As Alex opened his mouth to apologize, a slamming force just under his rib cage drove him into the air. He felt himself instinctively reacting to thousands of hours of CIA training. This situation called for the physical skills he had learned from Repetitive Martial Arts Drill #28. The CIA had designed such responses to counteract each of the seventy-two most common forms of physical attack, and had drilled them into workers chosen for the violent work of the Agency.

Alex threw his legs uphill using his stomach muscles and twisted his body over the force, driving his assailant under him as they fell. Now for the part that took the longest to master: The impact of Alex's fall must be broken, lessened somehow. His right arm was extended, slightly bent. Just as the impact of the man hitting the ground was first sensed, Alex drove his right elbow into the mass of the head and neck beneath him. The impact of that blow went through his assailant's face, into the dirt where it landed. Bone could be heard snapping as the force of impact from Alex's fall was countered. Judo was based on Newton's principle that for every action there was, or at least should be, an equal and opposite reaction. The slowing of his fall allowed his feet continued to swing over the base of the conflict, and then tighten their arc to hit their landing spot as his upper body twisted along in the earlier arc of the feet, the arms of the assailant no longer grasping him tightly. Alex rolled lightly to his feet in a balanced crouch, looking around him. Brooks had spun his back to the scene and was also standing in a crouch, hands raised, looking for others. There were none.

"What the hell was that?" Caitlin yelled, looking at the large cowboy still on the ground, inert.

Alex dropped to one knee to reach for the neck of the cowboy. He felt a strong pulse and noticed a shard of bone sticking from his jaw. There was a steady trickle of crimson flowing from the bone to the gravelly soil, quickly absorbed.

"Darned if I know, but he appears to have hurt himself in the fall," Alex said with a frown.

As Brooks helped LuAnn to her feet, he brushed the gravel from her. There was a pounding of feet as three cowboys rushed around the maintenance shed. They skidded to a stop, as they saw their friend, Jeeter, lying motionless on the ground. They looked at LuAnn, unsure what was going on. "What the heck?" one of them yelled to LuAnn.

"I tripped and skinned my knee," LuAnn said, pointing at her bloody kneecap. "Jeeter must have thought that Alex here was acting up and tried to defend me. He missed the tackle, and there he is."

After a little confusion, the ranch hands started trying to figure out how to move Jeeter. Seeing his jawbone protruding from his face and dripping blood into the soil, there was some muttering among them and hostile glances at Cuchulain and Elliot, who stood with the women, watching. Another ranch hand showed up with a canvas stretcher, and they began to move Jeeter onto it.

LuAnn led her three guests quietly toward the ranch house. On its wide porch, Virgil Clemens, her father, leaned against a column and watched them approach. As they got to the porch steps, he said with a little grin, "Hell, LuAnn, you just got here and there's trouble already. I'd better buy everyone a drink before things get out of hand. Cocktails start now and dinner is in ninety minutes. That should give you time for a few drinks and a change of clothes. I expect that my foreman will fill me in on the details of the excitement before then."

The Clemens' Ranch

Dawn

Cuchulain walked out toward the corral with the angled light of early dawn throwing long shadows from the sprawling log house across the rough grass. He wore a faded pair of Wrangler jeans and a blue-striped cotton button-down shirt. His still-wet hair was slicked back, black and shining.

Someone was sitting on the corral rail, smoking a hand-rolled cigarette. His wide-brimmed hat was pushed back on his head, and a steel-gray brush cut was beneath it. A large rectangular silver belt buckle on his jeans caught an early ray of sun. There was lettering of some sort on it.

"Howdy," he said, jumping down from the rail. He stuck his hand out. "I'm the foreman around here."

"Hello," Alex said as he reached his hand to greet him. "I'm Alex. How is the cowboy who fell yesterday? Jeeter—that was his name, right?"

Alex felt his hand suddenly being squeezed hard, and he instinctively returned the pressure. He could feel thick calluses against his own as the pressure increased. The man was strong.

The pressure leveled, and then dropped as the foreman gazed into Alex's eyes, then he nodded almost imperceptibly and jumped nimbly back up on the rail.

"Well, his jaw hinge is shattered and the jaw's broken," the foreman said as he settled himself. "But I reckon he'll live." He flicked his cigarette to the dirt. "How do you pronounce that last name of yours?"

"Coo-HULL-an," Alex said. "Why?"

He studied Cuchulian. "They ever call you Cooch?"

Alex shrugged. "Seems likely with a name like mine," he said.

284

"I was in the Marine Corps for twenty-some years. Word gets around. You that Cooch?"

Alex sighed, and nodded. "I'd rather not make a fuss about it, though," he said. "That was a long time ago. I'm an investment manager now."

"I figgered. I've *broken* hands usin' less pressure than that. My name's Proctor Mikey. They call me Mikey. Took me awhile to figger you out. Then I remembered that your buddy Elliot was a Seal; the boys was all excited about that. They thought maybe they'd have a fight in his honor."

"It's not too late," Alex said with a smile.

Mikey dug a small sack from his shirt pocket, unfolded a paper from an orange pack, and began to roll another cigarette. "I never got to meet your daddy. Never met a man with the Medal. Wished I had."

Alex looked at the dawning sky for a long moment and said, "He was a good man."

"The boys sort of gave up on the fight in Elliot's honor," Mikey said quietly. "They figure you fucked up the ranch's honor when Jeeter got hurt going after you. Jeeter's jaw is wired shut, but he wrote a note at the infirmary. It just said, 'Protectin' LuAnn.' They're planning to work on you some. They call it 'riding for the brand,' They like that LuAnn girl."

"Hell, I like her too. It was an accident, or at least it wasn't what it seemed," Alex said as he sighed and looked away. "Well, does recovering honor for the brand include guns and knives? If not, Elliot and I will deal with it. But you'd better call around and get some more folks for your side. If that guy who jumped me was one of the bad guys, you don't have nearly enough folks to make it fun."

Mikey snorted a double laugh and then coughed violently. He hawked a big wad of phlegm and spat it on the dirt. "I reckon the boss would be highly pissed if he had a bunch of hands in the hospital or the hoosegow," he said. "Anyhow, they're fixin' to have you ride a horse that will do the job for them. You ride much?"

"Only a little," Alex said. "I've ridden more camels than horses."

"We got us a big horse named Cottonmouth. Good name. He's meaner than a blind fucking snake. They got him in mind for you, for a bumpy little ride across the prairie. And Cottonmouth's a biter."

"Hell, the fight's sounding better all the time. Any advice for a fellow Marine?"

Mikey sat for a while, pondering. "My claim to fame around here is that I was national high school rodeo champ a thousand years ago," he said, and pointed to his belt buckle. "I know horses."

"And?" Alex asked.

"Two things," Mikey said. "First, if you punch a horse really hard just between his ears, high up—and if you punch right, he'll go to his knees. Maybe a trained guy like you would kill him, but he'll behave if you don't. Second, and sneakier—but you may be able to pull it off if the rumors about your hands are true—and I just seen some evidence that they might be. You just whisper a bit in Cottonmouth's ear while they are holding him and run your hand up just between his ears and press hard. The place is called the poll; it's where nerves cross under a horse's skull plates. The plates don't quite meet there, and there's a little dip, so there's room to push a strong finger down in. Horses don't like pain; it makes them behave."

"That's good to know," Alex said. "I don't suppose you could show me how to do that on a horse."

Mikey smiled. "I reckon I could, both of us being Marines, and all. It's the least I can do to stop a massacre on my ranch."

Mikey eased himself from the rail, ground his cigarette into the dirt with his heel and walked toward the stables with Alex beside him.

Mikey stopped just as they reached a stable, and turned.

"I need to ask you something, but it's really none of my biddness," he said.

"Sure." Alex shrugged, and smiled. "Asking is free."

"Do you have any contacts left? Where you can give someone a heads up to see if anything is funny?"

"Funny, how?" Alex asked. "Who would want to know?"

Mikey studied Alex. "There was a different crowd of Mexicans came to town about three days ago. Not like most of the coyotes that bring illegal workers across. They're a bunch of bad asses, plus a guy who dresses funny and speaks bad Spanish. The locals are scared to death of them."

"Yeah?" Alex said.

Mikey said, "Yeah. We get a pretty steady stream of illegals coming through this part of Texas. We're on a good smuggling route from Mexico. It's been going on for quite awhile, and it's really none of our biddness, so we stay out of it. The immigration game changed with this crowd that just came in. One of my guys, Gomez, is a former Marine, who did his four years and got his citizenship after doing his Iraq time, twice. He was in town when those guys came into the cantina. Gomez thinks that the funny-looking guy was speaking *Arabic* to one guy who translates to Spanish. The bad guys were pissed when they did it in public, but still treated those two like royalty."

"So," Mickey said, "if they're bad asses, they're too expensive to be moving illegals. What are they moving? It don't smell right, and my nose works pretty good for smelling trouble. Gomez took a picture with his cell phone. Quality's shitty, but it's a picture."

"Did he now? Well done!" Alex said with a tight little smile, as he dug out his wallet and found a wrinkled business card to hand to Mikey. "Ask him to email the picture to me. It could be anything or nothing. Still, it's a change in behavior for them, isn't it?"

"Yup," said Mikey. "And it might be worth looking into—or not. You know anyone to alert? Word is that you were doing spook work for a while and were good at it. I thought there might be a loose connection or two that you could tweak. Immigration is one thing, but they don't need those guys for that. What they might be planning to bring across, is what worries me."

"I'll make a call." Alex said. "Maybe someone will take a look. Are you and Gomez available if someone wants to talk to you?"